Praise for
Taylor Chase

"Taylor Chase's writing is fresh, exciting and utterly
engrossing. Highly recommended for those looking
for something new and absorbing."

ANNE STUART

"A beautiful prose style . . ."

SUSAN WIGGS

"This fast-paced, absorbing novel sizzles—
a perfect brew of passion, danger and
gritty details of life in Elizabethan England."

PENNY WILLIAMSON on *Heart of Deception*

"A must read!"

CONNIE BROCKWAY on *Heart of Deception*

Other **AVON ROMANCES**

BEFORE THE DAWN *by Beverly Jenkins*
BELOVED PROTECTOR *by Linda O'Brien*
HIS UNEXPECTED WIFE *by Maureen McKade*
AN INNOCENT MISTRESS: FOUR BRIDES
FOR FOUR BROTHERS *by Rebecca Wade*
THE MACGOWAN BETROTHAL:
HIGHLAND ROGUES *by Lois Greiman*
THE MAIDEN AND HER KNIGHT *by Margaret Moore*
SECRET VOWS *by Mary Reed McCall*

Coming Soon

THE BRIDE SALE *by Candice Hern*
A SEDUCTIVE OFFER *by Kathryn Smith*

And Don't Miss These
ROMANTIC TREASURES
from Avon Books

THE OUTLAW AND THE LADY *by Lorraine Heath*
THE SEDUCTION OF SARA *by Karen Hawkins*
SOMEONE IRRESISTIBLE *by Adele Ashworth*

TAYLOR CHASE

Heart of Night

AVON BOOKS
An Imprint of HarperCollins*Publishers*

AVON BOOKS
An Imprint of HarperCollins*Publishers*
10 East 53rd Street
New York, New York 10022-5299

Copyright © 2001 by Gayle Feyrer
ISBN: 0-06-101290-4
www.avonromance.com

First Avon Books paperback printing: December 2001

Avon Trademark Reg. U.S. Pat. Off. and in Other Countries, Marca Registrada, Hecho en U.S.A.
HarperCollins ® is a trademark of HarperCollins Publishers Inc.

Printed in the U.S.A.

10 9 8 7 6 5 4 3 2 1

*For Danielle Girard—the sassy one
and Sonia Simone—the wild-eyed scribbler*

Love ... in spite of darkness brought us hither.

JOHN DONNE

Prologue

London, 1586

*K*nave! Poxy peacock!
      Flushed with anger and humiliation, Lady Claire Darren fled down Bedlam's corridor. Her soft shoes made a frantic whisper on the thick rushes.

Just as she reached the door, Sir Reginald's agitated voice sounded from the floor above. "Claire! Where are you, Claire?"

She opened the heavy oak door, then stepped through and pulled it shut behind her, silencing Sir Reginald's calls. Freedom—if only for a moment.

Rain no longer splattered down in Bedlam's courtyard but sharper cold followed its departure. Despite the heat of her emotions, Claire shivered within her cape of sable-lined velvet. Her exhalations hovered like lost spirits, then dissipated in the chill air. Breathing shallowly, she tried to warm the air she drew into her lungs, to filter the taint that seemed to coat them. February's cold had done little to suppress the stench of

1

the nearby sewers. Inside the asylum had been worse, the odors of fouled straw, sweat, urine, and blood contaminating the air. The areas the visitors saw were kept clean, but the reek was omnipresent, heavy as a threat.

Claire rubbed her bare hands together and realized she must have dropped her gloves when Reginald kissed her. It was unlike her to bolt. No doubt her betrothed would find her soon, infuriated at her flight and petulant that she had not shared his lecherous response to the whipping of the asylum's inmates. Watching the correction of the madmen was becoming quite the fashion, he'd said. Everyone must go at least once. Well, she had gone once, lured by shameful curiosity. But she despised the base cruelty on display. All it stirred in her was pity for the victims and revulsion for the perpetrators. But something cruel stirred in Sir Reginald.

And something crueler still in the man who ordered it done, Bedlam's overweening master, Edward Quarrell.

Remembering his unnerving gaze, Claire shivered again. She thrust him from her mind. Soon she would leave this wretched place and never see him or it again.

Sir Reginald Fitzroy, the Baron Lord Thaxton, was the man she must contend with, now and for the rest of her life. Queasiness lingered, and Claire determined to avoid him for a few moments longer. She looked around for a hiding place. The courtyard of Bedlam was bleak, the stones of the old priory grim and gray as the clouded sky. A few skeletal trees grew close by the chapel in the center of the courtyard. Gusts of wind shook the bare branches, a tuneless clatter. Lifting her skirts of garnet damask, she wove her way between the muddy puddles left from the morning's rain and secluded herself on the far side of the chapel, invisible from the asylum. None too soon, for she heard the door open. Reginald's nasal bark sounded in the courtyard.

"Lady Claire! Are you here?"

She could picture herself inching round the chapel wall as Reginald circled it, and felt a fool. She was twenty-three, not a green girl running from a forward kiss. Nonetheless, when she heard the sound of Reginald's footsteps stalking across the courtyard and into the chapel, Claire hurried back and pushed the asylum door wide, shoving some rushes under the bottom with her shoe. It did not swing closed, and she hoped it would stay so till Reginald reappeared. Quickly, quietly, she returned to her hiding place. After a moment she heard him emerge from the chapel and curse when he spotted the open door. He took her bait and ran back inside.

Claire felt a surge of relief, a thrill of petty spite to have tricked him so easily. When he found her unmolested, any concern would evaporate in anger. The whole situation was absurd. He was, finally, inescapable. Because of that, she did not leave now, but only hid away, huddling in the warm folds of her cape. Claire remembered his wet mouth on her own, his tongue prodding her lips, insolent and graceless. She detested him.

But Reginald did not detest her. His extravagant praises compared her ordinary chestnut hair to a blazing autumn sunset. Her eyes he likened to glowing emeralds, though they were more brown than green. Her breasts—what he could see of them—he called white apples. Such gaudy flattery quickly faded, its brightness meaningless when Reginald had a dull ear for music and a dull mind for thought.

There was no evading the contract. Claire had been betrothed to Reginald at seven and confirmed consent at twelve. Only his long tour of the continent had delayed their wedding so long. Legally, she could marry no one else. His rich, ambitious family would not release her. Her own was sinking ever deeper into debt. Her rapacious mother was endlessly extravagant in pursuit of fashion, her beloved father in his quest for the secrets of alchemy. The honor of housing Queen Elizabeth's progress last year had all but beggared them. The Barony of Thaxton offered great wealth in return for the prestigious connection to the Earldom of Brightsea. Claire would marry Reginald, give him an heir, and then pray she would be left in peace to play her lute while he debauched himself in London.

What did it matter whom she married? The man she loved cared for her only as a sister. She could not change Rafe

Fletcher's lack of passion for her, or her own lack of feeling for her betrothed. Tears stung her eyes, a frustrating alloy of anger and self-pity. She blinked them back. These stolen moments alone were useless if she was as miserable by herself as she was with Reginald. She must find a moment's peace. Pushing the unhappy thoughts from her mind, Claire shut her eyes, evoking the complex strands of the new madrigal she'd learned at Court. As always, the beauty and order of music captivated her, soothed her. Plucking invisible strings, her fingers danced the melody.

Suddenly a bell clamored. Men shouted at the gate. Claire started as the raucous noise shattered the delicate musical pattern she was following in her mind. She opened her eyes as one of the sisters and a guard emerged from inside Bedlam and hurried to the entrance. The gray-haired sister unlocked the iron gate and moved aside. The guard joined the two without, helping to pull their struggling captive into Bedlam.

Claire stepped back against the chapel wall, appalled as the madman was dragged across the courtyard, naked except for his wet linen. The thin white shirt was ripped open and his hose plastered to his skin—both streaked with blood and dirt. Traces of blood marred his face, too. His wet hair clung to his skull. The guards were massive, the man almost their match for height, but slender and sinewy. She guessed he was little more than thirty. The madman twisted wildly in their grip, possessed of a violent strength of his own. They slapped him at every protest, jerked him off his feet and kicked his legs, his ribs. Claire's alarm twined with pity and outrage at the brutality of the guards.

Suddenly, the man broke free and ran, the guards pursuing him. He reached the gate, but it was locked. As a guard tried to seize him, he dropped into a roll, then regained his feet and bolted across the courtyard. This time, his tormentors converged from both directions. Seeing himself trapped again, the man stopped, flattening himself against the wall across from her. The guards formed a semicircle and moved forward to capture him. One of them cursed; another laughed as if it was all a joke. Filled with trepidation, Claire edged along the side of the chapel, glancing toward the door through which she'd fled Bedlam. Part of her wished herself out of danger, part wished to give the poor madman a witness to their cruelty. He would be taken into the asylum, locked in one of the foul cells, and beaten for his defiance. But what could she do? He was not her charge.

"Leave me be!" he cried. "Oh, God! Don't touch me again!"

His voice stayed Claire. Despite his panic, it rang rich and clear, filled with a wild, compelling music that sounded within her. An angel might rail so, being held by the devil's minions. Claire knew the notion was but a romantic conceit, but his plight moved her profoundly. Why had a gentleman been dragged here? For it was a gentleman's voice, well modulated even in these bizarre circumstances. A melodic accent rolled beneath the English syllables. An Irish lilt?

"Don't touch me! No!" His voice shattered as one of the guards seized his arm and dragged him forward. Demoniac, he fought, his coherence lost in feral cries. Then even those were stifled as one monster of a guard locked a forearm across his throat.

A hot pulse of anger sent Claire stalking across the courtyard. Her resolution firmed as she approached. She would not tolerate this injustice, this senseless brutality. "Release him," she demanded.

The guards turned. Two glared at her, the other only laughed. "We went to enough trouble to catch 'im, m'lady. We're not likely to let him go."

"You've barred the gate. He cannot escape. Give him a moment to calm himself." Thinking quickly, she offered the guard a good reason. "Perhaps he is hurt, and his pain drives him wild."

"We leave him be, you'll be lucky if 'e don't jump on you, m'lady."

"Why drag him in screaming, if he'll walk?" She knew the answer to her own question—because they relished their cruelty.

"We've no shackles on him yet, m'lady. If he can walk, he can run."

"And jump," another added with a leer.

"Release him," Claire commanded again, pitching her

voice low. They did not have to obey her, but she was an Earl's daughter. Even if they did not know her rank, they yielded to the authority she projected, to the aura of privilege draped about her, rich as the cape of velvet and sable.

The leader of the guards muttered his disgust. Turning, he gestured for the others to release the man. Grinning viciously, they shoved him forward. Murky water splashed her as he landed in a puddle at her feet. Claire gasped and stumbled back a foot, even as the man lifted himself from the muck and scrambled away from her. The laughter of the guards made them both halt where they were, her from pride, the madman from fear. For a moment she wondered if her efforts to have the guards release him would do any good. The man only crouched and trembled, staring about him wildly. She doubted he knew what was happening.

"Any second 'e'll bolt, and we'll just 'ave to chase 'im round the courtyard to catch 'im again." The guard scowled at her, then added, "M'lady."

"Who is he? Do you know his name?"

"Tom O'Bedlam will have to do for now. Word came 'e was wandering about half-naked, like 'e is now. Raving. Nobody knew who he was, so they called us to come take him. So we did. Fought us like an animal. You saw, m'lady." His voice accused her.

Defended himself against beasts, Claire thought, then chastised her own foolishness. Well-bred looks and an angelic voice did not make the man sane, only added pathos to his plight. As she watched, the madman bent forward, rocking, arms pressed to his body, fingers sunk into his rain-drenched hair. His forehead was cut and bruised.

"Sweet Christ," the man whispered. "What is happening?"

There was such despair in his voice that Claire's heart seemed to twist in her breast. She moved toward him, gesturing the guards away when they protested. The man shuddered, violent tremors racking his whole body. Claire glanced up at the sister cowering by the gate, and said quietly, "Bring a blanket for him."

At the sound of Claire's voice, the man lowered his hands. She saw, before he balled them into fists on his thighs, that his fingers were long and elegant. His frenzied gaze met hers and stilled. She could see him struggling for control. His eyes were fascinating, filled with shards of color, blue and green, gray and amber. Emotions, vivid and disparate flashed within them: fear, anger, confusion, hope. Beneath the dirt and blood were fine-honed features—high slanting cheekbones, a straight nose, and supple lips. With his brows and eyes at a tilt, he looked not so much an angel but some faerie changeling grown to manhood—either way a creature who found this ugly realm too terrible to bear. He seemed to hate being touched, yet his misery called out for comfort. Perhaps it was only kindness he needed.

Claire knelt on a drier patch of ground in front of him, strangely calm even as she wondered at her own actions—probably as lunatic as those of the tormented creature before her. She reached out tentatively, her fingers brushing lightly over his. "What is your name?"

His hands turned and grasped hers. The long fingers gripped tightly, bone pressing bone, yet she could hardly tell which fingers were hers, which his. A shock rippled through her, and another, as if deep notes sounding at her core rose up, vibrating through her body. The world plunged into shadow. Claire felt engulfed in darkness, aware only of his face before her, his strong hands meshed with her own. A quivering stillness held them. Within the quiet lived both beauty and terror. She trembled, resonating in the echo of a great heartbeat, or the throbbing of a deep wound, before the next stroke of pain. Yet for the moment she was suspended, safe. Wonder filled her. There were only the two of them, sheltered within this strange haven. The grip on her hands eased to gentleness. The man gazed into her eyes as if he sought to read her very soul. As if he could.

Had anyone ever looked so deep?

"*Mo cride.*" His voice was no more than a sigh on the strange words. "Claire . . . "

"Claire, are you mad!" Reginald's shout rang across the courtyard.

The harsh sound jerked her back as though sharp hooks caught her spirit and yanked it back within her flesh. Claire had not been aware of the world around, only of the man kneeling before her, his fingers linked with hers. They tightened. His gaze pleaded, too bright, too compelling. Her heart quickened, beating a frantic rhythm. She began to lean toward him, then pulled back, astonished. Could his madness cast some sort of spell? She snatched her hands away guiltily, severing the last of the bond with the man before her.

Claire gasped as loss struck her, sharp and sudden as lute strings snapping. A painful discord, then a terrible silence. Her whole body felt hollow, empty, bereft of the shimmering harmonics of his touch.

"No—" Panic ignited his eyes. Seizing her arms, he pulled her against him.

Stunned by the impact, Claire did not even try to struggle. The softness of her body molded against the sinewy strength of his torso, his lean, taut thighs. Fear swept through her, and a wild exhilaration. Her hands tightened on his shoulders. His arms encircled her, pressing her closer. She felt held by a magnet, as if every particle of her being fused to his. Trembling coursed through her limbs, fiercer than before. Terrifying. Exquisite. She gasped as she felt the touch of his lips.

He tastes of rain, she thought.

Thought vanished as he kissed her deeply. Kissed her as if he would devour her soul. His mouth, his teeth, his tongue consumed her. Breathless, she drank his breath. The heat of his body seared through her clothes and she felt naked against him. Brightness flashed through her, a sheet of flame. Sensation scorched away thought, incinerated fear. She flowed against him as flesh and bone melted in the blaze, molten, liquid at the core. She was fire clinging to fire, fusing with fire. Lost in delirious pleasure she wanted only to burn. Burn hotter. Burn brighter. Brighter—

"Damnation!" Reginald's curse shocked Claire back to cold awareness.

Shaken, confused, Claire tried to draw back from the close

embrace. The man held her fast. What was happening? This was a stranger. A madman. She must be mad as well.

Reginald splashed through the mud and grabbed her arm, dragging her back. Claire's knees gave way. She sagged against him, then instantly tried to pull free. She hated his touch.

Holding her fast, Reginald kicked out, his foot slamming the madman in the chest and knocking him into the mud. "I want him whipped!" he yelled, and the guards rushed forward.

"No! Don't hurt him!" Claire cried out, breaking loose.

They all halted, if only in stupefaction.

"Don't hurt him?" Reginald stared at her, flummoxed. "He's a crazed animal. I stopped him from ravishing you."

"No," Claire whispered, but fear returned. She curled her shaking hands into a knot, pressing them to her lips. Her lips felt bruised. The taste of rain lingered in her mouth. Mud clung to her cheek and streaked her hands. She was afraid to touch the stranger now—ashamed of the strange desire that obliterated all resistance. But she could not bear to see him punished again. "He's not fighting back."

Crouched in the mud, the madman gazed at her with remorse, with desperate need.

"It's not fighting he wants now," Reginald sneered. His gaze went to her lips.

The captive reached out to her again, his fingers brushing the hem of her skirts. His voice was a hoarse whisper. "Help me."

"Keep your hands off her." Reginald grabbed her and jerked her away. She held him tightly, but only to keep him from kicking the beaten man.

"How can I help you?" she asked over Reginald's protests. "Who are you?"

He pressed the heels of his hands to his temples. "You must believe me—"

"That is most unlikely," an unctuous voice said.

They all turned as Edward Quarrell approached. Director and head physician of Bedlam he ruled his domain like a king. *Like a tyrant*. Claire's thought seemed to draw his gaze, a cool, mocking survey that lingered on her muddy cheek. He pulled a handkerchief from his sleeve, and offered it to her with a bow. A heavy scent of cloves and violets drifted from its folds. She did not like the scent. She did not like him. When she did not take the offering, he moved forward to survey the kneeling prisoner.

Grateful the physician had turned away, Claire studied him obliquely. She supposed that most would call Master Quarrell attractive, but his face was subtly strange, a little too broad at the temples and tapering too much at the jaw. Pale skin fit softly over the hard bone, like wax starting to melt. His large wide-set eyes were oddly sinister, their irises the opaque gray of a night fog. Beneath high, arched brows and low, heavy lids, their expression was lazy, almost somnolent. Despite his size and solidity, there was something insectile about him. From the first his presence had discomfited her, even before he'd ordered the whipping of the inmates. Then, as the lash fell, as Reginald pawed at her, she'd caught Master Quarrell smiling. A terrible, smug little smile. Reginald was merely disgusting, but the physician's cold lust raised a prickle of fear.

That is why I ran, Claire thought, surprised. *I was afraid.*

Turning to the head guard, Quarrell spoke with disdain. "It seems we have a lunatic at large. Do you have an explanation, Cross?"

The man shifted, cleared his throat roughly, "Umm . . . m'lady told us to let him go."

"That seems doubly unwise." Master Quarrell gave her a small, amused smile.

"The man might as well be naked." Reginald broke in, gesturing at the prisoner.

"Lord Thaxton," Quarrell acknowledged the censure with a miniscule bow of the head.

He loosened the tie of his cloak. "I told the sister to bring a blanket," Claire said defensively. She glanced at the madman. The wet linen clung to his skin, molding to carved muscle and long, elegant bone. It showed the latent power of his masculine sex. Claire looked away, but even now she could feel the imprint of his body against hers—his hard thighs, the grip of his hands, his fierce kiss.

But she remembered his gentleness too. When he first took her hands, his fingers had pressed bone to bone, but then eased. He did not mean to hurt her.

"Listen to me." The captive rose to his feet, dignified even in his immodest linen. His voice seemed firmer now, authoritative. His eyes had a clear intelligence.

"Who are you, that we should listen?" Master Quarrell asked.

The madman frowned, concentrating as if the knowledge seemed just within reach. When the words did not come, he shook his head. "You cannot treat me this way."

"Oh, but we can," the physician replied with mocking kindness. "It is for your own good."

With a smooth gesture, Quarrell removed his wool cloak and swung it out. It swished through the air, unfurling like a black shadow, then settled down over the captive's shoulders.

The madman sank to his knees again, as if the cloak were a leaden weight. For an instant he crouched, trembling beneath its darkness.

Suddenly he leapt to his feet, screaming like an animal in pain. His face contorted far beyond anything Claire had yet witnessed, terror and rage warping his features. She gasped, backing away from the madman even as one of the guards surged forward and grabbed him. The madman bared his teeth, snarling. Twisting, he seized a dagger from the guard's sheath and slashed at the arms that gripped him. The guard bellowed. Blood spurted into the air.

Breaking free, the madman lunged toward Quarrell. His arm lifted, dagger striking for the physician's heart. Quarrell dodged, careening into her and Reginald and knocking them apart. Raising the blade again, the madman lurched for Quarrell.

"No!" Claire cried out. Beside her, Reginald unsheathed his sword. She gripped his arm. "Stop!"

The madman halted at the sound of her voice, and turned toward her, the dagger still raised. His eyes met hers, filled with vicious fury and desperation. *There was no recognition in them.* Her stomach hollowed, a cold emptiness. Would he kill her?

"Please," she whispered. No light came into his gaze, but

his ferocity changed to bewilderment. He began to lower the blade.

"Seize him," Quarrell commanded.

Cursing, the guards grabbed the man and shoved him back down into the mud, twisting his arm to force him to drop the weapon. He struggled, moaning as they beat him, then bound his hands. The moans rose to tortured screams as they wrapped him in the black cloak and carried him into Bedlam.

Claire stared after them, shaking inside the warmth of her furs. She was still dazed from the fantastical experience and its hideous aftermath. How could the poor man be controlled one instant, raving the next?

"You fool!" Reginald hissed at her, prying her fingers from his sword arm. "Why did you hinder me? That lunatic would have killed us!"

"I thought I could stop him," Claire said. If the madman had killed the physician, she feared he would be slain in turn. "And I did. You saw."

"I saw him try to stab Master Quarrell, then turn on you instead," Reginald said.

"No." He had lowered the blade.

"He was already covered in gore. Who knows how many he's slaughtered."

"It looks to be his own blood," she argued, remembering the head wound.

"Why did you ever allow him so close? Your folly began all this."

Your obscene groping began all this, she thought, then flushed. However coarsely Reginald had behaved, her conduct must seem doubly bizarre. The madman had kissed her in front of everyone. His embrace should have been repellent, terrifying. But it was not. Not at all. Her cheeks burned with shame and confusion. "He was suffering. I wanted to help him."

"Help him? Weeping angels, Claire! The man's a deranged killer, not a lost puppy yelping in the gutter. Let Master Quarrell tend to him." Reginald sounded pleased now, anger giving way to condescension. To chastise her folly was to salve his pride.

"Yes, Reginald." Arguing was pointless. She could do nothing further today. Tonight was his family's ball. Perhaps tomorrow one of her brothers could find out the captive's identity. The man might have relatives who would tend him more kindly.

She frowned. Had the madman whispered her name? Perhaps she had heard nothing more than a sigh. It was confusing . . . disturbing. But not as disturbing as the magnetic power of his touch. Flame and ice licked at her spine. Claire shivered and drew her cape tighter.

" 'Tis not the most congenial spot to lollop," Reginald said peevishly. "Best we leave."

"Yes," Claire acquiesced, wishing she did not feel traitor to a stranger.

A guard unlocked the gate, and they returned to the hired litter that waited in the street. Claire's maid, Dorcas, watched over the gifts she'd bought earlier, while Reginald's plump manservant, Barnaby, guarded his master's precious tobacco. Dorcas fussed with Claire's cape and muddy skirts, and stole glances at Reginald. Her maid was a sweet, silly goose who thought the Baron the handsomest man she'd ever seen, and pouted if Claire did not sing his praises. With all Dorcas' flusters and blushes of late, perhaps Reginald had bedded her. Claire found she did not care, except that Dorcas would end up in tears—and pregnant, no doubt.

Clothes arranged and parcels counted, Claire and Reginald settled back against the wooden seat, allowed a blanket to be draped over their knees, and newly filled foot warmers to be placed beneath them. On the way here, Reginald had cuddled close. Claire was glad he now sat as stiffly as she did. "To the Cockscomb." Reginald waved the bearers toward his favorite tavern. They set off, the servants walking behind. Although Claire did not protest the detour, he added, "We need a drink to warm us."

"Most considerate," she murmured sweetly.

Too sweetly, perhaps, for Reginald sat in reproachful silence, his glances alternately sour and suspicious. He had provoked her, but she had been provoking in turn. Knowing the marriage was inevitable, Claire resolved not to make an enemy of him. She could not endure to flatter and flirt, but neither would she stir his animosity. Instead she endeavored to be bland and boring till they reached the Cockscomb

"Wait here," Reginald said, and disappeared inside.

Claire examined her parcels, taking pleasure in the gifts she'd bought this morning. She'd found an illustrated treatise on fencing for her favorite brother, Gabriel, and a rare alchemical text for her father's collection. That extravagance had all but emptied her purse. A pomander of a dried orange rind stuffed with a potpourri of violets and rose petals made a sweet prize for her mother. Holding it to her nostrils, Claire sniffed, wishing its fragrance would banish all memory of Bedlam's hideous stench and distressing events.

But not her madman's kiss.

Hesitantly, Claire pressed her fingers to her lips. Her mouth felt sensitive, quivering with the memory of his hunger. Reginald's most sweetly courting kisses left her cold. She had desired Rafe, and thrilled at the tender, fraternal salute of his lips on her hand. But even that longed-for touch did not compare to the brief, devastating embrace of the stranger in Bedlam's courtyard. Its power seemed impossible now. Overwrought by the surrounding horrors, she must have imagined the intensity.

But if the ugliness had affected her so deeply, why had she been drawn to her madman rather than repulsed? Why had she imagined his arms a haven, a true asylum?

"Here you are." Reginald reappeared, handing her a sloshing cup of spiced beer. He held no cup for himself, but brandywine tainted his breath. He watched resentfully as she sipped the hot drink, tasting cinnamon and juniper berries. "We must hurry if we are to catch the tide."

As if *she* had delayed them. Claire handed back the cup with a curt nod, too sick of Reginald to bother with civility. Claire hated the thought of dancing with him tonight at the ball—the palmy touches and mock kisses, his sweaty hands lifting her high in the volte. How would she endure a lifetime with this man? Yet law and duty demanded it. Catching an uneasy glance from her betrothed, Claire imagined he was wishing for a way out as well. Or at least for a bride who would relish kissing him in a madhouse.

Flushing, Claire turned her face away. She had proved all too well she was willing to kiss, and in a madhouse. Not Reginald but a nameless madman with haunting eyes and music in his voice.

They both sat in silence as the litters carried them down to the Thames. At the dock, Reginald chose a wherry with bright red cushions and helped her into the boat. Barnaby aided Dorcas, then climbed in after. They set off on the river, the afternoon tide bearing them swiftly toward the bridge.

"Which bank will ye' be stopping at—north or south?" the boatman asked.

"Neither," Reginald answered. He thrust his hand into his purse and drew out a fistful of pennies. "Shoot the arches."

The boatman drew a swift breath, his gaze fixed on the glimmering silver, easily a week's earnings. Dorcas gave a mew of frightened pleasure. Claire frowned. It was a tricky business, guiding a wherry safely through the narrow arches where the rushing water quickened its force, and churned into rapids with the shifting tides. Young gallants loved the wild ride, but there were accidents aplenty. Sensible travelers stopped their river journey at London Bridge and walked around, resuming their boat trip on the other side. "Don't be foolish, Reginald," Claire protested, annoyed at his recklessness.

"Foolish, me?" He glowered at her.

Claire quickly tried to mollify her tone, "Please, Reginald."

Too late. His lips twisted in a smirk as he challenged their boatman. "You've the skill for it, haven't you?"

The boatman had the greed for it, thought Claire. She did not like the uncertainty on the man's face, though it was better than Reginald's callous defiance. Spots of color flushed high on his cheeks, bright as an old lady's rouge. If Claire would not return his desire, he would frighten her and so feel manly in his daring.

She glared at him, then turned to the wherryman. "Take me to the shore."

"No!" Reginald exclaimed. "Take us through the arches, boatman, or I'll pay you nothing."

"I'll pay you," Claire countered, opening her purse. But she had spent most of her money on the gifts.

Reginald scowled at her, and added a golden angel to the silver in his hand, jingling the coins. The man quickly guided the wherry to the center of the Thames. Obviously, neither her betrothed nor the boatman cared a jot about her trepidations. Only Barnaby looked worried. Claire started to reach for her earrings and hesitated. She could bargain with her jewelry, but Reginald might outbid her again. The more he spent, the angrier he'd be. The rift between them could widen irreparably. Subduing her nervousness, she settled back on her seat, trying to look compliant. Boatmen often shot the arches.

And often crashed. Not everyone cheated death.

They swept down the river. The great bridge loomed ahead, shops and residences piled six stories high atop it. Beneath its arches were the twenty narrow channels. Claire saw the surge and foaming of the water, then felt its pull as they plunged forward, funneled toward the shadowed arch. Her stomach plummeted and her limbs went soft as jelly. She cried out, truly frightened now. Reginald looked back, obviously relishing her distress. He gave her a wild grin, full of brandywine courage. Claire bit her lips to keep from crying out again, and exchanged a glance with the ashen Barnaby. Dorcas made up for their grim quiet with shrieks of giddy fear and excitement.

The boat crested a surge, lifted, and bounced, spray spattering them like freezing rain. Reginald shouted his excitement. A foaming arm of current thrust up, tilting the boat and spinning it sideways. Struggling against the force, the boatman tried to aim the prow forward, but the rush of gray water pummeled them ferociously. Reginald's glee turned to terror as the oar broke loose. The end snapped back and struck the boatman, knocking him unconscious. Claire gasped as another surge of water smacked the wherry, then hurled them against the bridge. Wood cracked, but the boat rebounded, meeting a sudden swell that lifted them high. Dorcas screamed as the boat leapt and flipped, tossing them high.

Claire cried out but heard no sound. Time shifted. The pounding of her heart, the pounding of the water thundered the same deafening silence. She was falling . . . falling slowly as a snowflake. Everything drifted, the boatman, Reginald, the servants airborne, the boat rising over them like a flying coffin. The images swirled in a solemn dance of descent. Other visions wove through her mind. She saw her father with his potions, her brother laughing beside her at the theater.

She saw her poor madman, his serene and ravaged gaze drinking in her soul . . .

Then the water lunged up and wrapped about her, a slavering beast dragging her into its dark maw. Cold stunned her, driving out her breath. Claire struggled not to inhale. She felt the sodden weight of her clothes dragging at her as the current tumbled her through the roiling torrent. Pain raked her hand, her arm, as if some ghastly sea creature clawed it. She screamed as the piercing intensified. The river rushed in, filling her mouth and lungs with icy water. She choked, mad for air. Panic seized her, a tumult within to match the manic frenzy of the churning rapids.

I am going to die—

Then the powerful swirl of the water slammed against her and hardened into an impenetrable mass of darkness.

Chapter 1

◅ ‿◡◠‿ ▻

Seven months later

Blackness claimed him as the hood descended over his
face. The hangman's noose settled about his throat. The
rope shifted back and forth, caressing his neck with loving
malice. Slowly it closed, drawing tighter and tighter, choking
off hope. Adrian fought for breath and found none. His throat,
his lungs burned as he swallowed the scorching darkness.
Consciousness funneled into a tight spinning circle, blacker
and blacker.

The rope eased, and he sucked air through the coarse fabric of the hood. One breath.

The noose jerked tight, lifting him off the floor and making
him dance. . . .

The pain was so palpable, he might as well be the one throttled. But he could also feel the thickness of the rope clenched
in his hand, the weight of the body he worked like a puppet.

18

Trapped in a sickening vertigo of terror Adrian watched . . . he inflicted . . . he suffered.

Adrian woke with a cry, gasping with relief as the air filled in his lungs. But when he looked up, Edward Quarrell crouched over him, watching him in silent fascination.

Waking was no escape. There was only nightmare.

The doctor's hands were pressed palm to palm, as if in prayer, but Adrian could feel their hot imprint lingering on his brow. Quarrell had touched him, stroked his forehead, brushed back his hair. Knowledge intensified the sensation. Adrian's skin burned as if peeled by acid. His stomach churned with nausea.

The doctor had been indulging his taste for torture.

"I wanted to make sure you were sleeping well, my lord," Quarrell's sonorous voice poured over him, thick and smooth as oil. The sound engulfed Adrian, covered him. Weighted by sickening fear, he sank down into an ever deepening well of darkness.

Again Quarrell reached out toward him, then paused. The pale hand cast a dark shadow over Adrian's face, like a raven of ill omen. He could smell the physician's skin, perfumed with clove and violets, sharp and sickly sweet. The hand descended. Fingertips skimmed his hair and Adrian shivered, closed his eyes to shut out the fog-gray gaze of the physician, intent and devouring. With each stroke of Quarrell's fingers, the sense of suffocation increased.

Adrian struggled for breath, for awareness. This was not as terrible as some of the blood-soaked memories the doctor brought to him. Yet it was terrible enough, for this time he recognized the victim, and shared her torment.

Vivian Swift—

The door creaked as someone came into the cell. "How is the patient?"

It was Sister Mary's voice, calm, concerned. Quarrell stopped stroking his hair and Adrian opened his eyes. Quarrell's brows creased into a frown, then smoothed to blandness. He turned to face her. "Our Adrian was suffering from a nightmare, I thought I might help."

"He dreads physical contact, Master Quarrell," Sister Mary said quietly, stepping into the cell. "He always seems worse if we must handle him."

She offered this as if Quarrell did not know it. The doctor answered in the same fashion. "Indeed? But such fear is unnatural. We must not coddle our inmates, sister."

After the outlawing of Catholicism, Bedlam's sisters were no longer nuns, but they retained the honorary title. To Adrian, Sister Mary was in God's service, and there were moments when her plain face took on the compassionate aspect of an angel. The faint, warm scent of pears she wore promised a sweet earthly freedom beyond these stone walls. Yet she was only human, a woman under the physician's authority.

Adrian knew Quarrell would do nothing blatant in front of her. He presented a polished façade of deception ornamented with hypocrisy. Adrian doubted if even the worst of the guards knew the depths of the doctor's depravity. Whatever Sister Mary might suspect, she was protective of her charges. Quiet, stubborn, she came a step closer, determined to bear witness.

The doctor need only dismiss her from the room—but tonight he ceded the game and moved to the door. "I must leave. Do as you think best."

When he had gone, Adrian gave Sister Mary a grateful glance. "Thank you."

"There is no need to thank me." Her head tilted to the side, a quizzical gesture. She did not understand why touch was such a torment. Quarrell was the worst—but anyone might submerge him in their pain, their grief, their viciousness. By simply touching him, Adrian became a part of their emotions, feeling them as if they were his own. His curse was unpredictable. He never knew if a touch would be simple skin to skin, or if flesh would suddenly peel away and some flayed soul would slide over him like a caul of agony. He did not know if he would be shown a moment or a lifetime. Even objects—a handkerchief, a ring, a shoe, might bring a barrage of horrifying images meshed with more horrifying emotions. Adrian had never risked exposing his secret to Sister Mary. He trusted her goodness, but not her silence. It was his greatest fear that one of his keepers would discover the truth and inform Quarrell.

Yet today I revealed my secret to a stranger. . . .

"Sister Mary, can you tell me how the new inmate fares?"

"Mistress Vivian? I am not allowed to visit her, Adrian." After a hesitation, she added, "I am told her delusions make her dangerous."

"She is not deluded," he said, although Vivian Swift was dangerous indeed. One touch had told him that she ruled London's underworld—or had till her rival imprisoned her here.

Sister Mary regarded him silently, seeming to weigh what he said. Adrian knew the sanity he had regained was always measured against his former violence, his supposedly false claims of nobility. She had seen him at his worst. Seven months ago they had dragged him screaming into Bedlam. Or so he had been told. He remembered nothing of that day or the week after. He did not know how long he had been wandering the streets before they brought him to Bedlam. The last thing he remembered was riding to meet his father at the docks—

Adrian frowned, raising both hands to rub his throbbing skull.

"I do not think Mistress Vivian will survive the night," he warned her.

It would not be the first time, or the last that a patient died here mysteriously.

Sister Mary drew a small, sharp breath, then shook her head. "I cannot tend her, so I must pray you are wrong."

There was nothing he could say. Nothing she could do.

"Try to sleep, Adrian," she said quietly, and then departed.

But he found it difficult to sleep, wondering if Quarrell would return with his soul reeking of Vivian Swift's blood. . . .

Adrian had met her only this morning, in the common room. Those confined there were seldom the peacefully mad and harmless idiots allowed the freedom of Bedlam's grounds. Nor were they so violent that that need be locked in their cells. Dreading contact with their madness, he sequestered himself in a corner and willed himself invisible.

Vivian Swift entered defiantly, clutching some semblance of dignity even in manacles. Wary as a cat, she paced the alien territory. Her hair, newly cropped by their keepers, stuck out about her face like a black burr. Her gaze was keen as she stalked about, examining everyone. Was she hunting for some imagined persecutor, or searching for someone with a semblance of sanity? She came to him, spoke to him, but he drove her away with veiled threats.

Next she'd approached crazy Isotta, who seemed sane, but was not. The madwoman leaped on Vivian, her fingers hooked like talons. Foolishly, Adrian rushed to a stranger's rescue. When he pulled Isotta away, her despair and fury engulfed him. She believed her husband had killed her child—her lover's child—baked it up in a mincemeat pie, and forced her to eat it. Mocking laughter rang in his ears. Adrian could taste the spiced meat in his mouth. A surge of nausea rose, acid in his throat. He choked it down, but the memories, emotions, kept flooding him. All around him, the denizens of Bedlam erupted into manic laughter, shrieks, and groans. He stood, immobile, trapped in Isotta's mind. Betrayal beyond comprehension. Her dead child.

Her memories stirred others within him—images he should understand, but could not. Ghastly flashes rising from his own darkness.

A babe stared up at him, eyes sightless, tiny lips blue.
A scarlet ribbon slithered like a snake. . . .

The guards hurled cold water over him, followed by a deluge of curses and blows. "Back off, my lord!"

It was Vivian who had saved him. She took his hand and pulled him back to reality with a jolt bright and lethal as lightning. The burning clarity shocked him back to his senses.

New visions shot through him, and he pulled his hand away. One thing he was certain of, this woman was entirely sane, if not entirely safe. Adrian retreated to his corner, trying to sort through this new barrage of images.

Vivian followed, questioning him. "The guard called you 'my lord.' "

He hesitated. But for the first time in months, he felt a sense of hope, however lunatic that emotion might be. He could not read the future in a touch, only the past, or the present moment. Yet he'd hoped they might help each other. "I am Sir Adrian Thorne. My father is the Baron, Lord Roadnight. I protested my rank overmuch when I found myself in Bedlam."

She eyed him askance at that. Her skepticism was natural. Why was he not locked up in some quiet room at home, carefully tended by the servants?

Why indeed?

"I did not expect you to believe me. Soon I will no longer believe myself." He laughed a little, a rusty sound. "My cousin apparently does not believe me either. From the window I watched him arrive and leave again, and I am still here. Perhaps he was a delusion as well."

"I do not know if I believe you or not," she said simply. "If you speak truly, then your cousin prefers your madness to your sanity, and looks to be lord in your stead?"

"So it seems." When the darkness came, he did not even fully believe himself. "After my cousin left, Master Quarrell told me that Adrian Thorne is dead. I have no proof but my own memory—and the look in Quarrell's eyes when he said it. Sometimes I wonder if I killed this Adrian Thorne. I wonder if his death spilled those memories into my brain."

Perversely, Adrian provoked her, then cursed himself for it. She seemed his last hope. Dangerous as it was, he knew he could make her believe him. So he told her who she was— Vivian Swift, notorious Queen of the Clink, ruler of thieves and whores, reigning brightly in the dark shadows of her underworld kingdom. Out of the images in his vision, Adrian described the most vivid. She sat before a mirror, a man reflected behind her. Her lover. Her betrayer.

"Rafe—" Her voice broke off abruptly. Her eyes flashed with both anger and pain. "Rafe Fletcher."

"Rafe," Adrian repeated. "You gave him a gift, a brooch, because you saw him in the mirror, staring at it."

"A golden dragon," she whispered, suddenly amazed. She believed him now.

"The dragon is important—I don't know why." It was something he never understood, how some objects were laden with significance, as images in a dream could be. He could feel the dragon watching him, waiting. He could almost reach out and trace its curving spine.

"What else?" she asked.

He shook his head. "Nothing else. Sometimes I see whole histories, sometimes only scattered pieces of a mosaic. Sometimes there is meaning, sometimes not."

"When you touch someone? Anyone?"

"I never know. Most often it is through touch. Sometimes an object will reveal things." Quickly, he added, "I have not told my keepers, for fear they would think me even madder than I seemed." And for fear Quarrell would understand the truth fully, and do away with him.

"I will not tell them," Viv swore. She gave him her most audacious smile. "Tell me, Sir Adrian, have you given much thought to escape?"

He felt a sudden surge of hope, and returned her smile. "A great deal, Mistress Swift."

Then Quarrell had come and taken her away. . . .

Adrian leaned against the wall of his cell, shame crawling through him as he remembered his own relief to be spared a confrontation. For his cowardice he suffered doubly. Quarrell had come anyway, oozing with Vivian's suffocating fear and pain.

But she was not dead. Not yet.

Or if she was, it was not Quarrell who had killed her. Adrian would have sensed it from the physician's touch if he had.

Quarrell had some curse like his own, so that he perceived the suffering he inflicted in some extraordinary way. He absorbed it, then poured it forth when he touched Adrian. But Quarrell did not suffer. He remained separate, a depraved glutton relishing the pain and misery of his victims. A ghoul fattening on death.

It seemed Quarrell understood the essence of Adrian's experience well enough to torment him, but not to feel threatened. Adrian wondered how long he would live if Quarrell comprehended just how much he knew of the doctor's secret crimes. Locked in Bedlam, Adrian could not put his knowledge to use against Quarrell. Even if he were free, he had no proof the visions of torture and murder were anything other than Quarrell's fantasies.

For that matter, Adrian had no proof that they were not his own.

Quarrell's touch had drained the energy from him, as it always did. Adrian felt himself drifting into sleep, craving that oblivion even as he feared the nightmares lurking in the dark. Half awake, he wondered if he should pray for Vivian, as Sister Mary said she would do. Vivian had offered him hope. Sister Mary had offered him kindness. Such rarities here.

When he closed his eyes, their faces blurred together, slowly becoming another woman. She came to him often at the edge of sleep. Ever elusive. Ever desired. She was good, though he could not say how he knew. She was beautiful, though he could never fully see her face. Her name hovered on his lips, but however much he tried, he could never quite recognize her. . . .

Adrian sat at the base of a great oak, it roots spreading around him like claws. He leaned back against the scaly trunk, and felt a fierce heart pounding within. His own heart leapt, beating wildly. Fearful, he looked up and saw the tree was a great dragon, twisted and knotted about itself. It gazed down on him, fiery eyes gleaming. Its tongue unfurled like a scarlet ribbon as it opened its fanged maw and swallowed him whole.

He was alone in the darkness. Waiting. Hunched in terror.

Then hands reached out, a woman's hands, slender and firm. They clasped his own. With their touch, terror vanished. For a moment, there was peace.

Then a new pain filled him, a longing, a hunger terrible in its sweetness. He searched for her face, but he could not see in the darkness. There was only her touch, her presence, which was a light burning in his heart. The only brightness. . . .

Her soft voice asked, "Who are you?"

But he could not find his voice. Slowly, the darkness dragged her away, an implacable tide. Her fingers slipped through his own like water. Her words became his own, echoing over and over as he called after her— "What is your name?"

If she answered, he could not hear her.

The light in his heart faded, its glow dimmer and dimmer until all sense of her vanished.

He was alone again in the dark.

Adrian woke abruptly. The faint sound of iron scratching on iron crept down his spine. Quarrell had come for him. Fear twisted through him with sinister images as the cell door swung open—but it was Sister Mary who stepped through.

In the torch-lit hallway he could see Vivian Swift. Beside her stood two men. One small and slender, with suspicious brown eyes. One tall, muscular, dark-haired. His equally suspicious eyes were blue.

"You are being rescued, it seems," Sister Mary said quietly, kneeling beside him. She fitted the key to his chains. "I pray that it is the right thing."

He stared at her in stunned disbelief. Surely this was yet another dream? But he answered her concern, murmuring, "I shall do my utmost to remain sane."

The chains fell away and Adrian rose, rubbing his wrists. Amazed, he walked to the open door and stepped out of his cell where his rescuer waited with her distrustful companions. It was all too solid, too particular for a dream—the grimy hallway, the guard sprawled unconscious. Vivian gave him a quick, fierce smile.

Escape. Suddenly it became real. His heart lurched wildly as rejoicing tangled with a surge of panic. He was not free. Not yet. Adrian struggled to stay calm, imperturbable, at least on the surface. Returning Viv's smile, he answered, "You are most resourceful, Mistress Vivian."

"I'm as surprised as you are." Her voice sounded rough, and he could make out bruises on her throat.

Remembering the hood, the noose, he swallowed hard. He took a breath. "And as grateful, then."

"Later." One of Vivian's cohorts nodded toward the unconscious guard. "Let's be gone."

Adrian followed the others as they ran along the hallway, past the now unlocked doors and slumped guards. His heart pounded violently. *Hurry.* Now that escape was in sight, he could not endure even the thought of the cell. The brown-eyed man glanced over his shoulder, another suspicious glance. He had a kind, clever face. Viv called him Izzy. The other man she ignored with such concentrated ire that Adrian would have known something was amiss. Even if Rafe had betrayed Vivian in the past, now he was helping her, helping Adrian, escape.

The stairs were in sight. Only two more sprawled guards, one last set of doors. The others went through. Adrian tried to pass, but one of the men was only faking unconsciousness. He grabbed Adrian's bare ankle, jerked him to the ground, and wrenched him back. Adrian gasped as anger and fear jolted through him, half his own, half the guard's craven wrath. The guard's hand slipped, pulling off his shoe. Adrian kicked out viciously. His bare foot rammed the man's jaw. A stunning echo of pain sounded through him. The guard grunted and let go. Adrian rolled to his feet. Doubled perceptions rippled through him in a nauseating backwash. He staggered to the wall. The guard rose, lunging at him. Adrian gathered his strength and punched him. The guard stumbled, shook his head, and charged him again, grabbed his throat. Growling with rage, Adrian jabbed his knee into the guard's crotch. With a guttural croak, the guard fell to his knees. Suddenly Izzy appeared and struck the man's skull once, twice, with his weighted purse. The guard toppled face forward onto the stone floor.

"C'mon, then," Izzy urged, tossing Adrian the fallen shoe.

He pulled it on and ran after, his mind a reeling chaos. The others were gathered at the foot of the stairs. He leaned against the wall, struggling for breath, for control. Only a little farther. . . .

"Make it look like we forced Sister Mary to help," Viv ordered.

Adrian and Izzy led her into an office, tied her up, gagged her. "You don't want 'em guessing we're being easy on her." Izzy said, double-knotting the ropes. "Don't worry, I know how to make it look good but not hurt."

"Nod if you're all right," Adrian said, troubled.

Muffled by the gag, Sister Mary nodded and glanced at the door.

"That means hurry." Izzy slapped his shoulder and ducked out the door.

Adrian did not want to leave her behind, but all he did was whisper, "Thank you."

Her eyes urged him to flee, and he did, following the others through the door, across the courtyard, out Bedlam's gate, and down the street into an alley where Viv's cohorts waited. *Freedom waited. . . .*

Outside, the suffocation of Bedlam lifted. The sickening stench of the sewers clung like the lingering dread of capture, but breezes carried myriad aromas that never penetrated Bedlam's heavy walls. Adrian inhaled heady gulps, drinking the green scent of trees and shrubs, a hint of roses, pungent drafts of cooked onions, fish, and ale. Izzy popped a cork from a bottle and Adrian smelled the acid richness of red wine.

He felt vulnerable as a new-hatched chick, fearful and

wonderstruck. His senses were overloaded. Excitement blurred the names—there was a man called Smoke, a boy named Tadpole. Viv vanished and reappeared, bright as a flame in gaudy satins and a red wig. Izzy thrust a wine bottle at him, "We need to look like revelers."

Adrian baulked at touching it, but worried he'd seem peculiar. "Then I will sing."

He thought it a good solution, but Izzy frowned, then examined the bottle. "It's not mucky, and you've no need to drink unless you will."

I must act sane. Adrian forced himself to reach out and close his bare fingers around the neck of the bottle. Smooth glass—nothing more. He glanced at Vivian, who watched him anxiously. He smiled, feeling foolish, feeling wildly relieved.

"You need a disguise." A woman pressed a cloak into his hands.

No images flooded him, but his tension instantly doubled. They could be caught at any instant. Adrian draped the cloak loosely over his shoulders, covering Bedlam's telltale indigo uniform. He shrugged, arranging it to touch cloth, not skin. The tension eased, exhilaration rose, lifting him above the fear. Playing at sots and strumpets, they all made their way down the road toward Bishopsgate. Adrian might as well have been drunk. He was intoxicated with freedom, shivering with excitement. Looking up at the expanse of night sky, he turned slowly, watching the stars reel. Giddy delight rushed through him, and he fought the impulse to laugh wildly.

Freedom. . . .

"Where's that song?" Izzy asked, lifting his bottle high.

Yes, he promised them a song. And why not? One of the inmates had taught him a lewd ditty about sailors and mermaids—sins of the fins and sins of the flesh. He sang it loudly, feigning a drunken slur as they made their way to the city gate. It was all so easy. Izzy gave the night sergeant a full bottle of wine and they were through the portal without a single question. They played their game all the way to the Thames, where wherries waited near the Bridge. The night wind chilled Adrian as they crossed the river to Southwark. Hunching, he drew the cloak closer. Apprehension splashed over elation, rocking him like the choppy waves. What would he do if Viv turned and bade him goodbye and good luck?

But she didn't. Not yet. The wherries landed on the opposite bank, and Viv led them through her domain, the Liberty of the Clink. Criminals had once fled to the liberties to escape London's law—so it seemed fitting that a madman did so now. Adrian followed the others through a maze of back alleys to an inn called The Buzzing Hornet. The innkeeper was obviously nervous, but promised to do right by Vivian and her friends. It was determined that Viv, Rafe, and Izzy were to sleep elsewhere, and Adrian was to stay here with the others.

"Will you be all right tonight?" Viv asked Adrian. "Tomorrow someone will take you where you choose."

He nodded—then Vivian Swift was gone to tend to her own troubles. A sudden feeling of isolation dulled the edged excitement of escape. Adrian's blood hummed wildly, but his stomach felt hollow. He must trust these strangers who helped him only for Viv's sake. The innkeeper led the way upstairs and unlocked the door to his room. After the hideous cell in Bedlam, the simple lodging was a palace. Gratitude surged up in him and he smiled at the innkeeper. "We've set watchers to keep you all safe," the man assured him. "In the morning, I'll see to getting you better clothes. A decent doublet and breeches."

"Gloves," he said quickly. Sometimes a muffled aura emanated through cloth, but no vision had ever come unless there was some contact against his naked skin.

"Gloves?" The man gave him an odd glance, clearly wondering why he should fuss about such a trivial thing.

After the madness claimed her, his mother had always worn delicate kid gloves. Protected, she could pretend that she'd never touched another's life in a comb, a glove, a ribbon. Never learned secrets in the clasp of a hand. Never felt her mind shatter at a death too terrible to bear.

"I must have gloves." This time his voice was calm, easy, despite his anxiety. He had trained the tone since childhood.

"If you must, you shall," the innkeeper said.

As soon as the man left, Adrian flung aside the cloak and stripped off the hated indigo uniform. He washed over and over, sponging away the grime of imprisonment. Cleansing away degradation. Bedlam had been a living death for him, and rescue a resurrection. Quarrell must not drag him back. Adrian doubted he would rise again from that grave.

Somehow, he must make contact with his father without risking capture. Tomorrow he would write a note, and arrange to have it delivered secretly. It seemed better than trying to reach him without warning. If his father was even in London. Suddenly time cracked—

Candlelight flickered uneasily in a low-ceilinged room. The air smelled of brown ale and sweat, tar and the Thames. His father sat at table, his face carved with grief. In the wavering shadow, his black eye-patch looked like an empty socket. . . .

Adrian shuddered, then thrust away the disturbing image. Was that the last time he'd seen his father? Just thinking made his head ache now. All his energy bled away, leaving overwhelming exhaustion. Too much had happened too suddenly. Tomorrow would be soon enough to plan. He must sleep.

Adrian regarded the bed warily. Who had slept in it last? Its clean linen could not be any worse than Bedlam's filthy straw. Naked, he crawled between the sheets. They were old and worn, soft against his skin. Myriad sensations blurred into a blanket of comfortable fatigue.

That night he slept without dreams. . . .

Adrian rose at dawn and watched the sun rise. It was a long time since he had seen such a miracle. Light gilded the rooftops and stained the clouds to hues of autumn fruit, the luscious yellow and coral of ripe pears, streaks of apple red, rosy plum. Could one dine on a banquet of clouds? Surely his spirit feasted on this sweet and terrifying freedom.

A knock sounded at the door, shattering his euphoria. But it was only the innkeeper, bringing a light breakfast and the promised clothes. Draped in the blanket, Adrian thanked his generosity, and sent him off with the hated indigo garments to be burned. Taking the food to the window, he devoured the sharp yellow cheese and dense bread, washing them down with the rich brown ale. Then, slowly, he ate the apple, juicy and crisp, better than any sweetmeat. Belly full, he plucked through the garments gingerly, but no images spilled forth from their folds. When he put on the linen shirt and drawers, he felt slightly drunk, but that might be his own relief to find nothing dubious lurking within them.

The rest was serviceable, clothes for Adrian Noname: doublet of green fustian, balding in patches, mustard netherstocks, and brown breeches. He put on boots, overlarge, and wiggled his toes inside them, absurdly amused by everything. Had the shirt and shoes belonged to the same tipsy fellow? Last, he donned new gloves of dark red leather that fit snug and smooth, as if made for him. He moved about the room, touching everything. No images penetrated the thin leather shield. Scrubbed, newly clothed, his hands armored in a second skin, Adrian felt ready to face the world, brimming with plans. In control.

But control was fleeting. Within the hour, Vivian came to the door. Rafe stood by her side, his gaze doubly wary. Vivian must have told this man his secret. Before, Adrian had only been a curiosity to Rafe, now he was a freak. Adrian wanted to close the door on them, but he stood aside to let them enter the room. Viv had promised not to tell the guards at Bedlam, no more than that. She had rescued him when she might have fled alone. Judging from her expression, she now meant to claim the debt he owed her. Reluctantly. And reluctantly he would pay it.

She faced him. "You said objects would reveal things to you."

"Sometimes," he answered, knowing she wanted something more specific than muddled emotions. "Rarely—but it is as potent as touch when they do."

Did he think Viv would spare him? She turned to Rafe. "Show him the brooch, Rafe."

The dragon brooch. Adrian knew that was what it would be before Rafe raised his hand, opened his fist. The golden beast gleamed, coiled about its mound of amber.

"Nothing may come of this," Adrian warned as he took off his gloves. But foreboding filled him as he reached out, closed his hand around the brooch.

He became someone else—became Gabriel Darren searching out clues to treason in a stinking wharf-side alley. He heard what he needed. But the conspirators heard him as well, seized and held him as the dagger went deep, opening a well of blackness inside him. He fought free, ran into the night. He knew he was dying. But he had to tell Rafe. He held a few words fast as he stumbled through the streets to reach him. Only when he fell into Rafe's arms did he give them up, precious as silver coins, as gems. He prayed that Rafe hear him, for he could no longer hear Rafe. He felt the blackness opening wider, and he sank slowly into it. Like final blessings, the faces of those he loved rose from the depths, then floated slowly away. . . .

But Adrian did not die with Gabriel Darren. He emerged from the vision with Rafe Fletcher gripping him, as he had held his dying friend. Adrian felt Gabriel's deep affection tangled in his own gratitude, as if Rafe had been his companion for a decade. Dazed, aching, he offered the brooch to Rafe, who quickly plucked it from his palm.

"This was your gift to Gabriel, and before that your father's to you," Adrian said. Without thinking, he laid his hand on Rafe's shoulder, only to have him pull away, fear and mistrust showing through his concern.

His reaction hurt Adrian, illogical as that was. Bitterly, he told Rafe, "I do not know sometimes if my soul is my own.

But it is not because I am a warlock who has bartered it to the devil. I never asked for this curse. It has brought me nothing but grief and pain. I did not want to be locked in Bedlam, but that's where it took me. I did not want to feel your friend's love for you—or his death."

"But you did," Rafe whispered.

"Yes." Then he told them what he had seen in the vision, the full import finally sinking in. Treason. A plot against the Queen. The fragments meant more to Rafe and Viv than they did to him. Exhausted, Adrian sat on the bed while they discussed what to do. His own emotions were small concerns compared to a kingdom in the balance.

Viv came to him, laid her hand on his shoulder, careful to touch only cloth. Her hand was warm and firm. "Thank you."

Rafe approached as well, still tentative. "You've had this . . . ability all your life?"

"Only since the night I was injured—or attacked. They took me to Bedlam because I could not remember who I was."

"It only began then?" Rafe asked.

"For me—but my family is cursed with it." He faced them. "My mother could do this thing, but it destroyed her."

"Destroyed her how?" Viv asked.

Always a fragile spirit, like a creature of Faerie, finally driven mad by her cursed gift. "She had an infant daughter, born too weak and sickly to survive. My father said she felt the babe's death and could not bear it. She went mad. She died mad."

He waited for them to shrink away, to cast him out. Call him cursed. Lunatic.

"You just survived the touch of death, Adrian," Vivian said. "Not of your own child, it is true, but of a painful murder. You have the strength to bear this gift. And because of it the Queen of England will live."

"We must go," Rafe said. But he reached out and gave Adrian's shoulder a squeeze.

He looked up, startled that Rafe would offer the acceptance. Yet he knew that the man had a generous heart. Would they accept him if he told them his mother had all but blinded his father? If he told them his great-grandfather had died lunatic as well? This time Adrian held his tongue.

"Farewell for now." Viv gave him a full purse. "If we do not return, this will help."

"Godspeed," he said, knowing their mission could well prove fatal.

Rafe and Viv went to stop the treason. Adrian stared at the closed door, wondering if they would ever return. The thought pained him, as if he had known them for years. He wished he could have gone with them. But the vision had left him as weak as if a surgeon had bled him. He would be more hindrance than help.

Drained, Adrian lay back on the bed. Images rose up to haunt him, but he was too tired to push them away. He let them wash over him, a flooding of pain and sadness that overwhelmed even the months of Bedlam's misery. He hovered again on the edge of that final dark mystery, filled with visions of a dead man's life and his last hour. Gabriel Darren's last-remembered faces rose up, gazing into his mind's eye. Adrian's heart ached for the sorrow of their loss and for the easing solace of their love. Their images spun slowly. Rafe, closer than a brother, laughing as their swords danced in play. Gabriel's father with his gray beard and wise blue eyes, turning the crinkled vellum of an ancient manuscript. *Claire,* his cherished sister, loyal and lovely.

Very lovely . . .

Her face drifted by him, pearly pale as a blossom taken by a breeze.

So familiar, Adrian thought. He might have known her always. A rush of tenderness poured through him, a longing that seemed to rise from his own darkness and reach toward her luminous presence. Even her name was familiar, as if his lips had tasted his sweetness before.

Claire . . .

His eyes closed, weighted with sleep.

A dragon uncoiled from a mountain of amber. It flew, carrying him on its back. The wind flowed around him

*and the world spread below in a glowing mosaic of
mountain, forest, and sea. Then the dragon folded its
wings and plunged down toward the mountain, its golden
scales clashing like metal as it landed in a dark cave.*

*At first Adrian could not see anything but the golden
sword he held. He lifted it and its faint glimmer revealed heaps of silver, gems of topaz and garnet.
Crowning the top was a perfect creamy pearl, worth a
soul's ransom. But a cloaked figure roved back and
forth before the treasure, insubstantial as a shadow,
black as a grave. The cloak flared like wings as it
whirled to face him, evil billowing from it like an acrid,
metallic stench. Adrian gasped and retreated.*

*Then, behind the shadow, he glimpsed a woman
standing on the dragon's hoard of jewels. Her face
glowed, more beautiful, more precious than any pearl.
She was slender as a willow, with the same supple
strength. Infinitely desirable. He yearned toward her.
She reached out her hands to him.*

*He reached out in answer. If he could only touch her,
he would be safe.*

Claire. . . .

*The shadow swept over them like a crow, beak and
claws gaping. Adrian lifted his weapon to defend them.
It ignited, blade and hilt molten hot, blinding him, burning through his hand to the bone. He dropped the
sword, and the shadow fell upon him, enveloping him,
dragging him into the void—*

Adrian woke sweating, disoriented, his stomach churning.
He felt as if he'd plummeted from a great height. The fall was
terrible, yet he ached to fly again. The room was dark. He'd
slept into the night and now was wide awake. He rose and
went to the window staring out at the stars. Deeply troubled
by the dream, he kept watch till morning, when the innkeeper
brought his breakfast. Adrian forced himself to eat, knowing
he needed to build his strength.

It was noon when Izzy knocked on the door, bringing news of success. "We've done it, my lord, taken the traitors. Caught 'em or killed 'em, every one."

"And you are all safe?" At Izzy's nod, relief flooded through Adrian, for his newfound friends and, selfishly, for himself.

"Rafe and Viv are still at Whitehall Palace, my lord, but they sent me to let you know what's what."

"You called me 'my lord' " Adrian stilled.

"Yes, my lord, Viv explained a thing or two to me." Izzy fidgeted uncomfortably. "How you were out of your head after being attacked, so they took you to Bedlam, but your cousin left you shut up there for his own ends."

"It would be best to go on calling me just Adrian," he said, though even his Christian name was a risk just now. Surely it was better that Izzy know he was a Baron wrongly confined than any stray madman Viv had decided to free from Bedlam. He must trust her judgment, or strike out on his own.

"I'll go back to doing that." Izzy hesitated, watching him with concern and wariness. "What with the other matter—the bit of treason—being taken care of, Adrian, we've been asking around, and we've some news for you. It's not good news, but you've got to know it anyway."

"If I have to know it, then you'd best tell me, Izzy."

"I'm sorry to say so, but your father . . . well . . . he's dead, my lord."

"Dead?" Adrian whispered, stunned. "How? When?"

"Done for by thieves—attacked the same night as you were, last February." Izzy paused. "You'd had an argument with your father. You remember the why of that?"

"No." He wanted to deny the argument as well as the memory. "No."

"You ran out the back of the tavern into the alley. Next thing was the watchman heard a splash. He caught two thieves trying to throw your father into the Thames. Shot one, the watchman did. Before he died, your father said they'd killed you, and tossed you in before him."

"They arrested the man who did it?"

Izzy shrugged. "Oh, the one left alive said he didn't kill either of you, he just found you both a bloody mess. Then he said his partner did it. They gave him a taste of the pinchers, and he confessed it, finally, for what that's worth. Maybe it was him, maybe it was the one they shot, but they're both dead, if it makes you feel any better."

Adrian shook his head. What if the thief told the truth? What if his father was protecting the family name, his own pride?

"Must be hard news to hear. I'll leave you alone now, my lord," Izzy murmured. Adrian barely heard him depart. Grief churned with uglier emotions. Terrible questions battered him.

Why did I not know my father was dead?

Why did I not let myself know?

Pain sliced into his brain. Time sloughed away. He was back in the wharfside tavern—

Fury overwhelmed Adrian. Sudden. Total.

"Don't look at me like that." His father backed away, slowly, fearfully.

"Murderer!" Adrian struck out, knocking him against a wall. Torchlight flickered wildly, scarlet ribbons of flame lashing, light and shadow writhing like snakes.

His father cowered. The horror in the one staring eye only enraged Adrian more.

The liar did not deserve to live.

Adrian's mind crashed shut like an iron door, but the fear had already escaped, rushing wildly through him. He saw his father's face in the darkness, blood running in scarlet steams. Imagination or memory? He pressed his hands to his temples, but he could not escape the rising horror.

Did I kill my father?

Did his murder drive me mad?

Chapter 2

❦

Claire made her way to the far end of the Privy Garden. Choosing an arched seat carved from a privet hedge, she laid her pillow in its hollow and settled there, her mourning skirts spreading around her like black water. She took her lute from its case and carefully tuned it, feeling the quivering vibrations as the strings came alive beneath her fingers. She should enjoy this perfect day. The September morning was warm, the breeze fragrant. Late roses still bloomed, and the scent of apples from Whitehall's orchard gave a rich aroma to the air. Crimson tassels of love-lies-bleeding brushed the hem of her skirts, the pendant blossoms tender and velvety.

Their delicate beauty did nothing to mellow the bitterness that rose when she felt the first twinge of pain in her hand. But that pain was expected now. Ignoring it, Claire began to play, plucking carefully at the lute strings with her plectrum. She chose the poignant melody of "Greensleeves." It was a tune the Queen often requested, for her royal father was one of many who had composed lyrics for the old ballad.

Alas my love you do me wrong,
to cast me off discourteously,
For I have loved you so long
delighting in your company. . . .

Claire stopped abruptly. "Greensleeves" did not salve her bitterness, but increased it. She would not play it.

Even as she considered another tune, giddy laughter spilled into the garden. She lifted her head, watching as three of the Court ladies drew a captured courtier into a game of blind-man's bluff. Satin and brocade gleamed flower bright in the sunlight as the young women hid behind hedges or columns, then darted out to poke and tease the groping blindman, trying to lure him toward the fountain. No doubt the gardener waited concealed behind a hedge, hands on the hidden mechanism, ready to send water through the pipes and sprinkle the courtly target when he ventured within range of the fountain.

A lady dodged behind a column—the chimera. A vividly painted heraldic beast s7urmounted each of the thirty-four decorative columns. Horns or tail gilded, their paws or hooves gripped a royal pennant. Unicorns, lions, gryphons . . . in the past, the mythic creatures had charmed Claire. In the past, she might have joined such a frivolous gambol. Now their merriment emphasized her sorrow. The columns hemmed the grassy walks like the bars of a cage. She felt imprisoned by protocol, trapped in the endless intricate dance of manners, when she longed to sit quietly under the chestnuts at home, to play her lute, to mourn. Queen Elizabeth wanted her to remain at court, but awarded small concessions. Claire had leave to sit alone and practice her instrument for an hour. Ignoring the ladies and their courtier, she turned her attention back to the lute—but she could not ignore her own grief.

The black she wore was not for Reginald Fitzroy. His heedless folly that winter day in the boat stirred fury rather than pity. She mourned her beloved brother, Gabriel, dead scarcely a month. She sorely missed his companionship and easy laughter. If he were alive, she would not be so weary of

Court. Instead they would analyze together all the nuances of the ceaseless social and political intrigues, and smile at all the vanities and foibles.

But home did not offer escape, only more turmoil. Despite Gabriel's death, her mother had urged Claire to accept the recent proposal of a rich but aging Earl. *The joy of a wedding will lighten our heavy hearts.* The facile words made Claire furious, and her answer had infuriated her mother. *Only the heavy weight of gold will lighten your heart.* Before the boat accident, Claire never dared to speak so bluntly. She would have made her wishes known, but yielded to duty. Now defiance bristled at every turn. Distressed by the arguing, her father had just granted Claire a year to mourn and to consider her future. But he would yield no further. He loved his daughter, but he worshipped her beautiful, tyrannical mother. Claire knew she must then choose a husband, or they would choose for her.

She did not want to think on that, not yet. Because she also mourned for lost love—for Rafael Fletcher, who was alive and happy but would never be hers. For years the dream of Rafe had glowed, a cherished secret of her heart. But that dream had been drowned in the pain and misery that followed her plunge into the Thames. Rafe had been away at war in the Netherlands when the accident happened, returning only last month to save his family when they were accused of treason. She had played a small part in uncovering that conspiracy. Seeing Rafe again, Claire wondered if that dream could be recaptured. If so, she would have defied her parents to marry him. But it was not to be. Yesterday the Queen had knighted Rafe, pardoned the notorious Vivian Swift, and decreed they should marry. Luckily for them, it was their heart's desire. Fate was full of strange conceits.

Perhaps my mourning black is also for my poor madman in Bedlam.

After the boat wreck Claire had hoped, desperately, irrationally, that something, someone else could be salvaged from the wreckage of that day. She'd sent Gabriel to Bedlam to ask whom the madman might be. But Gabriel was told the man was dead. Claire had wept inconsolably at the news, her misery doubled. It was a puzzle to her, how deep her grief had been, and still was. She'd never so much as learned his name, yet his tragedy felt inseparable from her own. His eyes, his voice, haunted her still. Sometimes, unbidden, her lips, the palms of her hands tingled, warm with the memory of his touch.

Pushing away such fruitless thoughts, Claire settled her lute into place and began a brighter ayre. As she played, a sudden pain lanced up the back of her right hand to her elbow. She schooled her face to remain impassive, her fingers to keep moving. Looking down, she could see the gnarled scars running from knuckles to wrist, their pink-edged whiteness gleaming strangely. Other scars were hidden from view beneath her sleeve, raking along her forearm. Her mother coaxed Claire to wear gloves to hide the visible ugliness of her hand, but she refused. The scars were hideous, but she would do nothing to hamper her movement.

Even seven months after the accident ravaged her arm, she could play only clumsily. Her index finger was paralyzed, the middle finger awkwardly stiff. Claire had learned to hold her hand so the crippling was not apparent. She had taught herself a new balance for such mundane tasks as holding her wine goblet, and she was determined to master her lute again. She had gained strength and agility in the outer fingers and thumb, using them to hold the plectrum. Simple tunes she could manage, but the swift, intricate plucking of the strings was now beyond her. Though she had lost that skill, the joy and the solace of creating music were not to be lightly relinquished. Her arm ached continuously as she played, and would afterward. She ignored it. To create music was worth the pain.

To be alive was worth the pain.

For two days after the accident, she had lain insensate while her family tended her body and prayed. They had all but abandoned hope when she awoke, emerging from the well of blackness with her throat parched, her head pounding, and her arm horribly mangled. But she survived. Reginald Fitzroy had dragged all the others with him into death, his manservant and poor Dorcas, the foolish, greedy boatman. It was another, more skillful wherryman who had dared the narrow arches of the bridge and grabbed Claire as the roiling water lifted her briefly to the surface. Or so she had been told. She remembered the churning current, a sudden weightlessness, the terrible plunge into gray icy water. Then nothing.

Nothingness.

That absence of memory was a black pit, a grave waiting to swallow her. The thought of it decimated her where the pain could not. Claire stopped her playing as cold sweat pricked her skin with icy needles and her hands began to quiver. She did not know how to fight the fear. The darkness rose around her, a voracious whirlpool sucking her down, drowning even her will to fight. She sat, clammy and trembling, the lute dangling by her side.

You are alive, fool, she chastised herself. *Alive.*

"Lady Claire?" The quiet tone summoned her back from the spinning morass of fear. A tall figure shadowed her. She looked up and saw Sir Nigel Burne, his face unexpectedly concerned. "Are you well?"

"As well as I might be." Claire bit her lips on the sharp retort. She should be grateful that he had banished the darkness, since her own will had failed.

He shifted his weight back a step, ready to depart.

"Forgive my rudeness, Sir Nigel," Claire said, stiff with shame to have revealed her weakness. He was not a man to whom she wished to reveal either frailty or temper. She respected him and valued his respect. No doubt, he was on his way to or from a meeting with Sir Francis Walsingham. Few were more privy to the plans of the Queen's secretary of state and spymaster than his chief intelligencer, Sir Nigel Burne.

"Your arm pains you?" He glanced at her discarded lute, then briefly at her maimed hand. She subdued the impulse to hide it in the folds of her skirt.

"I must challenge myself to regain what skill I can." It was easier to acknowledge the pain than the fear. She curved her lips to a thin smile. Years at Court had taught her the masks of courtesy. But since the accident, they pinched so tightly she wanted to cast them off and trample them—sometimes in pure ill temper, sometimes in a reckless hunger for freedom.

"Your efforts are admirable." His tone was sincere, his eyes kind.

From Sir Nigel both responses were rare gifts, but Claire hated to dwell on her injuries. "I have hopes that my playing may one day be admirable again."

She studied him for a moment. Sir Nigel was tall, attenuated almost. Pale ash brown hair was cut close to his head, and trimmed to a narrow beard and mustache. His features were small and regular, prim even. But his eyes were intent, a curious shade of green, pale and cool as grapes. The other ladies-in-waiting dismissed him as cold and contemptuous, but Rafe had lately declared that Sir Nigel was enamored of her. Startled, Claire had countered that he had never done anything untoward, not even flirted with her. He was a married man—though, perhaps more married to his cause than to his wife. The only overt passion Claire had ever seen Sir Nigel display was political. Her brother had died in his service, and she was sure it was for Gabriel's sake that Sir Nigel was unfailingly courteous to her.

"I have no doubt you will succeed," he said now.

To turn the conversation from herself, she said, "There is endless speculation at Court. Do you believe Queen Elizabeth can bring herself to order the execution of her cousin, an anointed Queen?"

"I think she must at last," he answered. "You know we have evidence which links the Scots Queen directly."

Claire nodded. "If executed, she may become a martyr. That is also a danger."

"Perhaps, but a martyr cannot claim a throne," he said.

"Tension at Court has eased this past week."

"Following the execution of her Catholic conspirators? Yes." He nodded his approval. "And those involved in the snaphance plot will soon join them. Treason is forever a threat. We must remain vigilant."

She heard the fervor in his voice. "We were lucky that Sir Raphael and Mistress Swift discovered the truth in time."

"They have earned their reward," Sir Nigel replied, somewhat begrudgingly. "The traitors are brought to justice. Your brother's death was not in vain."

Claire touched the brooch she wore pinned to the bodice of her gown, a golden dragon coiled around a small dome of amber. Rafe had first given it to Gabriel. Now, she treasured it in memory of the friendship they had shared. Perhaps it was that friendship she had loved, as much as Rafe. "I am proud of Gabriel," she said, though pain constricted her throat. "And of Sir Raphael as well."

"He is staying at the Dancing Fox, I believe?"

"Yes, that was the name they gave me," she answered.

Sir Nigel nodded, then rose and bowed. But after a second's hesitation he spoke again, his pale gaze intent, "Your brother uncovered the first links of a deadly plot against the Queen. The Crown is both indebted and grateful, as am I. If I can ever be of service to you, do not hesitate. You have a friend in me, Lady Claire."

"Know that I value your friendship, Sir Nigel." She felt gratitude—and relief—that he was kind to her simply for Gabriel's sake.

Claire watched as Sir Nigel walked away, then picked up her lute once more. She thought of Gabriel's quick wit, his kindness. Before the accident, he'd brought her new music; after it he'd helped retrain her injured arm. He had gone to wretched Bedlam to ask after a stranger, just to ease her mind.

Setting her plectrum to the lute strings, she began to play. The rippling music that spilled forth was a lovelorn Irish ballad. Unbidden, images of her madman rose again. She was certain that lilting undercurrent in his voice had been Irish. She sighed with frustration, trapped in coils of melancholy. Her madman was dead; her attempt to save him had come to naught. There she had failed.

Gabriel was dead, but his life was not poorly spent. Queen Elizabeth lived. Claire's own role in that rescue had given meaning to her life. But pride was a cold solace for grief. Suddenly, she hungered to see her friends. Rafe loved her as a brother. With Gabriel dead, that love had become precious indeed. For the first time she was grateful her infatuation had faded, so she was not torn with jealousy. Working with Vivian to foil the Queen's enemies had created a bond on which she might build a friendship rather than rivalry. Claire resolved it would be so. Surely, the Queen would grant her leave to visit them tomorrow.

It would be an adventure, of that she was sure.

Claire took up the lute and began to play again, forcing her fingers to a sprightlier tune.

Burne paused where he could observe Claire, but not be observed. Even under the black veil, her chestnut hair gleamed as she plucked her instrument. She was admirable in her courage . . . and utterly exquisite.

He considered their conversation. She had confirmed the name of the inn Fletcher had given him, but his own intelligence suggested it was only a blind. Fletcher and Swift continued to be troublesome, poking about in matters that did not concern them. Albeit he had reason to be grateful for their efforts on behalf of the crown, he disliked both of them. Mistress Swift was brazen and conniving. Fletcher preached noble sentiment while flouting authority. The man was reckless, mawkish, and ludicrously handsome—

Burne was jealous.

Lady Claire had loved Rafe Fletcher once, perhaps she loved him still.

Fletcher, fool that he was, had fallen in love with Vivian Swift. Burne had seen to it that he got her. When Burne suggested the match to Queen Elizabeth, she had laughed, saying it was her own thought exactly. He doubted it. The Queen did not like to see others married, since she was determined not to wed herself. She'd simply seized upon the union as the only possible way to control Vivian Swift, who looked to be a useful if dangerously slippery tool.

Elizabeth wished herself always first and foremost in the affections of her courtiers and her ladies. Despite her skill in statecraft, her deft manipulations, she had her father's vanity. She had commanded lusty hearts in her youth, but such adoration had faded with her beauty. Loyalty and respect remained—along with omnipresent greed and fear—but she must have constant flattery as well. Those who craved advancement danced to her tune.

Burne danced, but at a moderate pace. His rewards had been equally moderate. He did not have the flamboyance, the rash virility that the Queen rewarded in excess. Burne's devotion was to Protestant England, not Elizabeth herself. But if the Queen did not particularly favor him, neither did she underestimate his worth. Walsingham's health slowly declined. When he died or stepped aside, none of the impetuous gallants would be entrusted with his position, however much they flattered, fawned, and pranced before Elizabeth. Burne would become the Queen's secretary of state, member of the Privy Council, and England's spymaster.

Once, that was his reigning ambition. Once, nothing would have tempted him from the path to that goal, certainly not love. In the past, he had regarded that state with scorn, as if it were no more than lust prettily bedecked in silks and garlands. The crimes of love differed little from the crimes of lust. Yet lust did not make love's sacrifices. He did not know exactly when his admiration for Claire Darren transformed. But when he heard of her accident, his heart plummeted. He knew at once he would have dived into the Thames to save her, not caring if he survived. The thought of succumbing to such an impulse was in many ways more terrifying than the actual consequences.

Love.

Burne held his secret close, a terrible vulnerability he both treasured and loathed. Claire did not return his passion, not yet. She was not even aware of it. His hopes, his plots, were all directed toward the future. Claire was a prize for which he could wait. So far she had shown him only respect, a modicum of admiration. Slowly, Burne was nurturing those faint embers to a warmer glow. As much as he had hated the thought of Claire married to the callow Reginald Fitzroy, he knew she would have wearied of such a dull match—even as Burne had wearied of his wife, Margaret. With Claire so caged, Burne's appreciation of her intelligence, as well as her beauty, would have taken on new significance. Claire was honorable, but she was human.

Then Fitzroy had died, and Claire was free to choose for herself. Burne had feared that she might dare to choose Rafe Fletcher.

As the snaphance plot unfolded, Burne had often wished that one of the conspirators had succeeded in killing Fletcher—or that he'd done it himself when he had the chance. As an intelligencer, Burne had committed executions in the name of the Queen, even to preserve his own authority, his own secrets. But he had not murdered for personal gain—though jealousy had been a powerful goad. And fate had presented a better solution. Not murder, but marriage.

The wherry accident, her brother's death, Fletcher's betrothal, all had wounded Claire—but Burne would be there when she healed. Though he dreaded the fact that she must soon be looking for a husband, he could still make himself her staunchest ally. Someday his lover.

If he were only free, he would make Claire his wife.

Chapter 3

Claire gazed about eagerly as she crossed London Bridge toward Southwark. On either side, blocks of buildings rose six stories high. The street teemed with activity, merchants and their customers selling and buying, jugglers and singers performing—and cutpurses nipping. She wore doublet and hose and rode astride, as she had done since the accident, much to her mother's disapproval. But the even balance, the grip of her thighs and knees helped compensate for her weakened hold on the reins, as did a gentler mount. When riding at home, she made no effort to disguise her sex, but today she played the boy. Her hair was fixed beneath a large floppy cap with an overzealous plume that covered half of her face. Her small, high breasts were easily disguised by the stiff front of the doublet, as the swell of her hips was hidden by the puffy trunkhose. To the busy passersby, she seemed only a page on an errand.

The Thames was visible only between narrow breaks in the buildings. Strange, the churning waters in which she'd almost perished rushed beneath her, but she rode over them without a qualm. The busy river and its ships stirred no fear from this distance, but neither did the sight bring pleasure as it had before. The journey to Southwark would have been faster by wherry, but there her courage failed her utterly. She would not take a boat of any kind, unless there was no other way. Since the accident, she'd been on a boat but twice with her family, and been humiliated by her own trembling, sweating panic. She could barely stomach the smoothest passage. Once she had fainted. Trying to overcome her weakness, Claire had forced herself to sit alone in a boat tied to their family dock. That was little better, though knowing she could escape made her less desperate. Her fear did not answer to reason, and she had yet to bend it to her will. She had told no one of her weakness save the Queen, for fear Her Majesty might, unknowing, command her into the royal barge.

Passing under the shadow of the Tower Gate, she forced herself to look up at the grisly trophies impaled upon the spikes. Soon there would be more heads atop the ramparts—heads of people she had known, had helped Rafe and Viv to capture, and so to execute. But she would act no differently now, even looking upon their fate. They were traitors who had tried to take the life of the Queen. Claire's pity was that anyone should end so, a lump of carrion picked over by crows. The ugly sight muted her excitement, but did not ruin it. She rode on into the rough streets of Southwark. Though London law now ruled all the boroughs across the Thames, there was little evidence of its presence. Viv's domain, the Clink, was notorious for its gambling dens and brothels, and the Queen herself was known to come to the bear baitings.

Claire found the Dancing Fox with no difficulty, close by the Bridge and the courtyard of St. Saviour's. Inside, the customers were a rowdy lot, and she was glad of her disguise. But telling the innkeeper she had a message for Vivian Swift did not gain her access to the rooms, and she had to quietly reveal her identity. After a closer look at her face, he went to the stairs and beckoned. A lad with floppy brown hair descended.

As the innkeeper whispered in his ear, the boy looked over at her, eyebrow rising in surprise, then he gave her a wide grin.

"Tadpole at your service," he said with a wink, and gestured for her to follow him upstairs.

The room he unlocked was clean, but poorer than she would have expected. Entering, Claire found no one was within, though a fine satin gown lay draped over a chair.

"Mostly I'm just to summon 'em back here, if someone comes to call. But you, m'lady, I can bring to 'em directly," Tadpole told Claire, obviously impressed. With a conspiratorial grin, he opened the doors of a ponderous wardrobe. There was little on the shelves. He worked some lever and the back swung opened. Claire had seen such secret chambers before, for her father had one to protect his laboratory. Still, excitement tingled through her, deliciously sweet. "Viv herself designed this," Tadpole said proudly. "Step on inside."

He went through, and Claire followed him into a storage room. Tadpole closed the back of the wardrobe after her, then led the way down to a tailor's shop where they were given plain gray capes to cover what they wore. Tadpole pulled the hood well forward to cover her cap, tucking the plume within. With Vivian newly pardoned by the Queen, Claire could think of no reason for all this hugger-mugger, but she was enjoying the adventure.

The boy led her through a bewilderment of passages, tunneling between shops and weaving through back alleys until they reached an inn proclaimed by a yellow and black, wasp-shaped placard as the Buzzing Hornet. It looked prosperous, its sturdy wood frames filled with lime-washed daub and wattle. Tadpole cleared them with yet another watchful innkeeper, then led her upstairs. They stopped outside an oak door, and Claire heard the low murmur of voices cease abruptly at their knock. The door opened a crack to reveal a mild-looking fellow dressed all in russet, with hair and eyes much the same shade. Tadpole gave her name, which the other man recognized, for he stepped back immediately to let them enter.

Unerringly, her gaze went to Rafe, and then to Vivian,

seated so close beside him. Despite the sudden hollowness within, Claire smiled at them both. Envy, she thought, not jealousy. She wished them joy, but feared her own aching hunger would never be appeased.

Her mood lightened as she removed her cape and had the mischievous pleasure of shocking Rafe with her boy's garb. Viv took one look at Rafe's bewildered face and burst out laughing. "God's bones, Rafe, it's not the first time you've seen a woman in trunkhose."

"I had not expected it would become the reigning fashion," he said.

Viv rose in a blaze of scarlet satin skirts, but Claire knew the notorious Queen of the Clink had donned men's garb to strut about her kingdom. Viv inspected Claire's doublet, adjusting the pinked slashes with mock solemnity. She tilted the cap to a more rakish angle, then gave Claire a conspiratorial smile.

Recovering his manners, Rafe came forward to welcome her. "Lady Claire, however surprising, your visit is most welcome."

His smile was sheepish, but his large hands clasped hers gently. Claire let them rest there without fear. "Sir Raphael," she greeted, using his new title to both honor and tease him.

"You came alone," he asked, frowning a little.

Unchaperoned, he meant. She tilted her chin, "Yes."

"Lady Claire is well guarded now," Viv said to Rafe. "We must introduce the others."

Though her attention was on her two friends, Claire was aware of a fair number of people and a great deal of silent energy humming in the room. She had learned at Court to hear the subtle tones of silence as well as speech. This group had been plotting something.

"Our guest first?" Rafe hesitated, then turned and gestured toward the back corner of the room. "Lady Claire, allow me to introduce . . . Adrian."

Only a Christian name? As she turned to meet him, Claire wondered if this Adrian was a criminal, a fugitive, that he must hide his identity.

With one fluid movement he stood and moved to greet her. His face was arresting—and oddly familiar. Where had she seen him before? Roughly cropped, his hair mingled strands of dark blond and light brown, pale copper and polished bronze, and beneath it the upper tips of his ears were almost pointed. Winged brows and slanted cheekbones gave him the fey wildness of an elven prince. He regarded her with warm curiosity. The sunlight slanting across his eyes revealed irises alive with the colors of a quick-glinting stream, flecks of green, gray, and blue starred with amber.

The madman from Bedlam.

Claire's heart twisted painfully in her breast, and she stifled a gasp. No, it could not be, for that man was dead. This was but a chance resemblance. No—a striking resemblance.

Still disbelieving, she took in other details of his visage, the strong straight nose and finely carved lips. So similar. Had her madman been so tall? Yes—and broad-shouldered like this man, but not so gaunt. Clothes could tell her nothing. The man in Bedlam had been stripped to bloody, tattered rags. This one wore plain black velvet, an ambiguous style that could be mourning, subdued fashion, or Puritan severity. The clothes fit loosely, so perhaps they were borrowed—or stolen. Vivian would still number many thieves among her friends. Gloves of fine dark red leather covered his hands.

The room seemed filled with anticipatory silence. Adrian's eyes traveled briefly to the dragon brooch she wore on her mourning gown, and she saw recognition in them. Rafe must have been wearing it when they met, or told him something of Gabriel. The man's gaze lifted to hers again. He bowed and said quietly. "Lady Claire, I am most honored to meet you."

Claire drew a a small, sharp breath. His voice made memory certain—an angel's voice, mellifluous and flexible, yet strong. Each exquisitely modulated syllable seemed to pluck at her heartstrings. She would know his voice in the dark.

Not dead. Not dead. Her pulse beat the rhythm of the words.

And now her madman had a name.

"Adrian," she murmured.

He looked back at her, quiet and guarded, yet searching. Did he remember her? She could not tell. Was he hiding his reaction as she did hers, turmoil covered with the smooth mask of courtesy?

"You must meet the others, Lady Claire," Rafe said.

Claire turned to greet them, using the opportunity to calm her emotions. Next was the brown-eyed man who had opened the door for them. He seemed livelier now, with a sweet sly face and nimble movements. Rafe introduced him as Izzy Cockayne. "Master pickpocket," Izzy told her with a wink. "Though in future I plan to make a master innkeeper."

Two others remained, who Viv introduced as Smoke Warren and his sister Joan. Claire saw the family resemblance in their severe features and assessing blue eyes. Beneath her cowl, the woman's dark hair was streaked with gray, while the man's was pale as mist—or smoke. He had been Viv's captain when she ruled the Clink.

Claire smiled and spoke courtesies, wondering if Rafe and Vivian knew they harbored a madman. Seemingly, he had been cured of his frenzy, but what should she do? Rafe brought her wine, pressing the goblet into her hand. Images of that day in Bedlam's courtyard seven months ago flashed, lightning in a dark winter storm. She saw Adrian dragged in like an animal. Heard him railing like an angel against demons. Saw him crouched before her in the mud, reaching out to her. As the wine touched her lips, the reverberation of his touch, like a breath of heaven, a tongue of hellfire, licked at her lips. Flustered, she thrust those thoughts away.

She had abandoned him, but his memory had haunted her. Even after the accident—

Churning waves flung the boat high, spilled her into the icy air. She fell toward the water . . .

Suddenly the dark void funneled around her, sucking her down into terror. Her leg muscles wavered, rippling like water weeds. Claire leaned against the wall, praying it would hold her. Cold sweat wept on her skin. She gripped the wine goblet and stared into its garnet depths, despising herself for her weakness. Nothing had happened when she crossed the bridge, but now the darkness threatened to sweep her away. Fear, like Death, could claim her at any moment. Her arm throbbed. Claire had no idea if the pain was real or imagined. Her lungs felt suffocated. Forcing a deep breath, she looked up and found Adrian looking at her with a new intentness, as if he sensed the darkness swirling about her. He pitched his voice low to carry under the laughter of the others, calling Rafe, then gave the smallest nod in her direction.

Always quick to catch nuances, Rafe was instantly at her side. Knowing her pride was sensitive, he shielded her from the others as he guided her toward a bench. Claire was relieved to be out of Adrian's view, but she resisted the forward movement. Rafe stopped. He kept his voice as low as Adrian's. "Are you well?"

Her skin was damp and clammy, her hand cold in his grasp. But the worst was over. Drawing another deep breath to steady herself, Claire seized the opportunity. "I must speak with you," she whispered. "Alone."

Rafe pretended he had some favor to ask and guided her out of the room. Claire walked to the window at the end of the hall. Sunlight gleamed through the oiled paper, its warmth soothing her chilled skin. Nearby, she could hear the bells of St. Saviour's tolling noon.

Rafe came to stand beside her. "What is it, Claire?"

"The man who calls himself Adrian . . . I've seen him before, Rafe."

He gave her a guarded look. "And where would that have been?"

"The day of my accident, Sir Reginald took me to Bedlam. He thought it fine entertainment, but I hated it."

Rafe drew a deep breath, then said, "You saw Adrian in Bedlam."

"Then you do know." Relief surged through Claire, surprising in its intensity. She needed to protect her friends, but she had not wanted to betray the man within. Quickly, Claire described how Adrian had been dragged through the gate, how she had managed to calm him briefly, and how he had erupted in violence again.

But she did not tell Rafe that Adrian had kissed her.

"Perhaps there was reason for his violence," Rafe said, glancing away. "Perhaps some scent clinging to the doctor's cape disturbed him—a scent of blood perhaps."

"I cannot imagine an odor would drive him mad." What a curious thought.

"I do not know what caused him to react so, except that it could not have been you." Rafe gave her his most charming smile.

Sweet flattery, but subterfuge. Claire's temper flared. "I deserve better than such prattlings from you, Rafe. Speak truth to me."

"That was not a lie," he responded, startled. Her sharpness had its effect, for he answered her seriously. "I've never seen Adrian violent, though he has admitted he was in the past. He does not remember the first days he spent in Bedlam."

Disappointment dragged at her like an undertow, though perhaps it would be better for Adrian if he never remembered that day. "If he was released, then he must be cured."

Claire suspected it was not so, if only because Adrian's full identity was kept secret.

"He was not released," Rafe admitted. At her probing glance, he quickly explained. "I told you Vivian's enemies locked her in Bedlam, where they thought we would not find her. While she was there, Adrian defended her. When we rescued her, she had us free him as well."

Now the convoluted secrecy of her journey here became meaningful. Since Viv was no longer at risk from the law, the subterfuge was all to protect Adrian. But they must protect themselves as well. "But Rafe, how can you be certain—"

"He should not have been imprisoned there." He broke in, vehement. "He was wronged, Claire. His family might have saved him from Bedlam. Even if he was ill then, Adrian did not deserve to be shut in that pit of hell."

The cautious, soft-spoken man waiting in the next room seemed totally sane, and stirred her curiosity intensely. "Then you don't believe Adrian is mad, not now?"

Rafe hesitated. "He has spells—like a sickness—but he knows their cause. If he takes care, he can prevent them."

She frowned. "Spells? What provokes them?"

Rafe only shook his head. "Both Vivian and I are indebted to him. We will do all we can to repay that debt."

"So it is duty as well as compassion."

"If you will." He glanced at her, obviously weighing what he would say. "He . . . uncovered clues to the conspiracy, Claire. His information led us to Gabriel's killers and helped save the Queen's life."

She fought a painful rush of sorrow for Gabriel, and remembered how Adrian's gaze had gone to the amber brooch. "How? How could this man know anything, locked away as he was?"

Rafe pressed his lips together, stubborn. His continued evasion frustrated Claire. Obviously he did not feel free to say more, though what could it matter now that the plot was uncovered? Again, it must be to protect Adrian. But even under obligation, Rafe would not help someone he conceived to be a dangerous lunatic. And now he had shown that obligation to be hers as well. Gratitude mingled with her already chaotic jumble of emotions. Rafe's gaze followed hers toward the door. "I do not think Adrian recognized you."

She had seen him mindless as a beast—had seen the noble man emerge and be lost again in the ravings of madness. Even then she had believed the man could be reclaimed. "There is no need to speak of it unless he recalls it. I would not shame him, and no one remembers that day now but me. All the others with me that day are dead."

"Except those at Bedlam," Rafe said grimly. "Claire, you must not disclose his presence here."

"How could I now?" Rafe had manipulated her, but she was grateful he had told her of her own debt to Adrian.

"Some of this mystery will be revealed soon," Rafe promised. "But until our plan is set in motion, Adrian's safety and freedom are at risk. No one must know he is here. They will be searching for him."

"At Bedlam they said he had died."

"They lied. Deliberately."

"Yes." There could have been no mistaking so extraordinary an incident. Such cruelty, such injustice, infuriated Claire. A new determination swelled in her. With it came a hope and hot flare of excitement. So much had been lost, but perhaps some small portion of these last months' grief could be redeemed. She would make Adrian her cause again. She had intended so before, with far less reason. "I will help you."

Rafe frowned, and Claire could sense his protectiveness rising to the fore. Before it could gain sway, she argued, "Not long ago, you needed my help to prevent treason. You trusted me then."

"I trust you now, Claire. But I do not know how dangerous the situation may be."

"There was danger before, Sir Raphael." She faced him squarely, anger edging her voice. "I will not be thrust in some corner. I deserve better from you."

He opened his lips, no doubt to protest that she deserved safety, then closed them. "Very well—though the decision is not mine, but Adrian's."

"I understand," she agreed.

"Then I will let him tell you the rest of his story."

As Rafe started to turn, Claire placed her left hand on his arm, firm enough to stay him. "I want to judge for myself, without you present."

When he hesitated, she said, "Do you fear for my safety?"

"Not as you mean it."

"I hardly think he will seduce me in a hallway."

"Of course not," Rafe answered her, flustered. "But it is not seemly to leave you alone with him."

Claire covered her slip with a smile for his brotherly protectiveness. Only she remembered Adrian's devastating kiss. "Surely, when plotting, some propriety must be left behind."

"Very well, I will summon him," Rafe replied, with a continued reluctance that struck her as odd. He walked down the hall and beckoned within the room. When Adrian emerged, Rafe spoke to him quietly for a moment. Then he went in, closing the door and leaving them alone in the hall.

Claire tensed, filled with nervous expectation as Adrian approached. Was it fear or fascination that made her heart race? He stopped beside her. So close, he seemed even taller than he had before, almost intimidating. She tilted her chin, defiant of her own unease. But he did nothing threatening. His expression was gentle, almost solemn, though his gaze searched hers intently.

She decided to make the test. "You seem familiar, Adrian, have we met before?"

"Not that I remember, Lady Claire," he answered, "but I have heard you spoken of with great admiration and affection."

A gallant response that brought a rush of frustration, verging on anger. How could he not remember her? Not remember kissing her? She was all too aware of him. Her skin seemed to sting, as if abraded by his presence, a friction in the very air. She tried to hide her ugly, scarred hand in the folds of her skirts—and found trunkhose made a poor substitute. The doublet and hose constricted her, too tight, too confining. Could her boy's garb make the difference in how he perceived her? Impulsively, she pulled off her cap, letting her hair spill about her shoulders.

She saw a flash of surprise in his glance, and admiration that salved her vanity a little. Nothing more. Feeling foolish, she chided herself for her shallowness. Through injury or illness, Adrian had lost days, perhaps weeks of his life. What was one memory, however sweet, however intense? But she wanted him to recognize her—

The filtered light of the window gave his cropped hair a metallic luster and illuminated the vivid colors of his eyes.

When he spoke his voice was quiet. "Sir Raphael says that you have offered to aid us, Lady Claire."

She knew there was a fierce soul hidden behind the perfect manners, but she answered in the same measured tone. "Yes, I have."

"Sir Raphael and Mistress Vivian have reason to help me, as I have helped them. But why should you?" The caution in his voice made Claire realize it was not an innocent question. He must wonder how much Rafe had revealed.

Should she tell Adrian of their meeting at Bedlam? He might be embarrassed, or grateful, even angry, she did not know. Would the knowledge awaken his memory? She decided not to yield the advantage till she knew him better. For now, she answered with part of the truth. "I know that Vivian was falsely imprisoned in Bedlam, and helped you escape. I know that you gave Rafe some information that led to the discovery of my brother Gabriel's murderers, and helped prevent the assassination of the Queen. I will help you for their sake, unless I myself judge you unworthy."

"I pray that I never give you cause to think me so." His tone was earnest, but she saw him relax infinitesimally, confirming that other secrets were still hidden. State secrets or his own? Now he asked, "Do you understand what is at stake?"

"Not entirely," she replied. "Rafe says that your family kept you imprisoned in Bedlam, when they might have saved you much suffering. He has not told me your true name."

After a slight hesitation, he said, "I am Sir Adrian Thorne, now Lord Roadnight."

Fragments settled in Claire's mind, news and Court gossip gathered piecemeal after her accident. "Lord Roadnight and his son were killed last February—murdered by thieves."

"Supposedly. I do not remember that night, or much of that week . . . I learned only three days ago that my father died of his wounds." Suddenly, he paled. The bones of his face looked stark against his skin, his eyes dark-hollowed and haunted. He turned toward the window, his gloved hands clenched into fists.

"I am sorry, Sir Adrian," Claire said softly. "How terrible to learn it so."

A moment later, he turned back to face her. All the pain was smoothed over into an expression of gentle courtesy. She could hear only the faintest stress in his voice as he continued. "I did not die, as my father apparently thought, but my head was injured. I could not remember who I was. They found me wandering the streets and took me to Bedlam."

Claire regarded him intently, still hoping for recognition.

He took it for suspicion. "They tell me I was violent," he admitted. "In truth, I was ill for a time, but I am better now."

Unaware of their first encounter, Adrian could have kept her ignorant of that. She admired his honesty, and his courage. The admission did not come easily. She pushed a little further. "Rafe says that you have spells, but that you can control them."

"Yes."

Claire hoped he would elaborate, but the terse reply was all he gave. Had the injury to his head been enough to cause his former violence? Perhaps he had epilepsy and the falling sickness had been mistaken for madness? She understood he might not trust her enough to answer fully, but did he not want her trust as well?

Adrian looked down, rubbing his gloved hands together. Finally he said, "Certain things affect me . . . adversely. I have learned what to avoid."

He was evasive. What was he hiding? Doubt rose again, but battled weakly against her fiercer sympathy. Seeing his father murdered, being attacked and tossed into the Thames to drown—such terrible events could surely unsettle anyone's mind. And then to be abandoned for months in Bedlam! However ill Adrian had been, his family should have cared for him privately.

"A sane man might loose his wits in Bedlam, but you regained yours."

He looked up, meeting her gaze. His eyebrows lifted slightly, self-mocking. "So it seems."

"You lost a week, you said?" The week, the day, that she had met him.

He nodded. "When my memory returned, I explained who I was and asked for my father. My cousin, Sir James Thorne, was summoned instead. I do not know for certain what passed between him and my keepers. Perhaps he denied me, and said that I was deluded. But that would have been a great risk. I believe he bribed them to hold me where I was, so he could keep the Roadnight title for himself."

She drew a sharp breath. "Sir James Thorne was married this past month—to Lady Penelope Bellecote."

"Who was to marry me." Adrian managed a wry smile. It worked yet another transformation in his fluid features, emphasizing their keen-honed edges.

His handsomeness was too distracting. Claire kept her attention on their conversation. "So your cousin has stolen both your bride and your title."

"To do some small justice to my cousin, I think he truly believed me mad. My supposed death was preferable to my disgrace."

Sparked by anger for him, Claire came closer. "I would call that a great injustice."

He seemed to move forward to meet her, then took a step back. "My cousin might have had me killed. From what I know of Bedlam's keepers, it would have been easy enough to arrange. But he is not so cold-blooded."

"But he did nothing for your comfort either."

He gave a small shrug, as if it was of no import, but his lips thinned. She sensed he felt far more ire than he showed. "Now my cousin's connivance will work in my favor." Adrian continued. "If he had not lied, whether for greed or shame, Sir James could insist I was an escaped lunatic, and lock me up again with little or no proof."

His shrewdness increased her respect. "Instead, you will demonstrate your sanity, and your cousin dare not accuse you of madness."

"Perhaps. For the barony, he may risk admitting he lied."

"Even if he does, everything he says will be suspect," Claire said. "Most likely, he will achieve only his own ruin." Nothing in Adrian's responses suggested any trace of madness lingered. The only intense emotion he had revealed was grief at his father's death. Sir James' iniquity deserved his wrath. Even if Adrian quelled his rightful anger for fear of exposing any suspicious emotion, that very ability spoke to his sanity.

"He did not plot to destroy me, only took advantage of circumstances." Seeing her dubiousness, he shook his head sadly. "I have lost father, mother, others. I will not destroy my cousin unless he forces my hand."

"Will you have the marriage annulled?" she asked. Her cheeks heated at her own impudence, though her heart chilled at the thought of him married to the vain and grasping girl she had met at Court. But there was no denying Penelope's beauty.

Adrian shrugged again, but this time with a smile, seeming unmoved by the loss. "I had been engaged to Lady Penelope since childhood, but I seldom saw her. Sir James often praised her, and I wondered if he were jealous. I believe he loves her as I never did. I desire my freedom."

Learning he had been trapped in an unwanted betrothal, sympathy flared through her. She, too, knew a hunger for freedom. Her fear was a small dark cell she had yet to escape. *A boat the size of a coffin, forever flooded with black water.* She pushed the thought away. "How will you explain your disappearance? Many will be curious."

"A truncated version of the truth. When I was attacked by the ruffians, I suffered a memory loss—kind strangers took me in and tended me till I recovered." Adrian nodded to the door.

"Vivian Swift was an outlaw till but a few days ago. It will be a scandal," she warned, though her lips quirked at the corners.

"I will reveal I was in training as a cutpurse. It is a far preferable scandal." He gave a soft huff of breath that was almost laughter.

"Piquant, certainly." Claire's own laugh was strangely breathless. His simplest remarks rippled with a subtle music that made her yearn to take up her lute and play. She imagined his singing voice a pure golden tenor. But even if he would, her playing would no longer make a match to his song. Pleasure faded as bitterness returned.

"It is even true," Adrian said. "A few lessons with Izzy helped pass the time, though he declares I'll make a better baron than a nip. He even gave me a set of lock picks."

He looked down at his gloved hands again, then drew them closer to his body. The protective gesture echoed strangely in her own nerves. Had his hands been injured in Bedlam, his fingers broken by some cruel torture? Her stomach went cold and and shivers rippled along her spine. Without thinking, Claire shielded her scarred arm, then deliberately released it. She forced her mind back to the moment.

"Your first appearance should be public, Sir Adrian. There should be sound witnesses to testify you are no lunatic should your cousin risk revealing his deception."

"We have a plan already in place, for a few days hence," Adrian told her.

"Their masque—you will confront him then." Queen Elizabeth, with all her ladies, had been invited to the false Lord Roadnight's first ball. However, Claire doubted the Queen would honor the bland Sir James with her presence.

"Yes. Vivian made secret contact with Samuel, my old steward. He brought us an invitation that should get us as far as the door."

"I had not planned to attend the masque, but now I will," Claire said. "I can be your intelligencer. When you arrive, I will step forward, offering my recognition. Afterward, I will mingle with the other guests and discover their responses.".

"Yes. I would like to know the crowd's response." He frowned a little. "My cousin will know that Sir Raphael and Mistress Vivian are lying, certainly, but I doubt any of you need fear retaliation. His nature is self-protective rather than vengeful."

"Has he ever had such cause for revenge before?" Claire suspected Adrian was too unwilling to believe the ugly truth of his cousin's betrayal.

"He has more cause for shame."

"I pray it is so. But however it falls, I am determined to be part of your venture, Lord Roadnight." She had no lack of courage for this, whatever other fears tainted her life.

"If you are to recognize me, where might we have met before, Lady Claire? Other than here?"

It was an innocent question, but it loosed a flood of memory. Unable to meet those compelling eyes, Claire dropped her gaze, feigning thoughtfulness. Too vividly she remembered the hard press of his chest and thighs against her own. Her mouth felt tender and stinging from his searching kiss, as if seconds, not months, had passed since his embrace. She could almost taste him. She bit her lip till the sting of pain distracted her from such imaginings, and then made herself look at him directly. "Were you in London last year, in the summer?"

"Yes, I was here."

"I will say my brother Gabriel introduced us at the performance of a play. He used to take me to the theaters." Pricked by grief, she added, "I wish you had known him."

"I feel as if I do," Adrian said softly. He glanced again at the dragon brooch. "I know that he was loyal and gallant. I know he cared deeply for his family. He loved you, believe that."

"He told me so," Claire said, grateful for her brother's open affection. She touched the smooth amber with her fingertips, then looked into Adrian's eyes. "We have both suffered losses."

"Yes." His voice was barely more than a whisper, but the one word enveloped her in an atmosphere of intimacy. Warmth suffused her whole body, her whole being, cocooned her in tenderness.

The intensity of her reactions to Adrian was unnerving, and foolish considering how little she truly knew of him. One moment she wanted to kiss him, to see if the touch of his lips could possibly be as wondrous as she remembered. The next, she wanted to seek the soothing comfort of his arms, to curl within their protective warmth as if he were Gabriel or Rafe, beloved brother, dearest friend.

As if he were her lover. Or her husband.

The thought stunned her, yet no one, not even Rafe, had stirred such fervor within her. Was it a true connection, or naught but flimsy woven from his mystery and her own compassion? Her fascination—for fascinate her he did. Adrian had lingered in her mind long after she believed him dead. Now he was resurrected, both in body and mind. Unbeknownst to each other, they had helped prevent treason against the Queen. For the third time, fate had twisted the strands of their lives together.

But what were these strange spells he spoke of so evasively? How fragile was his mind?

Her father had promised her a year before she must marry. It was a year in which she could grow to know Adrian. In that year he could learn to trust her. For that trust to be truth, she must tell him that they had met. Should she tell him now? Caught in her sudden confusion, Claire had let the moment stretch out, become awkward.

Frustration and relief tangled in her breast when Rafe came out into the corridor, checking on his wayward charges.

He looked at Claire, "What is your final decision?"

"Nothing is changed," she answered him. She turned back to Adrian. "I am determined to help you," she said.

"Lady Claire is already attending the masque," Adrian told Rafe. With a slight smile, he added, "She offers to be our intelligencer, before and after our arrival."

"That's perfect," Rafe said. "Let us tell the others what you have planned."

Claire nodded, and together they rejoined their fellow conspirators.

Chapter 4

Burne glimpsed Quarrell at a table at the back of the tavern, and moved toward him through the crowd. They had agreed on the Crowing Cock, which was disreputable enough that the patrons would be deliberately incurious about cloaked conversation, but reputable enough to frown if such talk led to open violence. He nodded for his guards to wait out of earshot, and presumed Quarrell had equally intimidating protection nearby. Unseen by Quarrell and unknown to his own guards, Burne had a secret agent keeping watch for the past hour. Blending unobtrusively into the crowd, Graile had taken a table that allowed a view of the door, and quick access to Quarrell if need be. Not that Burne intended to have Quarrell killed. For the moment the doctor was still too useful. But Burne was cautious always.

As soon as he settled onto the bench across from the doctor, a serving wench approached. Like Quarrell, Burne ordered wine. Like Quarrell, he did no more than sip the vinegary brew before he commenced. "So, Vivian Swift helped Lord Roadnight escape?"

"Yes. Her cohorts staged a raid to rescue her. They released him as well."

"You have bungled, Quarrell, not once but twice."

"It was one event only, even if two escaped, Sir Nigel. A man of your intelligence is aware that no one can plan for such oddities." The physician spoke with unctuous assurance.

"It is my business to plan for just such events," Burne snapped.

"You can see that the circumstances are bizarre," Quarrell returned.

"What can you tell me about Lord Roadnight's escape?"

"You may well know more than I do, Sir Nigel, since you have access to Vivian Swift."

"I am not her confidant."

"A pity." Quarrell paused. "Sir James may find his cousin's resurrection compromising."

"I am having the Thorne's town house watched, as well as the country estates." Burne had known of the Baron's confinement from the first. Quarrell kept him apprised of all such illegal arrangements he made with the nobility, and Burne consented to those that were politically convenient. Adrian Thorne was Anglo-Irish, a dubious breed. Burne suspected all Irish sympathizers to be Catholic sympathizers as well. Sir James was wholly English and staunchly Protestant. Far better that he hold the Roadnight title. It had seemed a most tidy solution—Sir Adrian confined, and Sir James available for future blackmail.

Now it was most untidy. Burne frowned. "Why did Vivian Swift free the Baron?"

"He went to her aid when another inmate attacked her in the common room," Quarrell explained. "Apparently, she felt indebted."

"She doesn't believe he is mad?"

"He can be quite charming in his quiet moments. If she saw no display of violence except in her defense, she would be inclined to think him falsely imprisoned."

As she had been. "Why didn't you inform me Vivian Swift was in your control?"

"Why should I? She is not the sort of personage in whom you normally take an interest, Sir Nigel—a common criminal."

"An uncommon criminal with great power."

"Her power was to be short-lived. The rival would have killed her."

"But as the worm turns, he is the one who is dead." Burne had made sure there was no chance link between him and Bedlam's master.

Quarrell probably suspected as much, but he went on placidly, "Nonetheless, in such matters I am circumspect. If anything, too much so, since you now complain I did not discuss other business arrangements with you."

"Vivian Swift not only lives, but tells tales to the Queen—embellished for drama's sake, no doubt."

Quarrell tensed. "Am I to be dismissed?"

Burne said nothing, letting the weight of his silence convey judgment. The Queen knew nothing of the use Burne had devised for Bedlam, though Walsingham had approved it. Burne let Quarrell stew in his own acid juices a moment, then said, "For now, you will keep your post. Mistress Swift did not speak kindly of you, but her words were outweighed by those more powerful. I made certain they spoke in your favor."

The physician relaxed into an ironic smile. "It seems I am in your debt."

"So it seems."

Quarrell leaned forward, newly intent. "Lord Roadnight must be returned to my care."

"One lunatic is not a matter of great priority."

"Ah . . . but he is a danger," Quarrell insisted. "He has many fears, many furies, and little rational control. Who knows what he might do from terror or revenge?"

Suspicion stirred in Burne. Quarrell was too tenacious. "The wreckage of a man you showed me could not have managed to communicate, much less commit murder."

"There were episodes of mania, of violence, in Bedlam.

One of my attendants, Sister Mary, has gone missing. I fear for her safety."

"Is there any reason to suspect Roadnight?"

Quarrell shrugged. "She was one of his keepers, a woman. Within Thorne's troubled mind, love might twist to hate, trust to fear. You know his family history."

"His Irish mother burned out her husband's English eye," Burne said grimly. "But you have no proof any harm has come to this attendant, much less that Roadnight caused it."

"None so far," Quarrell admitted.

"We have problems enough without such bootless conjecture."

"His madness is unpredictable. No one is safe until Lord Roadnight is under my care." Quarrell paused. "My position remains at risk. I must protect my own interests."

Burne tensed. Was Quarrell daring to threaten him? He would have him squashed.

"No," Quarrell said quickly, as if reading his thought. "In the past, I have mentioned my plan to establish a private asylum. . . ."

Irritated, Burne almost refused him, but reconsidered. "Can you assure me it would be secure?"

"In my own hospital I would have far more control." With a faint smile, he added, "And families of consequence would feel more inclined to give their poor fools into my care."

"Make the arrangements, then. I will see that you have sufficient funds within the month." Burne rose, giving the physician a last brisk nod. Quarrell was easy enough to control through his petty ambition and greed. "You know better than to cheat me."

"Indeed, Sir Nigel, I do." Quarrell inclined his head. "This new arrangement will be of great advantage, to both of us."

"Make sure of it."

Drawing the hood closer about his face, Burne moved quickly through the tavern. The two guards followed him outside, where a third man tended their horses. They mounted, and rode toward the Thames. A half mile later, Burne paused under the shadows of a tree and waved the guards beyond hearing range. He did not have long to wait before Graile appeared. "Did anything of significance happen before I arrived?" Burne asked his agent.

"Nothing," Graile answered quietly. "Master Quarrell spoke to no one."

"You're sharing watch on Thorne Hall tomorrow?"

"Yes. In the afternoon." Graile hesitated on a breath, then spoke. "Yesterday I had the impression someone was following me. If so, it was someone skillful. I eluded them and doubled back—but they escaped me in turn."

Burne could think of no reason for Roadnight to follow Graile, nor would Sir James' men be likely to leave their posts. Perhaps Quarrell had a watcher with unexpected skill. It was also possible Vivian Swift had sent someone. "You are certain?"

"No, not certain."

Burne nodded, not bothering with chastisement. Failure would make Graile all the more observant. "If you have the chance to capture Lord Roadnight, take care. Master Quarrell warned me his violence can erupt at any time."

"Yes, of course." Graile's replies were terse, but his voice softly modulated.

"If he can hide his lunacy long enough, who knows what political havoc such a Catholic sympathizer can wreak. It cannot be permitted." It was an order for assassination.

"I understand." Graile's expression was as detached as his voice. A shaft of moonlight turned his eyes to silver, cool and reflective. He almost seemed to be thinking of something else, yet Burne knew he missed nothing. Intelligence and dedication made Graile the best agent he had, but his background was dubious—a Catholic turncoat. Burne hoped Graile would remain loyal to the Protestant cause. It would be a shame to have him eliminated.

It would also be extremely difficult.

Burne issued a crisp order. "Report to me tomorrow night at this same spot."

"At the stroke of nine, Sir Nigel."

After Graile rode away, Burne headed his mount toward home.

Reviewing Quarrell's arguments, he doubted the situation was as serious as the doctor claimed. As long as Burne himself was not implicated in the Bedlam scheme, Lord Roadnight's escape was only an annoyance. Eventually his madness would reassert itself, and his allies would turn him lose or turn him over to the authorities.

Burne frowned anew at the trouble caused by Swift and Fletcher. Burne knew Claire had recently visited the Dancing Fox. Had she made contact with them there? Should he connive another meeting at Court, and see what she might tell him? He tensed with arousal at the thought. Seeing her would be both pleasure and torment. He tried to formulate a mock innocent question that would garner information, then rejected such an approach. If the opportunity arouse he would seize it, otherwise Burne dared not risk making her suspicious. The relationship he was slowly coaxing was far too fragile to survive it.

As he rode through the gate of his town house, Burne's heart sank. He'd hoped his wife would be abed, but candles glimmered in her chamber. He had married into the Cecils to advance his position. What had seemed the most sensible of liaisons soon became an aggravation. Now, with his heart and body clamoring for Claire, it was a misery. When he'd met Margaret, he'd considered her attractive enough. Now her tall elegance seemed little more than gauntness, her fair hair and skin pallid. Her elevated syllables grated along his nerves. Worse still, her mind had no subtlety. He could scarcely glean anything of import from her detailed accounts of Court gossip. All he learned from his wife was what everyone wished him to hear. Hungry for status, she wanted him to emerge from the dense shadows of Walsingham's wing into some sunny spot where he could be properly displayed, preferably in peacock satin and jeweled buckles. No doubt that was the reason she was waiting up for him now—to harangue him yet again about his office. Burne prayed the Queen would soon bestow a rich barony upon him, if only to quiet Margaret for a time.

As he rode forward into the courtyard, memory summoned Claire's low, melodious voice, her penetrating observations, and her deft wit. He saw the pure oval of her face, her tender mouth, and her wise, sad eyes. The touch of flame in her chestnut hair hinted of the flame of passion within. He already knew her loyalty, her valiant heart. In every aspect, her vivid warmth utterly eclipsed his chill and irksome wife.

All in all, he wished Margaret were dead.

As a warden of Bedlam, Quarrell possessed a suitably furnished residence, with attendant servants. But he kept a more isolated home on the outskirts of the city, rented under the benign name of Lamb. He dismissed the guard he paid to watch the grounds when he was not there, and released the chained mastiffs into the yard. He kept no servants on the premises, and had but only the simplest food on hand, a few clothes. Nothing he could not tend himself.

After entering, Quarrell lingered for a few moments in the great chamber off the hall, allowing a lazy anticipation to unfold as he drank a glass of wine—far better than the sour piss served at the tavern. But he drank only enough to heighten his other appetites. He was ready. Yet, despite the adventure ahead, dissatisfaction tainted his mood.

Quarrell found he missed Lord Roadnight. He had not expected to be deprived of his presence, but to enjoy it for months or years to come. Adrian was a delicious mystery. Somehow he could sense cruelty, and it terrified and appalled him, aggravating his madness. True, others had this effect on him—but Quarrell believed that no one else had so deep an impact. He wished he had understood Adrian's responses better, so he could have savored them, enriched them. With his other victims, Quarrell found the paroxysm of death itself necessary to his satisfaction. But Adrian's fear was so exquisite, its flavor so complex, Quarrell would have kept him alive as long as his suffering could be stoked.

He would reclaim Lord Roadnight yet—and punish those who had deprived him of his favorite inmate. But now he had other matters to attend to.

Quarrell went into the hall and worked the catch on the secret panel, then descended the stairs into his hidden cellar. He enjoyed the quiet here, and the rich aroma of decay. There were no windows and the walls had been well padded. The earth floor muffled a good deal, and had swallowed many secrets. He could sense his other victims' presence, so close beneath his feet. Soon they would have company.

Sister Mary was hanging suspended in her chains, as she had all day. She had fainted from the pain. Quarrell watched her for a moment as he stood by the white-draped table with its assorted implements. The lock of her hair he had clipped lay to one side. He picked up the mousy strands and stroked his lips with them, inhaling their scent of soap and pears. Then he put the lock back on the table beside the waiting black mourning ribbon, the carved box. When he finished with Sister Mary, he would bind the keepsake and place it neatly with the others.

It did not take much to revive her. Her moans evoked an exquisite reverberation along his nerves. He waited a moment, until she focused on him. She said nothing, only stared. "No prayers?" he asked, in his most courteous tone.

She whispered a few words, but then trailed off, too exhausted, too hopeless, to continue.

The rush of power hardened him. His whole body seemed to swell with it, huge and throbbing.

"You helped Sir Adrian escape, didn't you?"

This time there was no denial. Fear of pain made her respond with a faint nod.

It no longer mattered if it was true, albeit he had been certain she was involved. Under normal circumstances, he would not have selected her as a victim. It was difficult to find someone so competent to work at Bedlam. But she also possessed too keen a conscience, which would have caused him trouble sooner or later. All in all, she was most useful serving his most specific needs. When he was done, he might not bury her with the others. A new plan was taking shape, and he thought she might serve him better in some public display.

Meanwhile, fear was a most useful weapon. "Do you know where he is?"

The answering whisper was impossible to understand.

"Yes? No?"

"No . . ."

"I do not believe you." He did actually, but the small sob was gratifying. Revenge was a pleasure to nurture. He salivated a little, tasting his own rising excitement. The hours ahead would be most fascinating. Sister Mary had always been so quiet, so self-possessed. But now he would possess her entirely.

Command the body, and the soul would follow soon enough.

Perhaps she read the end in his eyes, for she closed her own, tears leaking from the corners. Instantly, he demanded, "Open your eyes. Remember you must watch me at all times."

She did as he ordered, though her gaze skittered desperately from side to side.

Returning to the white draped table, Quarrell examined his knives—shiny tools to peel away every resistance. After deliberation, he choose a most excellent scalpel. But when he showed the instrument to Sister Mary, she closed her eyes again, weeping silently.

"I did warn you, my dear," he murmured, flicking away her tears with the needle's tip, then tracing the delicate curve of her lids. "Closing your eyes will not help at all."

Chapter 5

Simmering with tension, Claire watched the dancers move through the sprightly steps of the galliard. Her duties at Court had prevented any further contact with Adrian and the others. Even messages were deemed too risky. Yet if the plan were abandoned, surely they would have found a way to let her know. She wanted their venture to succeed—and she wanted to see Adrian again. Her emotions were in confusion, longing and wariness circling each other ceaselessly. But she saw no possibility for quick resolution. Tonight she would not think of her attraction to Adrian, only of the challenge he must face.

Covertly, Claire observed her hosts amid their entourage. So far, the Thornes' evening was a great success. The theme of the masque was the Golden Age, which suited their heraldic colors of yellow and green. Spangled yellow gauze draped the walls, and fragrant green garlands decked with ribbons and golden fall flowers hung in swaths throughout the rooms. The flames of a thousand wax tapers burned within the great chamber and illuminated the garden without. A dozen musicians played with a deft skill Claire envied. The guests danced, jewels flashing and rich fabrics gleaming in the candlelight. Everyone dressed in costume, or at least a fanciful mask. In one corner a lacy primrose butterfly flirted with a lion, his face framed with a mane of ribbons, and a tail protruding from his tawny velvet round hose. In another corner a molting canary tried to reattach feathers to her hair.

Fearing to be too conspicuous in mourning weeds, Claire had the Grecian tunic she had worn to a masque last year died saffron, but draped it over with a black veil held by a wreath of rosemary, weeping willow, and nightshade—remembrance, sorrow, and truth. The wreath was for Gabriel, but she made a passable Eurydice, lost in the underworld and mourning for her minstrel Orpheus. There were others in the same antique mode. Mercury bowed to finish the dance, gold wings on his heels, Dionysus renewed the wine in his goblet, and their hosts wore classic garb as well.

Penelope Thorne, the false Lady Roadnight, had chosen the role of Venus to her husband's Mars—beauty and strength, Claire supposed, though in myth the two were illicit lovers. Lady Penelope held court from a dais on the far side of the great chamber. Sheer ivory silk and cloth of gold draped her comely figure, and a ransom in emeralds glittered at her throat. As a maid, Penelope had been much admired at court. Praises were sung to her thick ash blond hair, her round blue eyes. Her cheeks were soft and smooth, her mouth small but full, like a ripe strawberry. But Adrian had not seemed to be deceived by that softly enticing exterior. That itself was good testament to his sanity.

Despite the masque, Claire could perceive tension beneath Penelope's smiles. Now and again, she would glance toward the entryway or look out toward the garden. In the torch light, guards patrolled the wrought iron gate and any spot where an escaped madman might scale the wall. Then she would look to her husband seated beside her, seeking reassurance he could not give. Had she known from the first about Adrian's imprisonment, or had her husband only revealed the truth when he must?

Looking at Sir James, the usurper, Claire detected signs of stress under his polished manners as well. Beneath the gilded armor and green hose, he did not much resemble his cousin. His compact figure lacked Adrian's height and sinewy grace. Sir James' complexion was ruddier, his hair a sandy hue. His eyes shone a guileless blue, and his round, boyish face was deceptively trustworthy.

The galliard ended, and the musicians paused for the guests to regroup. As the moment approached, a ferment of excitement and apprehension filled Claire to the brim. Seeking a better view of the entry, she wove her way through the press of the crowd toward the hallway. More guards were stationed along the walkway outside. Without obvious cause, it would be rude of them to question the arriving guests and demand they unmask. Invitations were checked against a list of guests kept at the door, but once her friends were that far, she doubted anyone could stop them. As Claire hovered, she observed Samuel, the old steward who had purloined their invitations, keeping watch as well.

Just as the music resumed, a new group arrived at the door. A tiger and tigress led, garbed in orange velvet napped like a feline's pelt and slashed with black satin. Green glass eyes glowed from their masks. A formidable menagerie followed behind—a golden hawk with smoke-colored hair, a gaudy popinjay, and two massive bulldogs guarding the rear. In the center of this bestiary stood a black-clad figure, head and shoulders covered with the white head of a unicorn.

The green-eyed tiger mask lifted to reveal Rafe's face. He smiled disarmingly as he produced the invitation for the ushers. As soon as they went to check the names against those on their list, Rafe slipped his mask back in place and stepped aside. A jester in yellow and green motley somersaulted forward through the opening—Izzy with his face painted and a popinjay's beak on his nose. With a jangle of bells, he sprang to his feet, reached into the wide slashes of his trunk hose, and produced three glossy apples. Tossing them into the air, he juggled the fruit in a blur of crimson.

The instant the ushers were distracted, the rest of the party spearheaded into the hall with the masked tiger at the head. Behind him, the small fierce tigress and the golden hawk flanked the horned figure of the unicorn, with the bulldog guards bringing up the rear. Izzy in his jester's motley pranced behind. Suddenly the apples vanished back into his trunkhose and three knives plucked from his belt whirled in their stead, warning off any who approached from behind. Two guards followed warily, annoyed but loathe to interfere with important guests—or spinning weapons.

When the group reached the great chamber, Samuel stepped forward. Looking frightened yet triumphant, he announced in clarion voice, "Sir Adrian Thorne, Lord Roadnight."

A shocked hush fell upon the crowd, every gaze swerving to watch the procession. Claire inhaled sharply, caught up in the shared suspense. "Yes," she whispered under her breath, urging him on.

Although the invaders had their faces covered by masks or paint, all eyes were on Adrian. At the announcement, the unicorn had stepped to the fore. His gilded horn gleamed like a spear. Save for that horn, the unicorn mask was pure, shining white over his garments of mourning black. Their midnight darkness created a stark contrast against the warm colors of his companions and the golden assembly in the hall. The procession was deliberately staged to give the guests much to talk about afterward, but the very care and deliberation of their entrance also argued against any charges of wild lunacy that James might dare to fling. Claire watched Adrian lead his party forward, decisive power in his graceful stride. This was no tattered madman fleeing Bedlam.

Claire turned to look at the couple on the dais, anger at their cruel injustice cutting through her sharply. They deserved far worse reprisal. James Thorne turned deathly pale and shrank back against his chair. Penelope stiffened too, but there was more anger than fear in her eyes. They knew that in a moment their purloined world could crash into ruin. Penelope hissed something at Sir James. Belatedly he rose, waiting as his cousin came down the hall toward him.

The golden menagerie paused. Alone, the unicorn walked the last few paces to the foot of the dais. Slowly, Adrian lifted black-gloved hands and removed the gleaming white mask. Murmurs rippled through the crowd as the true Lord Roadnight was recognized, excitement restrained only by their awareness of the drama still unfolding. Adrian looked only at James, but his clear voice rang out through the gathering. "As you can see, cousin, I am not dead."

A red flush colored over Sir James' pallor, but he drew breath, years of training coming to his aid. He stepped to the edge of the dais, extending his arms as if to step down and embrace his cousin. Then he halted, perhaps reading some warning in Adrian's eyes, and instead opened his hands in a gesture of wonder. Like Adrian, he spoke for all to hear. "Cousin, my heart is as amazed and delighted as my eyes are to behold this miracle. Before he died, your father himself testified to your death at the hands of the thieves who threw you into the Thames."

"I understand your mistake perfectly, cousin. If you did not know I lived, how could you come to my aid?" Adrian asked with no apparent irony, though James paled again at the words. His voice still pitched to carry throughout the room, Adrian gave his own explanation. "Indeed, I was most sorely injured. At first, I did not know myself . . ."

Claire thrilled at Adrian's deftness. In control of himself? How smoothly he controlled the entire room! And his poaching cousin as well. Sir James released a pent-up breath as he realized Adrian would not expose him as a usurper.

"But fortune was kind, for I found caring friends who tended me until I recovered." Adrian's lips curved into a smile as he gestured to his companions.

Rafe and Viv raised their tiger's masks, though the rest of the menagerie stayed hidden. A fresh shock wave rippled through the crowd, as the newly famous couple that had uncovered the snaphance conspiracy was recognized. Handsome, and the hero of the moment, Sir Raphael would be much sought after. With Viv pardoned, those not scandalized by her criminal past would delight in her notoriety. Claire smiled. To deflect any unwanted queries about their mysterious association with Adrian, they need only give a subtle warning that some answers were too confidential, too incriminating, or too scandalous to voice.

Enjoying her own part in their drama, Claire stepped forward. Adrian turned as she approached, and gave her an elegant, courtly bow. She spoke clearly for all to hear. "Let me be among the first to celebrate your resurrection, Lord Roadnight."

"Lady Claire, I am most grateful for your kindness." Adrian gave her a conspiratorial smile. She could read his excitement in his quickened breathing and the bright glitter of his eyes. Fascinated she watched as the candlelight heightened first one color, then another within the irises, flashes of green and blue, of gray and amber. Surely as magical as a unicorn's eyes.

It was foolish to dally so. Claire smiled and moved away a pace or two, though it seemed she moved into a colder region. Now that she had opened the way, the other guests stepped forward to greet Adrian and acknowledge his claim. Claire noticed that Rafe and Viv moved closer, flanking Adrian with Izzy, and the others close behind. Keeping within that protective shell, Adrian greeted everyone with the same gracious ease.

When the tide of well wishers at last subsided, Penelope and Sir James came to Adrian's side. Smiling broadly in his vast relief, Sir James gestured to the whole company. "As fate would have it, we have arranged a ball in honor of your return, Lord Roadnight." With those last words, he relinquished the title he had stolen.

James might be happy to be spared retribution, but Claire saw Penelope's smile fix into a grimace. "It is our joy to welcome you home, Lord Roadnight."

"And I am overjoyed to have safely returned," he told her, then turned back to James. "Why do we not let our guests enjoy the dancing, cousin, while we speak privily?"

Adrian gestured to the musicians to begin playing. They hesitated a fraction at receiving their commands from a new source, then began the measured strains of a pavane. Adrian walked through the hall toward a private chamber, his menagerie of guards falling in behind. Penelope watched Sir James follow in their wake, then moved among her guests. Claire watched as she feigned surprise, explaining that she knew no more than they did. After all, she fluttered, had she known of her former betrothed's survival, would she have dared to wed? Claire moved after her, conversing with the other guests, gathering their reactions. She bristled when she overheard several veiled insults about his Irish ancestry, but was reassured to find the majority considered Adrian more capable than his cousin. Many sensed chicanery, but the gossip would soon fade when Adrian resumed his rightful position.

After a few moments, Penelope abandoned her guests and went to join her husband in his confrontation. Knowing she could not follow, a surge of frustration filled Claire. Curiosity, yes, but the need to protect Adrian rose with startling ferocity. He was not yet out of danger.

Adrian's heart pounded as exhilaration and relief, apprehension and anger swirled within him. Nonetheless, he played his part and nodded in greeting as he moved through the guests. He'd dreaded facing so large a crowd, but it was far simpler than confronting Bedlam's inmates—or their keepers. Quarrell had taught him what evil could lurk beneath a cultured exterior. Adrian doubted anyone here possessed so twisted a soul, yet they all had known or inflicted suffering that might besiege him, intensified like light through a prism. He did not fear the vicarious pain greatly. He had endured it before. But his own unpredictable responses could destroy all he'd regained tonight. One bizarre incident could tip the precarious balance and give James the opportunity to declare him lunatic.

His guardians, Rafe and Vivian, Izzy and the Warrens, stayed close behind him. He sought a glimpse of Claire and found her, slender as a nymph in her antique gown. As always, the sight of her warmed him, beckoned him. But he could not turn aside. Not now.

Adrian reached the door of the library. Once inside he would be beyond the help of his friends. Pausing, he brought his hands together, almost a gesture of prayer, feeling the thin but precious shield of leather. Nothing had breached his barriers since he had begun wearing gloves. The greatest danger had been facing James. But there had been no kinsman's embrace, no hypocritical kiss on his cheek, to break through his barriers. The warning in Adrian's gaze had kept James at a distance.

Adrian opened the door to the library and entered, noting that it had been expensively refurbished since last he saw it. His cousin hesitated, then followed him within, closing the door but standing close by it. His gaze darted anxiously about the room.

"Shall I summon a witness?" Adrian asked, wondering if there were any they would both trust with their secrets.

Still uneasy, James shook his head.

Adrian moved to the far side of the desk, putting that physical barrier between them as well as asserting his position as the master of the house. James relaxed slightly, but remained close to the door. Now that he finally confronted his cousin, Adrian was far angrier than he had expected. But anger was a weapon he must wield with care. However justified, any violent emotion would ring alarms Adrian did not want sounded. So he smiled instead, albeit bitterly. "As you can see, cousin, I am neither dead—nor mad."

"I was told first the one, and then the other, and in both cases I was given proof," James said in his defense.

"And in both cases the proof was false, despite what you preferred to believe."

James looked flustered, but he broke out suddenly, "Why should I believe you sane now anymore than I believed you mad before?"

"I doubt I seemed lunatic to the hundred witnesses without. At the moment you can but prove your own duplicity and greed."

"You were not sane when I went to Bedlam!" James exclaimed. "You cowered like a beast in the corner of your cell. You did not even recognize me!"

Shocked, Adrian strove not to show it. He did not remember James coming to his cell. But Quarrell often visited, savoring the mindless terror he could induce. Perhaps the doctor had ushered James in to see the result, which lasted far longer during those first weeks in Bedlam. To James he offered other plausible reasons. "I suffered a head wound. It played havoc with my memory. For that matter, there are potions that can make a man behave as if mad. If I did not recognize you, perhaps I was drugged."

"But Master Quarrell . . ." James obviously realized there was little reason to trust the doctor. "He told me you had attacked him violently before collapsing. Why should I doubt him? I thought to spare the family scandal."

"I believe Master Quarrell profits greatly from preventing such supposed scandals. As do the families." Adrian glanced around at the new tapestries hanging on the walls, the fashionable luxury of carpets laid on the floor as well as covering the tables. "I see reason aplenty in this room alone. Your good fortune came at a high cost to me."

"I admit I benefited from your suffering, but I did not cause it," James protested. "I never wished you harm."

"Then I hate to think what you might have accomplished had you been inimical. In your benevolence, you have claimed my title, my home, and my betrothed for yourself."

James looked both shamed and beleaguered. "I did what I believed was best."

"Best?" Adrian asked sarcastically. "Bedlam was best for me?"

"I did not think you knew where you were."

"I did not see you come to my cell, James. But, once, from the common room, I saw you enter and depart from Bedlam. After you left, they told me that Adrian Thorne was dead. You buried me alive in that pit of hell!"

James flinched away from the burst of anger. "One last time, I brought money for your upkeep myself. Master Quarrell dissuaded me from any future visits—too painful."

Suddenly weary, Adrian went on, "Even if I was still dazed from my injuries, had you brought me home, I might have recovered sooner."

"What if it was but a partial recovery? Should I have brought you back and chanced letting Penelope marry a lunatic? Forced her to bear children that would carry the taint you get from your mother's blood?" James spoke with fervor, caught between pleading and accusation. "She died insane—and her grandfather before her. She tried to murder your father!"

Dim light hovered around Adrian—wavering candles in a dockside tavern. He stood at a table, his father across from him. Between them, a carved wooden box. Adrian took it, his fingers brushing over dark wood carved with intricate knots and serpents of wisdom. He pressed the latch. Opened the lid . . .

"Adrian?"

The fragment of memory ebbed. Adrian found he had braced his arms on the table. He wanted to reach after the image, though he sensed something ominous in it. He hungered for the days he had lost—and feared them too. Could he have murdered his father? How could he bear that guilt? Yet guilt was better than this uncertainty, the gnawing fear that sullied his grieving and made him feel a liar even when he spoke the truth.

James was looking at him with renewed suspicion. Adrian could not afford to be distracted. "Her memory haunts me too," he said in a low voice. Better to admit the fear than the actuality, that he was already cursed as his mother had been.

There was sympathy in James' face now, mixed with mistrust.

A quick rap sounded at the door, then Penelope entered the room. She moved to stand beside James, as if soliciting his protection. But Adrian saw little fear in her face, no gratitude, and no guilt. Instead he saw anger and humiliation at having her celebration turned against her. Her chin jutted obstinately. The emeralds that had belonged to his mother gleamed on her throat, green as the hills of Ireland. Anger stabbed again, sharp in his chest.

James had given way to him now; but once alone with Penelope, he would begin to regret the loss of all he'd stolen. Adrian must make it profitable to believe him cured. "I cannot deny the history of my family is troubled. Our wishes may be more in accord than you now believe."

"Accord? In what way?" Penelope asked.

Adrian gestured around him. "London life is not what I desire. I will leave to you the intrigues of Court and retire to the country. Your marriage is consummated. I will not demand an annulment. The legal tangle of betrothal contracts versus the sins of consanguinity is nothing I wish to argue in court."

"You would surrender Penelope?" James could not conceive it.

Penelope looked both relieved and insulted.

"Certainly your wife is beautiful. Who could not notice? But I see that you love her." Unfortunately, Adrian saw no love in Penelope's gaze. James' yearning had been apparent to Adrian when he was only betrothed to Penelope. He did not want her, even then. In this one thing, James had unwittingly been kind.

"What are your demands?" his cousin asked.

"For the moment I will remove to Roadnight Manor. I will choose the servants needed to attend to its needs and mine. I will keep the other estates in Somerset, Wiltshire, and Avon, as well as those in Ireland. However, there are unentailed properties in Hereford and Hampshire, which I will deed to you entire. If your income will not be as rich as you had envisioned, it will be greater than what you inherited from your own father. You can cut a figure at Court and wield some influence. You may also keep this house to do with as you please."

Penelope glanced around the room, her expression covetous. "You are generous now, but you will change your mind when you wed. Your wife will want a London residence."

"No. I will not wed." He did want a wife, children, but he would not risk passing on the taint he carried. And he did not think James would be able to resist this final offer. "Though you may never be Lord Roadnight, your son will inherit the barony."

James was stunned. "I do not believe you."

"I give you my word on it."

"If you are mad, your word is of no value," Penelope challenged him.

James lowered his gaze, mumbling, "Your heirs would still inherit if you betrayed your word—or forgot you had given it."

"We do not want your word," Penelope said curtly. "We want a legal contract."

"Very well." Anything that would bind them fast, even if he must be bound as well.

"I doubt it would hold up against a challenge," James said to Penelope.

"You refuse my word, you doubt a contract—but I need not have offered you either." Seeing James' hope at war with suspicion, Adrian added, "This is a far more equitable arrangement than you in control of my fortune and me locked in Bedlam."

"Master Quarrell came to us after you escaped," James said hesitantly. "He says you are cunning—and dangerous."

"Quarrell's cunning is more in evidence than mine. Whether you believe me or not, I tell you now he is far more dangerous." The last thing Adrian wanted was to be forced to confront Quarrell. Who knew what response the vile doctor could provoke in him? To try and explain that vileness to James would only be taken as proof of madness. Viv could testify to Quarrell's cruelty, but James would probably believe Adrian had bribed her with promises of wealth. He must remain well guarded until all this was settled, and he was far beyond the doctor's reach.

He had to believe that was possible.

Leaning forward over the desk, Adrian deliberately released his anger. "You cannot begin to imagine the indignities, the cruelties, I suffered at that man's hands. Quarrell will not set foot in this house again. If you take any steps to bring him here, I will bring the brunt of the law down on you for your lies about my death."

James paled, but Penelope's eyes flashed defiance.

"I will strip you not only of your stolen title, cousin, but all your stolen wealth." Adrian went on relentlessly. "If I must, I will strip you of your stolen wife."

Penelope gasped, and James went whiter still, though Adrian knew it was the one threat he would not carry out. Knowing that James' deceit had been to secure and protect the woman he adored was the only thing that mitigated Adrian's anger.

"We agree to your terms," James said, moving closer to his wife.

Adrian settled back, looking from one of them to the other. "Within a week, I will retire to Somerset. After that, you may go on with your life in London as before."

James nodded, looking exhausted now. "We will have documents drawn up this week, to make your agreement as binding as possible."

"For both of us," Adrian agreed. "In these documents, you will admit you knew I was alive, and chose to leave me in Bedlam. I will concede you did this in the mistaken belief that I was mad, because of my mother's fate. And because of her, I will cede the barony to your heir." He would also stipulate terms as to who would attend him if he must be shut away. He would not place himself at their mercy again.

"And after that?" Penelope asked.

"Once the details are settled, we will meet in six months, in a year, and again in two. Each time I will release more property into your hands. You will see that my care of my tenants remains sound, and I will oversee your actions until some trust is restored."

"Time will be the proof," James agreed.

"Until this is settled, Sir Raphael and his lady, their entire party, will remain here."

"But—" Penelope protested.

"This is still my home," Adrian kept his voice low, but let the edge of anger cut through sharply. "Everyone in it is my guest, including you."

James backed away, guiding Penelope with him. "Very well."

"One final thing," Adrian said. "Lady Penelope will return my mother's jewels."

Penelope's hand went to the emeralds at her throat. "If you do not intend to marry, you will have no need of them."

"Nonetheless, they are not yours." Adrian nodded that the interview was over. James and Penelope went out the door. Adrian drew a breath to calm his agitation. If his luck held, a week from now he would be at Roadnight Manor. He would be safe.

After a moment, Adrian went out into the hallway, where he found Viv and Rafe waiting with their companions. Claire was not with them. Adrian scanned the crowd and caught another glimpse of her talking to the guests in the great hall. As if aware of him, she turned and smiled, then started toward them, moving with fluid grace. Her familiarity haunted him still—though surely this trust, this tenderness was only a strange bequest from her dead brother.

"Have you reached an accord with your cousin?" Rafe asked, giving a nod toward Sir James, who stood within hearing.

"We have, but until it is documented, I ask that you stay here as my guests."

"Of course, Lord Roadnight." Vivian answered, for it had been agreed to beforehand. "For as long as you need us."

Whether or not Quarrell had told James that Viv led the escape from Bedlam, his cousin knew neither she nor Rafe Fletcher was to be lightly crossed. Adrian was deeply grateful that they had delayed their own plans to help him.

He had never had close friends before, only acquaintances, congenial companionship with no hint of true intimacy. Too close an affinity had stirred glinting flashes of the awareness that overwhelmed him now. Always before, those glints had been a signal to withdraw, smiling but aloof, and let the friendship wither. Bedmates who could stir more than his flesh were quickly discarded. For long years he had not even comprehended it was fear urging his retreat. He had realized it alone, in Bedlam, when all his defenses were stripped away. Compared with the emotional poverty of the past, his present friends proved precious indeed.

His heart warmed as Claire joined them, exquisite and evocative in her clinging Grecian gown. It was easy to imagine Orpheus journeying to hell to rescue so lovely a Eurydice. On impulse he said, "You were the first to welcome me, Lady Claire. Would you do me the honor of being my guest as well?"

"Yes, Lord Roadnight, with pleasure." Claire smiled, her face bright with surprise, for this had not been agreed upon. "I will send word home of tonight's extraordinary events."

Her glow conjured light within him. Adrian smiled in answer, then belatedly realized his own jeopardy. Claire was beautiful, compellingly so. Whenever she was in the same room, his gaze was drawn toward her. To be in her presence was to move through the remembered paces of a dance, surrounded by music sensed if not heard. Music perhaps heard only in dreams.

Claire was also unmarried. He must not allow himself to think of her in such a fashion, or he would regret too greatly the future he would soon be signing away. It was too painful. Too dangerous. For him—and for her.

James and Penelope were watching him even now, proof of

how unwise he'd been in displaying his attraction. Deliberately, Adrian went into the great chamber and sought out a man who'd been a sometime companion at Cambridge, extending the same invitation to him as well, though this time he was refused. Though the fellow was obviously curious, he had already promised to attend a hunt. There was no one else who was more than a fringe acquaintance, so Adrian returned to the hall. He hoped that it would appear that he was asserting his rights by gathering his own guests, and protecting himself from any violent schemes.

But glancing at Lady Claire standing in the hallway, Adrian silently confessed that he had thought only of her unique loveliness, her vibrance. His gaze caressed the graceful flow of her figure, her high breasts and supple hips. He could no longer pretend it was her brother's tender affection he felt. His own yearnings were not chaste. She stirred his blood as no one had ever done before, an arousal that permeated his whole being. He supposed there were other beautiful women here tonight, but he had seen them only as potential allies, potential enemies. Claire he sought at every turn.

She fascinated him with her complex mix of directness and subtlety, of cool intelligence and warm spirit. Already he would recognize the husky timbre of her voice in the darkness. He would know the tantalizing scent of lavender, musk rose, and nutmeg that clung to her. It was far too easy to picture that veil discarded, her chestnut hair flowing loose about her pale shoulders. Her neck was smooth and elegant, and he pictured the emeralds circling her throat. The green fire of the gems would conjure an answering flash in her dark eyes. He would loose her gown and let it fall in a pool, leave her clothed only in the jewels.

No—

Quickly, Adrian turned away. Lust was a torment he did not need, love a luxury he could not afford. Not now, not ever.

Safety was his only desire.

Chapter 6

The morning was still cool and touched with mist when Adrian went outside. In the garden, two men were trimming the yew hedges while a lad gathered the clippings. Adrian paused to greet the gardeners and accept their welcome, then dismissed them for an hour. He wanted to be alone, free to wander where he choose.

Looking back at the stone walls of the house, he felt no regret at giving it to James and Penelope. He had come here first as a grieving child, separated from his mother, and found it unwelcoming. Already his cousin had altered the two places for which he had the most affection, the library and this garden. The grounds were now fashionably formal and contrived. Along with the stiff walls of hedges, there was a great deal of topiary sculpted in geometric shapes, and two new elaborate knot beds of hyssop. Some things remained familiar. Pennyroyal still grew between flagstones, releasing its aromatic scent as he walked along the path toward the secluded rose arbor. Rows of bright flowers bloomed on either side, purple heartsease contrasting with shaggy orange marigolds.

Adrian had been locked in Bedlam for seven months, hidden away in the Buzzing Hornet for over a week. As he wandered in this peaceful solitude, the touch of scented breezes on his face, the warmth of the sun dissipating the mists, almost dizzied him with pleasure. Here all was benign and beautiful. Feeling deprived of touch, he took off his gloves and reached out to stroke the varied textures of living things—the crisp outline of the hedges, the dewy velvety petals of the heartsease. He inhaled deeply, drawing in cool air sweet with greenery and flowers.

It was a small taste of the greater freedom to come. Soon he would be back in Somerset, safe at Roadnight Manor, with its tousled gardens and abundant orchards. In autumn the air would smell of harvested hay and newly pressed apple cider. There he would ride moorlands, purple with heather, and lose himself in the tangled forests of oak, elm, beech, and chestnut. He would climb the rolling slopes of the Quantocks to their crest, and let his circling gaze encompass the rough heaths, craggy limestone cliffs, and lowland fens. To the west, the Severn Estuary would meet the sea in a meld of blue-grey waters and misted sky. And beyond them, Ireland waited, with her green, seductive wilds.

But for now this walled garden was paradise enough. Coming to the end of the path, Adrian found the arbor untouched, the latticework still bearing a lavish burden of crimson musk roses. He sat on the wooden bench and buried his face in a full-blown bloom, drinking in the fragrance of the ruffled petals. Their perfume was as vividly intoxicating as wine, at once utterly pure and purely voluptuous.

A sudden noise made him spring up, reaching for the dagger at his belt. But it was only a cat chasing a squirrel across the garden, both of them squeezing under the gate, its black wrought iron framed with yet more roses. Adrian sank back onto the bench. Despite the success of last night and the tranquil atmosphere of the morning, his nerves were bowstring taut. Though he was safe enough with his friends here, he still could not trust James and Penelope.

Worse than that, Adrian could not trust himself. He looked

at the fine steel blade in his hand, its handle etched with a winged phoenix. It was a new dagger that Rafe had brought him, innocent of blood. Holding it, he perceived only the weight and balance of a perfect weapon. He used to have great skill with a knife, greater still with a rapier. Now the thought of using them sickened him. But he could not afford such squeamishness, and determined to practice and quicken his sword arm. Rafe had promised to train with him this afternoon.

Another sound—footsteps this time. Adrian was on his feet instantly, standing close to the arched bow of the arbor, dagger at the ready. But it was Lady Claire coming down the path. His trepidation melted to delight. She moved with cygnet grace, a sleek black swan. The skirts of her mourning gown swayed with each step, the flowers bright around her feet. Adrian sheathed the weapon before Claire could see his alarm. She was alone, seeking the same quiet as he had, perhaps. She paused, bending down as he had to caress the glossy petals of the heartsease. Gold flashed on her shoulder. She wore the dragon brooch again, the one that had belonged to her murdered brother. The amber glowed from within, as if the warmth of her shoulder animated the golden resin. Had it taken on a new life, now that she had claimed it?

Lady Claire saw him, a warm smile lighting her face. As she approached, a shaft of sunlight draped her chestnut hair with a veil of fire, and picked out the gleam of green in her hazel eyes. She extended her hands in greeting, as he had seen her do only for Rafe. Warning clamored within him, at odds with the impulse to meet her touch. He knew the dangers well, yet shrank at the insult of standing back and tugging on his gloves. She saw his hesitation, and her puzzlement shamed him. He wanted ease between them. Always, she seemed so familiar. Her presence brought a sweet warmth like glowing dawn after darkness, green spring after frosted winter, something fresh and good. But her goodness was no guarantee that some pain of hers might not cut into him fiercely.

Yet he moved toward her, reached out, because he did not want to deny her.

Because he did want to touch her—

Her hands slid into his clasp, smoothly, like a key into a lock. He held the slender branching of her fingers, the tips slightly callused from playing some stringed instrument. Her right hand felt oddly stiff. Rafe had told him that Claire had been injured in an accident, and so Adrian kept his clasp gentle. For an instant he felt no more than her firm elegant hands resting warm within his, and the pleasure of her presence increased by the pleasure of the touch.

Then a terrible vertigo seized him, twisting him inside out. He sank to his knees, taking Claire with him—

The smell of blood filled his nostrils, fresh blood and old. Images, sensations, blows came in a furious barrage as the guards hauled him through the gates of Bedlam. Explosions of rage crashed against sickening jolts of fear as they punched him. Malice and cruelty battered him. The men dragged him across the courtyard, cursing and kicking him relentlessly. One of them jerked him up by his hair, then threw him down, kicking, kicking. He saw himself dying, stomped beneath their boots. Their wish, their intention—or only his own fear?

Frantically, he jerked free and ran across the courtyard. Flight only heightened his fear—terror not only of the present but of the faceless, pursuing past. But there was no escape. The gates were locked, the walls too high to scale. The guards cornered him, moved in on him, their hands flexing.

He yelled at them not to touch him. Laughing, they seized him anyway, their brutal force slamming through the shreds of his control. Gripped by their scorn, their mindless hatred, he fought with new violence. Desire for freedom knotted with the urge to smash, the lust to torment. An arm pressed across his throat, thick and hard as an oak branch. He struggled against the body and mind trying brutally to crush his will.

"Release him." Her voice rang like a bell. She commanded them—and they obeyed.

Freed from the throttling hold, Adrian fell to his knees. Tremors swept through him, a cold tide. He rocked, whispering prayers, trying to press his gutted emotions back inside his body, to hold his own thoughts within his mind. Trying to shut out the brutes. Trying to remember his own name.

Silk whispered as she knelt before him on the filthy ground. Her expression of stern command softened. Her voice calmed him, mellow and warm as sunlight. Soothing comfort spilled forth from her like balm. His desperate need for isolation became a desperate need for touch. He grasped her hands tightly, fingers twining, flesh and bone linked. Her touch was compassion, tenderness, sanity—a true asylum. Her face shone luminous as a candle flame in darkness, kindling an answering light in his mind, his heart.

The swarming terrors hushed, and peaceful stillness enveloped him. The shroud of shadows retreated, driven back by her radiance. In that glow, even the hovering dark transformed. It became a mysterious cave housing, not horrors, but unimaginable wonders. It became the shadowed realm of a night forest that by day would glow with sunlit greens and browns, the colors of life. He gazed into her eyes, knowing everything yet nothing about her. Nothing but her name.

"Claire. . . ." A prayer. An answer.

Her hands tightened in his, and Adrian knew she shared the moment, in thrall as if they had been transported back to that day. The darkness shimmered, now no more than the cool shadow of the arbor surrounding them. Muted sunshine gleamed beyond and a soft breeze floated over them, filled with the sweet perfume of roses, the musky spice of marigolds.

"Claire," he whispered, as if discovering her name for the first time.

His hands clasped hers still, though he could not feel, only see, their separateness. Her eyes were wide with surprise. No fear emanated from her, despite what must be the overwhelming strangeness to her—this disappearance of boundaries. Her quiet was more than matched by her courage. It had been worth it, worth the madness, worth Quarrell's torments, if it brought him to her. Her light, her warmth, would burn away every shadow. She was there now, in his heart, a pure flame to light the darkness.

Kneeling still, Adrian bent his head and pressed his lips to her fingers. She whispered his name. He looked up to find her eyes glowing with wonder and her lips parted, moist and tempting. Irresistible. He kissed her, claiming that yielding softness. At the touch, the flame in his heart blossomed like a rose, filling every atom of his being in an instant, opening petals of light, fire, music. Pure and burning joy.

The need for her unfolded from deeper and deeper within him, fathomless. His arms went around her, molding her against him. Her warm lips parted to take the thrust of his tongue, filling his senses with her taste and scent. He pressed her closer still, needing to feel her flesh and more—needing to melt it into his own, to become one with her. He would lose himself in her. He would find himself. His hand sought her breast, small and tender beneath the strict form of her bodice. He felt the wild beating of her heart sounding in rhythm with his own.

The pure fire became substantial, suffusing his flesh. His loins throbbed as if the sun pulsed there, radiating heat. She pressed against him, and her softness hardened him even more. He strained toward her, aroused in every atom of his being. It was as if their clothes had dissolved. As if he filled her already and she sheathed him. One flesh, one soul.

She gave a soft cry, pleasure and wonder, then broke away suddenly, utter amazement on her face as she stared at him. He was shocked, bereft, the pain of loss twisting his heart. His body ached with need, his manhood throbbing.

"Claire . . ." He did not know what else to say. He was suddenly aware that he had been about to ravish her in the garden. Nothing, no one, had existed for him save her.

"Adrian," she whispered in answer, as much at a loss as he.

Drawing a deep breath, he released it slowly. He had thought her familiarity, his own instinctive trust, were emotional bequests of her brother. But he had seen her himself, months before. "You were there, the day they locked me away. I did not remember until now. I lost those first days."

"Sir Reginald took me there, the day of the accident." She drew a breath, then added, "Afterward, I tried to find out who you were, but in Bedlam they said you were dead."

"Why didn't you tell me?"

"If you never recalled that day, I thought perhaps it was better that I not tell you." She looked away for an instant, then back at him, her gaze intent. "I hoped you would remember me."

"Now I do." How could he have forgotten her? Adrian wanted to embrace her again. Then he remembered how their meeting had ended—her presence obliterated by some dark swirl of engulfing evil. Madness had taken him, even then. Tremors coursed through him. He prayed that Claire could not see them. But she was not looking at him. She was looking down, frowning. A blue vein showed on the slope of her brow like a delicate river coursing under her skin. He watched the faint quiver of her eyelids, the fringed line of her lashes dark against the smooth curve of her cheek.

Then her gaze lifted, her eyes questioning him. "You knew my name then, though no one had said it," she said. "You knew my name."

"That was all. Your name, and that you were good, when everything else was horrible. I discovered nothing else."

"What else could you discover?"

Only truth was possible. Adrian spread his hands open in front of her. "My affliction, my madness, comes through touch. I feel the emotions of others, their grief, their anger, their suffering. Sometimes it is what they are feeling, sometimes pain from their past. Even some objects can carry a terrible tale."

He feared she would be shocked, frightened, but she answered quietly, "I know such things are possible. Does it happen so with everyone?"

"No, but I never know who or what will affect me."

"But it is not always pain?" Her eyes glowed with hope.

"Not always. Not with you," he whispered. After such closeness, it seemed she must know all that had flooded his mind. But that was never the way of it, though she had understood more than anyone else had, it seemed. There were few he had dared ask. "What did you feel when you took my hands?"

Color stained her cheeks, but her gaze held his. "Sometimes when a song ends, for a moment it echoes, in the mind, the heart. The whole song is there, and all the emotions it conjures. Perfection. I was there, with you, in that moment that was both painful and beautiful. But I do not understand it anymore now than I did then."

Adrian understood it far better. She was the beauty. He was the pain. That was all he had to offer her.

Claire gazed up at him, her expression puzzled but tender. She truly did not understand, for she reached out hesitantly toward his face. Open as he was, all resistance would dissolve if she touched him again. Surprise flashed in her eyes as he pulled back abruptly. Her hand fell back to her side, and she waited for what he would do, what he would say.

I love you.

Adrian knew it was already too late to change his heart, but his mind was resolved. He had emerged from the horror of Bedlam into this peaceful garden, and the enchantment of her presence, but madness might yet be his fate—if not in Bedlam, then in a tower carefully guarded. His mother had been locked away for two decades, sometimes singing, sometimes screaming. Never sane even when she was peaceful. His great-grandfather too, had died a fool babbling of creatures crawling from the walls.

Despair and desperation swallowed him. He could not be so selfish as to inflict such uncertainty on Claire. He would not marry. He would not have heirs.

He rose to his feet, but did not help her as she stood in turn. Adrian could feel his face take on a mask of smooth and meaningless politeness. "Lady Claire, forgive me. This should not have happened."

He saw her tender expectance change to hurt. Her lips parted to speak.

Turning, he walked swiftly back into the house, ignoring her call. His heart was a dark, aching hollow. His arms, his body ached where hers had imprinted. One flesh—and he had severed them from each other.

Breathless with shock, Claire watched Adrian retreat. His falsely polite words stung, sharp as a slap. What had happened? Only a moment before, they had shared that exquisite resonance, two instruments vibrating to the same music. Separate yet utterly attuned, as intimate as lovers must be. Then he had coolly detached himself, had abandoned her.

Shaken, Claire followed Adrian into the house. He had vanished. She inhaled a breath that shuddered like a sob. Confusion, pain, and anger plucked at her nerves till her whole body quivered with the rejection. She searched for him, but found only empty rooms and locked doors. Her uncertainty grew with each failure. Not wishing to walk in on Sir James or Penelope, she asked Samuel where Adrian had gone.

The old steward answered with impassive politeness, "Lord Roadnight gave orders he was to remain undisturbed, my lady."

Claire turned away, cold anger and hot shame rushing through her in conflicting currents. Surely he had told the servants no more than that, a general command, not an order to deny her admittance. At court, Claire had seen women who could not hide their obsession for a man, and had determined never to be one. Whether Adrian had taken refuge from everyone or just from her, she was searching for a man who did not wish to be found. Clutching at the raveled skeins of her emotions, she turned and walked blindly down the tapestried passage. An open door showed her the music room and she plunged into the offered sanctuary. Its bow windows overlooked a swath of green lawn, and late morning sun turned its oak paneling to a rich swirl of dark grains and knots. A vivid carpet from the Orient lay in the middle of the floor. Equally extravagant and exotic, an inlaid screen shadowed the closet window seat. Grateful, Claire sheltered behind its privacy.

She took up a lute from the window seat and plucked a few delicate notes. Sharp pain clawed at her tendons and her hand faltered. She began again, and came to the same wincing end. Music promised soothing escape from the chaos of her emotions, but that same turmoil made concentration impossible. Laying the lute aside, Claire struggled to reclaim calm, but the morass of her emotions sucked and pulled at her like dark river muck. Adrian could discover hidden secrets through touch. That much she understood. Their handclasp had finally drawn forth the memory of their meeting at Bedlam.

What else had he glimpsed?

A light footfall made her look up. Adrian came through the doorway. He glanced around quickly, but did not see her within the shadows of screen. She watched as he crossed to the far side of the room, where an Irish harp stood on a table. For a moment he only stood there, his gloved hands gripping the edge of the table. With unguarded grace he bent to the harp, his long fingers gliding along the polished smoothness of the wood. Any other man, she would have envied the fine instrument, but now she envied the harp the caressing touch of those fingers. Reaching out, he plucked a string on the harp. The single pure note softly filled the room and shivered sweetly along her nerves. Another note, lower. A pang of arousal shot through her. She imagined stripping the gloves from his hands, imagined their glide over the curve of shoulder, breast, hip and thigh. Imagined their heat cupping the heat at her center.

Taut as a harp string herself, she rose and stepped forward.

Adrian whirled, hand flying to the hilt of his dagger. They stood so for a moment, the tension between them growing till the air thrummed. Then he lowered his hand, and the startled wariness in his face smoothed to a perfect mask. He bowed gracefully. "Lady Claire."

Assuming this courtly manner, he made their kiss in the garden no more than a flirtation. Shallow. Meaningless. Ignoring his posing, she deliberately looked to the dagger, hoping to provoke some unfeigned response. "Do you think me so dangerous?"

"A beautiful woman is always dangerous." A compliment. Followed by a small, tight smile. Followed by a dismissive shrug. He glanced toward the door.

She stood where she was, fighting the urge to bar his way. Her lungs compressed, her breathing grew reedy and shallow. Even if her mind could frame a rejoinder, she could not give voice to it.

He faced her again, but his eyes were empty as glass, refusing to see her. His tone was formal. "Lady Claire, if you are disturbed about my conduct in the garden, you need not fear. I will not affront you in such a fashion again."

Anger snarled with hurt, twisting and knotting inside her. His detachment was the affront, not the impassioned kiss they had shared. "Better that fashion than this."

He lifted an eyebrow at her sharpness, her refusal to bow to the rules of civility.

Her nerves janged like foolscap bells. "Why this cool façade? I hate it."

"Do you? You have not complained of my manner before."

"Before, it was warm." Anger yanked against the weakened grip of her control.

"Forgive me, lady. I would have said it was too hot."

She surged forward to slap him. He caught her, his gloved hand clamping her wrist. His eyes flashed green fire. Desire? Anger? Then their color dulled as his passion closed off. Claire saw no relenting in him. She pulled against his grip. He released her arm, stepped back a pace. It might well have been across the room.

"You call me wanton?" She goaded him, furious at his withdrawal.

"It was my manner that was in question." His chill only increased her heat.

"And mine, with you," she challenged. Anger was like wildfire, a quick fierce heat rushing through her, a burning vividness that swept from her center out through her limbs. It was frightening to be out of control—exhilarating to be free. She wanted to slap him again, force some response from him. She wanted to pull him against her, feel the sweet fire of his kiss, the hot press of his body. She wanted him. Fiercely.

But he did not want her.

Shocked at her own wayward emotions, at her rash behavior, Claire covered her wrist where he'd gripped her, pressing it to her breast. The touch of his gloved hand still burned against her skin. Her weaker fingers refused to curve to their path. Looking down she saw her pallid scars, ridges ugly as worms crawling over the back of her wrist, up under her sleeve.

"Is it because I'm crippled?" She bit her lips, but it was too late to call back her question, her accusation.

"What?" He looked blank. An attempt to don his poseur's mask again?

Words would not come, lost in a crazed buzz of emotions and images. They swarmed like hornets, stinging. Over and over her mother flinched to see the slowly healing wounds on Claire's arm. The aging Earl who asked for her hand brought her perfumed gloves to cover it. The maids of honor, the dashing courtiers, turned their eyes away as well, hiding their pity, their repugnance for her, their relief for themselves. Again and again Claire shrugged away the stings. Mere vanity. The scars were nothing to the loss of use. Her father no longer asked her help with delicate experiments. She plucked feebly at the strings of her lute—and her music came forth weak and crippled too.

The swarm descended, the stings burning, burning . . .

She held up her stiff, scarred hand, confronting him, confronting herself.

"No, Claire. No!" Adrian looked totally stunned. "Of course not."

What then—her infatuation with Rafe? But if Adrian sensed that, he must also have sensed that its last glow had faded before the desire he himself had evoked. Did he think her fickle? Or was it some uglier flaw? She was glad Reginald Fitzroy was dead. She mourned the others his arrogance had killed. But she hated him, hated the reckless folly that had marred her body and spirit. Did Adrian think her selfish, heartless? Could he have discovered her terror of the river? Did he know she could not even enter a boat without wanting to flee, and despise her cowardice? If Adrian was not repelled by the scars on her skin—was it the scars left on her soul? "Is it because I—"

"No." Now his voice was soft, sincere. "You have done nothing."

The anger that had lifted her burned out, leaving her with shame. Disbelieving herself, Claire burst into tears. Fighting for control, she retreated back to the window seat. The livid scars glared like an accusation. She covered her hand in the folds of her skirts, but there was no way to cover her soul, raw and exposed to view.

Adrian started toward her, then checked himself and stood watching while she cried. He held himself rigid, his hands knotted into fists. She hated her tears, hated that he did not comfort her. Claire did not understand what was happening to her. She cried seldom, and alone. Her mother staged scenes to get her way. Claire would not. She swallowed down her tears, wiped angrily at her face. She had no right to ask, but she must. "Tell me why."

"You do not know my whole history," he began. His voice was formal, distant. She could see him struggle to conceal his distress behind the smooth mask.

"Don't—don't hide." Claire closed her eyes, too weary now to weep. Abruptly, he halted. When she opened her eyes, his face was grim.

"You say you are crippled—" His voice cracked.

Against her will, she flinched.

"Your hand will not obey your will. I do not doubt you feel damaged, weakened, even if others only see your strengths. So understand this. My mind is crippled, Claire. Madness is in my blood. My mother died lunatic."

For a moment she could only stare at him, stunned. "Your mother?"

His face did not change, and yet it did, the bones sharper, as if stark memory cut through his flesh. "The lunacy struck suddenly, the night my baby sister died."

"What happened?" The cadence of her heart sounded cold and inexorable thudding filled her breast. Consuming dread of what he would say warred with the terrible hunger to know him, to know what had shaped him.

"I woke to screaming. When I ran out, I saw my mother being dragged up to the tower. I saw my father—his face burned and bloody." Adrian lifted a hand, covering the left side. "I cried out to them, but the servants carried me away. In the morning, my father came to me, his eye bound. I remember the white bandage stained with seeping blood."

"How dreadful . . ." she whispered. Sick misery churned her stomach. Too vividly, she imagined the child whose safe world had toppled into chaos in a single night.

"My father said my new sister had died. My mother could not bear feeling the babe's spirit fly to heaven. In a rage of grief, she had attacked him with a candle, blinded him in one eye."

"How old were you?"

"Five," he answered.

So young his life had been blighted. "Do you remember her before . . . ?"

"I have memories of her being happy, of being happy myself. Glowing bits and pieces." He sighed. "Sometimes it seems my life began that night."

Her breath caught, a small sob.

"My mother never remembered any of what happened. Ten years melted away like wax. She remembered nothing of her marriage. Nothing of me."

Claire leaned toward him, the slightest movement and he moved back. His glance was wary. She pressed her arms closer to her body. *Do not touch him.*

She feared his confiding was at an end, that he would retreat behind his façade. But at last he went on, his voice harder. "My father brought me to England, and I saw her but seldom after that. She was kept locked in her rooms at Treise Castle when she was calm, shut away in the tower when she grew violent. Such may be my future as well."

"Do not imprison your future in your past," Claire entreated him.

He looked at her directly. "I have asked you all to help me regain what my cousin seized. In truth, I am desperate to do so. I will take up my title, my wealth, my power, not as a sword to go forth in the world, but as a shield against it. They are my protection. If I go mad again, I will not be sent to such a hell as Bedlam."

"That is the extent of your hopes?" she asked, stricken. Coldness filled her, as if the river swallowed her into its maw. She fought to stay calm, to make sense of this, to discover some path to lead them both out of misery.

"Fear shapes them, such as they are," he answered.

Claire saw shame in his face, a shame she understood all too well. He loathed the fear that ruled him, as she loathed her own. Even as she watched, he drew into himself, smaller and tighter into a confining shell. Without it he must feel defenseless—yet he must break free. "What if you have reclaimed your sanity? What if the future you fear does not unfold?"

"How can I know? Even if my control does not deteriorate, I have a duty to the future. My blood is tainted." He looked at her with naked longing, with deep sorrow. "I must never marry. I must remain apart, from you most of all."

You most of all. . . . He had thought of marriage, and of her. Her breathing caught, then quickened. She did not dismiss his words, only tried to compose a new form for them. Melancholy they might be, yet not a dirge. "I see your gift has brought the curse of suffering with it, to both your mother and you."

"Gift?" He shook his head, disbelieving.

"Yes, for gift it may be, as well as curse." She urged him to see it so. "Tragedy destroyed your mother, but you have gained strength. You would have recovered sooner were you not brutalized by your foul keepers in Bedlam. You emerged sane from a place that might drive others mad."

Something in his twist of a smile tightened all her nerves till they vibrated under her skin. His voice was so bitter she could taste it. "So Vivian said. But I never told her my mother's grandfather died lunatic as well."

Claire inhaled sharply. His great grandfather too? Such a dark history could not be ignored. Yet it was not inevitable that he would pass on his strange ability and its difficulties, still less that it must lead to lunacy. Was he right to deny himself and her? Intellect urged caution, but her drowning heart cried no. Adrian was not mad—could not go mad. Claire had always thought herself sensible. Now she wanted only to cast away all the weight of reason and live on a wisp of faith. She was the very thing she had vowed never to become, a fool for love. She wanted to cry for the moon, to beg for the sun. To plead for the shining light of his presence in her own darkness. But his pain, his need was greater than hers. "This gift came the night you were injured?"

He hesitated. "Not precisely."

"What would be precise?" She demanded to know the truth. There was no hope for him, or for her, without it.

"When I was a child such sensations were rare. Even so, to tell my father an object felt strange, or that a dream felt too real, earned me a beating and dire warnings. I smothered every response I'd learned to fear as mad, until they all but vanished. Now I think they were only whiffs of smoke. The fire burned on beneath."

"Until the blow to your head unleashed your power somehow?" she asked. "Could the cause be purely physical? Perhaps, as your father thought the thieves had killed you, you saw them strike him down."

A green streak flickered in his irises as he glanced at her, and a fear so palpable she had to restrain herself from moving toward him. But gray clouded the colors, and his face was suddenly weary. In a flat voice, he said, "It began before that night. It began with my mother's death."

Adrian fell silent. Claire could see that he did not want to talk of it. "Tell me."

"Word came that she was ill, but not that her illness was mortal. My father went alone to Ireland. I was not there at her bedside, but I can name the night, perhaps the moment, of her death. She came to me in a dream, young and beautiful, but full of sadness. . . ."

Claire held her breath, filled with awe and wonder. The memory seemed to hover in the air between them. His voice was no more than a whisper. "She took my face in her hands and kissed me on the forehead, as she did when I was a child." He opened his hands, staring at them. "She wore no gloves in the dream. Her hands, her lips, were cool as mist."

He closed his eyes, anguish etching his face.

"And then?" Claire softly called him back.

Adrian opened his eyes. "And then she vanished. I woke calling out to her. But I knew she was gone."

"The undeniably sane have seen the dead bid them farewell," Claire said, aching to comfort him. "Even animals have been known to cry out at their master's passing."

"Perhaps it was not the beginning of the madness, but I sensed some awful knowledge—within me or without. I went to meet my father at the docks, trying to pretend I did not know the news he would bring me from Ireland." Frowning, he put a hand to his face as he had before, covering one eye.

"Do you remember something new?" she asked. "Do you remember meeting him?"

"Images haunt me." His frown deepened, creasing deep into his brow. His voice shook as he answered, "But I do not know if they are true, Claire, and it torments me."

Ache overcame caution. She stepped toward him, reaching out.

With unexpected quickness Adrian moved back. Though the false coolness did not return, resolution was in his eyes. "There can be nothing more between us."

Once more he turned and walked away.

Chapter 7

New understanding lessened the pain of Adrian's rejection, but not the pain of need. Claire had lost too much to let him go so easily. Only her desire for Adrian had made her face how bitterness was crippling her spirit. She would fight to keep him. But if she pursued him now, she sensed he would only retreat further. Her own emotions were still too raw, too chaotic to trust. She must regain a portion of calm, and think on what to do.

No one but Adrian knew the full extent of the suffering that drove him to retreat. Yet Claire did not share his conviction that he must remain alone. Their timeless moment of sharing had brought joy, and beneath the flame-hued swirlings of desire, a clear light of peace. Her heart cried out that he was denying the very things that might heal him. Yet he had made it plain, no words of hers could ease his fears. He would not allow her touch.

To be so vulnerable and yet so isolated must be appalling. Although skeptical by nature, Claire knew such extraordinary talents existed. She should have considered such a possibility earlier. Adrian had hinted at the truth. Even Rafe—

A new thought struck her, forceful enough to send her rushing from the music room back to the guest wing of the house. Determined to question Rafe, she knocked at his door. Would he still lie abed? It was morning, neither early nor late. After a moment, the door opened and he looked out. He was bare-chested and remarkably disheveled. Not only that, Claire could hear a rustling within. She guessed that Vivian, still only Mistress Swift, had made use of the connecting door between their rooms.

"I can speak to you later," Claire said, flustered.

Rafe seemed to sense her disquiet was more than mere embarrassment. "No. Wait. I'll be out in a minute."

The door closed. She heard muffled laughter within. The happy sound conjured the image of her and Adrian among tangled sheets, dawn kindling the sea fires in his eyes. Claire realized she had never heard him laugh.

She walked to the end of the hallway, looking out a window at the garden. Not so long ago she had gazed down from her own window, tendrils of mist coaxing her to come enjoy the cool morning. The mists had vanished, the garden transformed by the sun. As she was transformed. Adrian filled her heart and mind. She had offered him her hands, unthinkingly, the impulse to touch him stronger than any fear of pain. But with the clasp of his hands, the touch of his lips, everything had changed.

She was in love, suddenly and completely, with a stranger. Enchantment permeated the air she breathed. It coursed through her blood like a song whose notes only she could hear, wild and compellingly sweet. It beckoned her into a forest, deeper and deeper, till she was alone and lost. Afraid of the encroaching dark.

Touching Adrian in the garden, she felt she knew everything about him.

In truth she'd known almost nothing.

She turned as she heard Rafe come out into the hallway.

Fully dressed now, he strode toward her, concern stamped on his features. "What is it, Claire?"

"I know about Adrian's gift."

Rafe drew back a step at her abruptness, and then stepped closer. In a low voice he asked, "Adrian told you?"

"He . . . touched me." She flushed again, remembering the heat of Adrian's hand pressing against her breast, her nipple tender, her lips feeling the intimacy of his kiss. With the rush of sensual memories, Claire's impulse to confide shifted to reluctance. Afraid Rafe might intuit the reason for her blush, she gestured. "He touched my hands."

Rafe moved closer, ever the protector. "Without his gloves?"

"He wore no gloves." She remembered how Adrian had sometimes rubbed his gloved hands together—that guarded, almost secretive gesture.

"Is he all right? Are you?"

"Yes." She frowned, uncertain.

"Tell me what happened," Rafe insisted.

"Adrian remembered when I first met him, that day in Bedlam. And I . . . felt like I was back there with him."

Rafe shook his head, frowning. "I did not share anything of what he felt."

"You?" She gripped his arm with her good hand. "Tell me what happened." His gaze went to the dragon brooch, and then he turned away, gazing over the garden blindly. A chill went through Claire, but she persisted. There had been enough evasion. "It's Gabriel, isn't it? You told me that Adrian led you to Gabriel's killers, but not how. Tell me now."

Rafe met her gaze again, reached out and touched the dragon brooch she wore with his fingertip. "Gabriel wore this the night he died. Adrian held it in his hand and saw who murdered him. It hurt him, Claire. Adrian could feel it all, as if they stabbed him as well."

Sympathetic pain for Adrian knotted with Claire's still raw grief for her brother. "How terrible."

"He collapsed. For a moment I thought he would die in my

arms as Gabriel did." Rafe paled. "I could see Adrian was in pain, but I was not drawn into it."

No one had been dearer than Gabriel. If Adrian's touch had not already forged this strange bond between them, this new knowledge would have done so. "You should have told me. I am greatly in his debt."

"It is his secret—his to reveal or not. But I have a responsibility to you as well." Rafe dragged his fingers through his hair as he did when he was worried. "He swears he is no warlock, Claire. I believe there was no evil bargain with the devil. If he is a witch, he is a white witch, and wishes to do good."

Adrian's gift did not disturb her so much. Although wary of her father's obsession with alchemy and magic, she was accustomed enough to strange talents not to fear them. "My father's studies have brought him in contact with many people who claim such unusual abilities. None were mad. None evil—not as you mean. Certainly many were greedy charlatans, but some convinced even me. Dr. Dee casts horoscopes and can see the future in a scrying glass. He is trusted by the Queen herself. There was an old lady from Cornwall who could find lost objects as if the world were transparent. She did nothing but good."

"In truth?" Rafe asked, obviously nervous.

"These people were neither saints nor devils," she chided, fighting a smile.

Rafe's look asked how could she be sure, but he went on earnestly. "Adrian does not intend harm, and so far I have seen only good come from his gift. But it torments him, Claire. Some visions are too horrible to bear and he must escape them somehow."

"He endured the horror of Bedlam and survived," Claire said. "Surely, the danger is not weakness of mind, but the strength of the impressions he receives."

"Yes, but even a moment's carelessness may lead to catastrophe."

Claire regarded him defiantly. The moment she shared with

Adrian was not a catastrophe. Nor what happened with the dragon brooch, for all it pained him. "You said yourself, great good can come from his gift."

"Yes." Despite agreeing, Rafe shook his head. "I both pity and admire him, Claire—but I worry too. He may be driven to violence again."

"I cannot believe he is dangerous now," she said, willing it to be true.

"Danger may seek him out, Claire. None of us can predict what he will do."

Adrian surged forward as Rafe did, steel ringing against steel as both rapier and dagger locked hilt to hilt. For a fraction of a second, they were caught in the clutch of snarled blades—the next second they leapt away. Rafe attacked instantly, *stromazione,* a light cut for the face. Adrian double-parried and countercut, blocking the thrust of Rafe's sword with his dagger, sliding his own rapier over and around to cut at the shoulder. Rafe deflected his thrust and landed a dagger slash to his sword arm.

Adrian danced back cat-quick, then counterattacked, his rapier blade in constant motion, cutting tight figure eights before him to ward off the other blade. The quick slashes and forward rush forced Rafe back briefly, but a sudden feint broke through Adrian's guard. He parried Rafe's rapier as the point aimed a crippling drive to his knee. Adrian blocked low on the outside, but Rafe slipped the blade under and thrust up, aiming for his heart. A swift *battere* beat the lethal thrust aside. As Rafe countered, Adrian dropped into a low *passato sotto.* The blade sheared over his head, a narrow miss. From the lunge Adrian thrust out, his own rapier point touching in a killing thrust to the belly.

"Ah!" Rafe exclaimed, both pleased and annoyed. "Good strike!" With thumb and forefinger, he removed the balled practice point of Adrian's sword from his padded vest and stepped back. "That's enough for today."

"Thank you." Dripping sweat, Adrian rose from the low

lunge. His muscles began a low aching hum as his tension ebbed. It was an ache he used to relish, but today it burned fiercely. Rafe had given him renewed confidence in his skill by not pressing his exhaustion.

"You need to rebuild your strength, of course," Rafe said. "But after so long without training, you have excellent speed and fluidity."

"But?" Adrian already guessed what the criticism would be. After his earlier encounter with Claire, he had wanted not to think for an hour. Or to think of nothing but the sword. He had not achieved even the latter.

"But your concentration was poor," Rafe admonished, sword point tapping where his dagger had scored a touch. "True, I'm dead because I underestimated your distraction. However . . ."

"Understood." Despite his bleak mood, Adrian returned a disarming smile. He did not want his manners to suffer as his bladework had. But then, he had been practicing at mastering his emotions far longer than mastering the rapier.

When he was a child and the English boys taunted him for being half Irish, he'd fought fiercely—only to find there were no victories in such battles. In their eyes, the fights he lost proved him inferior, those he won proved him savage. Instead, he'd learned to swallow his anger, to blunt sharp words with smiles and easy banter till it was second nature to him. There were subtler taunts and provocations later, but if any temper frayed, Adrian made sure it was his opponent's rather than his own. They looked foolish indeed when he proved himself more the perfect English gentleman than they. The skill he'd developed at fencing allowed the same finesse, and a sharper revenge. In this, at least, he'd been granted respect.

Rafe regarded him judiciously. "Tomorrow we'll have another short round with rapier and dagger."

Adrian nodded agreement, gratified now that he'd managed some exercise in Bedlam to work his muscles. Strength and speed would return. His concentration was another matter.

Rafe rested his hand on the shoulder of Adrian's heavily

padded fencing doublet. A friendly gesture, yet Adrian surmised the pressure was significant. Blue eyes searched his own. "I'm glad you decided to tell Lady Claire the truth."

Another layer of the truth—

"It was necessary." He wondered if Rafe knew what had prompted his so-called decision. Some but not all, he conjectured, given how discreet Claire was. Rafe was protective of her, a friend assuming as best he could the place of a dead brother. Adrian knew Rafe's conflicting feelings about him might never be resolved. The familiar weight of depression settled over him, far heavier than Rafe's hand. Ignoring the bleakness, he smiled pleasantly, "She is all that is admirable. I will miss her greatly when I retire to the country."

"You could always invite her to visit." It was not a statement of the obvious. It was a question.

Adrian answered it as such. "I doubt it would be wise."

Rafe frowned. "I'd hate to see her married off to another currish coxcomb like Sir Reginald."

"Few men would be worthy of her."

Rafe made a noncommittal noise, unable to make the stretch that Adrian would be a worthy match. He chewed his lip, worrying over some unspoken sentence, finally settling on a comradely salute with his sword. "Until tomorrow, Lord Roadnight."

"Tomorrow." He returned the salute.

Back in his room, Adrian stripped and sponged off the sweat. His body was exhausted, but his brain would not cease churning. He donned the clothes the manservant had laid out, fine linen deeply edged with lace, velvet trunkhose and doublet of mourning black decorated with jet buttons. He could control the image he presented to the world, but not the flotsam of emotions that battered him like storm wreckage, the shattered collision of past and present.

Desire. Regret. Grief. Fear. Floundering, he turned from one only to be struck by another. Images returned—images of Claire and the destruction he had wrought in her heart. He did not want to think on her sudden, startling tears. Yet it was better to think on her tears than on the kindled passion in her eyes—hazel eyes, with green fire flickering within the rich brown. Better to think on her angry slap and scornful words than on the melting tenderness of her lips, the lithe curves of her body pressed to his.

He had hurt Claire, humiliated her. And to be kind he must continue to be cruel. He must avoid her company, even the friendship he once presumed to court. It was far more than friendship he wanted.

He must not touch Claire. He must remain untouchable.

He'd told her that his life began the night his mother went mad. Like a mortal cast out from Faerie, his golden, innocent world vanished like a dream. He wandered, lost in a gray fog, afraid to search for the light. And so, instead, he found the dark. He thought of Quarrell's eyes, gray as fog, the pupils at their center like a tunnel into the blackest hell.

But he had escaped from hell. Life seemed to begin anew the night he fled Bedlam. Despite the fears snapping at his heels, the world suddenly glowed with that long-forgotten brightness. He'd rediscovered the joy of simple things—a clean body, good food, a deep sleep. He'd rediscovered trust, and friendship—which were not so simple, but held the promise of a deeper joy. These past days he'd felt alive, vital, as he had not for years. Without admitting what was happening, he'd let himself hope for too much.

He'd begun to hope for happiness.

Glowing bits and pieces, he'd told Claire—those halcyon days of childhood when his mother ruled Castle Treise, a flame-haired queen of Faerie with golden stars shining in the center of her green eyes. Such stars were the touch of magic. He had them too, she'd said, and danced away, laughing with delight.

Always in his memory she was dancing. She spun him round on the hillside on above the sea, then tumbled with him in the long grass spattered with orange and yellow wildflowers. Her dress was green as the grass. In Ireland all the colors were so bright. The blue sky arched overhead, and below the waves leapt and frolicked like sea ponies tossing their white manes and tails. "Do you see them?" his mother had asked. "Do you see the chargers of the sea folk there, prancing in the water?"

Adrian remembered Castle Treise ablaze at solstice, the hall gleaming with a thousand candles and scented with boughs of evergreen. He could taste the Christmas wassail, so rich with spices it made him dizzy. His mother took his hand and bade him lead the dance with her, though he stood no higher than her hip. Standing by the mantel, his father raised a cup in toast and smiled, happy—

Glowing bits and pieces. Beautiful in themselves, if you did not think how the whole was broken.

With Claire, Adrian could imagine such simple joys, hearth and home, love and laughter. Children. But such imaginings were futile dreams, as far beyond reach as the lost kingdom of Faerie.

He would not make a child that would be dragged into the gray mists.

Dragged into the darkness of the night.

Chapter 8

Edward Quarrell drew his hood closer to his face as he approached the precincts of St. Paul's. Rising from a churchyard that covered more than twelve acres, the vast cathedral dominated London's skyline and served as great hall and marketplace to the citizens of London, as well as a place of worship. Lady Penelope had summoned him here, after her masque took such an unexpected turn last night. As he entered the open doors, Quarrell found it amusing to picture himself as an angel arriving in answer to a lady's prayers. He would save her from the troublesome Irish demon wreaking havoc in her life.

Adrian . . .

A sea-swell of voices rose around him, echoing in the tall arched ceiling of the nave. Streams of light filtered through the high windows, glazing the array of bright cloaks and skirts. Quarrell avoided the conspicuous promenade of Paul's Walk where the gallants strutted, and headed toward the back quadrant. Frowning away beggars and pickpockets, he wove his way amid the booths of ribbon sellers, perfumers, and purveyors of gewgaws who crowded this section. There Lady Penelope was, waiting with obvious impatience beside a pillar. As her note said, she wore a pale green cloak, and carried a red rose. After giving her a deferential bow and introducing himself, he guided her to a niche beside a marble tomb, a spot well shielded from curious ears. In a furious whisper, she recounted Adrian's dramatic reappearance. Quarrell listened— and watched. Under the cloak, the lemon satin of her gown was embroidered with tiny strawberries. They glowed like drops of blood against the flushed softness of skin. That image pleased him. He enjoyed his incipient arousal as she prattled on.

"If only he would show his madness, people would not blame us. It will be worth the scandal of having lied about his death to have him out of the way." She eyed him with sulky ire, this exquisite creature. "He promised Sir James our heirs would be his own, saying he'd never marry, yet the next day he almost seduced Lady Claire in the garden. After what I chanced to see this morning, I have no faith Sir Adrian will hold to the contract! He'll marry and beget his own debased brood."

"You saw him with Lady Claire Darren?" Quarrell asked sharply.

"Yes." She pouted. "He took her hands. Then he kissed her. She let him. The rich baron she was betrothed to is dead, and Lady Claire has her sights set on Sir Adrian."

Quarrell's anger seethed like a nest of vipers. Quickly, he closed it off. He could afford to reveal nothing but his supposed concern for Adrian, perhaps a touch of greed. Not possessiveness. "This lucidity is only a phase. While it endures he will be most cleverly manipulative—but still dangerous."

"You know he's half Irish. Madness runs in their blood. He must be gotten out of the way before he taints our ancestral house."

Quarrell suppressed a smile at this transparent pose. Was she urging a kidnapping, or more? He guessed she wished the present Lord Roadnight dead, but had not quite admitted it to herself. If she hoped he would lead her to that plot, she would be disappointed. He had other plans. "Better I take him quickly, before this contract you spoke of is signed."

"Yes. Even now it is being drafted, and will be brought to the house tomorrow. My husband feels guilty over the deception he committed—as though he had no cause! He says Sir Adrian will not interfere with our marriage. To him, that is what is important."

"You did make him fall in love with you, did you not?" Quarrell asked silkily. "He values you more than life itself. What greater testament to your charms?"

"You are impertinent," Penelope chided, but she looked at him with new interest.

He doubted it was lust. She was cold, her desire all for wealth, status, admiration. Her beauty, her round, sweet body, were currency to be invested for the desired return. He wondered if she would bed him to achieve what she wanted. Although the thought was tempting, it could also be a dangerous miscalculation to pursue it. The pleasure of copulation was shallow compared to satisfaction of his greater appetite. And if Lady Penelope scorned to bed a supposed inferior, he could lose the hold he now had. Far better to tickle her vanity with his flattery, and so draw her to him as an ally. No doubt she felt a sweet excitement in planning out wickedness, in believing that he did not condemn but admired her ruthlessness.

Darkness uncoiled in his loins as he lured her further. "Will you help me return him to my care?"

"To Bedlam? Impossible, he has friends now. Everyone who was at the celebration will testify he is not mad. Sir Raphael and Mistress Swift have the Queen's ear."

"Not Bedlam. My private hospital is being readied. Even now, he can be taken there and kept under guard. Bring your witnesses there, the more impartial the better."

"But you said his affliction came and went, that he had times of lucidity, such as this," she complained. "If he speaks as he does now, he will be freed in an instant."

"Yes, but I know remedies to make him better—or worse," Quarrell assured her. "Anyone who comes will see a madman who must be locked away."

She grasped it instantly. "What must I do?"

"How many sup with your husband and Sir Adrian tonight?"

"Sir Raphael and Mistress Swift, as well as Lady Claire." She added with some acidity, "The cook is full of plans for rich roasts and sumptuous pastries to welcome the master home."

"Excellent." From his purse Quarrell took the five small vials he had brought for just such an eventuality.

"Oh." Her eyes widened. She gave a quick glance over her shoulder, and then held out her hand. He watched her furtively slip the vials into her purse. Her flesh was smooth and white over bones as delicate as a bird's. Such dainty fingers. The slightest pressure and they would shatter with a lovely, delicate sound. *Crack . . . crack . . . crack.*

"How are they to be used?" Her whisper was sweetly conspiratorial.

"Before supper, pour them into the wine, one to each beaker. If your own wine is also tainted, take only a sip or two. Be prodigal with the guests. Call for toasts, so that they will drink deeply. Make sure the servants drink some as well. It is a celebration, after all." He met her gaze, and found it wide with excitement. Her open vulnerability made the darkness in his loins stir, aware and alert like the opening of a fiery eye. An idea woke in his mind, flexing a tentative claw. "Can you drug the wine without being seen?"

"It will not be difficult."

"The concoction is harmless but effective, the taste spicy, somewhat like cloves. Soon after they have drunk, they will grow drowsy and retire. I assure you they will sleep soundly." He paused for effect, letting her imagine them all quiet.

She licked her lips.

"Is there a back entrance to your town house?" He already

knew the answer, but his murmur evoked the stealthiness of night.

"Yes, a wrought-iron gate. One guard watches it. It will be a bit more difficult to drug him, but I will manage it."

"I will find the gate. When they are all asleep, you will open it and let me in." Salamanders of dark flame crept through his body, licking, licking with little tongues of sweet poison. Quarrell exulted silently. Yes, it would be so easy, with the guards and servants all asleep, the husband who loved her so dearly sprawled in his chamber. How better to seal Adrian Thorne's madness than in blood? "I will take Sir Adrian away. In the morning, you can admit your deed. You need only say he made some threat, or spoke strangely when you were alone. So strangely that you knew you must have him put away."

"Yes, yes, for my safety." She was all eagerness.

"I'll warrant your safety means everything to Sir James." Another smile played about his lips. He almost hummed with the growing pleasure, the coalescing of the salamanders into the fiercer dragon. Its power surged through his loins, hardening him.

A small frown creased her brow. "This new hospital will offer greater comfort than Bedlam?"

"Yes," he said solemnly. "No one will feel you are mistreating him."

"That is important, too." She smiled with genuine delight. Yes, she was like a small bird, so vain and so innocent in its soft plumage.

"Tell no one of our plan until it is accomplished." This was crucial. He must impress it upon her. "Give me your word, my lady. Sir James' conscience plays the gadfly, and you do not know which of your servants you can trust."

"The older servants are over fond of Sir Adrian, and he has charmed some of the new ones as well. Any one of them might warn him. But my maid is faithful. She can help me."

"No," he insisted softly. "Even if you can trust her to protect you, you cannot trust her not to make some mistake. Sir Adrian has an uncanny ability to perceive danger. You must

take care to conceal your own intent, still more to guard
against a fidgety servant."

She frowned. "Very well."

Quarrel could easily dispatch one servant girl, but he was
indeed afraid she might talk to the others first. Penelope must
not confide in anyone at all. That would be disastrous. "All
will be as I have asked, then?" She nodded. "Good. I will
come at midnight."

"And that will be the last I see of Adrian?"

"I promise you it will be so," he murmured.

Claire lifted her goblet as Rafe and Viv called for a toast to
Adrian. She took only a sip, and even that sat uneasily. This
morning she had a small taste of passion, and it had proved
too rich a stew. Emotions seethed and roiled her stomach,
making it almost impossible to eat. Remembering Adrian's
rejection, hurt bubbled up, then anger, then fear. Remembering his kiss, desire burst forth—the pungent spice that permeated all else. Such overwhelming emotion should be a surfeit,
but she was starved. Thwarted, her desire for Adrian only increased. She craved his look, his touch, his presence. No one
else would satisfy.

The whole banquet had taken on the fantastical quality of a
dream. Her perceptions were blurry one moment, painfully
sharp the next. She stole glances, keenly aware of his masculine beauty—like a splendid elf king, golden, tall, and slender,
presiding among lesser mortal lords. His hair was smoothed
back, gleaming with hues of burnished metals and sun-
ripened grains. Colors gleamed in his eyes like the waters of a
sun-splashed sea, now green, now gray, now blue, now gold.
His black velvet doublet showed the breadth of his shoulders.
Tight kid gloves gleamed on his hands as he gestured, luring
her eyes to their long-fingered grace. Their masculine power
she knew well. It was emblazoned in her flesh.

Claire forced her gaze away, afraid it lingered too long.
The appearance of the next course was a welcome distraction.
She watched the servants clear away the last of the oyster pie

and replace it with crisp roasted duck in rose sauce, served on a bed of fragrant petals. She applauded with the other guests, but she still had no appetite, despite the magnificence of the food.

Sir James and Lady Penelope offered a second toast. James showed better humor than Claire would have credited. Even Penelope displayed a restless energy, rather than a sullen temper. The high spirits of Rafe and Vivian must be infectious. They were in love and their joy overflowed, adding brightness to the air. Once Adrian was secure, they would be free to set their wedding plans. Flushed and happy, they drank deeply from their goblets and talked animatedly with Adrian over the fine points of rapier work. Curiously, all three had trained with the same famous swordsman. Claire found it amusing, though not as amusing as the free-flowing wine made it for her friends. There was an excess of clove in the blend, Claire thought, taking another small sip from her goblet. Too much clove gave her a headache.

The duck was removed in favor of a fresh sallet of spinach and lettuce leaves scattered with radishes, mint, and marigold. Claire picked at it with her fork, trying to attend to the conversation. For a time they talked of the repercussions of Mary Queen of Scots' trial. But that was grim business, and they soon moved to lighter topics. Rafe sought Adrian's advice how best to develop an orchard. Viv asked Claire's opinion of master woodworkers, if there was a family who did furniture as well as fine instruments? A new dish went round, a fine shield of brawn, the forepart of a boar, served with a sauce of mustard and capers. Claire ate a bite, no more.

Again, Penelope urged the servants to refresh the wine. Claire allowed a splash to top her cup, sipping as she stole another glance at Adrian. When he turned, the tilt of cheekbone and brow accentuated the slanted edge of his ear. She had a sudden urge to nip the peak, to trace the rim with the tip of her tongue, then suck the smooth tenderness of the lobe. Would he shiver as she did at the very thought? The pleasurable chill trickled down her back, then flared to heat as her mind conjured images of caresses far less innocent. She wanted to feel the long sinews of his thighs, the muscular curves of his buttocks. She had felt attracted to men in the past, but never with such wrenching immediacy. Her own desire was a revelation —a feverish joy, and a continuing misery.

Claire caught no yearning glances cast at her. No one could fault Adrian's courtesy, but his demeanor was smooth and impenetrable. When he turned to her, his face became a mask, his eyes bits of colored glass, reflecting without seeing. She wanted him to look at her as if she truly existed—as if no one else existed. She wanted his gaze to acknowledge those moments of beauty they had shared. Thinking on it, her heart quickened, almost a separate entity, painfully alive within her breast. Each time his gaze eluded hers, its sharp beat resounded throughout her body, slowly growing to an unbearable ache.

Claire made herself look away, to try and quell the pain. She welcomed the reappearance of the next course, a rich array of sweets to finish the feast, and made a show of vacillation between the delights. Finally she took a pear tart and forced down a a bite. Laughing, Viv fed Rafe a bit of gingerbread. Looking at the elegant curves of Adrian's mouth, Claire wished she could play such a game. She wanted to feel the touch of his lips against her fingers, the moist pressure of his tongue, the edge of his teeth.

For once Adrian's eyes met hers. Her heart leapt with hope, a bright hot pang that burned through breasts and belly. Her nipples hardened, stiff and sore in the confines of her gown. Desire glowed like a coal between her thighs. Her tenderest flesh felt scalded and yet suddenly moist. Her response shocked, excited, frightened Claire all at once. If the exchange of glances could ignite such desire, what would his touch be like on her breasts, or there, at her burning center? Need threatened to consume her where she sat, a devouring blaze, but she did not look away from him.

Adrian's eyes flashed with an answering fire, but his lashes quickly lowered, closing off his response. Closing her off from him. Dousing the flame with a sudden wash of coldness. Blindly, Claire crumbled the rest of the tart with her fork, pretending to eat. When the steward came, she let him refill the cup, but drank no more from it. The chill wake of rejection left her feeling ugly, clumsy, marred. Her arm throbbed and its scars seemed to crawl all the way to her heart and down to her belly, brambles cutting with dagger-sharp thorns.

Pain twisted her inside out, turned Adrian into the enemy. He was an elf king who bewitched her, then left her bereft, retreating to his crystal fortress that no mortal sword could shatter. What was she to do? It was as a musician she had trained herself, not as a seductress with the guile to penetrate the walls Adrian now built about himself, or the power to shatter them. She could not endure to make a fool of herself, pounding futilely at that glassy hardness.

She was lost in a labyrinth. Her attraction to Rafe had been painful at times, yet they had always confided in each other like friends. She had wisely held her tongue about her infatuation. Though betrothed to Sir Reginald, she'd had flirtations at court, enjoying the banter of wit she most enjoyed. With the heart not in play, such games had no risk. She had never entered into the delicate and dangerous intricacies of seduction. She glanced at Lady Penelope, laughing as she poured wine for her husband with her own hands, brushing coquettishly against him. For a moment, Claire envied Penelope the arts that had broken through Sir James' guilty hesitations and won her the husband she wanted. But Penelope manipulated with deft ease because she did not love, and Claire did not envy her that. Nor would she envy Sir James when he discovered it.

Claire had often been told she was beautiful. She did not gainsay either beauty's power or its limits. Her life was easier in some ways because she pleased the eye, but once she had despaired because she knew Rafe had a penchant for soft blond beauty such as Penelope possessed. Yet Rafe had married a dark sprite who stirred him body and soul.

She wanted that total consummation. She wanted it with Adrian. She could no longer imagine it with anyone else. His withdrawal hurt her. His glassy smooth mask angered her. But he did care. He must. The connection between them was too strong to deny. Fate had returned them to each other, and Claire could not but believe their lives were entwined. His arguments of the morning troubled her, but not as much as the thought of life without him.

She dared a glance at him. He looked suddenly weary, suddenly alone. Not the elf king aloof in his crystal palace—but the unicorn obscured in a shadowed wood. But how was she to reach him? Could she seduce him? She could imagine herself the maiden luring the unicorn, and wondered if he would emerge from his secret forest to lay his head in her lap. Yet in that myth, the maiden was false, her love a trap, a betrayal. Adrian needed trust, not duplicity, even if it pretended to serve his true needs. Lust prompted such a scheme, and hurt, and anger. Not love. The maiden did not have to lure the unicorn. The maiden could join the unicorn in the wood.

Doubt came like a chill wind, filling her mind with ominous whispers like the rustling of leaves. Adrian understood far better than she did the darkness he fled. But there was no escape for her. The dangers to him were threats to her happiness. His shutting her out could not spare her that. And if he knew the dark, its teeming density was clotted with fear. Blinding fear. Claire could bring the light to that world, show him a new way. . . .

Calmness came with the resolution to seek him out again. Always, she had valued friends to whom she could speak with honesty and directness. She wanted the same trust in a lover, in a husband. She must speak her mind, her heart, and hope he would do the same. Though in truth, she still did not know what she would do, what she would say.

But that was tomorrow. Tonight drowsiness stole through her, urging her to sleep.

Claire woke near dawn, a dull headache pressing about her skull like too tight a cap. She lay abed, rubbing her temples and listening to her maid's fluttery snores. She smiled a little, for usually the girl was up at the first beam of light, scuttling about like a mouse. Finding it impossible to sleep, Claire rose from bed and went to the window overlooking the garden. The world was filled with a thick fog like pale gray smoke, the wakening light muffled.

She looked over toward the rose arbor, catching a glimpse of the trellis where Adrian had kissed her with such passion, only yesterday. The first thought of him kindled desire. Her skin flushed inside and out, as if licked by fire. Her heart quickened, and a pulse echoed between her thighs, tender and aching. If he touched her there, she would melt, she would swoon. Even the thought of it made her dizzy. She leaned against the sill.

Fog swirled and parted below, showing glimpses of the garden. If she went down, would Adrian join her there again? Would he be unable to resist, as she could barely resist going? Claire sighed with exasperation. He had been resisting her far too well. The very romance of the idea tempted her, but it was just such a contrivance as she had determined to avoid. And if he resisted the lure, she would be utterly shamed.

The garden looked curious in the hazy light. Thick swaths of fog wound about the clipped geometry of the topiary, their dark shapes more like ebony chess pieces than living foliage. Then she saw a movement, a cloaked figure slinking through the obscuring mists. A man, she could tell that much. Not Adrian, someone bulkier. The man glanced back, his face shadowed beneath the hood, then turned and vanished into the fog. A guard? He'd worn dark clothes beneath the cloak, not the bright Thorne livery. Claire frowned uneasily. There was something sinister in his movement, she thought. She would wake Adrian.

Claire hesitated. What if her fears were induced by the mist? How foolish she would feel if the man were only a guard after all. Worse still—perhaps this was only an excuse to seek out Adrian, sleepy and vulnerable. She could go question the guard instead, or wake Rafe and Viv. But it was

Adrian whose life was filled with secrets, Adrian she was concerned for. Even if nothing was wrong, feeling foolish or embarrassed was better than wavering here by the window.

Silently, Claire opened the door and entered the empty hallway.

Chapter 9

Blood drenched him, trickling along his skin, tracing winding, branching paths like rivers. It had voices that sang to him, shrill, shivering screaming music. Roses bloomed, roses of dew, sparkling dark on a lady's fair skin. Petals fell, spattering blood red at his feet. Drops became a stream, a tide, a swollen sea. Crimson swallowed him, saturated him, permeated him to the soul. Monsters arose from it, birds with dripping pinions, a white unicorn that bounded free in terror, a great, moiling dragon that gathered, stretching its claws, expanding scales that flashed scarlet and gold and opened its huge jaws, showing teeth of adamant.

Adrian fled in terror, but he could not run. He was bound. Reek filled his nostrils, dark metallic sea of death. He screamed, but the sound was stopped, choked by a gag. Pain beyond imagination's reach cut into him, stripping him, peeling away sanity. Silent wails shrilled through him, rising higher and higher with each gleaming stroke of the blade. De-

light twined with the agony, worming through the coils of his brain with obscene laughter.

And all the while someone touched him, stroking his hair. . . .

Adrian moaned. Groggy, he started to lift his head, then sank back onto the pillow. He felt defiled—his mind clotted with sickly sleep and nauseating emotions. Disoriented, he wondered if even now he was trapped within some perverse nightmare. Flickering candlelight danced hectically across his eyelids. Muffled screams choked his mind. He hovered, afraid of both dreams and waking, but the enemy must be faced. He pushed toward awareness. His face was damp with sweat. Something clung to him. He realized he was still half-dressed, his clothes clammy, sticking to his skin.

This must be a dream. The air still reeked of blood.

Adrian opened his eyes. Penelope was lying beside him on the bed, staring at him. Staring at nothing. He sat up with a choked cry. Her eyes were wide and fixed, their bright blue dulled. Death set her face in a rictus of pain, bruised mouth stretched wide in a helpless scream. Her blond hair spread out smoothly on the pillow. Her skin was marble pale—to the base of her throat. Below that she was naked, clothed only in blood. The crimson garment did not cover skin, but muscle and nerve. She was flayed. Only her hands and feet were still whole, like delicate white gloves, little white boots.

He was drenched with blood, not sweat. Her skin draped his body, clinging in a grotesque embrace.

A bloody knife lay beside his hand—the dagger Rafe had given him.

Adrian cried out again, flinging the grisly rag of flesh from him, knocking away the knife. He leapt from the bed, stumbling, falling, then dragging himself up by the bedpost. In the corner he saw his young manservant lying with his throat slit. Shudders convulsed Adrian until the open bed curtains swayed. He fought against the waves of nausea, the urge to vomit out the horror. A thick fog of terror dazed him so that he could hardly move or think. The walls pulsated, shrinking closer around him like a devouring maw.

He struggled to the window, opened it, and gasped in the wet, foggy air. Forcing himself to turn back, he saw the carnage illuminated the muted dawn light. He stared at the corpse laid out like a demon's bride. His nerves vibrated with echoes of silent screams. Adrian crouched, closing his eyes. He covered his ears with his hands, pressing them tight against his skull. Crush it and the images, the shrieks that quivered in his brain would end. The ghastly thing on the bed would vanish forever.

Penelope . . . A swell of pity overwhelmed his revulsion. Penelope was only a selfish child. She did not deserve this hideous fate. Adrian forced himself to open his eyes again, to look at the white mask of her face. Dark bruises marked the corners of her colorless mouth. She had been gagged so the household would not hear her cries, but he had sensed her agony. Her clothes lay scattered, a slipper overturned on the carpet, a blood-streaked shift of knotted silk tossed by the bed. In the corner, the poor servant looked startled at his fate. Dark blood smeared his boyish face and spread like a bizarre beard over his chest.

Shudders rolled through Adrian. His skull felt brittle, as if it might crack and all the madness come oozing in to drown his throbbing brain. Or was the roiling madness within, wanting to break free? How could he have done this? He remembered nothing of it—as he remembered nothing of the night his father died.

No! He remembered everything before sleep—eating supper, drinking wine, feeling exhausted, waving away the lad. Sinking onto the bed. Sinking into dark coils of dreams that wrapped him in the smell of blood, the panic of choking, and endless pain. And slithering through it like a serpent was an obscene delight glorying in the agony it created. Could Quarrell's spirit have invaded him? Was the physician an incubus that fed on blood and fear, and had consumed him whole?

Adrian fought against the rising terror. Why would such vicious madness overtake him now? He was close to safety. There was no reason to attack Penelope. Could she have touched him while he slept, filled with ill wishes? Plots to send him back to Bedlam, and to Quarrell? Thoughts of murder?

He stared at the bloody residue of Penelope's skin and his own flesh seemed to writhe against the bone. Even if she wanted to kill him, Adrian would not have done this butchery. At his worst he had only reflected back what others had cast on him. This sickening deed mirrored no intention of Penelope's childish cruelty. Perhaps in some mad extremity of fear he might have killed her, but he would never wreak such slow, deliberate torture. He would not even know how to commit this atrocity.

Quarrell's presence pervaded everything, like a stench of sulfur.

Other dreams returned to haunt Adrian. He had seen such horrors before in visions, and had prayed it was no more than sick fantasy, a twisted dream. But here was the reality. The doctor entertained himself in this fashion. Quarrell took the pain of others like some intoxicating drug, inhaling the aroma of blood like a rank perfume.

Murdering Penelope and casting the blame on Adrian was exactly the sort of scheme that would delight him. Quarrell wanted to reclaim control of him, one way or another. Panic swept through Adrian, and he fought the urge to bolt. He must focus his mind. Who would believe him now, except for Vivian? No one else had experience of Quarrell's cruelty. Once they saw Penelope's mutilated body, his friends would doubt him. Their trust had been based on Vivian's judgment, not their own. Would Rafe believe him now? Would Claire?

Adrian's heart twisted. Claire had seen the cruelty of Bedlam, but she had also seen him a crazed lunatic, beyond control. He could not bear for her to think him so demented, so evil. But this madness was not his. It was part of the horror of Bedlam, part of Quarrell's touch.

Then a new fear stabbed him. Were they alive? Had Quarrell killed others in the house as well, killed his friends? Killed Claire?

He must find her. She must be alive!

Adrian turned toward the door. It was open, and the curtains drawn back from the bed, framing Penelope lying exposed on the blood-soaked sheets. He realized Quarrell had displayed his gruesome crime for whoever first walked along the corridor. Panic streaked through him, doubling his fear. He must not be trapped here.

Heart racing, legs heavy as lead, Adrian stumbled toward the door.

Claire moved quietly down the hall, wondering again why she could hear no servants moving about. She was surprised to see the door to Adrian's room open. He must have risen early as well. As she came closer, Adrian appeared in the doorway. He supported himself against the frame, swaying slightly. Blood matted his hair and smeared his face. Clots of darkening crimson covered his shirt and hose. He stared at her, his eyes like glass, voids within.

"Adrian!" Fear jangled through her, and she ran toward him.

He lifted his hands, warding her off.

She stopped, fearing she might hurt him if she touched him. "Where are you wounded? Who has done this to you?"

He only shook his head.

"Let me help you!" She stepped closer, then saw the room behind him. A human shape lay on the bed, covered in blood. Flayed. Though the face was turned away, the thick ash blond hair was Penelope's.

And Adrian was covered with gore—

Images from Bedlam flashed in her mind. The crazed way he'd grabbed the knife and attacked the physician who'd covered him with the cloak.

"Claire . . ." His voice was a hoarse whisper. She shrank back against the wall. Her breath caught in her throat, and her heart beat a wild racket, like a sparrow struggling to escape the hawk's talons. If Adrian came after her, she could run into her room and draw the bolt. She could flee down the stairs. She could scream for help and someone would come. Why was no one else awake?

Adrian sank to his knees before her. The motion made her slide further away along the wall, but then she stopped. Even at this distance, she could see the shudders wrenching him. Because of them, she did not run, did not scream. Through the fear, part of her still yearned to reach out and protect him. Truly, love was a kind of madness—

He could barely speak. "Claire . . . I did not . . . do this."

She found her voice. "You're covered in blood. Penelope's blood."

"Yes—no." He looked toward the room, then turned back, his hand raised as if he would ward it off. "Quarrell killed her."

"Quarrell?"

He looked despairing. "Bedlam's master."

She remembered. "The doctor. You tried to stab him."

Adrian moaned, fingers clutching his head. She took another sideways step toward her room, but he lifted his head again. "He killed Penelope. I swear to you."

"You saw him?" Against the evidence of her eyes, she wanted to believe he was innocent.

"I can sense him . . . as you could smell smoke from a fire." He held out his hands, pleading for her to understand. "In Bedlam, he would come to my cell. He would bring . . . nightmares . . . with him." He gestured toward the body on the bed. "Nightmares like that."

"You dreamed of doing such things?" Fear prickled her skin, cold and sharp as needles.

He shook his head. "Never unless he was there. I would wake and find him gloating."

Memory flooded Claire. When Reginald took her to Bedlam, it was Quarrell who ordered the whipping of an inmate. The doctor had smiled—a smug little smile, as if he knew something secret and watched as Reginald tried to kiss her. Angry, disgusted—and frightened—she ran from the room and out to the courtyard. Then the guards had dragged Adrian through the gate. She had touched him, and her touch had restored his sanity. Then Quarrell appeared, unfurling his cape and draping it over Adrian.

That was when Adrian attacked him.

Perhaps a scent of blood lingered. . . . Rafe had said, when she had described the incident to him. Perhaps to Adrian, more lingered than just a scent. Perhaps Quarrell had covered him in horror too great to be borne. Horror such as waited within that chamber. Claire held the thought tightly. "You know he killed Penelope as you knew who killed my brother."

Hope ignited in Adrian's eyes. Her heart gave a pang. Oh, she wanted to believe him, though her mind argued furiously and fear gibbered at her, wanting her to hide away. There was no knife in his hands, but he might lunge upon her, throttle her. . . .

But he did not. He waited. He trusted her.

Fear spawned monsters, and wishes idle fancies. Only the quiet of an open heart might perceive the truth. Claire saw his hands streaked with blood, but there was less there than covered him elsewhere. Surely if he had butchered Penelope so dreadfully, they would be coated with gore. But he might have wiped it off. The blood on his linen did not spatter him, but looked almost as if someone had painted him with it. Fear cried flight. Reason debated the evidence. Her heart urged her forward. Trembling, Claire moved toward Adrian.

Kneeling in front of him, she took hold of his hands as she had in Bedlam, as she had yesterday in the garden. His fingers interlocked with hers and she felt their lives weaving in the gesture. Adrian was quaking still. She wished she could know exactly what he saw, what he felt, even if it was terrible. Yet reverberations lingered like some diabolical music just ended. She let them sweep through her, sensing echoes of their savage and sinister resonance. Did that darkness emanate from him or another? Another quiver of fear rippled through her and Adrian's fingers tightened around hers. Pain stabbed up her injured arm, making her gasp.

Instantly, his grip eased. Where was the violence that could slaughter Penelope? Claire thought of Reginald's mean laughter, of the anger and arrogance that had heedlessly destroyed others, and almost killed her. She thought of Quarrell, with his smug, secret smile that iced her heart. There was nothing of that in Adrian. There was fear, there was anger, but not consuming hatred. Not vicious cruelty. Not madness. He could not have killed Penelope.

Tranquillity enveloped her, a center of peace in the tumult surrounding them. Fear was gone. She had touched Adrian's heart, his core. Darkness swarmed all around them, but the center was golden. Pure as the note of a bell ringing in her heart. Gently, Claire loosened her hands, and Adrian released them. He was no longer trembling.

"You give me strength," he whispered.

"We find it together." Brightness filled her, their faith in each other bringing light to the terrible darkness. Then she remembered. Quickly, she rose to her feet, drawing him with her. "Adrian, I saw someone— a man leaving the garden."

"Could you see his face?" Adrian asked urgently. "Was it Edward Quarrell?"

"I don't know—the fog obscured everything," she had to tell him. "But I came to wake you because he seemed so furtive."

"The guards should have stopped a stranger. Perhaps he killed them." He glanced toward the open door. "He murdered the poor boy sent to serve me."

"We must have been drugged at supper," Claire said. "My own sleep came suddenly, and heavily."

"Drugged?" Adrian frowned. She could tell he was having difficulty concentrating. He raked a hand through his hair. "That means a conspirator within."

"Your cousin? He would not have known what Quarrell would do to Penelope." Claire tensed as she glanced down the hall toward James' room. "Perhaps he is also dead."

Adrian swallowed. "Yes, it is possible, but Penelope might have gone to Quarrell alone."

"Unknowingly inviting her own death?" Claire shuddered.

"Perhaps he planned all along to murder her and present the deed as mine. Or perhaps he thought finding the body would be enough to drive me mad again." Looking as if he might be sick, Adrian gestured at his gory clothes. "The proof seems all on his side."

Queasy in turn, she struggled not to show it. "Then we must find our own. Can you take some object he's held and find a clue to expose him?"

"He left the knife beside me. I knocked it aside."

"Perhaps, if you touched it now?"

He shook his head. "I dare not risk losing control now."

"Then I will get the knife, and keep it hidden." She rose, though even the thought of crossing the threshold made her stomach threaten to heave.

"No. Do not go in there." Adrian stood and blocked her way. "I will go back and get it. I will put on my gloves." Drawing a harsh breath, he looked toward the door. "I must cover the bodies, too. They are terrible where they lie."

Visibly bracing himself, Adrian went back into the bedroom. That he could face what lay within showed Claire how strong he truly was. She hovered near the door of her own room, trying to keep a view of the stairs. She still heard no servants awake. Remembering how generous Penelope had been with the wine, her suspicion sharpened.

After a short while, Adrian came out of the room. He closed the door, then walked to stand beside her. He had washed his face and hair, and put on the black doublet from the night of the masque, with a cape about him. There might be visible streaks of blood on his linen, but at this early hour, they could easily be mistaken for a dueling wound, or dirt from a scuffle. Once again, he wore his gloves. He held something concealed beneath the cape.

"I've written a note saying I did not do this thing, and accusing Quarrell. But I do not think James will believe it." A sound downstairs made them both whirl. At last, the servants were stirring. "I must go. I will try to get a message to Vivian, to let you know if I am safe."

"No. Go to my father's laboratory," she said. "You will need help to prove Quarrell is the murderer."

"James will arrest me, or shut me away," he protested. "I don't want you involved."

"No one will know," she said. "Adrian, I want to help you. I am in your debt."

She saw him hesitate, but he desperately needed a refuge. When he nodded, she told him the directions to the laboratory near their townhouse in Westminster. "The key is hidden to the left of the door, in a niche below the small gargoyle."

"If your father appears, what shall I say?" Adrian asked.

"Tell him part of the truth—that I have given you sanctuary, and will be there soon. If he hesitates, tell him that you helped find Gabriel's killers." Adrian frowned and shook his head. Claire could see that he did not want to take advantage of that. "If you tell him of the murder, he will fear for my safety. But you can trust him with the truth of your talent. He has long studied alchemy and strange magicks. He will not think it madness."

He smiled ruefully at that. "A small blessing."

"You must hurry," she urged.

Gently he took her hands, but no emanation of emotion came through the protective leather gloves. His eyes gazed intently into hers. "Thank you for believing me."

She wanted to kiss him, even in the midst of the horror.

Abruptly, he released her hands. Turning, he ran down the stairs and out the door.

Now that he was gone, new fear seized Claire. The ghastly corpse in the bedroom preyed on her mind. It was easy to believe a spirit so tormented would cry out for vengeance. She went back into her room and locked the door. Cold chills trickled down her back, as if invisible fingernails raked an icy path.

Asleep, her maid snored softly, with a whuffing sound like a pony curling its lip around a thistle. Claire pressed a hand to her mouth, holding back hysterical laughter. She started when she saw blood on her fingers, and quickly looked at her robe. None there. She could not help Adrian if she was implicated in his escape. She dipped the corner of her black veil into the water pitcher and carefully cleaned the few smears, fighting the churning of her stomach. She had seen wounds and injuries, and it was not like her to be squeamish. But the depraved cruelty of Penelope's death was beyond her experience.

When her hands were clean, Claire crossed to the window and looked out. If only she had seen the intruder more clearly—if only she could identify Quarrell on her word of honor. That would hold more weight against suspicion than the vague figure she had glimpsed. Would James pay it any heed? Claire returned to the bed and lay down, shivering. She counted seconds in breaths, making sure Adrian had time enough to lose himself in the mists.

It was perhaps only ten minutes when she heard footsteps in the hallway. Another minute more and the screaming began.

"No. . . . No. . . ."

Claire watched as Sir James wept, his body rocking with denial. Slowly, he raised his head from his hands. His ravaged gaze traveled from Claire to the others blankly, as if seeing nothing clearly but the hideous vision in the bedchamber. His suffering caught at her heart. They stood about his chair in the hall where last night they had reveled, Penelope's waiting woman moaning into her handkerchief, the servants horrified and mute. Rafe and Vivian stood close together, watchful.

"God in heaven," Sir James entreated hoarsely, "how could you allow such a thing to happen to her?" His bloodshot eyes roamed their faces, pleading for an answer. He paused at Claire. "It is a judgment. I knew Adrian was mad. I saw it with my own eyes, and yet I let him in the house, gave him free-dom to work his lunatic designs."

"Remember Sir Adrian's sane behavior," Claire said, judg-ing her tone carefully. Thorne teetered on a brink. "He was no madman when he wrote the note you found."

"Then why did he flee?" Sir James's voice cut through the open space of the hall. Claire saw Rafe start as if under a lash. The words hung there.

"Fear that in your grief you would think as you do now." Claire kept her voice neutral.

"What else am I to think? That Master Quarrell, who never spoke with Penelope, never met her, crept into a locked and guarded house and did—this thing? I would be mad, myself, to believe such lunacy."

"Not guarded," Rafe spoke thoughtfully. "Our sleep was not natural. Mine came over me too suddenly, and this morn-ing the household stirred late. None of the servants woke even once during the night." He glanced at Samuel for confirma-tion, and the man nodded.

"I believe we were all drugged," Claire said.

"By this treacherous doctor, from outside the house?" Sir James attempted a scornful laugh, but it was a cry of pain. "If we were drugged, it was by Adrian Thorne."

Vivian's shoulders twitched. Though she was reining her-self in, her impatience fairly crackled around her. "Are you certain Master Quarrell had no motive?"

"For killing Penelope, a stranger to him? Quarrell is a re-spectable physician, and bears me no grudge. If only I had lis-tened when he warned me of Adrian's violence!"

Claire exchanged a glance with Vivian and Rafe. Dis-traught as he was, Sir James did not even realize his indiscre-tion. He had confessed his knowledge of Adrian's confinement in Bedlam. Perhaps he believed so absolutely that his cousin was a demented murderer that he no longer saw any wrong in admitting the conspiracy with Master Quarrell.

"Adrian wanted vengeance. I robbed him of Penelope. He

knew she meant more to me than all the world." Sir James lowered his head into his hands. Sobs racked him.

Vivian stalked forward. Her dark eyes glowed with pity, but her hand clenched on her skirt, as if closing on the haft of an invisible knife. "Sir James, I have seen a far different side of Edward Quarrell than what he showed to you."

Sir James battled for control, and raised his head. "What do you mean, Mistress Swift?"

"Quarrell is not master of Bedlam out of his altruism, or even for profit alone. He indulges a secret vice of his own there, a thirst for cruelty."

"Some inmates suffer at the guards' hands—poor wretches without influence."

"I do not speak of such ordinary brutes. Edward Quarrell singles out certain of his patients, and these he torments to satisfy his own lust—"

"No doubt you have many sources of intelligence, but the tales of inmates?" Sir James broke in. "Those cannot be reliable."

Claire suspected Sir James's own culpability for wronging Adrian made him eager to lash out. Sir James had wanted Penelope enough to cheat his cousin, and so was sure Adrian had felt the loss enough to destroy her. If Adrian was guilty, vengeance might be had. Nothing less was tolerable to the man in his frenzy of grief. He gestured he would hear no more.

Vivian stood her ground. "It is not another's tale, Sir James. Before we uncovered the conspiracy against the Queen, the traitors imprisoned me for a short time in Bedlam. I experienced the doctor's taste for suffering for myself. He gloated over my fear, my pain, and suggested ways to embellish it. I swear to you, Master Quarrell is the madman."

Comprehension widened Sir James's eyes. "It was in Bedlam you met Adrian."

Vivian pressed on. "Lord Roadnight was one of those Quarrell tormented. We escaped him. It is the doctor who has wreaked vengeance."

"Who else but Adrian would have drugged us?" James asked. Then, seeing the glance Claire exchanged with Rafe and Viv, he cried out. "Penelope? No! Impossible!"

"Not impossible." Quietly, Claire willed him to look at the truth.

For a second James stared at her, horrified, but then his eyes went blank. Ignoring her, he rounded on Vivian, the easier target. "Now I see how it stands! You helped my lunatic cousin escape. How much money did he offer you?"

Rafe shifted angrily, but Vivian darted him a glance. To James she said, "None."

"Mistress Swift is not the only one who saw Quarrell with his inmates," Claire spoke firmly, adding her weight to Adrian's cause. "I was shown Bedlam as a sightseer. I too saw his enjoyment of cruelty."

Sir James shook his head. "No. Your heart is too tender. You saw no more than the force necessary to control violent lunatics."

Despite her pity, exasperation flared. Claire managed to keep her voice even, "Sir James, do not forget the man I saw leaving this house at dawn."

"That was Adrian escaping. For us, Lady Claire, perhaps there is some excuse for falling under my mad cousin's persuasion. We wanted to believe the best of him. But Mistress Swift here saw him in Bedlam, in his mad fits. This greedy Queen of the Clink, what has she done to turn a profit?" He fixed Vivian with the voids of his eyes. "My cousin is not the first of his line to be violently demented. His mother—"

"I know. Her mind broke when her child died," Viv said tersely.

"She tried to murder her own husband. She put out his eye! My uncle had to keep her under lock and key. And what of her grandfather?" James declared.

"Her grandfather?" Viv turned toward Rafe, who was obviously as much in ignorance as she. When Rafe looked at Claire, she glanced away.

"Yes, Mistress Pickpocket. He died raving, and who knows

how many before him." James sneered at Vivian. "Know that your greed has turned loose a murderous lunatic. Penelope's death is on your head too."

"Adrian Thorne is—"

"No more!" Sir James cried, rising so violently his chair fell backward with a crash. He clutched at the shreds of his control. "No hue and cry has been raised yet, nor the bailiff been summoned. I will keep this shame secret if I can, but not if it means that monster escapes. I will send for the Crown's men to investigate—but I can bear no more of you. Begone from this house by noon."

Claire watched the last of his household go after him, breath knotted in her throat.

"We'll be more use to Adrian elsewhere," Viv muttered to Rafe and Claire, her voice still husky with the anger she had not vented. She nodded toward the door. "Come."

"Wait." Rafe looked troubled. "Let us speak where we can be sure of privacy. Will you come to our chamber, Claire?"

She followed them up the carved oak stairs to the bed-chamber. Once the door was shut, Rafe turned to Claire. "You know more than you have said."

"I spoke with Adrian before he fled. Quarrell had covered him in Penelope's skin, drenched him in her blood." She shuddered. "It was almost too hideous to be borne."

Vivian squeezed her shoulder, a quick, almost rough pressure, but comforting.

"I owe Adrian a great debt. I would like to believe in his innocence," Rafe said. "But we cannot be certain of his sanity."

"But that is my point," Claire returned. "Hideous as it was, especially to Adrian's vulnerable senses, he did master his horror. He was in shock, but he was not mad."

"You know where he is?"

"I am certain he will let me know," she prevaricated. Rafe's doubt stopped her from saying more. She could tell he was not convinced of Adrian's innocence.

"You must tell us, for your own safety," he urged. But

Claire could not trust him with the secret. Rafe saw it and was hurt.

"There is no chance you can identify the man you saw in the garden?" Vivian asked.

Claire shook her head. "I only glimpsed him for a moment. But Adrian told me he sensed Quarrell's presence."

"He was sure of it?" When Claire nodded, Vivian's eyes glittered dark. She told Rafe, "I'll stake all I own that Adrian Thorne is innocent, and that he is right about Quarrell."

Rafe frowned. "I cannot so easily stake your life, or Vivian's. Adrian may not even know what he does when a fit comes on him. You heard what Sir James said about his mother."

Vivian snorted. "Who knows the truth of that?"

"Adrian himself said she died mad," Rafe argued. "I am grateful for the help he gave us with the brooch, but such powers are not natural. A dark, unholy force may work through him."

"What is this?" Vivian retorted, exasperated, "Your Puritan grandfather's cautions? Are you saying Adrian's possessed by demons?"

"Cases of demonic possession are documented." Rafe looked defensive, but did not back down. "Adrian has admitted gaps in his memory. His own horror at evil may be real, but that does not prove that something did not use him as its instrument—and will not do so again."

"If there is a demon, he comes in Edward Quarrell's form." Vivian narrowed her eyes. "I, for one, will not be satisfied until his guilt is proven, and he is dead."

"Vivian—" Rafe's warning tone suggested that this was an argument they'd had more than once. "You swore to me you would not murder him."

"Don't tell me you want him to live? Not after this!"

"He must testify," Claire broke in, fearing Viv's rough justice.

"Do you think he will tell the truth?" Vivian stalked to the door. "The house and garden should be combed for anything Quarrell may have left behind. Sir James would never believe in any sign our men might find, but I'll have Izzy put the idea of a search into the servants' minds." The door shut none too gently after her. Rafe started to follow, but Claire caught his arm.

"Adrian gave you Gabriel's killers—and so helped uncover the plot against the Queen. You owe him the benefit of the doubt."

Rafe sighed and ran a hand through his heavy mane of hair. "I feel the obligation, Claire. But the connection you feel to Adrian is more than that, is it not? I've seen the way you look at him—and he at you."

Claire looked into his concerned eyes. "Yes," she answered simply.

"Do not let your emotion blind you to possible danger. Adrian's powers may not be demonic, but they might be more than he can tolerate and remain sane. Be careful, Claire."

"I will." Then she turned and left.

In her room, Claire helped her distraught maid to gather their few things. When they were ready, Claire rang for a servant, and a whey-faced lad in livery came and carried their baggage downstairs. She planned to speak to Sir James before she left, but his secretary met her in the hallway outside the bedroom. He was as sickly pale as the boy had been, and his voice was unsteady, but he made an effort at decorum. "Sir Raphael and his companions have already departed. The Master bade me speed your ladyship on your way. He himself is too indisposed. He trusts your ladyship will understand."

Claire did understand Sir James' misery. She also understood that nothing they'd said had changed his conviction of Adrian's guilt. Further attempts to reason with him would be pointless. She must bring Adrian the news, making sure no one from this house followed her.

"Tell Sir James that despite our disagreement about the murderer, my heart is with him in his loss," Claire answered.

The man nodded glumly, and escorted her toward the stairs. As they reached the landing, there was a knock at the door and old Samuel moved to answer it. The secretary stopped short, and Claire and her maid did as well, allowing the steward time to dismiss any but the most important visitor. From the landing, Claire could see a tall, cloaked figure on the threshold. "Tell Sir James I wait on his pleasure." The voice was sonorous, oddly familiar.

"Sir James cannot receive visitors."

"Perhaps he will make an exception—for Master Edward Quarrell?"

Claire laid a hand on her maid's arm and silently urged her back out of sight.

Decorum forgotten, the secretary hurried past them. "Physician of Bedlam?"

Master Quarrell's gaze fixed on him as he descended. "Yes, I am he."

"Perhaps he will see you after all. Wait here, please." Forgetting Claire, the secretary disappeared quickly down the hall.

Cautiously, she moved forward enough to study the physician's build, comparing it with her glimpse of the man in the garden. It was no use. The figure had been too dim, and nothing about its shape, or Quarrell's as he stood in the threshold, was remarkable enough to stand out.

The doctor stepped inside, and not as one who had never seen the place before. Giving only a brief look about him, he removed his gloves and unfastened his cloak. His movements, what she could see of his face, conveyed impatience. Or a concealed eagerness.

Sir James himself came into the hallway. In a few terse, strained words he told Quarrell of Adrian's return, and what had been discovered at dawn in his room. Quarrell's show of shock was convincing. "I scarce know what to say." He sighed grimly. "If only you had sent for me as soon as Lord Roadnight emerged from hiding."

"He seemed sane! How was I to know?"

"Lunatics have their lucid moments. Long experience has taught me what astounding cunning some of them possess. I thought that I had warned you of this."

"You are right, of course. If only I had listened to you!" James' voice broke.

"If only . . ." Quarrell extended the moment out, as if pleased to make Sir James dwell on it. "If only Lord Roadnight had been confined safely in my private hospital, Lady Penelope would be alive even now."

Sir James faced him, silent and pale, his conscience bearing the full brunt. Claire's stomach twisted with nausea at Quarrell's manipulation.

"Let us lose no more time. My new asylum is ready to receive its first inmate. It is safest to have Lord Roadnight committed immediately."

Sir James ran a hand through his hair. "He has escaped."

Quarrell's head snapped up, vaporous gray eyes so wide they were transparent. "Escaped?" he choked out.

Claire was convinced that for the first time his shock was real. Whatever his pretext for coming here, he had expected a neatly trussed Adrian delivered to him. The enormity of it all cast a miasma of soul-sickness over Claire.

"I shall call out the asylum guards at once! This lunatic must not be suffered to run loose. There is no telling what he will do! Will you lend me your men, Sir James?"

"They are already searching."

"Send them to me if you will, my lord. I will organize a combined search." Quarrell hastily drew on his gloves. "Sir Adrian will be apprehended and locked away, I promise you."

"I would rather see him dead," James said flatly.

Without answering, Quarrell bowed farewell. As he turned to go, he caught sight of Claire on the landing above and looked up. Until this moment, she had only vaguely remembered his features from the day Adrian was dragged into Bedlam, but now she recalled them vividly. The eyes especially, with their high arched brows. Their arrogance was not outright but shrouded, impenetrable as a roiling gray cloud. His nose was slightly crooked, his chin jutting and deeply cleft. A strong visage, but the skin seemed to slough over the bone. His glance swept over her like a touch, not sexual but as intimate as cool, clammy fingers probing for—what? She saw recognition in his sardonic smile.

"My lady." He sketched her an ambiguous bow, and was gone.

Chapter 10

Fog enveloped the streets, a dank brume muffling sight and sound. Moving along those clouded pathways, Adrian became convinced someone was following him. Subduing panic, he wove through the streets and doubled back on his own path, trying to confuse his pursuer but retain his own sense of direction. After a half hour of such tactics, he slid into an alleyway and waited tensely, obscured by the chill mists. No one passed by.

Under his cloak, Adrian clutched the wrapped knife closer. He wished he could fling it away, yet feared to lose it. The burden weighed far heavier on his mind than in his hand. He waited a few moments, then hurried on. Although he glimpsed other souls moving through the pale gloom, he could not be certain that any one of them was hunting him. Suspicion receded as the gray mists thinned, and he wondered if his pursuer was but a figment his mind had conjured from the sinister haze. Would fog forever evoke the opaque coldness of Quarrell's eyes?

Adrian's sense of dread eased when he glimpsed the sun, a pale golden blur low in the sky. If he was being followed, he would be more visible, but its light and warmth soothed his nerves after oppressive murk of the fog. He continued on, checking behind himself as he walked the whole way to Westminster. Porters and shopkeepers were busy with morning tasks, but a single wherryman might remember him and his destination too clearly. Better to blend with the growing flurry of activity on the streets.

Slowly, the rising sun warmed the air, and by the time Adrian discovered the quieter residential area with its chestnut-lined lane, the fog had dissipated into delicate tendrils of mist. Soft patches of cloud daubed a milky blue sky. How curiously benign the morning had become. Unless he concentrated his will, the abominations of the night crept up from the deep recesses of his mind, almost blinding him with darkness.

He fixed his mind on Claire, on the grace of her presence that cleansed his soul. Relief filled him when he found the stone tower she had described, draped with ivy and sequestered behind a low wall. The ivy-bordered shutters of the lower windows were closed. As she had said, there was no sign of anyone within. To the left of the door he discovered the chink between two stones, below a gleeful gargoyle and almost hidden by the dark green leaves. Reaching with his gloved finger, Adrian found the key her father kept for emergencies. Apparently the mind of Sir William Darren, Earl of Brightsea, soared too high amid arcane lore speculations to plod among ordinary practicalities like remembering his keys.

Adrian opened the door to darkness, then paused, glancing once more at the street, before he stepped inside. No one had followed him here. Within, the tower was silent. Slowly his eyes adjusted. Strips of light from the cracks of the shutters shone on whitewashed walls and a flagstone floor, bright enough to discern a stool, the edge of a table, a thick beeswax candle standing upon it. But there was no fire from which to light it. The aroma of old parchment mingled with scents of harsher chemicals and pungent herbs. A curve of light from a window above outlined a winding staircase. Near its base another door opened to the outside. He disliked tresspassing further, but he needed to find water. Remnants of dried blood on his skin and clothing filled his nostrils with a stench, and his mind with a horror, fainter now, but encroaching when he relaxed his will. Fragments of images he saw were bad enough, but it was the delight—Quarrell's malignant ecstasy—that threatened to drive him mad.

Unlatching the door Adrian found a little walled garden, overgrown but peaceful, fragrant with the scent of herbs. As he had hoped, the alchemist had water at hand for his experiments, a round well sheltered by a small tree. Laying the bundled knife aside, he drew a bucket of clear, cool water, stripped, and washed away the last of the blood. When he could discern no streaks left on his body, he turned to his clothes. He had put the black doublet over the gruesome linen, not wanting to leave his stained garments as another false clue pointing to him. He scrubbed them as best he could, sickened by the ruddy tinge of the run-off water.

Beautiful, greedy Penelope. Her inability to conceive of an evil like Quarrell's had only heightened the gruesome pathos of her death. Hideous images sliced across his mind. He shuddered, thrusting them away. When he dressed, he donned everything but his gloves. The damp garments chilled him further, but at least nothing remained but the discoloration.

And the far darker stains the memory left on his mind and soul.

The knife waited, its pull an insidious undertow tugging him back into the darkness he'd just escaped. If he touched it, he would feel Quarrell's vile lust and his victim's pain. Adrian wanted to bury it, forget it, but the knowledge would haunt him. He wished Claire were here, an embracing shore of sanity within his reach. Yet he did not want her to watch as he exposed himself to the invisible horrors of the blade.

He did not want her within range of the blade in his hand.

With that dreadful thought the worst fear returned. What if

Quarrell's essence had overtaken him completely, acted through him? In the ghastly tangled nights in Bedlam, Adrian had suffered Quarrell's malevolent delight as well as his victim's pain. Some confrontations he remembered. Sometimes he woke after the doctor's evil obliterated all awareness. Yet some kernel of his identity must have fought against the darkness. It must have—

Kneeling, Adrian unrolled the cloth to expose the knife. Bracing himself, he laid his hand over the hilt.

Crimson roses dripped over the iron gate, framing a pale face alight with anticipation—Penelope. So eager.

"Lead on," Quarrell murmured. He followed her through the mist-shrouded garden and into the house. Her silk skirts whispered intimately as she walked up the stairs, down the hall, and into the bedroom. Adrian lay drugged on the bed. Helpless.

Gloating filled Quarrell, thick and sweet. He rested his hand on Adrian's forehead, then turned on Penelope. Swiftly he captured his unsuspecting prey, gagged and bound her in silk, and hung her from the bedposts like a white chrysalis. He witnessed the first metamorphosis— the gleam in her eyes transformed from wicked delight to amazed terror. Taking up the knife, he began the true revelation. She emerged like a butterfly from a pale cocoon, damp and glowing, displaying her true color. Lovely crimson. Lovely, lovely, lovely. . . .

Quarrell drank in the anguish that poured forth from her, body and soul.

Adrian hung, suspended in terror, in agonizing pain, watching his flesh peeled away. Pain harrowed his flesh, his mind. . . . But he could also feel the hard handle of the blade clenched in his hand, the hot flow of blood over his fingers. The silent screaming, the unbearable anguish, the obscene, lascivious delight rose to an excruciating crescendo—

Adrian plunged into blood-spattered blackness.

Slowly, consciousness returned. Adrian opened his eyes and saw the knife. Its sharp blade gleamed like ice in the sunlight. With sight came memory. His stomach roiled and acid sickness welled up his throat. If only he could vomit forth the grisly images and be free of them. But he fought down the sickness. The memories would stay, and he would only be weaker.

How long had he lain here in the garden? A few moments? The light did not seem much changed. Adrian covered the knife, closing it off from his sight. He washed the flecks of blood from his hand, scrubbing as if the touch had drenched it. The aftermath of the visions left him chill and exhausted. Yet, terrible as they were, he had found surety of his innocence and clutched it tightly.

Sapped of energy, Adrian entered the tower, looking for a place to rest. He climbed the winding stairs and discovered a room with a mullioned window, sparsely furnished with a wooden chair and narrow bed. Tapestries of fanciful beasts added color and richness. Feeling curiously protected, he shrugged off the doublet and removed the damp shirt, setting it by the window to dry. He slipped off the precious gloves, his shoes, and then lay down on the bed. A quivering ran through all his limbs, but his mind was clear of drugs. Though weary, Adrian was sure his taut-strung nerves would respond if anyone entered. As his eyes closed, his last sight was a scarlet lion whose mane and eyes were crimson, and facing it a white eagle with outspread wings raised like storm clouds. He prayed they would stand guard over him.

Adrian awoke, alert. There it was again, a scratching sound outside. Walking unsteadily to the edge of the window, he looked below. Bright afternoon sun streamed down, burnishing Claire's chestnut hair as she probed for the key he had replaced in the cranny. Joy and relief surged through him. He shoved his feet back into his shoes, pulled on his shirt, grabbed his gloves, and then hurried down. The door opened, and his heart gave a pang when he saw the sunlight framing her with a bright halo. Without her valiant intervention, without the generosity of her belief and the core of peace he found within her touch, he might now be shut away in an asylum, or in prison.

At the threshold she tensed, peering into the dimness, then entered when she saw him safely arrived. As she moved closer, he could see the misery of the morning engraved on her face. Her lips were tightly pressed, and a blue vein branched on her forehead, signaling her stress. Adrian had known that he would bring her pain. He should feel anger, rage, at Quarrell for all he had wrought. Instead, a thick clotting guilt hampered thought and breath. He halted at the foot of the stairs, quashing the fierce urge to embrace her, to press his lips to the blue rivulet on her forehead and breathe the scent of her sun-warmed hair. His troubles had descended on her, wreaking havoc in her life. Yet the impulse was more a selfish need to snatch comfort than to offer it.

"Your journey was uneventful?" Claire asked tentatively.

He heard her full meaning. Fear of pursuit was only part. Yet she did not fear him, she only feared for him. "I arrived without incident."

"That is good."

"Tell me what occurred after I left." In answer to Claire's searching gaze, he said, "I can bear it. Words are nothing to what has already passed."

She nodded, accepting his judgment. Adrian listened as she told him of James' refusal to see anyone as a suspect save him. He was heartened that Viv defended him. "And Rafe?"

Claire frowned. "He wishes to believe in your innocence, but he is concerned for Vivian's safety, and for mine."

"I imagine I should feel the same." It was as Adrian expected; though he'd hoped for more support from the man he'd come to think of as his friend.

"He is afraid some demon possesses you against your will."

"The demon is Edward Quarrell."

"You are certain now," she said, reading something in his face.

He had proof—though few would believe him save Claire. "I touched the knife. I saw him."

Emotion swarmed in her eyes, pride, consternation, curiosity. "What did you learn?"

Adrian forced himself to look back into that hideous snake pit of writhing images and untangle the least venomous. "Penelope opened the garden gate to Quarrell. I doubt it can be proved."

"Now we have somewhere to hunt. Perhaps there is a scrap of cloth, a footprint to be discovered there."

He nodded. "Perhaps."

"Is that all?" she asked.

"I saw myself through his eyes, asleep on the bed. I cannot imagine inventing such a convolution." He could not bear to venture further. "The rest we know already."

Claire compressed her lips, understanding him all too well.

He went and looked out the window at the herb garden, willing the loathsome memories away. Just how much it had cost him to keep the darkness at bay and his mind clear was not information Adrian wanted to share. Or how close the fear of losing his control still loomed. Although he was convinced he had played no part in Penelope's murder, he also knew the violent emotions of others had driven him to violence.

A cold chill swept through him. . . .

A scarlet ribbon fell from his fingers—red as heart's blood.

A surge of rage swept through Adrian and he lunged forward.

"No!" His father backed away, arms raised to protect himself.

Adrian gasped, his heart lurching. Fortunately Claire was rummaging in a cabinet and did not notice. He turned his back to her, calming his breathing. Would he ever learn the full import of these memories? Would it be better if he did not? He heard a click like a trigger. Startled, he turned round—

Flame bloomed between Claire's palms. Dexterous despite her injured fingers, she lit the candle. Seeing his interest, she showed him a small box in her hand, from which a trickle of smoke and the odor of phosphorus rose. "A contrivance of my father's. Convenient for striking a flame—when it does not flare up and burn the hand that holds it. An unpredictable blessing."

She lit several candles, and by their glow began searching the interior of a chest. She brought forth folded clothes, her father's he supposed. Offering the small pile of linen, doublet and trunkhose, she said, "I can see faint blood stains on your shirt. These will fit you well enough, and they are inconspicuous, neither too rich nor too coarse. If you will wear them?"

Gratefully he took them, his gloved hands touching hers. Though he felt no more than the warmth of her hands through the leather, a wave of simple human longing rose to a swift crest, rushing stronger the higher it mounted. It was all he could do not to snatch off the muffling gloves and share the healing peace of communion with her.

But he had already drawn her far too deeply into the snare that held his own soul.

"Thank you," he said quietly, and turned from her.

He changed upstairs, but there found no sheltering isolation. As soon as the shirt touched his bare skin, emotions assailed him. Not evil this time, nor another's pain—the presence that enveloped him burned as clear and warm as the light Lady Claire had cupped in her hands. The fleeting images were of vibrant life, but having lived the man's death with him, Adrian recognized him. This clothing had belonged to Claire's brother, Gabriel.

Adrian sat on the bed, struggling to find an inner balance. For once the dark emotions were all his own, apprehension and regret knotted about a core of loneliness. The clothing he wore shimmered with an easy delight that he had not known since he was a heedless child in Ireland, before his mother was locked away. Echoes of another man's happiness filled him with a poignant nostalgia. But he could not reclaim the past. It was survival he must think on.

Claire called his name. Adrian answered, knowing he was taking too long. She would suspect just such a thing as had happened. Swiftly, he tugged on the other garments, doing his best to disregard the new jumble of images. Adrian paused at the head of the stairs to steady himself, then slowly descended. Claire had lit several candles, and by their glow was searching through a cupboard. Hearing him, she turned, and he braced himself for pain when she saw the spectre in her dead brother's clothes. But she only smiled, reassured by his return. Adrian discovered an echo of the dead man's brotherly tenderness, a deep and abiding affection for Claire mingled with his own feelings. That closeness wrapped about him, intimate as touch, sweetly precious. The contact told him no childhood secrets, but deepened the sense of trust, the hunger for contact.

Impulsively, he moved forward, gathering her into an embrace. With a murmur of surprise and pleasure, Claire wrapped her arms about him. He held her close, at first taking comfort as Gabriel might have, in a safe haven. But where her brother had felt only innocent affection, Adrian's blood quickly stirred. His nerves lanced with bright darts of desire as she molded to him, pliant as a vine. He pressed her closer still, feeling all the supple curves of her body, the enfolding warmth of her arms, the soft crush of her breasts and belly against his torso. Her lips met his eagerly, opening to yield the honeyed warmth of her mouth. Her tongue stroked his, a subtle dance, its touch softly clinging, velvety moist. Shy and yet wise in its melting caresses. Her hips pressed to his, the vee of her thighs framing his loins. Her heat radiated through him and he stiffened with arousal. His tongue probed the cove of her mouth with more insistent thrusts, a rhythm of longing. He wanted to plunge into her more deeply, to penetrate the wet fire within her with his flaming sex.

I must not. Cursing silently, Adrian drew back. Need ached in him.

"Adrian?" Claire looked up, desire and puzzlement writ on her face. Her fine brows drew together, and the blue vein curved up her forehead.

Though his awareness of Gabriel had faded entirely in the rush of his own emotions, Adrian used the other man's feelings to force distance between them. Ruefully, he rubbed his collar. "I feel dizzy. My own emotions mingle oddly with your brother's."

Tears sprang to her eyes, but she smiled at him. "I loved Gabriel. I miss him."

Gently, he said, "I cannot bring him back, but you should know that his last thoughts were of those he loved—of your father, and of you."

Her tears spilled over, but Adrian dared not reach for her again. "I am sorry."

She wiped her eyes, "No. Such pain I will gladly bear. It promises comfort."

"Gabriel had a gift for finding joy." Without forethought this time, his hand moved to a sleeve, rubbing the fabric. The touch brought a glimpse of Rafe Fletcher, sword in hand, laughing at the enemies he faced shoulder to shoulder with Gabriel. Adrian keenly regretted he had never had such a brave and honorable companion.

"Yes." She nodded. "But if you can perceive that, why do you look so sad?"

"I feel I have lost a friend I never had."

"Gabriel would have been your friend, I am sure of it."

"No. I would have turned him away," he said, surprised at his own bluntness. "For years, I shut my gift away, and any such affinity threatened to unlock the door."

She nodded, understanding. "And now?"

Salvation. "Now I threaten you all instead."

"You would protect me from Master Quarrell?" she asked.

"With my life," he said instantly. And then, with reluctant truth, "But I do not know that I have the power to defeat him." Death was preferable to madness, but only his own death.

Claire's life was priceless. The thought of that failure was like an abyss opening. He dared not look into its depths.

"Then you must let your friends protect you," Claire replied seriously. "It is our right."

So gentle and so valiant. Adrian's arms ached with the lack of her—a yearning less palpable than sex, less identifiable, just as undeniable. Love. But this time he controlled the impulse to draw her to him. For her sake, love and desire must be denied. To avoid answering her claim, he asked, "How did your brother's clothes come to be here?"

She looked as if she meant to say more, but then inclined her head, accepting his change of topic. "Gabriel kept extra garments several places for convenience in his intelligence gathering. Father knew, but did not approve."

"It proved a deadly occupation."

"Yes," Claire said. "But it was not the danger. My father thought Court intrigue, and politics in general, unworthy of my brother."

Adrian glanced around the room, at the old, moldering tomes filling the shelves, the odd bits of metal piping and vessels piled on a central table. "Rather than a worthy ambition like trying to change lead into gold?"

"For the best, there is more to it than greed. My father would tell you material gold is but a symbol for the secret wealth of mind and spirit." Claire answered with a small smile, but it vanished as she continued, "He labors ceaselessly without attaining his dreams. As his disappointments grow and the years remaining to him grow fewer, he spends more and more of his fortune on chemicals and essences, rare volumes and elaborate equipment."

Adrian comprehended her frustration, but in fairness he remarked, "This is not so much."

"This chamber is not his laboratory, merely his study. And every estate where we spend any time is equipped with everything he needs. But he has a particular fondness for this tower."

Adrian could well imagine it. The old stone walls were imbued with tranquillity.

"Adrian . . ." Her voice was hesitant, her expression determined. "There is something else you must know."

"What is it?" The chill returned.

"Before I left Thorne Hall, Master Quarrell came to the door. He pretended shock at the news of Penelope's death, but he was truly surprised when he learned you were not trussed and waiting for him to carry you off."

"Did he recognize you from Bedlam?" Panic squeezed his heart.

"Yes, I think so," she answered.

"You must guard yourself—and I must seek another hiding place." Already, he had entangled Claire in his anguish. Now he was repaying her generosity by putting her at risk. Adrian prayed Quarrell had not learned the part Claire played in his escape. Penelope's murder proved the fiend would stop at nothing. No one was safe, for the doctor was obsessed enough to seek ways to fix the blame elsewhere, and clever enough to find them. Even as he brooded, something in Claire's demeanor triggered alarm. "What else?

She hesitated and said. "It seems he has plans for his own private asylum—where he will have even more control than he did at Bedlam."

The grate of the key startled them. They tensed, looking at one another. A rapping came, and a voice called, "Claire?"

"It is well," she whispered, relaxing. "It is only Father."

Lady Claire slid back the bolt, admitting a tall man of about sixty. Sir William Darren, the Earl of Brightsea, was slender and broad-shouldered, with unruly hair turned silver gray. Adrian knew his visage already, the curved nose that gave him a hawklike expression, the clear blue eyes. New traces of grief etched into his face, making him haggard.

"Back so soon?" Claire's father asked, kissing her forehead. "This morning your message reached me that you were staying—" seeing Adrian, he stopped short, head up, eyes sparking dangerously in the candlelight. "What is the meaning of this? A stranger here—in my laboratory? What are you thinking of, Claire?"

Lord Brightsea's daughter took his anger seriously, Adrian saw with misgiving. She had counted on his not discovering them here. He must trust his daughter's sense of honor, for he made no comment on their lack of chaperone, but his gaze searched every cranny of the room. The violation of his laboratory outraged him. Claire faced his wrath steadfastly. "This man helped discover Gabriel's killers. Now he needs our help."

"Did he indeed?" Her father's rigid posture relaxed, but he regarded Adrian gravely. "Does he have a name?"

Claire glanced at Adrian, uncertain whether to give it. He rose, "My lord, I am Sir Adrian Thorne, Lord Roadnight."

"The newly restored Lord Roadnight is so soon toppled?" he asked, puzzled. No news of the murder had reached him apparently. His scrutiny traveled over Adrian again, glinting as it marked the borrowed clothes, the gloves worn indoors, but pausing only to search Adrian's eyes. "What had you to do with my son?"

"I never met him, but I was able to describe the men who attacked him," he answered.

Lord Brightsea gave him a sharp look, but to Adrian's relief did not probe further. "Vengeance means nothing to me. Since I cannot have my son alive again, what justice can there be? Yet, perhaps Gabriel rests the easier for it." Removing his cape, he slung it over a chair. "By the look of it, you are hiding. Who are your enemies?"

Adrian hesitated, despairing of a way to tell his tale that would not call his sanity into question. But it would be far worse if Lord Brightsea heard it from another source.

"Lord Roadnight possesses a gift," Claire began as if it were no more extraordinary than possessing a hawk or horse. She told of Adrian's wrongful confinement in Bedlam, James' deception, and of the lies Gabriel had been told when she sent him to inquire after her unknown madman. Her voice caught as she told of the brooch, of Adrian's experiencing of Gabriel's death. For a moment her father's eyes blurred with tears, and he reached and took her hand. Then he swallowed back his grief and nodded for her to continue. Claire finished with the last terrible events, presenting her glimpse of the man in the garden as if it were a certainty.

"Dreadful," Lord Brightsea said. "Dreadful."

Adrian waited under his penetrating gaze. For Claire's sake, and perhaps even for his dead son's, he knew Lord Brightsea wanted to believe his innocence. But he could not be happy to have found his daughter alone with a suspected murderer.

"Remarkable," Lord Brightsea said finally, accepting things as they were for the moment. "Your ability is not unique, Sir Adrian, but few possess it in such strength. Is its reliability constant, or only sporadic?"

"Only sporadic," he answered reluctantly.

The Earl nodded. "Difficult . . . difficult."

Conscience bound Adrian to make his host aware of the danger, and he finished with the tale of Penelope's terrible murder. "My cousin wishes to believe me mad," he said. "His wife's death will continue to grieve and torment him, and he has not your wisdom about the hollowness of vengeance. He and Edward Quarrell will hunt me. The force of the law is on their side. Protecting me is dangerous."

"Where else can you go?" Claire asked. He saw her lips tremble, but her voice was firm and calm. "Not to Mistress Swift's, she will be watched. You cannot stay hidden long without allies."

All his friends would be suspect, and to chance revealing his affliction amid strangers would be dangerous. Adrian made his face impassive. "I must leave England."

Lord Brightsea flapped a hand, brushing away the words. "If this Quarrell hunts for you in London, he might also send men to search the seaward roads. I owe you a debt, Lord Roadnight, for Gabriel's sake, if no other." His worried glance at Claire told Adrian that dreamer Lord Brightsea might be, but he was not unobservant of others' feelings. He picked up a candle in its holder. "Come with me."

Adrian followed him up the stairs, and Claire came quietly after, a determined shadow. Inside the bedchamber, the Earl pulled back one of the tapestries, revealing what seemed a plain oak-paneled wall, until the older man pressed, and a section swung inward upon a narrower twist of ascending stairs. Curious, Adrian climbed behind the Earl to a chamber where expensive implements of brass, silver, and glass gleamed from the shadows cast by the moving candle, and strange symbols were painted on the walls. "Do not be alarmed," said Lord Brightsea, "this is not witchcraft. Alchemy is a study of the spirit as much as of matter, but it is a science." He set the candle on a table. "However, it is often misunderstood, so I conduct my most important work in this secret chamber. If your enemies arrive, retreat here. They might eventually discover this room, but not before help could arrive from my town house, which is not far away."

"Your men could not stand against the official forces Sir James might gather. Nor would I wish to put you in that position. I would not repay the Lady Claire's kindness by bringing danger on you. I must go soon."

Lord Brightsea mused, frowning. "I cannot deny your logic, neither will I give in to the howling pack. As long as you want a haven here, you have it. Only do not touch my alembic." He pointed to a vessel with a long tube and bulbous receptacle projecting from it. "Nor my athanor." He indicated a contraption half furnace, half miniature tower. "Their purity must be preserved from uncontrolled influences."

"I understand," he said.

Nodding at Adrian's gloves, Lord Brightsea smiled grimly. "Yes, I imagine you can."

Adrian tensed, and confined his answer to the request. "I shall respect your wishes."

"Your gift troubles you more than Claire's account suggests." He glanced briefly at his daughter. Claire said nothing, letting her father question him as he would.

With his hold on himself so tenuous, Adrian did not wish to share the truth. Yet the Earl spoke as if such abilities were familiar to him. "Yes, it is troublesome."

"It came only recently on you? With some sudden shock, perhaps?" At Adrian's nod, he said, "It is sometimes so."

Adrian moved closer. "Do you understand it? Because I do not."

Lord Brightsea gestured to a seat at the table, and took the one opposite. "I have no such abilities myself, but my work brings me in contact with some who do. I watched the Queen's astrologer Dr. Dee scry, creating visions in a globe of crystal, and a fishmonger's daughter lay her hand upon condemned men's foreheads and unerringly tell which would be executed and which pardoned. I have seen enough to know the possession of such a gift is not, in itself, madness."

Adrian kept his voice calm, but his fingers knotted tightly. "Yet it may drive one mad?"

The alchemist's swift glance told him it was so. But he merely said, "You have not yet learned to control your ability."

"Control it?" Hiding a stab of hope, Adrian unlaced his gloved fingers. "How?"

Lord Brightsea shook his head. "That I cannot tell you. Each must find a separate way, I think. However, you are undergoing a transformation, and I do know somewhat of transformations." He pointed at a shapeless lump of dull gray metal on one of the shelves. "Lead is stable, reliable, yet heavy, without beauty or surpassing value. Consider it the dross of ordinary sentience, the unawareness of common mankind. The aim of the alchemist is to refine that dross, in himself and in the material world. How is this done?" With a sweeping gesture, he indicated his powders in crystal phials and his many-hued liquids in curiously shaped cruets, the furnace of his athanor. "Heat is introduced, pressure, along with tinctures of many volatile sorts. This has happened to you. Your perceptions are no longer dull lead, but awakened by some fire that lay dormant in your spirit."

A cold frisson raced through Adrian's nerves. "I do not wish it so."

"Refusal may indeed drive you mad. Transformation means the death of the old. You cannot walk naked through winter and call last summer's sun to warm you."

Adrian saw his mother, disheveled and distraught in her remote tower prison, and in quick succession, his father's face haggard with grief, then an open box with a red ribbon curled in a corner. Another shudder passed though him, fiercer than before.

"Alchemical wisdom symbolizes revelation by discovering a mountain. In the instant of discovery, a most vehement wind shakes the mountain, shattering its stones to fragments. Terrible beasts are encountered then, a blood red lion with his maw corrupt with death, a pale eagle with cold, rending talons. At this point, resolution is essential. When the earthquake shatters the world, you must not fall, for when you see the dragon of flame, the treasure is near."

Adrian looked to Claire and found her gaze intent upon him, willing her strength. She was a treasure beyond his worth. To her father he said, "I have tried, Lord Brightsea—"

"The treasure is near," Lord Brightsea repeated, his gaze intent on the outlandish tools of his study. "Yet it is not attained. Each attempt brings you closer."

Adrian shook his head. His only safety lay in resisting the curse. The only security for Claire lay in removing himself from her life before it was too late for them both. "The toll is great. I fear it will break my sanity."

"Only fire may consume the corruption. Confront the cataclysm, and become fire. If you can achieve that secret, then after night will come dawn, and the daystar shall arise. By its light will appear great treasure. Chief among its jewels will be the Elixir of Life, which turns all things to most pure gold."

Confront the cataclysm? Adrian thought. *Not possible.* How could he control the visions? The bloody knife rendered him unconscious, and it was but an object. Quarrell's effect was decimating. His touch rendered Adrian powerless. Despair trickled through him, and with it, fear of all the Earl said. From long training, Adrian attempted the distance of irony. "If Quarrell makes an aptly corrupt lion, my cousin James hardly amounts to an eagle."

Lord Brightsea's expression was benevolent. "Alchemical treatises are symbolical, do not take the emblems too literally. Despite your vulnerability, you do not strike me as a weak man, Lord Roadnight. Fear can grasp even the strongest in its clutches, can it not?" He looked back and forth between them. Adrian nodded agreement, but for some reason Claire averted her gaze and turned away. Adrian had to subdue the impulse to go to her, hold her.

Her father leaned closer. "It is not a question of whether you are strong enough to confront it. It will confront you at every turn. If you wish to prevail, seek your strength in the purifying flame."

"I thank you for your advice," Adrian answered, knowing Lord Brightsea meant it kindly, but he did not realize what he was urging. In Claire, Adrian had found the purifying flame, and the elixir of life. In seeking her out, Adrian was endangering her. The Earl lived in a world of eccentric theories that harmed no one. He had not felt Quarrell's evil, nor wakened to feel himself cloaked in the bloody remnants of his lust—

Adrian forced the ghastly memory away.

"I see you need rest," Lord Brightsea said. Turning he took Claire's hand, cradling it between his own. "If you want anything, you will find my daughter and me downstairs."

Adrian remained where he was, sunk deeply in thought, sorting through plans and discarding them. He had friends and resources in Ireland, but would he be sought there for that reason. France then? He did not hear Claire's soft footfall on the stairs, but sensed her presence and turned. "Have you been there long?"

"No, a few seconds only." She offered him the plate she carried, soft cheese and bread, a plum. "Are you hungry?"

"A little."

Claire set the plate on a small table beside him. "May I stay?"

He smiled, inviting her before he thought. He must end this. "I must go tonight."

"Yes," she agreed. He glanced at her again, startled. Her determination filled him with foreboding. Whatever she intended, he suspected it did not include letting him go alone. "My father believes you . . ." she hesitated.

"But he would rather we were not alone in the tower?" When she nodded, he said, "It is a show of faith that we are alone in this room."

She came forward, pressing her hand lightly to his arm. Her warmth suffused him through the linen, sending a sweet fire through his blood. "I have a friend who can help you."

Adrian longed to strip off his gloves, his clothes, and burn away his fear and confusion in the glowing flame of her. Instead he drew away and shook his head, forcing himself to heed what she said. "When Quarrell widens his net, no one who befriends me will be outside it."

"This man will be. Sir Nigel Burne."

"Walsingham's spymaster?" Startled, Adrian considered the implications. "He could help me leave England undetected, certainly, but why should he?"

"Sir Nigel promised me his aid, should I need it," she answered. "A debt of honor. My brother was killed in his service."

"Even so, he is a suspicious man. If he thinks me mad, and a killer, would he not consider it a service to you to turn me over to the Crown's jailers—or to Quarrell's care?" He fought the surge of panic that came with the thought.

"You do not know Sir Nigel Burne. It is because he is so endlessly suspicious that he will be open to considering Quarrell's guilt." Claire smiled slightly. "Save for Sir Francis Walsingham, no one in England is so thorough an investigator. Unlike your cousin, Sir Nigel has nothing at stake himself. Once doubt is raised, he will sift out the truth."

He did not know Sir Nigel Burne, except by reputation. The spymaster's subtlety was respected, his power generally feared. Adrian had only Claire's assurance he would involve himself in such a dubious matter. It was staking everything on a mask of sanity that Adrian was not certain he could preserve.

"I have considered carefully. When Sir Nigel offered me his support, his promise was sincere." Claire pressed his gloved hand. "You must let me help you."

Adrian did not need to remove his gloves to feel the brightness of Claire's spirit, the certainty of her emotion. It shone in her eyes, and was confirmed in the tender, serious curve of her lips, in the pressure of her fingers, in the thrilling note of urgency in her musical voice. It was too late, he realized with a sweet despair. She loved him as he loved her.

He assented. "I will surrender to him if he will keep my presence secret."

She sighed with relief. "I was afraid you would refuse."

He rose, came around the table and knelt beside her chair, drowning himself in the forest hues of her eyes, dark evergreen and rich loamy brown. "I will refuse you nothing except myself, Claire. I can offer you no future."

"We will prove—"

He broke in. "Even if I am proven innocent, Claire, I cannot marry. I dare not have children."

She titled her chin, and her voice was firm, defiant even. "I have thought hard on it, Adrian. No such ability runs in my family. Who is to say it would pass to children of mine?"

"No such blight runs in my father's family either, but mother's family carries its curse."

"Must it be a curse?" she asked.

"It destroyed her, Claire. It may yet destroy me."

"You survived a childhood devastated by a terrible shock, and darkened with ongoing fear and neglect. Surely any child we had, sheltered with love and given guidance, would have the chance to grow strong," she reasoned.

He dared not believe her. "I refuse to sentence any living being to this hell."

Never looking away, she gently touched his lips with her fingertips. Radiance shot through him, arcing high and luminous as a rainbow against a clouded sky. He shivered as his barriers dissolved, freeing his spirit to spiral headlong with hers, flame twining with flame, melody vibrating within melody. Her words were feather soft, "Could it not be heaven?"

"Yes." The vehement whisper escaped him.

"Yes," she whispered in answer, urging him.

He opened his eyes, kissed her fingers tenderly, then confined them in his gloved ones. "No." He shook his head. "I do love you, Claire. But I can offer you no hope."

Her brimming eyes spilled over. She bit her lip, trying to cut one pain with another. Abruptly, she rose, steadying the dish she almost upended. "Eat something now. We will leave when it is dark."

When she was gone, he murmured, "The light goes with you."

Chapter 11

~~~oOo~~~

Sir Nigel Burne felt the usual increase of choleric humor as he approached his home. Once again the windows were arches of yellow light in the darkness. Margaret was waiting, wanting to know if he had been granted the barony, wanting to plot each step in his advancement. His horse snorted and pranced restlessly, and Burne realized his tightened grip had inadvertently conveyed his anger. Perhaps he should recount the more gruesome details of Lord Roadnight's deed. That might be enough to silence his wife.

Worry gnawed him about Claire and her involvement, however minor, with the murderous Baron.

He had heard of Lord Roadnight's flamboyant entry at the masque, and accepted there was nothing to be done until his lunacy revealed itself again. Another disappearance would provoke too many questions. A fatal accident would also be problematic, unless particularly well staged. He had even begun to doubt Quarrell's claim that Roadnight was still mad—but that doubt the Baron had most bloodily murdered.

Unfortunately, Burne had left but one man on watch outside Thorne Hall, and Roadnight had eluded him in the morning fog. Some hope remained for a quick capture. Better if Roadnight were already locked in the Tower, or Master Quarrell's new hospital, when his vile deed became general knowledge.

Burne regretted the gory chaos, but was pleased that Sir Adrian would be dispensed with soon. Although Sir James had been pale and lachrymose, persistent questioning had yielded certain leads that Burne would follow. Sir James was now greatly distraught, but once that passed, he could take up the Roadnight mantle once again.

Although Burne knew Claire had attended the masque, he learned only today that she had remained at Thorne Hall. Apparently Fletcher and Swift had embroiled her in their foolhardy rescue and restoration of Lord Roadnight. Burne had been furious to discover that Lady Claire had returned home with no more protection than her adolescent maid could provide. The murderous Roadnight might be lying in wait for her. Burne had seen what remained of Lady Penelope. What if the madman killed only women he knew? Sir James—and Sir Raphael Fletcher—should be throttled for not guarding Claire better. If anything happened to her, he would see them both dead.

Burne dismounted, tossed the reins to the groom, then stalked into the house.

Claire was there—standing beside his wife in the hallway.

He showed no more than mild surprise, of course, but his heart beat rapidly in his breast, alternating relief and delight, so that he wanted to muffle its betraying thump. He wondered if fear had driven her to seek his protection, but he could not see its shadow on her. Concern over a backlash against her friends, then. To secure her gratitude, he would stay his hand.

Beside her, Margaret looked smug and placid, so Claire had not revealed the gory murder. "My dear," he greeted his wife, bestowing a kiss on her cheek. Such small gestures often mollified her. Then he turned and bowed where his true interest lay. "Lady Claire, you honor us with your presence. You are well, I trust?"

Margaret read nothing into it, but Claire's gaze intensified slightly. He waited to see what she chose to reveal. All she said was, "I am as well as can be expected."

"We had a pleasant stroll through the maze before dinner," Margaret announced.

Why was his wife so proud of the stunted thing? One might as well call a grove a forest.

"Yes, Lady Burne has been most gracious in giving me a tour." Claire's brightness was too artificial. "The house and grounds are both impressive."

Save for the library, the rooms were filled with flowery colors. Burne would have preferred a domain that reflected the same somber dignity he favored in his own garb. He noted that Margaret was gowned in layers of insipid blue, the same watery hue as her eyes. Even in her mourning weeds, Claire glowed, vivid and vital beside Margaret's pallid elegance. His wife's lips were thin, and her collarbones jutted like brittle twigs beneath her throat. Wisps of limp, fine hair escaped from her coif.

He forced a smile and solicitous inquiry. "You have dined?"

"Of course," Margaret said. "Spiced pork, followed by pheasant in plum sauce."

"Most excellent fare, it was." Claire's smile was equally taut. These social inanities were wearing thin.

"Then perhaps we should retire to the library, Lady Claire?" Burne turned and nodded to Margaret. "If you will excuse us, my dear."

Margaret frowned. She was used to such late-night conferences, but they were not usually with a young and beautiful woman. Burne walked to the library and opened the door, indicating it would remain so for propriety. Claire entered and took a seat. With a rustle of satin, the soft scuff of heels on wood, Margaret turned and ascended the stairs.

Inside the library, Burne had a servant pour two goblets of his finest Xeres, then dismissed him for the night. He walked over to Claire and offered her the silver goblet of sherry. Given the circumstances, he could permit himself to study her closely. The rich chestnut brown of her hair gleamed with small shimmers of candle flame. A single rope of pearls looped her throat, creamy against her fair skin. She touched them once, nervously then took the goblet and sipped. "Thank you, I am fond of Xeres."

"Yes?" He continued to survey her, curious how she would approach him.

As usual she was direct. "You told me once I could call upon your friendship, Sir Nigel."

"Of course, Lady Claire. I meant it absolutely."

"No," she raised her hand, staying him. "Hear me out. If what I ask goes against your judgment or your honor, you must refuse me."

"It is difficult to imagine you making such a demand upon me, Lady Claire. I conjecture this momentous request is related somehow to the murder of Lady Penelope?"

She was not surprised. "Yes, it is."

"I interviewed Sir James this afternoon. Word will spread quickly, of course. Lord Roadnight has vanished, but we still hope to apprehend him before panic strikes."

"If you have talked to Sir James, then you must know of our theory."

"Your theory?" Burne frowned. He did not like to be missing any piece of information. "Sir James said little except that you had all been duped by his cousin—and to warn me to set watch on Vivian Swift."

"Sir Nigel, we believe that Sir James is the one who has been duped, and Sir Adrian is innocent. With your help, we can prove this and clear his name."

Panic flashed through Burne when he realized she had been aiding this butcher. Quickly, he subdued it. He had not suspected such a twist. Claire was alive, safe within his domain. She might only have been deluded by a clever madman, but a woman so sensible would have good reason for her belief. "If he did not kill Lady Penelope, who did?"

"Master Edward Quarrell, warden of Bedlam."

Burne stared at her, nonplussed.

"Sir James needs to blame, and so dismisses our evidence. We must find proof even closed ears will hear."

"Mine are not closed."

"That is why I have come to you." Fortifying herself with a sip of sherry, Claire began to tell him the story. Much of it he knew, but her version was different in one key point—that Sir Adrian had been injured and lost his memory. Confusion had been mistaken for madness when they first brought him to Bedlam. Claire told him of Sir James' collusion, but emphasized how Quarrell profited from the arrangement. According to Claire, Master Quarrell had tormented Roadnight, as he did other prisoners. "Mistress Swift will testify to this as well."

Perhaps the doctor had taken perverse delight in tormenting a nobleman. But Burne thought Quarrell was too wise to deliberately lie to him. "You may not know the whole story, Lady Claire. Lunacy runs in Lord Roadnight's blood. His mother was a mad Irishwoman—"

"As I understand it, his mother was sane until the death of her babe." With some asperity, she added, "I believe even English mothers have suffered such madness."

"Lady Roadnight was violent. She blinded Sir Adrian's father."

"That is no proof that Adrian is mad himself." She set the sherry aside and rose to her feet. "To be shut in Bedlam might destroy another man's sanity, yet he has survived it."

She defended Roadnight too fiercely—Burne did not like it.

"Lady Penelope's murder speaks against him," he told her. "Jealousy and revenge are emotions which compel even sane men to commit violent crimes."

"He displayed neither. He did not love Lady Penelope. I do not think he even particularly liked her. While he was angry at Sir James' betrayal, I believe he was relieved not to have to wed Penelope—even to rejoice in being free of her." She met his gaze directly. "That is an emotion I am familiar with, Sir Nigel, however ill it reflects on my character."

It was the most honesty she had ever given, to reveal this darkness. He gave her his own candid absolution in return. "Fitzroy was an arrogant fool."

If she did not embrace his acquittal, she accepted that he did not blame her. "If Lord Roadnight were a madman, he would have to be clever beyond belief to keep it from us daily. I think Adrian spoke the truth. He had no reason to kill her."

Burne controlled a flash of irritated alarm. "If Lord Roadnight did not hate Lady Penelope, perhaps he hated his cousin enough to strike where it would hurt the most?"

"I do not deny that Sir Adrian appears guilty, Sir Nigel," she said, facing him. "I only ask that you consider how carefully that appearance was arranged. Consider that Master Quarrell is a man who has exploited a position of power over the helpless. He has tormented two people that we know of— Lord Roadnight and Mistress Swift."

"Neither is a reliable witness."

"I would say both are. But surely you can have no doubt of Vivian's sanity."

"I have much doubt of her scruples." He took a sip of wine, deliberating. "Greed would be reason enough for such a woman to foster Lord Roadnight's plans to reclaim his title."

"Sir Raphael would not have gone along with such a scheme for greed."

"Granted." He acknowledged her assessment of Fletcher, who had a tedious tendency to moralize. "However, Mistress Swift may have lied to him."

"No. She would not." Exasperation edged Claire's voice, but she quickly countered his argument. "Certainly, Vivian is cunning, and could lie well for benefit or protection. But even if she had, her deception would have ended with Lady Penelope's murder. No one would risk such a hideous death for a bit of silver."

"True," Burne agreed, though he continued to hunt for weak patches in the weave.

Claire said, "I know Mistress Swift spoke to the Queen about Quarrell, but others came forward and spoke on his behalf."

"Others with far greater credence." He himself had made sure of it.

"Perhaps Master Quarrell has done them some unlawful service, as he did Sir James."

"Perhaps," Burne allowed. Even if Quarrell was innocent of the murder, he had begun to look like more of a liability than an asset. Could he actually be guilty? "But how did Master Quarrell achieve his end? Was the house not guarded?"

She told him how the wine had been drugged. "Lady Penelope could have tainted it easily. She urged us all to drink deeply. The whole household slept late."

"You are convinced of this?" he asked Claire. It was possible, of course. He himself kept small caches of physics for different purposes. A fortuitous delay. A necessary death.

"Yes, and I believe James would be as well, if he would let himself think clearly. He cannot face the implication that Lady Penelope unwittingly invited Death into their home."

"She had the same reasons as Sir James," Burne conceded. "Ambition, greed, and fear."

"And less conscience. I believe she admitted Master Quarrell through the garden gate, and then led him inside. With everyone drugged, he could do as he chose." She paused, then said in a more subdued voice, "Selfish as she was, I pity her end greatly."

He raised an eyebrow quizzically. "You do realize this complicated plot is more farfetched than a madman revenging himself upon a woman who has betrayed him?"

"Yes—but you are no stranger to complicated plots, Sir Nigel."

He smiled at that, and despite her concern she smiled in answer. Green lights flickered in her eyes. She was so beautiful, and her mind offered as much delight as her physical charms. "What is that you want me to do, Lady Claire?"

"You must investigate Master Quarrell," she spoke with renewed passion. "He is a killer who takes pleasure in suffering. Proving his guilt will prove Lord Roadnight's innocence."

Was it only a desire for justice that urged Claire to speak so ardently for Sir Adrian? Or was it a more intimate desire? Surely not. She barely knew the man.

"You know where Sir Adrian is, do you not?" Innocent or guilty, he did not want her close to Roadnight.

"I will not lead you to him." Claire twisted her hands in her lap, one hand stroking the injured fingers of the other. Burne felt a twinge of sympathy for her. A curious, vulnerable emotion. "If Sir Adrian surrenders himself, will you hold him secretly? Master Quarrell must not know where to find him."

"Master Quarrell has no allies here, Lady Claire," he assured her without reservation. "Meanwhile, I have resources for getting at the truth that are far greater than even Mistress Swift's.

She leaned forward, her gaze intent. "Perhaps Quarrell will be more reckless if he thinks Adrian is gone, and his own crime is unsuspected."

Again the Christian name. "How has 'Adrian' earned your trust so quickly, Lady Claire?"

A faint flush shaded her cheeks, but she held her head high. "There is a curious link between us."

Burne prickled uneasily. "Indeed?"

"I saw him the day he was brought to Bedlam. He was in great distress, but struggling to reclaim his dignity. The brutality of the guards appalled me. I sent Gabriel to inquire after him, but he was told the man was dead. They were hiding the truth even then."

"Or simply mistaking who was meant," he conjectured.

"No." Her response was quiet but vehement. "Impossible."

Thinking back, the doctor's efforts to reclaim Roadnight became highly manipulative. Quarrell looked to be a deadlier adversary than he had first suspected. "Tomorrow I will have a warrant drawn for Master Quarrell, and a search made of his home. The guards and sisters at Bedlam will be questioned closely."

"Sir Adrian told me of one named Sister Mary, who was kind to him, and might speak against Master Quarrell if it would not cost her position."

Memory stirred. Was that not the name of the woman Quarrell said had vanished? He implied Adrian was responsible for her disappearance. Had Quarrell killed her himself? Both theories remained possible. Either way, Quarrell was a distinct liability. "I will look for her," Burne said. "But what of Lord Roadnight?"

"Will you give me your word that you will not arrest him if he comes to you?"

"Although I find myself believing you, Lady Claire, there is yet no proof," Burne answered. "I give you my word that Sir Adrian will remain here in my keeping, unless I discover more conclusive evidence against him, or against Edward Quarrell."

Claire smiled at him, her eyes alight. "I cannot express how grateful I am."

He hoped one day to give her that chance. "Together we will serve justice."

"I will summon Sir Adrian. It has not tolled midnight yet; he will still be on the Thames. Do you have a lantern?"

After ordering a servant to bring the light, Burne escorted Claire through Margaret's formal garden, past the silly maze of knee-high hedges. A waxing moon showed now and again through smoky clouds. When they reached the dock, the Thames looked dark and murky, splotched here and there with wavering torchlight from the banks, and ruffled by a chill wind. Three times Claire covered the lantern with her cape and revealed the light, before setting it down. Its beam cast a pale path across the water. Soon, a wherry glided out of the night and slid up to the dock. Roadnight alighted. He smiled at Claire, and she responded in kind, her face radiant despite her worry.

Shock, anger, and jealousy twisted into a coiled knot in

Burne's stomach. He was certain it was far more than friendship Claire felt. She was not flighty. He had observed her often at Court, and knew her flirtations as little more than playful wit. Till this moment, he had had but one true rival, Rafe Fletcher. Perhaps it was only his irrevocable loss that had made her turn to this man. Perhaps misguided sympathy. Even if Lord Roadnight was sane, he was not good enough for her—this half-Irish lordling of dubious politics.

Sir Adrian faced him squarely, pure bravado perhaps, but his gaze was intent. Burne did not allow his full animosity to show, nor did he make a pretense of welcome. "Lady Claire has not fully convinced me of your innocence—but I do concede that Edward Quarrell may be behind Lady Penelope's death. I will order his arrest in the morning. He will be questioned and have his property thoroughly searched. For now, you are my guest, Lord Roadnight, but you must surrender your weapons, and accept that some sort of guard is necessary."

"I accept your conditions, Sir Nigel, and offer my gratitude." Roadnight handed over his sword, then brought out something wrapped folded in cloth. "Edward Quarrell used my dagger to kill Lady Penelope."

Sir Nigel extended his hand to receive the weapon. Roadnight seemed strangely reluctant to hand it over, then relieved when it was gone. The curious response heightened Burne's suspicions. But the man was no threat while within his control. "Follow me inside."

Despite his misgivings, Adrian smiled as Claire moved to his side. Shielded from view by her skirts, her hand slid into his gloved grasp briefly and offered a squeeze of reassurance before falling away. Together they followed Sir Nigel back to the house. As they came into the hallway, a thin elegant blond woman descended the staircase. "I saw lights on the landing, Nigel, and I see now that we have another guest."

"Lord Roadnight, have you met Lady Burne?"

"I don't believe so." He answered politely.

"We have met once or twice at Court, some years ago," she corrected him with a thin smile. "I have heard of your remarkable resurrection, my lord. I should love to hear the tale."

Adrian hesitated, for it was obvious that Lady Burne knew nothing of the murder. "It is a complicated story."

Quickly, Burne interrupted. "Indeed. And there are further complications that necessitate Lord Roadnight spending a night or two here. I will explain tomorrow, my dear."

Lady Burne obviously knew better than to argue. "Be welcome then, Lord Roadnight. I fear I am weary myself, and must retire."

Adrian bowed courteously. "I thank you for your generous hospitality."

There was a brief murmuring of good-nights, and then Lady Burne made her way upstairs. Burne turned back to Claire. "We will talk again in the morning, Lady Claire. But now, I wish to ask Lord Roadnight a few questions."

Adrian exchanged a quick, frustrated glance with Claire. Obviously she wished to remain by his side, as he desired her to be there, but she could hardly protest. Her gaze, her warm smile offered what reassurance she could. Burne beckoned to a servant and ordered that Lady Claire be escorted to the yellow chamber in the old wing, and a maid be sent to tend her. Without proof that Adrian was innocent of Penelope's murder, Burne was necessarily protective of Claire. She departed reluctantly, and Burne nodded toward the library. Adrian entered ahead of him, glancing about. His host picked up a bottle of sherry and carried it to the cupboard. "This is a fine Xeres, Sir Adrian. Will you share it with me?"

"Yes, thank you. The wind on the Thames was cold. It will warm me."

Burne did not summon a servant, but prepared the drinks himself. Handing Adrian a goblet, he gestured him to a chair. Adrian sipped the sherry. It was oversweet, but did take off the chill. Sitting opposite, Burne questioned him about what he remembered of the murder, no doubt testing his answers against Claire's, but Adrian knew they were in accord. He tried not to be evasive. His terrible gift was the one thing they agreed should be withheld from Burne. Claire felt Sir Nigel would only believe in Adrian's ability if he experienced it. Adrian could not guarantee he could feel something on command, or how bizarre his reactions might be if he did. He did not want the knowledge needlessly exposed to anyone, and certainly not to a man he felt would judge it as harshly as Burne might.

Adrian drank more of the sherry, trying to relax. He felt extremely uneasy—any man suspected of insanity and murder would be on edge in the presence of the Walsingham's most ruthless spymaster. Adrian sensed Burne did not like him, though perhaps he only disliked the situation. Nonetheless, Adrian hoped that Burne would go after Quarrell like a ferret after a rat.

At last Burne said, "Certainly you seem sane, Lord Roadnight, but so must Master Quarrell if he maintains his position. I know something of your family history. Have you never considered that some violent madness overtakes you unawares, and leaves you with no memory of what crimes you have committed?"

Adrian looked down at his gloved hands, the leather gleaming faintly in the candlelight. After a moment he lifted his gaze and said, "In truth, yes, I have known that fear. But I believe it is no more than fear. I cannot conceive that I would commit such savage crimes on woman or man. I can easily conceive that Edward Quarrell would do so."

"Did you see evidence of it?"

He hesitated, then said, "I saw him revel in power and cruelty."

"He tortured you in Bedlam?"

"Yes." Adrian searched for words to answer the straightforward question. "Physically, I was abused less than some. With me, his torments were primarily of the mind, but they were deliberately inflicted."

Burne frowned, dissatisfied. Unable to speak of Quarrell's midnight visits, Adrian told Burne of the whippings and other cruelties.

"Such treatments are standard for the mad," Burne said dismissively, though after a pause he amended. "Perhaps too extreme."

It was nothing Adrian felt he could debate until Burne believed him innocent and sane. But there were other, more immediate concerns. "Sir Nigel, I fear that anyone who has helped me—in particular the women—may be at risk from Edward Quarrell's revenge."

Burne understood him at once. "The warrant will be issued tonight. Lady Claire is safe under my roof. Tomorrow, I will have a watch set on her—and Mistress Swift, of course."

"Thank you." Relieved, Adrian sank back in his chair. The stresses of the day had taken their toll and he struggled to keep his eyes open.

"You look weary, Sir Adrian. Let me accompany you to your chamber upstairs."

"Indeed, I am growing fatigued." Adrian rose to his feet, swaying slightly.

Burne waited for him to recover. "It is late, and the day was long for all of us."

"Yes." Adrian dared to hope tomorrow would be better. Tomorrow, Quarrell would be taken. Now all he craved was the oblivion of sleep.

Summoning two guards, Sir Nigel led Lord Roadnight upstairs to the room he had chosen, well away from the wing that housed Claire. Roadnight entered without demur. Once he was inside, Burne locked the door and posted one of the men there, a great, burly fellow named Thomas. He handed him the key. "If his lordship attempts to escape, or if you suspect anything unusual, unlock the door and investigate. Summon help if need be."

Thomas drew himself up. "I won't be needing any help, my lord."

"You would be wise to call for it," Burne said.

Thomas looked dubious, but mumbled assent. Burne led the other guard back to the library, wrote out an order for Quarrell's arrest, and gave it to him.

"Tonight, my lord?"

"Not tonight. Go at dawn, with five men of your choosing. Master Quarrell may be dangerous, so make sure he is well secured. Take him to Newgate. Make certain the sergeant knows he's not to let this man slip through the cracks. They can have their garnish, but Master Quarrell's coin will buy him better food, not an escape hatch to the outside."

Quarrell would indeed vanish, but it would be Burne who would arrange it.

"Yes, my lord," the guard said, then left.

In the hall, the clock chimed midnight.

Back in his chamber, Burne lay down fully clothed on the bed. He waited one hour, two, thinking fiercely all the while. Slowly, the house settled into a deeper quiet, with only a few guards on patrol. At dawn, the servants would wake to prepare breakfast and tend to their duties about the house, and the squad would leave to arrest Edward Quarrell. Burne had a few hours in between to accomplish his plan.

He was not an impulsive man, but any intelligencer must be able to take advantage of circumstance. The design had fallen into place all at once, seemingly perfect, but there was no time to sort through all the ramifications. Was there some small but obvious thing that he was overlooking? This maze was high, its passages dark and thorny—but Burne believed he would walk through it unscathed.

In the darkest hours he rose, and made sure all was in readiness. He went to the door that linked his bedchamber with Margaret's, opening it quietly and entering. His wife lay sleeping, a pale, bleached thing lying amid the paler bleached linens. She slept on her back, stiff and prim like a nun. For once Margaret suited his convenience.

He pressed the coverlet more snugly about her torso, then eased onto the bed, pinning her arms within the brace of his legs. Taking the pillow that lay beside her, he pressed it lightly over her face. He increased the pressure slowly, carefully, wanting her starved for air before she awoke. More pressure and she came to life suddenly, thrashing beneath the covers. He held the pillow over her mouth and nose with one hand, pressing her forehead down with the heel of the other so she could not rise up. Somehow, she worked one arm free, her hand clawing at his, but he had anticipated that, and she scratched uselessly at his gloves. He increased the pressure, feeling her struggles turn to moribund shudders. It was over quickly then, though he held the pillow down a long minute after she stopped moving. When he lifted the pillow, her face gaped up at him, eyes wide and sightless. His fingers pressed to her throat, seeking the pulse point.

There would be no resurrection for Margaret.

Burne felt no regret—only grim satisfaction to be free of her. Wakening beneath it came a low buzz of anticipation for what that freedom might bring him. His heart quickened with new excitement, but he quieted it with even breathing. He would not think of Claire now. For the moment, the only thing of importance was that the rest of his plan unfolded smoothly. He gazed down at the corpse. Blood was going to be a problem, though there would be less now that she was dead. He stripped off all his own clothes and laid them safely aside, then removed Margaret's shift. Her skin gleamed bluish white in the dim light. He took out his dagger and began to cut, tossing the bloody refuse onto the rushes. The grisly act stirred revulsion, but it must be done. Margaret's eyes stared up at him, their paleness glazing. He could endure their stare, but there was no reason to. He reached out and closed the lids, then returned to his task.

It was a pity he could not use the previous murder weapon. Earlier today, he had seen Lady Penelope's body, and duplicated the atrocities as best he could. His efforts were amateurish butchery. As he worked, Burne became more and more convinced that Quarrell was the man behind the other murder. The physician had far more opportunity than Sir Adrian did to learn such anatomical techniques.

When he was finished Burne felt queasy and disgusted, but the sensations were nothing he was unable to master. Dipping Margaret's shift in the basin, he mopped away the blood from his hands and body. When he was clean he threw the garment onto the floor beside the flayed leavings, re-dressed, and went into the hall, closing the door behind him. He went to the next corridor and down to the door where the guard stood watch.

The man quickly straightened his posture. "My lord."

"I thought I saw someone moving about the grounds, Thomas. Unlock the door. I want to make sure Lord Road-night is within."

"I've heard nothing, my lord," the man assured him.

"Open it." At his sharp tone, the guard complied. Once within, they could see Sir Adrian, still partially clad, asleep on the bed. The opiate Burne had added to the wine was potent. It should last till morning. He nodded to the guard to check the windows. This time the man did not bother to argue but did as he was told. As soon as his back was turned, Burne grabbed the small marble bust that sat on the table by the door. Quickly, he moved up behind the guard and swung the statue down hard, striking his skull through the soft felt cap. With a groan, the guard slumped to the floor. Burne picked up the small tapestry covering the table, turned the guard with his foot and wrapped it over his face as if Roadnight had tricked him so. Burne smashed the guard's face through the cloth, then rolled him unto his stomach and struck three more blows to the back of his head, crushing it totally. He did not think he had gotten any blood on him, but he would have to check in better light.

After that was accomplished, Burne contemplated the un-conscious Roadnight for a moment, then swung the statue lightly, laying a glancing blow along his forehead, just enough to bruise and bleed a little. Roadnight moaned, no more than that. Before leaving, Burne opened the casement. He would say Roadnight had attempted to escape. The other guard had witnessed him and warned Thomas to summon help, but the dead guard had been vain of his strength. Not that Burne expected his version of events would be questioned.

He hefted Roadnight over his shoulder, carried him back down the hall into Margaret's room, and dumped him on the floor beside her bloody skin. Roadnight moaned in his sleep again, grimacing as if he smelled the raw flesh, but he did not wake. Burne left him there and returned to his own room. Carefully, he examined his clothes by candlelight, but found no blood. He would don the same garments when they summoned him to see the corpses. Any smear he might have missed could be explained that way—though it was unlikely anyone would suspect him. His hatred of Margaret had been quiet, governed by formal manners. When he could, he had chosen avoidance over argument, and even their arguments were supremely civil. An exquisite shiver of relief trickled along his spine. Never again would he have to listen to the incremental rise of Margaret's voice as she harped on some coveted goal.

How much sweeter were Claire's melodious alto, and the soft, exquisite lips that shaped her words. . . . With her image emblazoned in his mind, Burne returned to bed. He was too keyed up to sleep, but that too could work to his advantage. All the better if he looked haggard. His greatest concern was that lack of sleep not dull his wits too much, but going without sleep was a common occurrence when some great case was unfolding.

If all went as he had planned, this new crime would sever the relationship between Claire and Lord Roadnight. Although Burne chanced that her guilt at bringing his wife's killer here might drive Claire away, he hoped it would chain her to him instead. Together they had been deceived and together they would grieve. Together they would find solace. All the evidence pointed to Sir Adrian, but if Claire stubbornly refused to believe he was the killer, or if Burne had overlooked something, the open window allowed the possibility that

Quarrell had managed to make his way across the grounds and into the house. The blow to Sir Adrian's head could have been caused by Margaret in her struggle for life, by the guard, or by the doctor.

Ideally, Claire would blame Roadnight rather than Quarrell. It did not matter which man was guilty of the other murder. He would ensure that both were soon dead.

Most importantly, she would never suspect Burne.

Chapter 12

F loating, drifting shapes hovered just beyond touch, some mere outlines, some vividly textured. Birds glided on blue iridescent wings, their feathers melting into the sky. Coiled knots of burning gold bloomed into yellow flowers, then fell to powder sands licked by the sea. A vast black dragon with scarlet tongues of mane fluttering like pennants and distended nostrils glowing like the flames of a smith's forge. All as ephemeral as sea clouds, all unbearably beautiful, alluring. So close . . . yet so far, far away.

Adrian lingered in the exquisite open spaces of the sky, a perfect, lonely harmony above the fearful clamor so dim and distant below.

Hands grabbed him. An iron grip jerked him from the cushioning clouds of his dreams. Harsh voices. Bleak light searing his eyes. He was shaken so brutally his teeth clattered. Adrian moaned, struggling against the clinging stupor that blurred his sight. Shouting filled his mind, loud and hollow as

189

bells clanging. It reverberated over and over, overlapping so that he could make no sense of it. Someone threw water in his face. Bedlam—guards mauling him. He struck out blindly. Someone slapped him, knocking him back against the wall with savage force.

"Enough!" a voice commanded.

Not Quarrell, but the tone was familiar. Panting, trying to focus his eyes, Adrian could only wait to see if it would be obeyed. The blows ceased. Slowly the grain of the oak paneling sharpened to clarity. He gripped a carved ridge, dragged himself up the wall. His limbs were clumsy, weighted. His head felt too heavy to lift, yet his mind was light, spinning in a nauseous vortex. The scent of blood seeped into his consciousness. He struggled to wake.

Sir Nigel Burne stepped in front of him, face cold, eyes bright. Triumph glittered in them. But no, it must be rage. But why?

Adrian felt as if he were swimming in rancid oil. His sluggish tongue managed one word. "Drugged . . ."

"Drugged?" Burned scoffed. "The only drug is your murderous madness."

Blood. Everywhere, the odor of blood. Inescapable.

"What's happened?" A terrible fear seized him. Claire! Had Quarrell killed Claire? Adrian's heart twisted, wringing cold fear into his gut. He closed his eyes, praying.

"Look," Burne commanded.

Prayers would not change what was. Adrian opened his eyes, following Burne's glare to the bed. Carnage bleeding into the white linen—a woman's body, flayed as Penelope's had been. Fair hair streamed over the pillow in obscene seduction.

Not Claire. Thank God it was not Claire. But who?

Unlike Penelope, her eyes were closed, though her mouth gaped in a silent cry. Turning away from the terrible corpse, he caught sight of himself in the mirror and inhaled sharply. Blood smeared his face and shirt. How could they not believe him a lunatic? His eyes seemed to glow, too green, too bright.

There was a rustle, a gasp. He turned, clutching the wall

against his dizziness. Claire stood in the door. She stared at him, her eyes wide with shock.

"Come away, my lady," a guard said. "You should not see this."

"Adrian!" She dodged the guard and ran to him, clasping his hands.

Their warmth made him aware of the chill of his own. But that warmth was only physical sensation, flesh and bone. Always before when Claire touched him, awareness of her spirit had permeated him like sunshine. Now he was at the bottom of a cold dank well, and she was far above. In frustrated need he tightened his grip on her hands.

Pain flaring in her eyes, she pulled away. "Adrian . . ." she gasped.

What was wrong? He touched her but he could not reach her.

The guards dragged them apart. Burne stepped between them. "He's murdered my wife," he told Claire hoarsely. "He has deceived us both. I will see his head on a pike."

Impossible. Adrian could not even remember the woman's name. Lady Mary? No—Lady Margaret. He glanced at the impossible horror on the bed, and back to Burne's accusing eyes. His tongue labored around the troublesome words. "What reason?"

"Reason?" Burne snapped. "No reason. This is the wanton violence of a madman." His eyes gleamed in pale, chill wrath. "One who has acquired a taste for blood."

"No," Adrian pleaded to Claire. He could not have done this. Could he? Her face mirrored his confusion. His fear. She held her hand pressed to her breasts, rubbing her fingers. He must have hurt her, gripping her hand so tightly. "Forgive me."

"Forgive you?" Burne repeated in cold outrage.

"Claire," Adrian said. "Quarrell . . . this must be—"

"Quarrell?" Burne asked. "My wife invited a stranger into her chamber, so that he might murder her? Or was she, as well as Lady Penelope, in league with him to deprive you of your inheritance?" Burne turned to Claire. "Do you still believe in your theory?"

Claire winced. "Lady Margaret had no reason to help Quarrell."

"But . . ." Adrian hesitated. *No reason . . . no reason . . . no reason . . .*

Burne lashed him with sarcasm. "Master Quarrell discovered you were hiding here? He made his way across my grounds and into my locked house? Discovered what room you were in, killed the guard, drugged you, and carried you into the room where my wife slept?"

"The guard dead?" Adrian's thoughts swarmed. He tried to capture one. "Quarrell . . . must have found a way. He is a demon."

"Demons now?" Burne scoffed. "Such creatures are found more easily in the minds of the mad than in the daily world."

"I did not mean—"

Burne cut him off. "If such infernal creatures act through him, why not through you?"

"I only meant . . ." in confusion, Adrian looked to Claire. The doubt on her face cut him to the quick. "He is only a man, but infernally clever. Infernally evil." Even that truth sounded mad. His head ached. He pressed a hand to his brow, winced. "I'm bruised. Perhaps Quarrell knocked me unconscious."

"The guard struck out at you—or my wife." Burne broke off, averting his face.

"Sir Nigel, this is terrible beyond belief." Pain filled Claire's whisper.

Burne turned back to her. "I do not blame you, Lady Claire. Do you understand? It is not your fault. I myself was taken in by Lord Roadnight's semblance of sanity. He may be unaware of what he does, but he is undoubtedly the killer."

"I know it seems so." Claire shook her head, but to Adrian the gesture looked like confusion as much as denial. "But you will find it's not true. You must."

"Investigate Quarrell!" Adrian pressed his only hope.

"I have sent men to arrest him," Burne answered, "but I

know who is guilty. Lord Roadnight will be taken to the Tower and kept under close guard."

No! Not a prison cell. Images of Bedlam rose up. The brutal guards. The filth. Frantically, Adrian cast his eyes and mind about the room, searching for some clue that would point to Quarrell. The air reeked of blood and death, but Adrian felt no sense of the doctor's presence. He fought down the rising panic, trying to make sense of this chaos. Pretty fancies had filled his sleep, not the perverted dreams that came with Quarrell's invasive touch. Had he grown so used to those insane lusts that they lost their impact? Had they become a part of him, so that he became Quarrell in his sleep? Could he have done this? It was unendurable.

Adrian had wanted to be free of his visions. Now, he felt blind without them.

His glance came to rest on a bloody dagger lying on the floor, half hidden under the bedcovers. He quailed at the thought of touching it, dreading the hideous deluge of blood and pain. But if he took it in hand, he might find some clue that could be proved. Desperation overcame fear, and Adrian dove for the knife. As his fingers closed around the handle, he prepared himself for the shock of the touch, for Quarrell's lascivious cruelty to assault him.

Nothing.

He clutched the knife tighter, but no visions came. A guard grabbed his wrist, twisting till he dropped the knife. Instinctively Adrian kicked out, scrabbling to his feet. The man backhanded him, knocking his head against the door. Pain blurred his gaze, but he saw the snaphance jutting from the man's belt. He launched himself, knocking the guard down even as he grasped the gun. "Put down your weapons," he commanded, rising slowly, his aim not on the other guard who had drawn his gun, but on Burne.

The other guard glanced at Burne, and at a nod set his snaphance on the floor. Claire was only a yard away. Adrian bitterly regretted what he was about to do, but it was the only way. She would understand. She had to believe in him. But he did not know if he could believe in himself anymore. He lunged forward, grabbing her, pulling her back against him. She went still, and for a second he thought all was well. He stepped toward the door, and suddenly she struggled against his grip. "Claire," he whispered. "Claire, don't fight." She stilled again, her body tense. He could say no more in front of them. *Don't leave me,* he begged her silently, but knew she could not feel him, even as he could no longer feel her.

"Release her!" Burne commanded. Adrian saw fury in his eyes, and fear.

"I did not do this," he said, as much to Claire as to them. "I could not have done this!"

"Then surrender," Burne said, implacable. "What you do now only proclaims your guilt."

"I will not let you lock me away." If they did, he would not survive. The Tower would be his gravepit, as certainly as Bedlam. "Order your men to disarm," he commanded. When Burne hesitated, Adrian barked, "Do it now! Throw down that cape and put the weapons in it."

Claire made a quick attempt to escape his grasp, almost breaking free. He gripped her tighter. "Be still."

"You would not kill her—not in your right mind," Burne said.

"You dare not risk it," Adrian challenged. Holding Claire fast against him, he trained the gun between Burne's eyes. "Know this. If it means my own life, I will certainly kill you."

"Release Lady Claire," Burne urged. "Despite this, I will still investigate Quarrell."

"Pick up the cape," Adrian told Claire. When he released her, she whirled and looked at him, anger and alarm fused in her gaze. Despite the pain it caused, he kept the weapon trained on Burne. She bundled the weapons in the cloth, but he could not tell if she obeyed willingly or out of fear. Adrian locked Lady Margaret's room from within, then took Claire's arm, guiding her toward the adjoining door to Burne's chamber. "Come with me, but command your men to stay where they are," he said quietly to Burne. "Make sure they obey that order."

Burne faced the disarmed guards. "Lady Claire's safety is the most important thing," he said as if he meant it. "Stay where you are till I summon you. Make no attempt to follow."

Adrian moved them both backward into Burne's chamber. Claire did not resist. "Now, lock this door behind us."

Once Burne had done that, Adrian opened the outer door to the hallway. He saw more guards waiting at the foot of the stairs. The sudden shock on their faces reminded him of the residue of blood smearing his shirt and hose. The guards' gray and blue livery was subdued, and would not immediately catch the eye. "Have those two strip," Adrian said, gesturing to the nearest. Burne barked the order, and the two guards reluctantly complied, leaving their outer garments in a heap on the floor. "Order them all into the library."

They followed that command as well. Adrian descended the staircase carefully, checking that no one was hiding out of sight. Still gripping Claire's arm, he nodded at the library door. "Lock them in, Sir Nigel, and bring the key." When Burne's back was turned, Adrian grabbed one of the discarded cloaks and wrapped it around him, hiding the blood. "Put the rest of the clothes in the other cloak," Adrian told Claire. Hearing the sharpness the tension forced into his voice, he made an effort to calm it. "When I let you go, do it. Quickly."

"It seems I have little choice," she answered. Without looking at him, she gathered the garments and weapons, and bundled them into the cloth. Adrian took hold of her arm again, gently this time, but still she did not turn to him.

He watched Burne turn the key and remove it from the lock. The door would not hold out long if the men determined to break out. They hesitated for fear of causing Burne's death, but fear of failing to prevent it might propel them into action. There would be an armory somewhere, where they could equip themselves. Anything that delayed them earned Adrian precious moments—time enough to get a wherry down the Thames. Even a few extra minutes might allow him to disappear.

A muffled clatter sounded outside the front door, horses trotting into the courtyard. Adrian quickly pulled Claire between the front windows and the door. A glance out the window showed two guards on horseback. With the gun he gestured Burne to the door. "Were they to take me to the Tower?"

Burne looked at him coldly. "No. They were sent after Quarrell."

"Adrian—" Claire tensed against him, her voice low and urgent. "Do not fight them. Surrender now. If you are innocent, Sir Nigel will discover it."

If you are innocent—Her doubt gnawed his soul. Would surrender return her belief? If he ran, he might forfeit his only chance of using Burne's resources to catch Quarrell. But after Lady Margaret's murder, how could he trust Burne to investigate without prejudice? Keeping the gun on Burne's back, he stepped out of sight to one side of the door. Claire moved with him, not impeding him, but what he could see of her face was pale and grim. "Take two steps through the door—no more," he ordered Burne. "Stand where I can see you. Do not look at me. Find out if they have captured Quarrell."

Burne did as he said, greeting the guards coolly. "What news?"

"Edward Quarrell was not at Bedlam," answered a voice beyond the door, "nor at his residence. We left men waiting at both places. When he returns, they will take him."

Unless he sees you first, Adrian thought.

Claire exhaled, a heavy sigh of defeat.

Despair overcoming him, Adrian leaned back against the wall. With a clouded brain, he struggled to think what else would delay pursuit. He could steal the guards' horses, but last night Burne had his own wherry at the dock. The river would be a far swifter escape. When Burne glanced through the door, Adrian gestured him to send the men away.

"Return to your captain, and report back to me at noon," Burne said.

"Yes, my lord," the men replied.

The sounds of the hooves retreated. Adrian decided he would take Burne's wherry, go round the curve in the Thames and then—what? There were no friends who would harbor him now, neither inside of London nor without. Even if Viv still believed him, Rafe would refuse the risk. None of Adrian's own estates would be safe. Then he thought of a sanctuary. One place obscure enough that he might be safe from both Quarrell and Burne for a few days. One person who might take him in, perhaps even know some small way to help him.

Adrian stepped out onto the porch, keeping Claire beside him. He must have a few minutes alone with her. But not here, where capture was every second a risk. Better to take her across the river to Southwark. After that farewell, he would need a horse, money for food. He still had money, but not enough. "Sir Nigel, add your purse to the guns."

Burne cocked an eyebrow at him. "Thief now, as well as murderer?"

"Claim what recompense you will from my cousin," Adrian answered.

"Indeed, you have greatly deprived us both," Burne sneered as he tossed his purse.

"To the dock." Adrian motioned with the gun. "Now."

Burne walked ahead, his back rigid with anger. Holding Claire close, Adrian guided her along the path. She said nothing, but the nearer they came to the river, the more apparent her reluctance. "It will be all right." He tried to pitch his voice so only she could hear—though neither she nor Burne was likely to believe him, whatever his tone. At the sight of the waiting boat, Claire stopped short. "Don't be afraid," he whispered, urging her onward.

The guard attending the dock straightened as his master approached. Knowing he had but one shot, Adrian hid the gun under his cloak, but kept it trained on Burne. Under his breath, he said, "When we reach the dock order him to untie the boat, then stand aside."

Knowing he looked disheveled, Adrian pretended to be leaning drunkenly on Claire. The guard gave him a peculiar glance as they drew closer, but followed Burne's command. When the man bent down to unfasten the rope, Adrian quickly stepped forward and struck him hard with the heavy metal barrel of the gun. The guard collapsed onto the dock.

"Take his gun, Claire. Put it into the wherry with the rest, then finish untying the rope." Adrian released her, stepping back to keep Burne in his sights. She did as he said, then edged backward. Catching hold of her, he commanded, "Get in the boat, Claire."

"No!" Both Claire and Burne exclaimed in answer.

"You must come with me," Adrian dared say no more. If Burne realized how safe Claire truly was, nothing would stop him from preventing the escape. But how could Claire still fear him this much? She trembled violently. "Now, Claire," he said, gently taking her arm.

She glanced at the boat, the pupils of her eyes dilated. "Please—" she began.

"Take me as your hostage." Burne spoke quietly, but his face was livid with fury.

"No! I have already cost you Lady Margaret's life," Claire protested, but her voice shook.

"I will give mine freely to protect yours," Burne declared. "Do you think I could bear to find you dead and mutilated— as I found her?"

Adrian wanted Burne fearful, but not utterly reckless. "I will release her on the other side of the Thames."

Suddenly Claire surged from his grasp. She gave a low cry as he caught her wrist. Burne lunged the instant the gun wavered. Locking Claire against him, Adrian shoved the weapon into Burne's chest, pointed straight into his heart. "Don't make me shoot you."

Burne retreated, measuring him. Adrian did not want to kill

him. If Burne attacked again, he would aim for the shoulder. But he put the full force of his desperation into his eyes, hoping Burne would see death there. Slowly, Adrian backed toward the wherry. Claire twisted against him, but he righted his aim in time. This was too dangerous. A shot could easily go awry and kill. "Go back to the house, Sir Nigel. Live to fight me another day."

"Yes," Claire urged him. "Go—*go!*"

Burne moved back, but slowly. Peripherally, Adrian could see the boat starting to drift from the dock. The guard groaned, raising his head. It had to be now. Adrian dragged Claire to the edge of the dock, lifted her bodily into the boat, then leapt in after her. She cried out wildly, trying to climb over him to get back to the dock. Shame and frustration mingled in Adrian as he restrained her. Holding her pinned hard against him with one arm, he grabbed the oar with the other and pushed off into the Thames. Despite what she had just said earlier, Claire cried out to Sir Nigel. Cursing, Burne ran toward them, but the current took the boat, and even under Adrian's awkward one-handed strokes, they moved swiftly away. Burne watched in fury for a moment, and then ran toward the house.

Filled with apprehension, Adrian turned back to Claire. She had stopped struggling, but clung to the side of the boat, her face white, her eyes like darkened glass with terror. If she dreaded him so, why had she not tried to jump into the water? The current moved sleek and smooth here, but was not dangerous.

"Claire?" he said tentatively, reaching to touch her arm.

"No!" She gave him a wild look, and huddled down, as far from him as reach would allow, covering her face with her arm. Violent tremors coursed through her. Could she fear and loathe him that much, then? He felt like a monster. On her wrist he saw the ugly bruises his grip had made. "Don't be afraid, Claire. Please."

She stared her gaze wide and unfocused, her hand flung up to ward him off. Adrian did not know if she even comprehended what he had said. Even facing him in the hallway, with Penelope's bloody corpse in the room beyond, she had not been like this. He spoke softly, urgently. "Even if you now believe I killed Penelope and Lady Margaret, you cannot think I did it sane and awake. Claire, surely you know I will let you go."

Her breath came in hiccupping gasps, frightening him. She could scarcely breathe. He did not know whether to stay where he was or to try and reach out to her. Any gesture of comfort might be taken for an attack. Even as he wondered what to do, Claire gave a choked breath and fainted, slumping against the back of the boat.

"Claire!" Adrian was aghast. What had he done? He could not comprehend her fear of him. Did she have a weak heart? Had he killed her, forcing her to come with him? He crouched over her, feeling for the pulse at her throat. It quivered beneath his fingertips. Relief surged through him, followed by another pang of fear. Her skin was clammy, her hair drenched with sweat. Would she live? Why had his hated gift abandoned him now, when he wanted it?

Letting the boat follow the current willy-nilly, Adrian settled Claire as comfortably as he could. His thinking was still muddled. For a moment he floundered in a morass of guilt and fear and horrified revulsion. But none of that helped Claire or him. If he did not resume rowing, he would soon be captured again, accused of two grotesque murders. He seized the oars and bent his back vigorously, taking them around the bend of the Thames. Once they were out of sight, he rowed them in a straight line, putting as many boats as he could between him and the bank from which he started.

Claire moaned. Adrian reached out and stroked her cheek again—too cold, too cold

He paused long enough to strip off the bloody linen and splash himself with the river water, and then dress in the guard's clothes. Touch still seemed blind, but he wished for gloves. He sorted through the weapons, strapping on a sword and knife and taking an extra gun that could be easily hidden

under the cloak. He tossed the rest into the water. Looking behind, he saw a distant boat moving more swiftly than the other
river traffic. It was long, fast, and rowed by several men. They
did not seem to have singled out his boat from among the others, but if it was Burne, he was gaining. Back and arm muscles straining, Adrian crossed toward the other bank, rowing
fiercely until they reached a seedy part of Southwark. He
landed at a small, ramshackle dock. There was little time, but
finding help for Claire was even more imperative than escaping Burne and his men.

He had chosen a spot with as few people as possible, but
the two wherrymen sitting near their moored boats halted
their talk to watch him. Other craft passed on the river. Casting the boat adrift would be incriminating. Sir Nigel's boat
drew nearer, stark as a pointing finger. Adrian beckoned one
of the wherryman. Taking a few coins from his purse, he began weaving a slipshod story about a lover's quarrel, the lady
fainting, a promise to return the boat to the last stop before the
bridge. The man was rightly dubious of the story, but he liked
the look of the gold. Seeing the gleam of greed, Adrian
stopped spinning the tale and let the money speak.

"I'll row your craft over, and leave 'er by the bridge," the
old man grinned. "After that, I'll buy a wherry ride home for
meself, sittin' me arse on a fat red cushion."

Adrian pressed the gold coin into his hand. "Go quickly."

The boatman held the wherry steady while Adrian gathered Claire into his arms and disembarked, then took the oars
and pulled off across the Thames. With luck, the hunters
would not catch the man on the other side, and even if they
did, it would make a few more moments' delay. Adrian could
not go far with Claire in a swoon. Spotting the hanging sign of
an inn, he carried her there, whispering desperate, meaningless reassurance.

It was a rough section of Southwark. A group of sailors,
disgruntled soldiers, and ruffians filled the tavern below the
inn. Burne's livery and the declaration of Claire's family
name might protect them, or it might just as easily suggest an

opportunity for robbery or ransom. Instead, Adrian told the innkeeper he was a friend of Vivian Swift. Naming the former Queen of the Clink had the desired effect. The tavern keeper quickly gave Adrian the key to a room, and jerked his head toward the stairs. Adrian carried Claire up, away from prying eyes. There was a great deal of thumping and squealing from the other rooms as Adrian walked along the narrow corridor with Claire in his arms. This place was as much a brothel as an inn. A redheaded whore emerged from one of the rooms, lacing up her bodice. Adrian promised her some silver to open the door and help him lay Claire on the narrow bed in the center of the room.

They stretched her out on the tattered coverlet. Despite the poor light, Adrian saw that Claire's skin no longer looked like whey, and her breathing was steadier. Nonetheless, he asked the woman to summon a doctor. Instead she sat beside Claire on the bed, stroking her face and patting her cheek. She seemed kind, but her trade was all pretense. Frustrated, Adrian kept watch that she did not steal some bit of jewelry from Claire. He bit back a sudden upsurge of laughter, thinking of all he had robbed from Burne this morning.

But he had not taken what mattered most. That had been Quarrell's deed.

"A doctor should tend to her," he repeated. Anxiety swept through him, another abrupt shift of mood that convinced him Quarrell had somehow drugged him. The effects were wearing away, but his emotions were still ungoverned.

"Do more harm than good, 'n make you pay for the pain," she said. "I'll get one iffen you want, but I think she's just 'ad a bit of a faint."

"A moment or two more," he said. Perhaps he should summon Izzy from the Buzzing Hornet. He would know what doctor could be trusted.

"Stay here. I'll be right back—me name's Moll." With that, she slipped out of the room.

Adrian sat on the thin, musty mattress and held Claire's hand. Moll returned a minute later with some water and a cloth. Settling on the opposite side of the narrow bed, she began to bathe Claire's face lightly. Perhaps this woman was right—a doctor might bleed Claire to weakness, or funnel some noxious potion down her throat. Adrian stroked Claire's fingers till she stirred. He exhaled a vast sigh of relief. The whore stood back then, folding her own hands decorously. Something in the gesture made Adrian believe she'd begun in a far better life.

"Leave me alone with her," Adrian said, and gave her the promised silver. Moll went out, closing the door behind her.

Claire's eyes opened, but she seemed dazed. Then her gaze focused on his face, and for a second warm pleasure lit her eyes. Abruptly, fear flashed across her features, and she gasped and drew back on the bed. Though the drug still affected him, Adrian felt the stab of that fear. He fought the impulse to reach out for her. Instead he raised his hands, palms open, placating. "You fainted, Claire, and I brought you to the nearest inn—and a nasty place it is."

Grunts of rough lechery sounded through the thin walls on either side. She glanced about her quickly, and flushed when she realized what was going on in the other rooms. Embarrassment made him writhe within. "Do you want a doctor?" he asked. "I was afraid you had a weak heart. Do you need medicine?"

"You forced me into the boat." A shudder followed her whisper.

"Only so I could speak to you alone. I will not hold you against your will, truly."

"Too late," she said.

The words were quiet, but Adrian flinched away. She did not love him anymore. What he had done had destroyed her feeling for him. Hopelessness overwhelmed him suddenly. Hot tears welled and he blinked them back, fighting for control.

"I am sorry," he whispered. When she turned her face away, he went on, "If you are well enough, I'll escort you back to the Thames—"

"No!" she cried, shocking him again.

"It's the quickest way away from me," he said.

Claire paled, averting her face. She had turned her head just so when her father spoke of conquering fear. Adrian remembered then that it was a boating accident that had crippled her hand. "You're terrified of the river."

Claire whirled on him, her left hand flashing out to slap him. She gave a sharp cry, shocked at herself.

"It is the river you're afraid of," he said again. "Not me. Or the river more than me."

Claire saw the mark of her hand glowing hotly on Adrian's cheek. Emotions warred within her. She had been fearful and angry, waking alone with him in this wretched place. Now the glint of withheld tears in his eyes made her feel like weeping. Fury flared again that she should succumb to such weakness in herself. She balled her hand into a fist to keep from reaching out to him. "Sir Nigel said you feared you were the killer," she accused, refusing to confess her fear of the river. The sickening panic that overwhelmed her shamed her bitterly.

"Sir Nigel was filled with grief and anger, and twisted what I said. He asked if I had ever doubted myself. I could not deny the fear had gripped me. But when I think how those women were brutalized—" Adrian shook his head. "I do not have that sort of rage. Quarrell does."

"You forced me into the wherry," Claire accused again, drawing away from him. It was as close as she would come to voicing her terror of the water.

"I did not think about your accident."

"Did you not know—" she began, then broke off.

"From touching you before?" he asked gently. "No. What I perceive varies with each person, each time."

"And today?"

"The drug is only just now wearing off."

She looked down, biting her lip, grateful that he had not felt her cowardice, yet oddly resentful.

"Claire, if I had known, I would have taken the horses, or

left you behind. I thought if I could speak to you alone—" He stumbled, then began again. "Perhaps it would have made no difference . . . but I could not bear to leave with you so in doubt of me."

Claire realized she had lost track of time. "How long have we been here?"

"I'm not sure. A quarter of an hour perhaps," he answered.

Fifteen minutes. Already Sir Nigel's men would be searching for him. They might be downstairs this very minute. Adrian was risking his freedom, staying to help her. She had wanted him to surrender—but she did not want him caught. If she thought he was a murderer, where was the reason in that? For all her acceptance of the metaphysical realms her father explored, Claire had always believed herself reasonable. But realizing that Adrian had put his freedom at risk for her shifted her feelings despite the warnings of reason.

"You must escape London." She sat up, trying to push him away. He took her hands and held them, so that she exclaimed her frustration. "Adrian!"

"You believe me again?" He smiled a little, that ironic smile of his.

It made her want to laugh. It made her want to hit him. She struggled to make sense of her clashing emotions. "When you touched me—in Lady Margaret's bedroom—you felt far away, clouded. I feared at first you were a shell, just abandoned by whatever violent emotion or demonic spirit that had driven you to kill her."

"And now?"

"Now I believe Master Quarrell drugged you. There are ways to influence even a person asleep, with fumes, vapors, or liquid dripped from a string. No doubt he knows them all."

"A pity I cannot inquire what it was. My emotions have been in chaos, but they have been mine alone."

"Or you had less time to recover," she suggested.

"No." He pressed a hand to his forehead. "The dreams were different, too."

"You dreamed of the murder again?" A chill of fear trickled down her spine.

"No. I was totally oblivious, floating in a lovely ethereal world," he answered.

There was nothing lovely or ethereal about Lady Margaret's murder. If Adrian had killed her, some awareness of it would have touched him, however distorted.

"I cannot believe I killed those helpless women." Adrian took a long breath and released it. Holding her gaze, he whispered, "But perhaps I am a killer, Claire."

The cold seized her, icing every nerve, closing off her throat. She managed one word. "Perhaps?"

"My father . . ." His voice broke, too.

At first Claire was too stunned to protest, then she said, "But Adrian, the thieves—"

He held up his hand, but still could not continue. Finally, he said, "The night of the attack, I rode to the docks to meet my father. I had no way to know he would arrive then, and yet I was sure he would. Just as I was sure my mother was dead."

"Your mother's death opened this pathway within you," Claire said.

"I believe so." Adrian stood, pacing the small room. "That ride is my last memory of any certainty, but later I learned more from Izzy. My father and I went to a tavern on the docks. The tavern keeper says I went out twice. Once I came back carrying something, then a few minutes later I ran out the back—like the hounds of hell were after me. My father followed. And not long after, the watchman heard a splash. He went to investigate and found two thieves stripping my father. One he shot, the other he took prisoner."

"That thief confessed to killing you," Claire broke in.

"Under torture," Adrian answered harshly. "Before that he swore they had found our bodies lying there. My father and I may have fought. I may have struck the fatal blow."

"Before he died, your father said that they had attacked you both," Claire broke in.

"My father believed me dead and would have let the secret of my madness also die."

"The thief threw you in the Thames to drown, Adrian, and would have thrown your father after. His story can't be trusted."

"No, but that does not mean it is a lie." He looked at her, his eyes shadowed. "Since my escape images flash like shards of a broken mirror—I see my father's face, covered in blood."

"You are remembering the attack—" she began.

He stayed her. "I see him standing before me, and I remember being furious with him. Murderously furious. I have put all my will into seeming sane, so that you and the others would help me regain what I had lost. I needed a safe haven where I could hide away. But what if I deceived you and myself? What if I killed my father—and so went mad?"

Could it be true? She could see why the fear would haunt him. Yet, when he spoke to her so openly, her own fear of him dissolved. His warning went for naught and his pain stirred her protectiveness. Claire wondered at the chaos of the emotions that churned within her. Yet love was the strongest, sweeping her forward, undeniable. "I do not believe you killed him."

He sat beside her again, frowning. "There are other fragments of memory. Perhaps if I can discover their meaning, I can remember the truth."

"You were injured," she warned him quietly. "They may forever be fragments."

"Then I will spend my life on quicksand, never sure where my next step will take me," he said. "Without firm footing, I can never trust myself."

"I trust you," she said, knowing even guilt would be better than this terrible uncertainty he suffered.

"Claire . . ." His voice trailed off. She could read the craving in his eyes. The need for love. The need for her. She reached out, but he sat back, too vulnerable to accept her comfort.

"Where will you go now?" she asked, trying to be sensible. "I can still help."

"You have already aided me. I want no more blame attached to you."

"Tell me," she insisted. "I may need to send you news."

When he shook his head, she swore. "I will not reveal the place to anyone."

He hesitated, but did not deny her. "I go to Amesbury. Mistress Morna Boyle lives there, a nurse who tended my mother. She retired to a cottage near her granddaughter's farm—"

A visible shiver ran through him.

"What is it?" she asked.

"I do not know when I learned that," he murmured, surprised. "She would have stayed with my mother till her death. My father must have told me where she went afterward."

"The memories are returning." Her own hope increased. "We will uncover the truth, and prove you innocent of everything—your father's death, and these terrible murders."

"Claire, you must convince Sir Nigel to investigate Quarrell." His gaze was fervent, and he pressed her good hand more tightly. "Even if they capture me—kill me—he must be hunted down. I fear for you while he is free. For you and Vivian both. Perhaps Quarrell thought Lady Margaret aided me, and so killed her. Perhaps he was looking for you, and found her instead."

"If that is true, will I be any safer in London?" she asked.

"He may hunt for you, but if he stays here, your friends will be his targets."

"If you are wary, you will be safe. Keep guards close by to protect you."

"Master Quarrell has penetrated two guarded houses so far."

"Penelope was his unwitting accomplice," Adrian paused, then added, "I told you that the journey to your father's tower was without incident. That was the truth, but I thought for a time that someone followed me in the fog. After I circled round and saw no one, it seemed but a fearful fancy. Quarrell must have pursued me, first to your father's, then to Sir Nigel's."

"He will discover where the doctor entered," she assured him. "There must be evidence."

"Claire, I must go," he said. "But first we must find a way to escort you to safety."

"I am coming with you." She did not know it till the words were spoken. Surety came with the utterance.

"No!" His voice was firm, but desperation edged it. "I cannot let you so damage yourself."

Claire thought of her mother, delicate and implacable, plotting her future—another betrothal as quickly as possible, chosen solely for wealth and influence. Though she no longer regretted it, Claire knew she had lost her chance to win Rafe because she had not spoken. She had lost her musical skill because she had not fought for herself on the river. She had lost everything she truly wanted because she had never dared enough. If she left Adrian now, she was convinced she would lose him as well, and with him all hope for the future.

"I am damaged." She extended her hand, displaying the crippled fingers. "As yet my heart survives. If you love me, you will let me fight to keep it whole, to keep it alive. Let me choose my own path."

"I love you. That is why I will protect you as well as I am able." He drew back from her. "I will go by the river."

"I will follow," she cried out, incensed at his refusal.

"I do not believe you will." Adrian's voice was quiet but implacable. He rose to leave.

Claire glared at him, tears of fury brimming in her eyes. How dare he use her fear against her? Argument would avail nothing. They both knew she could not endure the water.

Before he could continue, a brisk knock sounded at the door. They froze, but a soft voice asked if they wanted ale. Adrian told her it was Moll, who had helped him tend to her. "I have no reason to trust her beyond that kindness."

He opened the door, and a redheaded woman stepped in. Despite her tawdry clothes, Claire liked the directness of her eyes and her easy smile. Adrian said, "I need your help, Moll, and I will pay you handsomely for it."

"Oh? And what help is that?"

"I need different clothes, a horse, and food for a day or two. And I must have gloves," he said. "In return, I will give you what I am wearing, and pay you well in coin."

Moll's smile grew broader. "On the run, are you?"

"For something he didn't do," Claire answered firmly.

The woman shrugged. "He's done me no wrong. That's all I care."

"Can you choose a sound mount?" Adrian asked.

"I know a stable master—comes here once or twice a week for a ride, himself. I'll take you to him and you can choose your own beast. But first I'll buy the clothes." She held out her hand, and Adrian paid her with silver from Sir Nigel's purse.

"Enough?" he asked.

"Aye. You wait here." With that, she was out the door.

They waited, wondering if their new ally might instead return with Sir Nigel's searchers in tow. Adrian seemed relieved when Claire argued no further, perhaps taking her silence for capitulation. The obvious strength of his relief warned her of the lengths he would have gone to keep her from following, so she schooled her face carefully, and did not allow him to touch her.

"I shall send Moll for Izzy before I go," he said at last. "Promise you will not leave this room until he takes you to the safety of the Buzzing Hornet?"

As Claire opened her lips to lie to him, the redhead returned with clothes bundled under one arm and a leather satchel slung over her other shoulder. "There be bread and cheese. You'll find a nice beef pasty for tonight."

Adrian thanked her and unrolled the cape of gray wool she handed him to reveal new linen, jerkin, breeches, and gloves of brown leather, a wool cap, and tan netherstockings. Moll sniggered a little as Claire turned her back to allow him to change, but had the consideration to do the same. Claire could not help but imagine Adrian's lean, broad-shouldered frame being revealed, and picture the pale gold of his skin taut over bone and muscle, his chest feathered with tawny hair. The image of his masculine beauty was compelling, and she wondered if he had imagined her as well, naked to his gaze and touch.

"The sleeves are short," Adrian said, turning round.

"Fussy, ain't you?" Moll rolled her eyes, but Claire saw bare skin showing between glove and cuff.

Seeing there was no help for it, Adrian handed Moll the stolen livery. "This will be risky to sell," he warned.

"Not in pieces, it won't." Moll folded the cape over her shoulder and stroked it. "I'll take you to the stable now . . . soon as I've locked this safe in my room." She went out, scratching the velvety gray mockado like a sleeping cat.

Adrian turned to Claire. "We may never meet again—"

"Don't say that." She took his gloved hands, gazing into his eyes. Their sea colors darkened with sorrow, and he leaned close to kiss her farewell. Claire started back, afraid the touch would convey her plan to him. He flinched, and the pain in his eyes struck deep into her soul. She put his gloved hands to her lips, clasping them tightly with her uninjured fingers.

"Yes," he said sadly, mistaking her reason. "Yes, it's better so." He touched her lips gently with his fingers, then turned away.

There was a quick rap at the door, then Moll opened it and beckoned to Adrian. He took up the satchel of food and was gone. Claire locked the door and waited, counting the minutes that separated her from Adrian. At last, she admitted Moll when she returned alone. "He's off. I'll go send word to Izzy Cockayne to fetch you."

"I don't want Izzy. I want a man's traveling clothes and a horse."

"It'll cost." Moll's eyes went greedily to the dragon brooch. When Claire's hand flew protectively to it, Moll's glance shifted to her pearl necklace.

"I have no money with me. The pearls must buy a mount

and a few coins for the road. You may have these clothes," Claire offered desperately. "These shoes have jet buckles."

Moll assessed the mourning velvet. Such rich black dye was expensive. "No message?"

Izzy might take Adrian's side and send men to bring her back. Rafe would surely do so. Yet leaving her friends no word of where she was going would be foolhardy. "Send to Vivian Swift herself, and tell her Adrian and Claire are together and safe. Ask her to send word to my parents. She will reward you well for your trouble—and your silence afterward."

"Looks like I'm in deeper than I thought," she said resentfully, but then shrugged.

"I must hurry," Claire urged.

Moll considered her. "The stable boy's about your size."

Claire seized on the idea. "Trading with him would be quickest, surely?"

"Nag and rags together." Moll grinned. "Follow me."

Not long after, a slender lad led a nondescript bay mare from the nearby stable. He wore a faded green doublet and hose, a shapeless cap pulled low, and a patched blue cloak. He stomped a bit as he walked, as if his scuffed boots were stuffed full of rags.

"No help for that," Moll said. "No smaller feet in the stable."

"They will matter less when I ride."

Moll frowned as she tucked a stray tendril of Claire's hair back under the cap. "Your figure's hidden, but that pretty face of yours will never pass a close inspection. So keep back."

Claire nodded. "I must go."

Moll caught her arm. "Stay here, m'lady. It's not safe on the road."

"I will be safe if I can find Adrian," she insisted.

"The stable master told him the back way to the main road. If you ride hard and straight, you should catch him." Doubtfully she added, "I hope for your sake he's worth it."

Chapter 13

◦──◦◝◞◦──◦

Beyond Southwark, Claire urged her mount into a gallop. The close smell of the city gave way to the fresh air of open grazing lands, and occasional patches of woods shaded her way. It was a freedom she had long craved, and if the situation were not so desperate, she would have reveled in the adventure. Passing a thicket of old oaks, she rode hard around a bend and saw the road ahead dip to a stream and shallow ford. A rider was wading his horse across. She slowed instantly, but he heard her hoof beats and turned. He hid his wariness so quickly she would have missed it had she not learned the subtlety of his movement. It was Adrian.

At first, he did not seem to recognize her in the stable boy's garments, but perhaps he had learned her posture, the set of her shoulders, with equal skill. He halted abruptly in the middle of the broad stream, turning his horse to face her. His face was a pale mask, his lips set hard. She had never seen him show his anger so clearly. It shocked her, but did not stop her approach.

Adrian sat very still in the saddle, waiting. As she rode down the bank he called, "If you do not turn back, I will take your horse and leave you here."

The stream was clear, and little deeper than his horse's fetlocks. Shuddering despite reason, she rode into the water. Covering her weakness she approached within two feet of him, letting the mare splash noisily. If Adrian could use fear to separate them, she could as well. "If you abandon me, I will continue searching for you on foot."

"Claire," he warned, his anger growing.

She refused to look at the current. This was not a river, but a stream no deeper than a bathtub. Even if she fell, she could not be swept away, would not drown—unless she swooned like a fool. With false bravado she circled him, ruthlessly adding, "Everyone will think I am still your prisoner. You may as well keep me for bargaining power."

"And what will you be worth, having been astray with a madman on the lonely roads?" he answered just as mercilessly.

"Leave me if you will. But I warn you, I will not leave you."

"Believe me, I do not want your company." He spoke with devastating calm, but by now she knew the mask that had come down over his face. He turned and rode up the western bank.

Claire followed, shivering with relief to escape the shallow stream. When the trees ended and the road widened she drew alongside. Taut with anger, Adrian did not acknowledge her, but his grudging acceptance was enough. He would not leave her alone on the road, vulnerable to thieves, or to Quarrell.

When at last they came to a dip between two hills with woods for protection and no one in sight before or behind, Adrian turned off the road and guided them through a field. There were sunflowers here. Claire gazed at them, bemused to see the exotic blooms growing wild. Years ago, her father had some of the first seeds smuggled into England, brought by Spanish traders from faraway Peru. Perhaps birds had even carried the seeds from her father's London garden and cast them here to take root and blossom into glory. They seemed a blessing somehow, a hundred glowing suns, dark-pupiled, benevolent eyes watching their progress.

Their golden beauty had no visible effect on Adrian. He barely spoke to her. They rode for the rest of the day, skirting the towns and traveling through the woods and farmland, buying fresh-pressed cider and apples from a cottage. When the sun set, and the blue shadows of dusk draped the trees, he stopped in a small grove on a rise overlooking the highway. "This stretch of road is relatively smooth. The moon will be waxing. After we eat, perhaps we can chance another hour or two by its light."

She slumped with weariness at the thought. Adrian looked exhausted too, though his face was still marked with anger. If Quarrell had drugged him, that must be taking its toll. But Claire said nothing, letting him set the pace.

Adrian dismounted, then helped her down from her horse. Aching leg muscles wavered as she landed. He gripped her arm firmly, steadying her. The warmth of his hand penetrated through glove and sleeve. Claire lifted her gaze to meet his. They were alone, more truly alone than they had ever been. Though he did not touch her directly, she heard the catch in his breath as he saw the passion in her eyes. Weariness fled, and Claire reached up, encircling Adrian's neck with her arms. He pulled back, but the next moment his mouth was seeking hers hungrily. The heat of his tongue invaded, sinuous against hers, greedy as if time, and fear, and denial, were no more. She reveled in his sweet ravenousness, and her own greed startled her. Her body bent to him like a sapling in a storm. Without the bulk of her skirts, the lean muscularity of his torso and sinewy thighs pressed hard against her. Her breasts crushed softly against his chest, and her nipples drew hard and tight. Desire coursed through her, a sudden bright heat blooming from her core. She moaned.

Adrian drew back and looked at her, his gaze a tumult of fear, anger, and desire. His grip tightened, holding her fast as he lifted her off her feet, dragging her close as his mouth descended again. His kiss was ferocious, ruthless, obliterating. Suddenly, the world swirled, coiling into a dark vortex. His embrace was the same pitiless grip that had dragged her into the boat, onto the deep water of the river. In a heartbeat, his thrilling strength became threatening. Claire went rigid as a cold wash of fear doused the heat.

Adrian tensed, as if the chill radiating through her froze him as well. The hold that had seemed inescapable eased for an instant, clenched tight, and then opened. He released her and stepped away. His chest rose and fell with his quickened breathing, but he did not say what was obvious to them both. Claire could feel how her fear wounded him, shamed him. She thought she had overcome her apprehension of him at the tavern, but now sour notes of doubt played havoc with her nerves.

"I'm sorry," she whispered. She had never been alone with him before at night. Fear crept nearer, though only a moment before that thought had stirred her desire.

"You must go back," Adrian urged. "You want to trust me, Claire, but you don't."

"I do!" she cried, to convince him and herself. "Even you admitted a moment of doubt."

"So I did. And I confess I no longer trust myself." His smile was mocking.

"You are trying to frighten me!" she cried, angry with him now. Had the fierceness of his kiss been meant to drive her away?

"Perhaps I am. This venture is folly. You are ruining yourself for nothing—and I am permitting it for pure selfishness. I will accompany you to the outskirts of the nearest town, and you can say I finally let you go."

"And have them searching for you with a far more accurate radius than London?"

He arched an eyebrow. "Then devise a story to misdirect them, Claire."

"No," she insisted stubbornly, hating the thrum of fear that lingered, a discord reverberating in her mind, fraying the true connection between them. Being forced onto the river had undermined her utterly, shattered her will and the confidence she had spent months building. Fear rose all too easily.

But she had not stopped loving him. She must hold fast. Yet this morning, after the horrific discovery of Lady Margaret's body, she had tried to reach him through touch, and could not sense him. Despite herself she wondered again why. If Rafe was right, some force had overtaken Adrian, and acted through him to destroy Lady Margaret. But Adrian said he had been drugged—with something different, or something more lingering than Quarrell had used before. That drug had blunted their connection—and intensified her damnable doubt.

Impulsively, Claire reached for him, yearning for a touch that would reaffirm the gentle strength she sensed at the heart of him, hoping for a touch that would show him her own sincere repentance.

Quickly, he stepped beyond reach.

Claire lowered her hand, but insisted, "I will not leave you."

Adrian sighed heavily. "Let us eat."

From the satchel he took the beef pasty that Moll had purchased and an apple, cutting them in half. Claire chewed on the meat and crust unhappily. It might as well have been leather and glue, and the split apple their divided hearts. After they were done, Adrian nodded toward a nearby oak. "You will sleep in that tree. I will give you all the weapons."

Was it because she had been afraid of him? Or did he fear to be alone with her if he held them? She was furious with these gadfly doubts. "We will be safer from highwaymen if you keep them."

"Perhaps, but you will sleep better." He handed them to her with a bow, withdrawing behind the amused irony he used to defend himself. "I will take the first watch. If you hear me climbing up the tree to get you, kill me."

She did not laugh at his shabby joke, but strapped on the steel and stuffed the gun's barrel in the stable boy's pants. Her brother Gabriel had taught her to shoot a gun. But now, with her stiff fingers, Claire could fire it clumsily at best. She would manage somehow, if she must. "My hand is no longer nimble, so when the highwaymen come, wake me quickly."

Kneeling, he boosted her into one oak, and then climbed another nearby.

That night she slept fitfully, she wedged in her tree, he in his.

The rising chatter of birdsong woke Claire at dawn. Pale light glistened on the leaves, barely revealing their changing autumn hues. The peculiar environment disoriented her for a moment, then she saw the guns wedged between the branches above her, and memory awoke. Safe in the crotch of the oak, she felt even more a fool for her doubt. If some evil force possessed Adrian in his sleep and drove him to murder unawares, surely he would have killed her last night. But no stealthy night prowling had disturbed her rest. Perhaps his movement this morning had awakened her, but he was not fixed on murderous purpose. Instead, he roved below her, laying out their breakfast on a smooth rock beside the softly plashing stream.

She supposed Rafe would argue that such a lurking fiend would be clever enough to know her perch in the tree and readiness of the guns protected her. She even supposed he could be right. But Quarrell was fiend enough for Claire. He was bent on destroying Adrian's sanity, his life. With her distrust, she had helped their enemy.

Claire clambered down and greeted Adrian with a tentative smile. "Good morning."

He accepted the weapons she returned. "You slept well I trust."

"Well enough for having a tree for a bed."

Adrian gestured for her to join him at the simple meal and settled cross-legged across from her on the rock. There were small chunks of bread and cheese, another apple, and a few wild blackberries he had found. She had hoped that the food was set out as a gesture of forgiveness, but it was only his unfailing courtesy. His demeanor was charming, detached, as if they were not fleeing deadly pursuit. The rising sun picked out glints of gold and copper in his hair, so tempting that she curled her fingers into fists to keep from stroking it. He offered her the fruit, his lips moist with the purple berry juice. Claire wanted to taste their flavor and caress their shape with her tongue. But Adrian's smile was remote, and his eyes full of shadows, like leaf-shaded water. An arm's length away, he seemed to sit behind a crystal shield that would repel any touch.

She would have no taste of him this morning, and must content herself with bread and berries. After a few bites, she asked. "How long will we stay in Amesbury?" There was no guarantee his old nurse would shelter him.

"I don't know. Sir Nigel has already spoken to my cousin, though I doubt James would know her whereabouts, or even think to give her name." He tore a chunk of bread in half. "His family always did its best to ignore anything to do with my mother and her kin."

"But you cannot be certain of his ignorance," Claire said.

"No, my father may have kept a record of her. Sir Nigel will follow any lead to track me down."

All the more because she was with him, Claire thought, nibbling her apple to make it last. Sir Nigel might believe her already murdered. Conversely, the searchers would be less likely to shoot Adrian out of hand if she remained by his side.

Adrian must be considering the same things, but what he said was, "Certainly, Sir Nigel will send men to watch the ports, especially any ships bound for Ireland. He will send men to search any estates my father owned. Perhaps he will investigate my past, and speak to friends I had at Cambridge."

"And would any of them shelter you?"

He stood up, dusting the crumbs from his hands. "None of them would risk so much for a man who offered no more than a pleasant acquaintance."

"Because you refused a deeper knowledge?" she asked, remembering what he had said to her in the tower.

"I chose the shallows." Adrian's voice was light, even as he added, "A relationship of any depth threatened drowning."

Chills coursed along her spine at the image, and Claire wondered if he tried to distance her deliberately. She suspected so, despite the smile that lay so lightly on his lips. Was this cool condescension the sharp-tipped weapon he used against those who approached too close?

Battling her hurt, her anger, Claire stood and faced him. "It is difficult enough to find true friends. Now that you have them, you will find they will stand by you."

"As has Rafe?" he queried.

"He protects those he has known longest and loved best." Compassion softened her resentment. How lonely Adrian must have been, always withdrawing from true intimacy. Meshed with his male beauty, that aloof demeanor must have made him all the more alluring to his admirers. Like an elusive prince of Faerie, he would have seemed forever beyond reach. His grace and charm were disarming, captivating, yet the sorrow behind them evoked a deeper longing. He must have broken hearts without trying.

Now her own heart was aching, but the fault was as much hers as his. Adrian had to know the game he played did him as much harm as good, but her regret made it difficult to challenge him. He did not blame her for being frightened, but he had needed her belief in him. Her doubt had wounded him, and Claire did not know when he would be open to her again.

They risked a few hours on the open road, not stopping, but soon took to the cover of the woods again, skirting around the towns. Both road and wood were dangerous, and they were lucky they encountered no highwaymen. Adrian kept one gun prominently displayed, the other hidden.

Now truly underway, Claire brooded on the future. What would happen if Quarrell's guilt went undiscovered? What if Mistress Boyle refused them sanctuary? They had been prodigal with their wealth in escaping London. Who knew how long they would travel thus. If such questions buzzed as persistently in Adrian's mind, he did not mention them. To distract herself, Claire began to recount this year's scandals at the court.

" 'Tis not unlike Bedlam," Adrian said sardonically. When she fell silent, he relented and began to ask more about her life, though he chose questions that allowed him distance. "Your parents were among those who hosted the Queen's progress last year, were they not?"

"It was a great honor," Claire replied. "One that could not be refused."

"Ah," he said, understanding the difficulties. "A great responsibility as well."

"Yes. Although my father does not pretend to be able to foretell the future, the Queen sometimes consults him on predictions made by her favorite seers. I believe she has a certain fondness for him, and offered him the opportunity to further impress her. He would have been happier tinkering in his laboratory, of course. His search is more for wisdom than power."

"And your mother?" Adrian asked.

"She was rapturous—but all the lavish, extravagant entertainments meant to curry favor went for naught when she committed the disastrous mistake of wearing a gown more opulent than the Queen's."

Perhaps she sounded smug, for he asked. "You are at odds?"

"Yes," Claire admitted. "Though I admire my mother's beauty and charm, as all do, her willfulness can be heedlessly cruel. She wishes to weave us to her chosen patterns, which none save my eldest brother ever fit. As a child I strove to win her smiles, for they made the world bright. But her pleasure was hard won. There was always something one forgot that would have made the attempt perfect."

His smile was so bitter, she had to ask, "It was the same with you?"

"After my mother was locked away, my father took me back to England. I tried to be the perfect son. There was little praise for my triumphs, much criticism for my failures,"

Adrian said, then added, "But I needed no special touch to tell that your father loves you, and sees your strength."

"And my weaknesses," she said. "My father sees us each unique."

"Your eldest brother, is he the perfect son your mother dotes on?"

"Ambitious, but not daring. Rock solid, save when she extends a fingertip to tilt him this way or that." Claire shrugged a little. "Tom bores her, though she praises him to others."

"And Gabriel?"

"Gabriel she chided but adored. Perhaps I loved him so because he had all her virtues and few of her flaws." Claire paused, for grief was still keen, but a warm rush of memories swept through her. She told Adrian of the music and laughter she had shared with Gabriel, and how she'd envied his adventures with Rafe. "Gabriel took me to the theater once, in the boy's garb I wore to the Buzzing Hornet. He warned me not to tell Rafe, for fear it would scandalize him. I discovered he was quite right."

Humor flickered in Adrian's eyes at the memory of her appearance at the Buzzing Hornet. "So, you ran off with me solely as an excuse to wear breeches?"

"To be sure." Her heart lifted at his unguarded warmth.

His gaze dipped, tracing the shape of her calf, then quickly turned away. Knowing he must be aware of her, she allowed her eyes to savor the lean muscles of his thigh pressed against his mount. He glanced at her askance, but his lips quirked with a smile. "Scandalous."

She laughed aloud. Despite the rift of last night, despite the carefully calculated distance Adrian had kept till that moment, despite the madness of their journey, Claire knew she belonged by his side. Here she would stay unless he truly did abandon her.

And if he did? If her love could not defeat his fears?

Indeed there would be a scandal, but Claire found she did not care. She would be sent from Court, and she would miss that service. Demanding as she was, Queen Elizabeth was also brilliant and fascinating. But Claire did not need to live amid that ceaseless buzz of intrigue. The quieter riches of a country life would well content her.

Given the importance of her family, she would not be entirely ruined, but her choices would be much diminished. Her mother would be on a rampage—an exquisite wave of black silk and frothy lace, sweeping everything in her path. She would be furious that Claire had twice lowered the price she could have commanded—first with a scarred hand, and now a mangled reputation. Lady Brightsea would search out a suitor for whom a little scandal did not overtop the desire to marry an Earl's daughter. She was entirely capable of locking Claire in her room to force her submission. Her father would always consider her happiness, but under these circumstances, he might well agree that a quick marriage was the wisest course.

Claire did not want anyone but Adrian. She would fight for her happiness, and his. "You should marry me."

He tensed in his saddle, but did not turn to look at her. "Not even to save you from dishonor."

"Not for my sake, for your own. We will prove Quarrell is the killer, but even then you will be vulnerable to James. If we marry, I can protect you—if the worst you fear happens."

"If we prove me innocent of murder, James will be all the more shamed by what he has done. If madness overtakes me, he will see that I am tended as my mother was."

"Shame is no substitute for love," Claire said sharply. "You cannot trust him."

His own tone stayed maddeningly calm. "I am selfish to refuse your generosity, but I would be far more selfish to accept."

"You asked me to believe that you love me." She challenged him to evade his own words. "Do you?"

He hesitated, then said, "From the moment I saw you, I believe."

"Then—"

"Let me love you enough not to inflict my father's fate upon you."

"And if your fear is for naught?" she asked.

"Then I will have protected your children from the curse I carry."

This was his greatest fear, but it was not hers. He had been taught to deny himself, and denial had increased his fear. She would love and accept any child of his. "You were taught to hate and fear this in yourself."

"My fear is not some idle fancy." He cupped a hand over one eye, like a patch. "My mother blinded my father in her madness. I may have killed him in mine. There is nothing more to be said."

"For today." She would agree to no more than that.

He turned to face her, desperation etched on his face. "I do not want your love to turn to hate. I do not want to loathe myself for making it so."

"I could never hate you, Adrian."

"I imagine my father thought so, when he married my mother. Instead her madness trapped him."

"And destroyed his love?" Claire asked.

He was quiet for a moment. "It wrapped around it, twisted and choking. Even her death did not free him—" Adrian reined his horse abruptly, his hands clenching the reins. His face drained of color and he closed his eyes tightly.

Claire held her mount, saying nothing as Adrian fought for control. When he opened his eyes, she asked, "Have you remembered something?"

"Yes." He drew a steadying breath, then spoke slowly. "I remember meeting my father at the docks. He wore mourning. I did not tell him I had already dreamed my mother was dead."

She sensed there was more and stayed quiet.

"He said she was . . . at peace." For a moment he struggled for breath, as if the memory smothered him. "He admitted that he'd . . . wished for her death. For his freedom. His peace." He paused again, pale and sweating, then shook his head. "That is all."

"Do you think her death freed him Adrian?" she asked quietly.

"His confession only proved its opposite. He had found no escape." Adrian looked at her, his gaze bleak. "You should escape while you can."

"You should accept that we are bound. Our peace will be found together, not apart."

The rest of the day, they spoke of safer things, politics, music, and the passing countryside. Sunset hues of saffron and carmine tinted the sky as they rounded the far edge of Winchester. The bold form of the cathedral showed stark beyond the dark-needled yews, the bright-leafed oaks and beeches growing thick on the hillsides. They followed another stream into the woods and discovered a pleasant clearing well hidden from the road. Claire waited while Adrian dismounted, but made no move to help her tonight. He had avoided touching her all day, even protected by his gloves. Being so close, man and woman, was a threat.

Claire got down from the saddle herself, her thighs aching from the long ride. Adrian handed her the packs and tended to the horses while she laid out the food. Even with her back turned, she was aware of him, her mind giving shape to the sounds he made, her body responding as if her nerves were randomly plucked. She glanced over her shoulder, and saw his graceful movements laced with wariness. Silently they ate the last of the bread and cheese while dusk turned the sky purple, and needlepoint stars pricked through. After the meal, Adrian once again handed her the weapons, but this time Claire handed them back.

"Climb a tree if you must. I have no need to escape you," she told him with some asperity. "Tonight I sleep on the grass."

He looked as he would argue, and then thought better of it. But he did look about. "We were on higher ground before. It's not safe here."

"We will share the watch." And since Claire could not trust him not to spend the night awake, she leaned back against the trunk of the broadest tree and wrapped her cape about her. "Sleep. I will wake you."

Darkness settled about them. At first Adrian seemed as restlessly aware of her presence as she was of his, but at last his breathing evened into sleep. As Claire kept watch, she listened to his quiet respirations woven into the sibilant rustle of the leaves in the breeze and the soft purling music of the stream flowing by. The moon rose over the trees, almost at the full. Hazy light silvered the grove, glistening in the water of the stream and giving shape to trees and rocks. The faint light showed her Adrian's form only when he moved. She found herself following the outlines painted by the moon, the high angle of his shoulders and slope of his back. Forcing her attention away from him, she listened to the rustles within the night forest. But it was not fear of human or animal intruders that made her quiver with tension. Strung taut with desire, her nerves vibrated. There was no conversation to buffer her awareness of his body.

Close. So close . . .

Claire had kept watch for perhaps an hour when Adrian started to dream. He moved restlessly, moaning low in his throat. She moved toward him instinctively, then checked herself and leaned back against the trunk of the tree. She whispered his name in the darkness, hoping to draw him up from the dream without quite waking him. His sleep did not ease. Instead, his moans grew more frequent, along with muttered protests. She rose and moved toward him, stepping as quietly as she could on the mossy ground near the stream. For a moment, she stood over him, uncertain. She need only call his name more loudly, or shake him. But she did not want him to wake, only to escape the nightmare that gripped him.

Kneeling beside him, Claire reached out and rested a hand on his shoulder, the thick wool of his cape faintly rough under her stiff fingers. She whispered his name again, a soothing murmur. Adrian moved restlessly, muttering something unintelligible, followed by another moan. The cloth was a barrier, she told herself. She waited a moment, calming her own breathing, letting her tenderness, her love for him well up inside her. Reaching up with her good hand, she stroked his forehead with her fingertips, gliding her fingers into his hair.

Under her touch, he sighed and quieted.

"Yes," she whispered. "Sleep."

She had not once thought that it might be some dark force in him struggling to the surface, some demon breaking free. Her fear was truly gone, she only longed to comfort him. And she had.

Now she should move away.

But what harm was she doing? Her touch soothed him. Claire continued to comb her fingers through his hair in a slow caress. Her own skin came alive, tingling where the strands flowed between her fingers. Still asleep, he turned his head toward her, and the moonlight caught the translucent gleam of a tear at the far corner of his eyes. A strange starvation gripped her, a need for taste as well as touch. She kissed the tear away, then licked the dampness from her lips, a salty drop of sorrow. It made her ache for him, deepening the hunger.

He exhaled a sigh even as she did. She shivered, but with a flush of heat that warmed her from the pit of her belly outward. Barely touching, the tip of her tongue brushed against his skin. Such a simple flavor, a faint salty sweetness, yet the sample made her desire more, to taste everywhere, lick everywhere. Her lips glided along the angle of his cheekbone, then down into curve beneath, feeling the roughness of his sprouting beard. As if magnetized, her hand reached to caress his other cheek, and glide down the column of his throat. His leather jerkin and linen were open at the front, enough that she could slide her hand into the opening and feel the strong line of his collarbones and the tender hollow between. The soft percussion of his pulse under her fingertips felt like a message from his heart. Her hand moved lower, and his soft chest hair brushed against her palm, tickling. In daylight she had glimpsed it through his linen, a darker bronze than the metallic hues that waved back from forehead and temple.

Now there was only the feel of it, rough-sleek as cat's fur, tempting her fingers to stroke.

Her hand slid deeper still, her fingertips skimming over the round of a tender-skinned nipple, softness of his chest hair. At her touch, the tiny nub hardened, thrusting up against her fingertips. She drew her hand away, pressing it over her breasts, where her own nipples had tightened at his response. Claire wondered if the hair below, the nest for his manhood, would be darker, more crinkled than the diamond-shaped patch on his chest? Would his sex rise to her touch as swiftly as his nipples? Would she dare such a touch? Heat pooled between her legs at the wanton image. The hunger to see him, to stroke him so intimately, was acute, devouring her resistance. Sight was impossible, but touch . . .

Adrian moved restlessly, moaning in his sleep. Warning clamored unheeded in her mind. Compelled by need, she stroked along his torso, feeling the radiant heat of his body through the linen shirt—then lower, her fingers moving along the worn leather of his breeches. A tremor coursed through her when she touched what she sought, the hardness of him swollen and straining against the leather. His heat was fiercer here, and she could feel him throb even through the leather.

Stop, she commanded silently. Futilely. Her hand tightened against the thickened shape of him, heat searing her palm. Her eyes closed, conjuring the hidden shape that she touched, then opened when Adrian gave a low moan. Apprehensive, Claire eased the pressure of her hand, but could not bear to withdraw it. Her heart racketed so loudly, the sound alone should wake him. Instead, he moaned again, his brow creasing to a frown. Did the nightmares encroach when she retreated? Her hovering hand descended, molded to him. At her touch, Adrian cast his head back, his lips parting as if he drank in desire with every breath. She wanted to fill his mouth with her kisses. Hot spiced wine could not be more intoxicating than his taste. She licked her lips and the wet sensation of her own tongue startled her.

Virgin as she was, she knew from the bawdy talk at Court

that she could caress him so, with her tongue as well as her hand. Knew that she could hold him in her mouth as well as in the throbbing core of her sex. Another flush of heat warmed her, spreading from that hot core up into her belly, down through her thighs. She parted her legs more, as if the gesture would cool her heat. This secret seduction was wicked. Yet his response seemed truer than all his denials. He did not wake because she was no threat. And if he did wake? When he did?

Stop! Her muffled plea faded to silence. Locked within this waking dream, part of her watched, part acted on desire. Her hands moved of their own accord, pressing against him till he moaned again. Not denial, surely, but assent. She felt their connection so deeply in her heart, in her spirit—but she was flesh and flesh wanted its match, its union. His leather gloves, his leather breeches were both impediments to the fusion of their being. She dared not try and remove his gloves.

Aroused, terrified, Claire whispered his name, asking permission for her invasion.

"Claire . . ." Adrian whispered her name on a breath, as if he granted it.

She waited, trembling, but he did not wake. She did not wake him.

With shaking fingers, Claire loosened his breeches. Slowly, she slid her hand inside. She could feel the coarser hair brush against her fingers, the sudden leap of his cock seeking her hand. She gasped at the burning heat of his skin, the thrusting carnality of hard flesh. His difference was so blatant, so shocking, that she almost pulled her hand away. The feel of his rampant arousal made what was happening more real—yet more unreal. His skin was hot satin, moist. Her fingertips traced along the length of him. Adrian drew a long hissing breath, arching in his sleep. She was trembling all over, trapped in a mesh of anxiety and desire. The pulse between her legs throbbed fiercely, demanding. She felt wet there, hot, alive.

All her frustration flamed into voracious desire. Her hand closed around the long hard length of him. A sudden urgency raced through her blood as he arched again, higher now. He gave a wild cry as he suddenly woke, reaching up to seize her arms in a fierce grip. He stared into her eyes, his own wide and glittering in the moonlight. His sex swelled in her hand. His lips opened in a silent protest—a silent plea. Her hand tightened. He gave a choked cry and she felt him pulsing, pulsing in her grasp. Warm wetness bathed her hand. His gaze held hers, desperate and amazed as he shuddered in the throes of pleasure.

His hard grip loosened. He sagged back, panting, still staring up at her. His hands tightened on her forearms, and she thought for a moment he would pull her into an embrace. Then he jerked back, knocking her hand away. Anger flashed across his face, and she shrank back. The next instant, it was gone, locked inside him again. He drew away from her, breathing harshly. The darkness of the grove deepened as the moon buried itself in a mass of clouds.

"Am I to believe you are a succubus, seducing men while they sleep?" His melodious voice dripped sarcasm. "Or was this yet another proposal of marriage?"

Claire was flaming hot now, but with shame rather than desire. How could she have let herself molest him while he slept, defenseless? What excuse did she have—her name whispered in his sleep? She wished he would rage at her, rather then regard her so coldly. "You were having a nightmare," she whispered. "Forgive me. I only meant to comfort you."

"Oh, I am marvelously well comforted." Cold as they were, his caustic words burned.

"It began so—" Without warning, the memory of his hardness filled her hand. She felt the leap of his sex as it flung forth its seed. Comfort was truth. So was the searing fire. She wanted more of him, his kisses, his touches. She wanted to feel him inside her. Her voice was choked with longing. "Adrian . . ."

"Forgive me if I do not offer comfort in kind." Abruptly, he stood and went into the woods, leaving her alone in the clearing. She sat for a moment, biting her lip to hold back her tears, then washed her hands in the stream. The minutes crawled by. Every rustling of the leaves boded his footfall, but he did not come. Her arms ached where he had gripped them. Tomorrow they would be bruised. But not so bruised as her heart. She wondered if Adrian was waiting for her to go back to sleep. She could not. Claire crept back to her post, waiting, watching the descending moon. Was he so angry that he would leave, walk off into the night? No, not that angry or that foolish. But the fear made her shiver. Finally he returned, walking cautiously in the moonlight. He went directly to his bed of leaves, doing his best to ignore her.

"Adrian," she whispered.

His faint movement stilled.

"Please—forgive me," she asked again.

He looked at her briefly. "You are forgiven."

She did not believe him. He did not forgive her, or himself. He was wrapped in anger again, like a dark, smothering cloak. "Don't lie," she pleaded. "You've never lied to me."

He must hate her. Quarrell had come to him in his cell, bringing nightmares with him. Even if she had meant no harm at the start, she had behaved like a wicked, greedy child.

"I dreamed of you," Adrian said, as if he could read her thoughts. "I wanted you. Perhaps I seduced you with my desire."

If so, it was not till her touch had lured him.

"You were asleep," she murmured. "I am ashamed to have betrayed you so."

He shook his head, "I betrayed you. Dragging you across the Thames. Letting you follow me. I did not want to let you go."

So he hated himself, not her. "You know that I do not want to leave you."

"Claire—"

"Listen," she pleaded. "If as you say, you will not marry me, this may be the only time we have. We do not need to risk begetting a child. We may still touch, kiss—"

"No!" He drew a sharp breath. "If I begin to touch you, I

cannot trust myself to stop." His tone was still harsh as he said. "Perhaps you can understand that."

She understood all too well.

"Sleep," he ordered her. "I will take the watch."

Hollow-eyed from lack of sleep they rose at dawn and set out once more, riding past Salisbury in silence. Impatient with their mutual brooding, Claire began again to tell Adrian more of what she'd learned of the science of alchemy and of her father's new interest in Giordano Bruno's books on the art of memory. It stirred his interest and the tension between them eased a little. But only a little. The morning was the pursuit of alchemical mysteries, the afternoon, the music theories of the Queen's new Italian lute master. By sunset, Amesbury was close at hand. Finding a quiet grove, they waited on the outskirts till nightfall, then crossed the River Avon and made their way to the small farm that Adrian remembered visiting, with the separate cottage built for Mistress Boyle. Dismounting, they hid their horses behind the barn and made their way quietly around the garden, searching for glimpses of the nurse. The window of oiled cloth did not give them a clear view, but it seemed that one figure moved within.

Claire reached out to touch him, then withdrew her hand. But the movement caught his attention. She said, "Let me go ahead. If Sir Nigel has sent men, it will not matter if they capture me. You may still be able to escape."

"If they knew to come here, escape will be difficult," Adrian answered her. "But go ahead. I do not know if Morna believes me to be dead or alive. It will be better if you prepare her than if I appear like a ghost."

"A most dusty ghost," Claire said lightly, and received a small smile in return. Cheered, she tugged her cap low on her forehead, raised the collar of her cape high. "Wait here. If it is safe, I will signal you." She gave one of the birdcalls she'd learned as a child, playing with her brothers. Adrian flashed a smile in response to the soft chirruping notes of the thrush, Claire grinned as their elusive accord returned.

She made her way to the wattle and daub cottage and knocked at the door. An older woman opened it, but only part way. Her body and face were broad and strong, her blue eyes intent. When she spoke, her voice was unexpectedly deep, its textured nap oddly comforting. "What do you want, lad?"

"Are you Mistress Boyle?" Claire asked, trying to keep her voice low.

"All my life, or the parts I can remember." Her tone was wary, but so she might be when any stranger knocked on her door late at night.

"I have a message from Lord Roadnight—" Claire began.

"And which one is it that's sent you—Sir Adrian, or Sir James?"

Morna Boyle knew Adrian was alive then. And knew what he'd been accused of, for she shut the door down to a crack.

"If you are afraid, or think it not safe to speak, I will trouble you no more." Claire moved back a step, wondering if the door would close in her face.

Instead, the old woman leaned forward, peering through the crack. "Who are you? Not a lad."

She decided truth would serve best. "I am Lady Claire Darren. Have you heard of me?"

"That I have. They said Lord Roadnight carried you off to murder."

"As you see, I am quite alive. And I am here now of my own choice," she said. "Whoever *they* are, they are hunting an innocent man while the guilty one goes free."

Morna relaxed a fraction, and the door opened a bit more. Claire realized the old nurse was holding one arm out of sight behind it, and wondered what she hid. A knife? An axe?

"Who told you of us?" Claire asked her.

"The two men who were here this morning, from the crown so they said."

"What did they look like?"

"There was a big pink lout named Flaxman, who made a lot of noise. The bearded one, Grey, didn't say much, but he was in command."

"Are they still in Amesbury?" Claire quelled the impulse to glance about. They were gone or they were hiding out of sight. But she was convinced they were not within the cottage.

"Been and gone. One made mention of riding to the Thorne estates to the west," Morna said. "I couldn't swear they've ridden on, but no one's seen them about town this afternoon. That I asked."

"They told you of the trouble in London?" Claire asked

"Aye. They said Sir Adrian's gone mad, like his mother before him. I said he'd not been here, and that I'd had enough of madness besides," Morna answered. "They warned me that he might come here and kill me as well."

"Sir Adrian is here, meaning no harm, but hoping for your help. If you cannot trust us, we will go."

Morna gave an exasperated sigh, and placed whatever she was holding down next to the door with a chunk. "Summon him, then. I have no reason to believe what two other strangers said—one too nice and the other too mean to be trusted."

Claire beckoned Adrian with her warbling birdcall. He emerged from the shadows beneath the trees and walked toward the cottage door with easy grace. Moonlight glimmered on his hair and caressed his face with opalescent light, marking the winged arch of his brows and high cheekbones, the sculptured curve of his lips. His unique beauty made her catch her breath, his visage a match for his luminous spirit, his quiet inner strength. But that beauty was sensuous too. Desire stirred with her memories of his skin against her lips, her fingertips.

Claire did not want to claim him dishonestly. Last night the temptation had been too strong to resist. Though she ached to reclaim him, ached in her very flesh, she and she alone had sundered their rapport. She dared not risk another such disaster. Like the unicorn, Adrian had disappeared when she pursued him. He might come if she waited. But would the soft invitation of her lap seem a sweet haven, or a trap?

Filled with uncertainty, Claire watched as Adrian approached Morna. The old woman gave him a beaming smile, and she held out her hands in welcome.

Chapter 14

⌒⌒⌒

Adrian walked to Morna and accepted the warm hand-clasp she offered. He still felt raw and vulnerable after what had happened with Claire, but there was no reason to be wary of her touch while he wore his gloves. Morna smiled, and Adrian saw the glimmer of tears in the corners of her eyes. Though leather lay between their skins, a sense of human comfort wrapped him, warm as a blanket. He had relied on her steadfast warmth as a child. As a man, he'd been grateful for her devotion to his mother. But he had not known if her loyalty would be resolute in the face of charges of madness. Looking into her wise blue eyes, he murmured, "Thank you."

Morna responded with a reassuring nod and stepped away so they could enter her cottage. Inside, the simple room was clean and neat, the flagstone floor swept clean. One candle cast a lopsided halo on the table and bench. A smaller light glowed beside the bed in the tiny room beyond. As Morna stepped back, Claire glanced down beside the door. Following her gaze, Adrian saw a hatchet resting there.

"They were frightening me fierce, those men," Morna said with a rueful shrug. "So I went and got that from the barn to protect me tonight. It wasn't just their wild tales about you, Sir Adrian. The lout was frightening enough just standing there breathing. The other one spoke soft and well mannered, but his eyes missed nothing. I'd not be surprised if he could number the plates in my cupboard. Grey he said his name was, though when they walked away the lout called him Graile." She repeated what she'd told Claire about the two men, then added, "But it was hard to believe what they said— that you'd murdered four women. You who always had such a gentle heart, my lord."

"Four?" Adrian said, aghast. "Penelope, Lady Margaret, Claire supposedly—"

"Vivian," Claire whispered, and Adrian exchanged a fearful glance with her. Could Quarrel have killed her in revenge?

"Vivian? No, that was not the name," Morna said, taking a seat on the bench by the table. She nodded solemnly. "There— a fine murderer you are, not to know your own victims."

Adrian was relieved that Vivian was not dead, but who was? He sat beside Morna. "Do you remember the name of the other woman?"

"Aye, for she was the one they used to warn me. 'Twas Mary they called her. They said she'd been your nurse in Bedlam and I'd be no safer than she."

"Sister Mary," Adrian's voice broke on the name. For a moment he could not speak, as memory after memory of her kindness returned. Then he said, "Quarrell has killed her as well."

"Who would this Quarrell be?" Morna asked.

"The doctor who held me in Bedlam." He fought the urge to reach out to Claire, to steady himself with her warmth and strength.

"That was true, then? You were locked away?" Suspicion returned to Morna's voice.

Adrian faced her. "My mother's gift came to me, Morna, though I did not want it."

"How long ago was this?"

Adrian looked away. "Seven, perhaps eight months ago."

"When my lady died?"

"After," Adrian said, though it had first stirred then. "The night my father returned from Ireland, bringing news of it."

Filled with misery, Adrian went to his father and embraced him, receiving a listless touch in return. Then his father pulled away. "It was a fierce ague which settled in her lungs," he said. "She's free at last."

"At peace." Adrian could barely form the words. The final acknowledgment stunned him.

"I wished for her death," his father said. "For my freedom. My peace."

Adrian was shocked his father would say so, but worried by his ghastly pallor, his listless tone. "Come into the tavern, Father. Have some hippocras to warm you."

"I could drink a cup before we go."

Adrian paid two sailors to guard the trunks removed from the Kestrel. He guided his father to the nearest tavern and got them a private room upstairs. The spiced red wine arrived quickly, but his father barely sipped it.

"You always had it, though you fought it long and hard." Morna sighed. "I did fear it would take you unawares."

"I still do not remember how it happened." Adrian looked away, his fear rising too close to the surface.

Claire moved forward protectively. "Adrian suffered a blow to the head. He lost his memory, so they took him to Bedlam. When he did recall his identity, his cousin denied him. Sir James let the world believe Sir Adrian had died."

"A Judas." Morna sucked in her breath. "They say we Irish cannot be trusted, and so betray us first."

"True enough," he agreed.

"Did your father bring you her bequests, then?" Morna asked Adrian. "When your mother was dying, she had me fill the box. I've no gift, but it seemed I could see her spirit moving into them."

"Her bequests? I never received them." Or had he?

"Outside on the dock." his father said, his voice heavy with grief and weariness. "What she left you is a small leather chest with the rest."

Adrian ran outside. On the foggy dock beside the ship, he searched through his father's trunks. Finally, he found a small leather chest and carried it back to the inn. His father waited, staring morosely into his wine. He did not even glance up as Adrian set the leather chest on the table, undid the straps and opened it. Inside lay smaller boxes of wood and metal.

"She gave you the dragon box," Morna said, "and put some mementos inside it."

Beside him, Claire drew a soft breath. Her father had conjured the image of a dragon.

Adrian remembered it at last, the mythic creature he'd loved as child. He'd sit by the narrow window of the castle with the carved box in his hand, tracing the sinuous curve of the dragon's back and tail, the sharp peak of its wings. He had not seen it for decades—

The dragon box rested on the scarred table of a dockside inn. Flickering light and shadow played like ghostly fingers over the carved scales, the talons.

He opened the box and a scarlet ribbon spilled forth, flowing liquid as blood.

Adrian rose abruptly, startling both Claire and Morna. He had seen the box, and the winged dragon had troubled his dreams ever since. He paced the small room, trying to drive away the images. For three days he had set his heart on this sanctuary. Now the impulse to move stabbed at him, goading him out into the night. Pivoting, he said to Morna, "We cannot stay here. I hoped they would not think of this place, at least so soon. Sir James must have recalled your name. Burne's men have visited once, and they will likely return."

He could not bring himself to look at Claire.

"You are both tired. Rest here tonight," Morna said. "You can go to my son's house at Marlborough, north by the Savernake Forest. I will take you there at dawn."

Adrian snatched at reasons for his change of heart. "That kindness would only raise suspicion. If you went away so soon, I think these hunters would come looking for you."

Instead, Morna told him how to find her son, and gave him a message that could come only from her. As she spoke, Adrian moved to the window. *What will I do when I get there?* he wondered. *Run again? Run, and drag Claire with me?*

"Did you hear something outside?" Claire asked.

"No, nothing. But I don't feel safe." Intuition, or only fear? "Burne's men could come back at any time."

"If that is what you believe," Claire said.

He looked with longing at the plain comfort of the cottage, clean and smelling of herbs and apples. But his skin prickled with warning. "I do. But you should stay here, Lady Claire. Enough money remains that Mistress Boyle can escort you back to London."

"I've made my choice," she said.

Desperation filled him. Why must she foolishly risk herself? What would dissuade her? "If the men return, you can testify that I have not harmed you."

"If they find you alone, they will kill you."

"Leave word with the local pastor, or with the constable," he argued.

"And have all hunting you. No."

"I cannot trust you," Adrian said cruelly. He did not believe she would try to seduce him again, but he could barely restrain himself from seizing her last night.

"You can trust me to follow you. To search for you," she

said, not caring if she shamed herself in front of the nurse. "I have proved it well."

He believed her. She had stayed with him despite his rejection, despite the ruin of her reputation. Worse, he wanted her to stay. Despite his denials, he thought constantly of marrying her. A wedding would save her from dishonor, and an unconsummated marriage could be annulled. But he was sure she would refuse the annulment. And he did not trust himself not to consummate the marriage.

But how could he endure it if, when, she married someone else? Worse still, if she was forced into a marriage without love because of his refusal?

When he said nothing, Claire spoke. "We began this journey together. We are meant to go on together."

He wanted her safe. But he wanted her with him. His own selfishness appalled him.

The urge to go snapped at his heels. "No."

"I will steal a horse if I have to," Claire said, trying to outguess his strategy.

He shook his head, defeated by her loyalty, by his own desire to keep her by his side, if only a little longer. "Let us go, then."

Quickly, Morna gathered up simple fare from her larder, pasties, cheese, nuts, and apples to take with them on the road. He tried to give her payment, but she refused, "When you're safe again, Sir Adrian, then I will take a gift from you."

"In future, I hope to give you more than gratitude for your generosity."

They gathered up the food and went out. Before they reached the gate, Morna hurried after him, resting her fingers on bare wrist. No images came to him, but he felt her earnest concern. "I know where it is you must go tonight, Sir Adrian. You must go to the henge."

Stonehenge—

The image of the ancient rocks rose in his mind, summoning him.

"No!" he said sharply. Then, after a moment, "Yes. Yes, I will."

Adrian brooded all the while that he rode, wondering if this night journey might be madness in itself. Clouds covered and revealed the bright full moon, its light guiding them toward their goal. In the distance, the henge seemed insignificant against the vastness of Salisbury plain. But as they drew close to the outer circle, the aspect shifted abruptly. The moon sailed free, revealing the awesome splendor of the gigantic stones. The rough-hewn blocks loomed up, over three times his height, the massive oblongs bathed in silver light, lintels laid across as if by a giant's hand.

"I have never been here before, but my father has spoken of these stones," Claire told him, her voice hushed. "I discounted the power of which he spoke, but now I feel it for myself."

He felt it too. The great stones emanated a primitive power, an ancient wisdom.

"In Ireland there are circles as well—stone dolmens," he said to her as they dismounted and led their horses toward the circle. "Not so tall as Stonehenge, yet they share the same essence. My father warned us away from such pagan places. But I could never resist them, and sneaked away alone. I felt safe within them for some reason I have never understood—especially since I was beaten for going there."

"If they gave you strength to endure, their safety was not illusory."

Claire beside him, Adrian entered the circle, feeling its ancient force surround him. Walking the perimeter, he reached to stroke the great stones, some textured, some worn smooth through the centuries by the touch of other hands. Their silent magnetism disturbed him, yet paradoxically the old feeling of safety encompassed him once more. Not from the world without—these giant blocks would not stop their pursuers. But he was calmed, as if while he stood here, humbly mortal before some power solemn and merciless yet not malevolent. Everything within him was aligned, his atoms one with earth, stone, wind, and cloud.

But once he stepped outside the henge, nothing would have changed.

Unless he changed it.

To the night, he said, "I run—but Death trails in my wake."

As if in answer, stillness settled over him, a quiet surety that did not deny the darkness that lay without this moment in time, this ancient sacred place. He turned to Claire, and felt a turning within his own soul. In the bright, pale light, the oval of her face looked pure and translucent as a moonstone. She might be the carving of an ancient goddess, but for the tender softness of her lips, the life that glowed in her dark eyes. Despite the fear he had evoked in her, despite the wall he had raised, despite his refusal of her passion, she had followed him loyally on this frantic journey. He was not worthy of the love she offered. Not yet. Perhaps never.

"I must go back," he told her. "Too many have died already because of me." Adrian grieved again for Sister Mary, her quiet strength and simple kindness. Quarrell had murdered her because that kindness had been offered to him. Would the doctor find Morna as well, as Burne's men had done? Would another innocent soul die because of him?

"Master Quarrell was a killer before he fastened on you," Claire said. "If you return, he will destroy you." He heard fear in her voice, the same fear he felt for her where Quarrell was concerned. But he heard another note as well. Hope? Approval?

"Sir Nigel may do so first, or my cousin. Master Quarrell spreads death and hatred like the plague. He must be stopped."

"How? How can you stop him?" she pleaded.

"I don't know." Anguish returned. "I always intended to do something—once I was safe, once I felt stronger. Instead I have run away, searching for a haven that doesn't exist."

"You are anything but safe, nor will you be while he lives," she agreed. "But are you strong enough now, Adrian?"

"I don't know," he said, and a shiver passed through him

even within this protective circle. "Until now my fear always weighed greater than my courage. I did not think I could stand against him."

"If he destroys you, he will not stop destroying others." She whispered, "I don't want to lose you."

"I think I have lost myself. Running seemed the only safety, but where is the end?"

"When Sir Nigel arrests Master Quarrell," she said.

"He may make no attempt, Claire, since he is certain of the identity of his wife's killer."

She began to speak, but Adrian hushed her. Horses were coming, their pace increasing as they neared the henge. They could mount and make a run for it, but was there any point in it now? If it was Burne's men, perhaps the time had come to give himself into their hands. But the riders might be thieves, following likely prey.

"We cannot be sure who they are," he whispered to Claire. He readied his snaphance and nodded for her to do the same.

Guns drawn, Adrian and Claire took cover behind the central stones. The dark forms of the riders crested the low hill, then split outside the circle, each moving midway round. Adrian heard the creak of saddle leather as they dismounted. A moment later, he glimpsed figures moving in the bright moonlight.

"It will be simpler if you surrender." The voice was low, but carried.

"Who are you?" Adrian asked.

"Servants of the Queen."

Adrian looked back and forth rapidly as the two men entered opposite sides of the henge, one moving smoothly, almost silently, the other lumbering. Their guns were drawn.

"Servants of Sir Nigel Burne, you mean."

"To be more exact." The dark-bearded man who spoke had a disconcerting calm. His eyes seemed almost expressionless, offering a perfunctory politeness that verged on disdain. "I am Grey, and he is Flaxman."

Grey, or perhaps Graile, so Morna had said. Adrian only nodded. "So, you were hiding near the cottage, waiting."

"Yes." Again, one soft-spoken syllable.

Flaxman stepped forward pugnaciously. "How was we to know the old woman was telling the truth? Even if she was, maybe you just hadn't gotten there yet." The man paused to glance at Grey. When he said nothing, Flaxman went on, "Better you hid here than on your own estate—with all them prying eyes and greedy fingers."

Greedy fingers? A reward then. A large one. From his cousin, or Burne, or both?

"You cannot escape us, Lord Roadnight," Grey insisted in the same quiet tone. "You have a gentleman's skill with arms. By necessity, ours is greater."

"Aye. We don't just prance about." Flaxman grinned broadly, but Adrian thought Grey's "ours" no more than professional courtesy.

Adrian had once been vain of his swordsmanship, but he had spent months in Bedlam with only such simple exercise as he could devise to keep up his strength. He would not choose to duel against a practiced assassin unless he had no choice. And this confrontation was with pistols. Grey's skill with a gun could easily overmatch his own.

All he said was, "I wanted to be certain you were not thieves."

"You have. Show yourself," Grey repeated. "Let Lady Claire come to our protection."

Adrian kept near to the cover of the great stones, but moved into view. Moonlight glinted on the barrel of his gun. "Lady Claire is free to go."

Claire did the same, standing close beside him. "I have no need of your protection," she told Grey. "I am safe as I am."

"In truth, we had just decided to return to London," Adrian said, unbelievable as that truth might seem to them.

Flaxman gave an incredulous snort. Grey tilted his head slightly, indicating curiosity.

Adrian explained, "Mistress Boyle just told me Sister Mary was murdered."

Flaxman pointed a finger at him. "You're the one what flayed her."

"No." Adrian ignored him, and spoke only to Grey. "I didn't. A physician named Edward Quarrell killed all three of them, and more besides."

Grey hesitated, frowning, then responded, "You fled London."

"I did not know that Sister Mary was dead then. She once risked her life to help me."

"And lost it," Flaxman sniggered.

"Yes. Exactly," Adrian said. "Now there is only one way to repay my debt to her."

"Most honorable," Grey murmured ambiguously. He moved slowly to the side.

"We 'ear you're good at spinning tales, my lord, but don't expect us to believe 'em." Flaxman laughed, moving the opposite way. "London's the other direction."

"You spun a tale to Mistress Boyle, telling her I was dead, though you can see well enough that I am alive and whole." Claire took a step toward Grey. "The truth is that we just decided to return to London."

Pausing, Grey appraised her. "Lord Roadnight abducted you from Sir Nigel Burne's estate. He promised to release you. He did not."

"He did release me. I chose to come with him."

"You do not seem to be his prisoner." Grey nodded solemnly. "But who is to say what threat he holds over you."

"None. He has not threatened me or harmed me, nor has he murdered anyone."

"So you say." He gestured to Adrian with his gun. "Your weapons, Lord Roadnight."

Adrian hesitated. They were likely to kill him out of hand if he resisted, and he could not risk Claire being injured or killed by mistake. He did not want to return in custody, but perhaps some benefit could be found in it. Stepping out from the shield of rock, he unbuckled and dropped his steel, then turned the gun and offered the butt of the weapon. With an uncertain glance at him, Claire did the same.

"Take the weapons, then bind Lord Roadnight," Grey ordered Flaxman. He looked at Claire as if he thought tying her would be wise as well, but did not command it.

Grey kept his gun trained on them as Flaxman grabbed Claire's gun and tucked it into his belt. Moving forward, he took hold of Adrian's bare wrist with bruising strength, and jerked the gun from his grasp. But Adrian learned the truth from that rough touch. He stumbled backward, disoriented by the jolt of brutal cunning. Claire grasped his arm and he turned to her quickly. "This is a trap."

She tensed, pressing closer to him. Adrian knew it was a risk to reveal what he'd learned, but their captors would want to separate them. Claire must know their intent. "If they did not kill me during capture, they were to make an excuse when you were out of sight—kill me and say I attempted to escape."

"Then I'll not let you out of my sight," Claire said. "I doubt they have orders to kill me."

Grey stood very still, his surprise showing in nothing more than a rapid blink.

"You spied on us?" Flaxman growled, baffled and angry. "When?"

"I must have," Adrian answered, though he kept his attention on the leader.

"My duty is to bring you back, alive or dead. Dead allowed more certainty than living," Grey's quiet inflection barely changed. "Since you have accused us in front of Lady Claire, it would not be wise of us to kill you—presuming such orders even existed."

"If Sir Nigel gave you such a command, it is because he believes Lord Roadnight guilty of murder," Claire told Grey. "He would not want him dead if he knew he was innocent."

"Presumably," Grey answered.

Adrian knew that guilt or innocence would not always be

Sir Nigel Burne's criteria. But the spymaster had no reason to order him dead other than revenge.

Grey still regarded him, his silvery gray eyes assessing. "Why did you surrender if you suspected we might kill you?"

Adrian did not answer.

Grey moved closer. "I don't like mysteries. Tell me how you knew."

Unlike Flaxman, this man would press for details. Adrian looked away, trying to think of a plausible lie. Another swift step and Grey took hold of his jaw, turning his face back. The surge of knowledge felled Adrian like a blow. He staggered against the assassin as the images battered him. The other man let go his hold and stepped back, uncertain what had happened, but aware of some current passing between them. Released, Adrian sank to his knees. Yet the power of the surrounding stones kept him in balance. The psychic assault did not decimate his mind.

"Adrian!" Claire cried out, suspecting what had transpired. Adrian lifted a hand to signal Claire he was all right. He could not speak yet. His body ached as if bruised. His lungs, his heart, his mind felt scoured.

"What's happening?" Flaxman called. "Has 'e gone mad in the full moon?"

"Nothing," the assassin answered, and then to Adrian, "Get up. Answer me."

He rose unsteadily to his feet as Grey watched with renewed suspicion. Adrian's new knowledge could mean his death, but it gave him power too. He moved closer, but the assassin lifted his gun, warning him to keep his distance. His voice a harsh whisper, Adrian said to him, "The blame is more theirs than yours. They hid his identity from you."

The response was also a whisper. "Whose?"

"Your father."

The pale mask of the assassin's face hardened into something implacable, and his eyes gleamed with cold, murderous fury. He pressed his gun to Adrian's heart. "Who told you? Was it Sir Nigel? Walsingham? Are you a rogue agent?"

"No," Adrian answered him.

The barrel dug deeper. His voice remained quiet. "Tell me how you know."

"The same way I know that Edward Quarrell kills helpless women," Adrian answered, keeping his voice low. "The way I know Flaxman wants to kill me. The way I know that of your many names, Graile is the oldest, save one. I know because you touched me and I felt it."

Graile stared at him, eyes narrowing as denial succumbed to belief.

"You are a warlock," Graile accused. His eyes flickered to the side, reassessing the ground on which they stood, the great stones that towered around them. "The murdered women were your blood sacrifices, and in return you have been given unholy power."

"No," he tried to think of an argument this man would believe. "If I were the warlock you believe me to be, and this place a diabolic circle, you would not have captured me."

"If you are the warlock I believe you to be, you will weave truth with lies to deceive me."

"I swear to you—"

"Your word is worth nothing!" Graile's voice grated, the vehemence fierce as a shout after his controlled tones. "You have sought sanctuary on unhallowed ground."

"This place is ancient, but not evil."

"What's going on, Graile?" Flaxman called out. "You need 'elp?"

"Stay there," Graile snapped over his shoulder. "Guard Lady Claire."

"Right. Just as you say." Flaxman's mutters were loud enough to carry. "World'd come to an end, and you'd not tell me."

"One shot," Graile said. His voice was quiet again, but Adrian could hear the strain. "You will be dead and everything you know with you."

"I understand your guilt." Adrian spoke softly. "It is a terrible burden."

"You understand nothing," the assassin hissed. His preternatural quiet suddenly teemed with violence.

Adrian knew that he was as close to death as he had ever come. Fear of Graile and pity for him mingled. He said quietly, "I understand perfectly, for I have the same fear."

Graile's face was the same smooth mask, but his eyes blazed even in the moonlight. "Lie or truth, either condemns you."

Adrian heard the hammer click back on the gun. An image leapt to his mind. "Before you kill me, know this. There is something here that is important—" The gun dug hard against his chest. His heart beat madly, as if to fly free of danger. "A talisman you will recognize."

"What?" Graile demanded. "What sorcery now?"

"I do not know why it is important, only that you have knowledge of it, or one like it," Adrian said. "Lady Claire must bring it."

"Flaxman, stay where you are," Graile ordered. "Keep your gun trained on Lady Claire, but let her come closer."

"They'll jump you," Flaxman growled, filled with distrust.

"Then you can shoot them."

Flaxman gave a bark of laughter, obviously relishing the thought.

"Claire." Adrian beckoned and came forward quickly, her gaze filled with concern. He wanted to touch her, yet dared not reach for that solace. Nothing must obscure the images so newly absorbed. "Lady Claire, will you show Master Grey the dragon brooch?"

Graile tensed at his words.

"Master Grey or Master Graile?" Claire asked with quiet defiance.

"Grey will suffice," their captor said.

She reached into her purse and took out the jewel she would not part with, and showed it on her open palm. Amber and gold glimmered, their yellow hues washed silver by the moon. But the details of the dragon were amazingly clear, limned in that clear light.

Graile inhaled sharply. For a long time, he simply stared at the brooch, disbelieving. When he reached for it, Claire closed her hand involuntarily, then opened it again. Graile took it in gingerly, as if it might scorch his hand, then examined it more closely. Finally he lifted the gun away and stepped back, looking between Adrian and Claire. His chest heaving as if he'd been running, but each breath shaped a word. "How did you come by this?"

Claire answered, "It belonged to a friend, who gave it to my brother. After he died I asked if I might keep it for remembrance."

"Rafe Fletcher gave it to your brother, Gabriel." As Burne's man, Graile could put together that much.

"Yes," Claire answered. "Both good men. My brother gave his life to save the Queen, and Sir Raphael risked his in the same cause."

"The dragon is a symbol of the Devil," Graile said, as if to refute her.

"For some the dragon is not evil, but a symbol of wisdom, of challenge, or of mystery. For me, this brooch is a symbol of a powerful and abiding love." Claire held out her hand, demanding its return. Adrian was filled with pride and fear for her.

Graile tucked the brooch away. "Later."

"So you say," Claire said, her voice edged with sarcasm. Her eyes glittered with anger.

"Your father is an alchemist."

"My father seeks truth, and has harmed no one in his life," Claire said. "If anyone here serves the Devil it is you, who would kill an innocent man without question."

"Perhaps the questions were answered to my satisfaction," Graile said to her.

"Perhaps you asked none," she challenged.

"Claire," Adrian said quietly, and tilted his head, asking her to move away. Obviously reluctant, Claire retreated out of hearing. Distressed that he had put her in greater danger, Adrian said to Graile, "Lady Claire knows no more."

"And what more do you know?" Graile demanded.

"I saw only a jumble of images from your past. I believe the dragon brooch sprang forward because it was the most powerful link between us," Adrian said, though he could pick more from the jumble than Graile would countenance. "But I will strike a bargain with you."

"A bargain?" Graile's voice, his expression, were ice.

"I swear I do not want your soul. I do not want you to commit any unholy act," Adrian said, aware of the peculiarity of swearing such oaths to an assassin. "Only escort us safely back to London. Return Lady Claire to her family—but allow me to escape."

"Unlawful, if not unholy," Graile said, then added, "And if I can devise this?"

"Once there, I will take the brooch—or any other object of your choosing—and find for you . . ." Adrian paused. The impressions he received were so varied he could not promise exactitude. Finally he said, "If I cannot give you an answer, then a clue, a path to follow. Something that you judge sufficient recompense."

Graile waited, as if he expected to be asked to sign an oath in blood. Finally, he said, "I will make your bargain, exactly as agreed. You will divulge what you find to no one."

"You have my word, whether or not you believe it," Adrian said. "No one will know but the two of us."

"For good or ill, I've made your pact. But if I find that you have lied to me, if you use your freedom to murder another innocent woman, I will hunt you down and kill you myself."

"I do not doubt it."

Graile frowned, but the slightly furrowed brow was less ominous than the expressionless mask. "You intended to return to London, in truth?"

"Yes," Adrian answered. "To return and to stop the murders, if I can."

"Which you say Edward Quarrell committed?"

"Yes. Do you know him?"

"I know who he is, no more," Graile said flatly.

"How—?" Adrian began, but Graile shook his head. Adrian knew it would be pointless to press him. Burne had sent men to question the doctor, so that was the most likely answer.

Graile nodded for him to return to Claire's side and he went to her. He longed to touch her and read the same longing in her eyes, but contented himself with clasping her hands in his own gloved ones.

"Are you all right?" she asked him.

"Yes," he answered, then turned to watch Graile approach Flaxman.

"We will spend the night here." Graile walked toward his cohort, sliding his gun into his belt. "In the morning, we will escort Lady Claire and Lord Roadnight safely back to London."

"You're crazy, Grey!" Flaxman hissed, keeping his gun trained in their direction.

"They've surrendered," Graile said.

Flaxman beckoned Graile closer, but his low mutter carried in the silence of the stone circle. "Why take him back alive? Dead's better. No chance of a corpse bolting on us."

"No." Graile's tone was quiet, almost disinterested, but it refused argument.

Flaxman's voice rose. "He's too dangerous. You know what he did—peeled those women like pretty apples and left them red and shiny on the floor."

"Perhaps. Perhaps not."

Now Flaxman's whispering took on a sly note. Adrian strained to hear. "Who's to say he didn't bring the lady here—rape her and slit her throat? We found her dead, and killed him. Simple justice."

Adrian tensed with fear and fury, and he felt Claire press closer to his side. But he was certain Graile would refuse this bargain of rape and unsanctioned murder. Adrian held his breath as Graile gave the other man a long, measuring look. Then in one swift movement, Graile grasped Flaxman's head and twisted it sharply.

Bone cracked. Without a sound, Flaxman toppled forward onto the ground, dead.

Claire gasped, going rigid beside him. Adrian was as stunned, as much by Graile's precision as the cold-blooded deed.

Stepping around Flaxman's body, the assassin approached them. He stopped just beyond reach, perhaps to reassure them. Nonetheless, Claire withdrew a step, then held her ground. Graile said, "I could not trust him not to shoot me, then murder you. The promised reward is quite large."

Adrian swallowed his shock, glad his voice was even as he asked, "My cousin offered it?"

"Yes, Sir Nigel let us know there was coin for your corpse, and conveyed to us that it might be better for all concerned if you did not return to London alive."

"Because he believed Sir Adrian had murdered me?" Claire asked, her voice ragged.

"He was concerned that you might already be dead," Graile told her. "If you were alive, our first duty was to guard your safety."

"And you have no interest in the reward?" Claire asked him scornfully.

"Not an immoderate one," he replied. "Would you have preferred I let him live?"

Claire looked over at Flaxman, then away.

"No, he was a danger to us all," Adrian answered for them both. Over Graile's shoulder, he could see Flaxman sprawled among the ancient stones. "Can we move him beyond Stonehenge?"

"Yes, that would be best," Graile agreed. "This location is too sinister. If his body were discovered here, the questions would triple."

To Adrian, Flaxman's corpse seemed a desecration. He did not say so to Graile, who thought the henge sacrilegious.

All practicality again, Graile said, "Last night Flaxman got in a brawl in Salisbury. It would be better if his corpse was found between there and Amesbury, not farther west. I will weight the body with stones and dump it in the river."

"Shall we wait for you here?" Adrian asked.

"No. I must formulate a plan." Graile considered for a moment. "Take shelter with Mistress Boyle. I will give you a list of things to gather—simple things which she may possess. They will enable us to travel in disguise."

"How long do we wait?" Adrian asked.

"If I do not return by dawn, you must make your own way."

"We have so far," Claire said to him.

"So you have," Graile answered. He told them what they would need, then had Adrian help him lift and tie Flaxman over his mount's saddle. Without another word, Graile mounted and rode into the night.

Brimming with distrust and anxiety, Claire turned to him. "What did you see when he touched you? Why did you show him the brooch?"

"I cannot tell you. I gave him my word."

"But because of that, he will help us?" When he nodded, she said, "Your touch changes lives. I know that well enough."

"I have promised to see what I can in your brooch, or whatever else he wishes. That was the price I offered for helping us, and why he will not just set us free." Adrian said it calmly, but a tremor ran through him.

"What of his word? Can he be trusted not to kill us once he learns what he wants?"

He hesitated, then ventured, "He has a sense of honor."

"I take it that is 'perhaps,' not 'yes'?" Claire said sharply.

"I believe you are safe. Like Rafe, our escort fears I may be some minion of the Devil."

"And t'would be more honorable to destroy you than keep his word?" she asked.

"Perhaps," he answered. "If I were such a minion, but I am not."

"If he believed you were such a minion. If he believes we are," Claire qualified.

"I believe he will keep his pledge. I will keep mine," Adrian said. "Let us go."

He could tell curiosity gnawed at Claire as they walked toward their horses. "What else can you tell me without violating your promise?"

"It is too difficult to filter out what would be acceptable," he said, not wanting to give Graile any excuse for anger. When she started to pose another question, Adrian said, "Whatever more you wish to know, Claire, you must ask him yourself."

"I would rather ask him for nothing more than the salt."

Adrian laughed a little, some of the tension easing from his body. Claire smiled at him despite her worry. They descended the rise, then spurred their horses across the moonlit plain.

Chapter 15

❦

Morna had not slept for worry, and welcomed them back. Claire frowned when Adrian told his old nurse that someone else might aid them. Adrian said no more than that for now, in case Graile did not return, and Claire almost hoped he would not. Quarrell's insane savagery was almost beyond her comprehension. Graile's calculated murder frightened her less, but angered her more. Perhaps because she had wished Flaxman dead, and so felt culpable. She wanted Graile dead too, but doubted he would oblige her.

Meanwhile, they shuttered the windows to hide the light within, then gathered what Graile had asked them to—flour, oil, egg white, beeswax, charcoal, and other oddments. They asked for old clothes for Claire as well, and Morna went into her bedroom to fetch what might be had. Claire found the cottage calming, ordinary in the most soothing way, even if they were shuttered inside in the small hours of the night. It had an aroma of goodness with its scents of scrubbed wood, fresh and dried herbs, bread, and autumn fruit. Claire was able to relax a little.

When Adrian went to feed and tend their mounts, she beckoned Morna to sit beside her on the bench. Here her curiosity about Adrian could be satisfied without pain to him. "Can you tell me what Sir Adrian was like as a child, Morna?"

She smiled, warmed by memories. "Such a sweet lad, he was, Lady Claire. He had a bright charm about him always, like his mother when she was a girl. A boy for all that, running wild out on the cliffs and moors. Though that was before all the troubles came crashing down and near crushed us."

"And after the troubles?"

Morna pondered. "For a long time he was too quiet, like a little gray ghost wandering about, always too careful, too fearful of both his parents. To speak the truth, I feared his father would smother Adrian's spirit. I saw him but seldom after he went to live in England. The light in him did kindle again, but always it was shaded."

"You said you knew he had his mother's gift?" Claire asked.

"Aye, so I did. 'Twas just the way he was aware of people, who he trusted and who he didn't. How he'd sometimes find a thing and return it without asking whose it be. Even when he was a little one, he saw it pleased his mother and not his father. Once she was shut away, his father would not endure it in Adrian. He hid it all away."

Claire's heart ached for the small boy who feared to be himself, who feared even to know himself, and for the man who now had no choice. "And his great-grandfather?" she asked. "He died mad as well?"

"He died of dragon's milk," Morna said with a sniff, "and he was well enough till that gobbled his brains. He had no gift at all, save for drinking and tupping wenches."

"Oh!" Claire fought to stifle the laughter of pure relief that welled within her.

"Did Adrian's father tell him such a lie?"

"Apparently so."

"Shame on him," Morna said, and then sighed. "But perhaps fear made him believe it."

They heard Adrian at the door, and Morna patted her hand. "You can tell him, Lady Claire, when you think the time is right."

"The time is right enough," Claire said. A change had begun at Stonehenge, when Adrian refused to run anymore. This news now seemed a good omen.

"What is that?" Adrian asked, looking from one to the other.

"Your great-grandfather," Claire began, and Adrian regarded her warily. She had to fight her nervous laughter again. It was not funny. "Your great-grandfather's madness was brought on by drink."

Adrian frowned as if this were some fairy tale she had invented to mollify him. Then, slowly, his brow cleared. He looked to Morna. "Truly?"

"God's truth," the old nurse said. "He had no gift at all, but his sister did. She died in her bed at eighty-eight, sound and sharp till the fever took her away. There are many tales of the sight in your mother's family—but no other tales of madness."

Adrian sank down on the bench, a look of bemusement on his face.

"Only your sweet lady mother had her gift turn on her so cruelly." Morna went on. "A madness of grief took her when her poor babe died. She had cause enough."

Adrian looked at her, and Claire knew his greatest fear still remained. The impulse to reach out to him rushed through her. As if he sensed it, Adrian stood and turned to his old nurse. "Enough of old troubles. Are you happy here, Morna?"

Morna regarded him quietly for a moment, as if she would make up her own mind about the old troubles. Then she nodded and began pleasant talk of the village, the newest babe, and the wealth of the harvest. " 'Tis good here, Sir Adrian," she finished, "but I miss the sound of the sea in my ears."

"I told my father you would," Adrian said, then shielded his face with his hands, rubbing his temples.

Another memory? Before Claire could ask, a knock sounded at the door, though they had heard neither a horse nor footsteps approaching.

Adrian said softly to Morna, "Answer, and don't be alarmed if you recognize the man who was here earlier. Let him in."

The whole enterprise was most peculiar, but Morna seemed used to peculiarities. In case it was some curious neighbor, Claire and Adrian slipped quietly into the bedroom. But Claire doubted the precaution was necessary. Few save Graile would arrive so soundlessly. The heard the door open and shut, and then Graile's voice telling them to come out. They returned to the front room, where Graile stood waiting. He nodded to them curtly, then turned to Morna. "If anyone comes asking, you only spoke to me and the other man but once."

"All my lifetime, I've been after knowing when to hold my tongue. So I will now, Master Grey." Morna nodded reprovingly. She gave no indication that she'd heard Flaxman say his other name, nor did she ask after his absent companion.

"Have Adrian and I been here?" Claire asked.

There was silence while they all considered. It was Morna who said, "Aye, you both came to the door after I was warned. Sir Adrian told me he was innocent, but I was afraid to let him enter. The threat of my ax drove you off. Later, I thought you could have harmed me if you wished, so I kept silence."

"Good enough," Graile said. He looked at what they had set out for him, then asked for one or two more items. Morna brought what he bade. When he took it without thanks, she could not forbear comment. "You were more civil when you came with false warnings."

"Civility was necessary then," Graile said coldly. He set about preparing their disguises, mixing up pastes and powers.

Claire trusted Morna's solid, sensible nature and loyalty and apparently Graile had decided to hazard the same. Aside from being more taciturn than ever, the intelligencer showed no apprehension. Nonetheless, Graile must be nervous; risking his identity, and possibly his life with people he barely knew and distrusted. Claire was nervous in turn, wondering if he might suddenly turn on them all. What if he decided that she and Morna and Adrian formed some unholy coven? They might never know till he snapped their necks. When Morna's ginger mouser, curious about the strange activities, mewed to be let in at the door, the intelligencer regarded its entrance like that of a witch's familiar.

Claire watched Graile make his preparations, skillful and precise as an alchemist, with no superfluous movements. Though she tried to observe him surreptitiously, he realized it almost instantly and turned to face her. She decided not to look away, but continued her perusal. The heavy beard was a close match to the ash brown hair that waved back from his brow, she guessed it was false simply because it hid too much of his face. She could see a strong hawk's arch to the long bridge of his nose, and glimpse thin, firm lips. His eyes were gray, a cool, silvery hue. He was Adrian's age, she thought, little more than thirty. As he met her gaze, his expression did not change; he merely studied her with equal concentration. When she refused to look away, he turned smoothly back to his work, conceding nothing.

Claire found his quiet politeness unnerving. She was beginning to believe he would honor his word to Adrian because of the deep effect of whatever had passed between them. But she had no doubt Graile would kill again—with the same cool indifference he had revealed in dispatching Flaxman. Her brother had been a spy for the crown, as had Rafe Fletcher. But looking at Graile she did not think spy—she thought assassin. Could they trust anything he said? She hoped Graile would deem lying to Adrian futile, false though that would be. Unless Adrian was touching someone he had only his own intuition, strong perhaps, but not infallible.

His concoctions complete, Graile had them sit on the bench, and began to age their faces and Claire's hands with the various mixtures, and to gray their hair. As he worked, he told them they would become farmers on the far edge of gentility. He would play son to their parents, traveling together back to London. Within an hour, they were both more wrinkled and gray than Morna. Claire tried on the serviceable clothes the nurse had provided. They were too big, but Morna padded them out to disguise her further. Adrian had only his own garments, but stuffed them tightly as well.

" 'Tis a fashionable look, such a well-padded peascod," Claire said, patting his stuffed belly. For some reason, Adrian looked as embarrassed as if she'd praised the volume of his codpiece instead, his cheeks turning pink beneath the glued webbing of wrinkles. The silliness of it all lightened Claire's spirits, though she must hope no one would penetrate their ruse.

Graile kept a disguise ready in his saddlebags, or had stolen one—if a disguise it could be called: plain, stolid garments of gray wool and buff leather. He added a battered hat, and with it put on a slouching posture and dull expression. The heavy beard covered much of his face. Still, it would be easy enough for Graile to age himself as well, and pretend to be a brother rather than a son. With a twinge of unease, Claire wondered why he had not.

Adrian must have thought the same, for when Morna began to make porridge, he asked Graile quietly, "You aren't worried Sir Nigel's men might recognize you?"

"Unlikely." Then, for once, Graile elaborated. "Certain of Sir Nigel's men know each other well, as is needed for complicated teamwork. Others he holds apart, to lessen the risk of exposure. Few of the intelligencers know me. Unfortunately, Flaxman was one of them."

Unfortunately for Flaxman, Claire thought. It seemed Graile had several reasons to dispense with the man. Preserving his mystery was motive in itself. At what moment had he decided on the murder? She forced herself to remember that she did indeed prefer Flaxman dead. She only feared that Adrian's neck might be as easily snapped.

Meanwhile, Adrian probed further, "Sir Nigel risked a

great deal, then, to track me down—to try and find Lady Claire."

"Yes."

Claire almost smiled at the terseness, since Graile could speak fluidly when he wished. But her thoughts strayed to Sir Nigel, and the debt she owed him. She felt both gratitude and guilt that he had called in so many of his men to try to rescue her. He must feel very guilty, himself, to see her snatched from his protection by the man he feared had murdered his wife.

She would have asked Graile more then, but Morna brought them each a bowl of porridge and stewed fruit. When their bellies were full, they exchanged farewells with her at the door, then mounted their horses. Darkness still veiled them as they stole quietly through the town and back onto the highway, setting forth on their return journey.

It was not difficult to feign age, Claire decided, when she was falling asleep in her saddle.

Hiding in plain sight, they'd joined a large pack train in Salisbury that was making the journey to London. Graile handled all the transactions, and they kept to themselves as much as possible. Disguising her voice, Claire exchanged only the simplest conversation with the other travelers. She spoke little to Adrian, but she rode beside him in an oddly companionable silence.

As they approached Winchester that evening, two local constables stopped the pack train, men as eager to seize the reward as Flaxman had been. Claire tried to look unconcerned as they rode up and down the pack train, greed glinting in their eyes. She tensed as Graile caught their attention, for he was vaguely close in description to Sir Adrian. One man declared that the beard must be false, the hair dyed darker. The other argued that Graile couldn't dye himself a new color of eyes, and so they turned away, disgruntled. Neither thought so far as false wrinkles. Claire breathed a sigh of relief as the pack train moved on into the old capitol.

"The first one was greedy enough to try and dye your eyes himself," Claire said to Graile.

"Or steal mine," Adrian suggested.

Graile gave a small snort that might have been laughter.

They shared a room of their own at the inn, so Graile could keep watch and to make it simpler to renew their wrinkles in the morning. Claire found it bizarre, trying to settle down with the intelligencer acting as their jailer. He laid a pallet on the floor by the door and gave them each one of the narrow beds, tying them by their wrists to the frames. It was not a great discomfort, for Graile only needed a warning should they try to escape, but it was strangely humiliating to endure. Claire would have complained more if she had not been so exhausted. Instead she sank like a stone into a well of slumber and did not wake till dawn.

The second day passed more pleasantly. Claire was refreshed enough to appreciate the color-splashed beauty of the autumn countryside, and be amused by their curious charade. She could still admire the fine, strong bones of Adrian's face beneath the sere mask, enjoy the precise cut of his lips, and dwell on the myriad colors glinting in his eyes. His hidden beauty was oddly arousing. She longed to pull him off into the woods and strip him of his padding, to comb her fingers through the soft mat of golden hair on his chest, and nip at the coral circles of his nipples till they drew tight and hard as her own. Probably her stolen glances had been too intent again, for Adrian turned to face her, those magical eyes gleaming, the sculptured lips curling into teasing smile. With a sudden sweet twist of her heart, Claire could imagine truly being old with him, and wrinkled—yet still filled with a tender and delicious longing. Had she been granted sight of their future? If this was her own particular vision, she took comfort in the thought that the thwarted longing of the moment would be transformed to years of fulfillment.

She hungered to touch him. But Adrian had made his own choice to retreat from her. Having misstepped before and violated his trust, Claire had resolved to let him approach when he was ready. She had not given up hope that he would relent. Since Morna's revelation about his great-grandfather, he had eased, if only one notch.

Skin to skin contact was far too intimate, and so Claire found herself continually tempted to pat his false belly. She chortled as she thought of it, and her amusement earned a wary glance from Graile. In truth, the soft-spoken and sinister intelligencer made any contact uncomfortable. Yet in a perverse fashion his presence lowered their resolve, for she caught Adrian casting longing glances at her, even in her padding and crinkled face, just as she had been eyeing him.

Close to nightfall they arrived at Guildford. Before Graile could order supper brought to their room, Claire walked into the common room. She knew it was a risk, but the thought of being confined with the intelligencer was too oppressive. Adrian followed her in and sat beside her at a dark corner table. Graile stood in the doorway. For a moment, he eyed them coldly, willing them to rise and walk away. When they did not, he finally joined them.

At first, the pack riders were the only travelers in the room. But as they ate their mutton pies, more farmers and laborers gathered for a pint and an evening's conversation. Graile listened to all that was said with a motionless quiet that made him nearly invisible. Adrian sipped his ale slowly, attending to his own thoughts. Claire felt a little foolish, for she did not want to encourage conversation that she could not answer truthfully. Still she preferred to be where she was, in the midst of ordinary human warmth, rather than be less than alone with Adrian under the intelligencer's bleak eye.

When the news of the town and district had been discussed to the satisfaction of all, one of the farmers called for a song. A lute was produced, and a few ditties plucked for the rough and ready singing of the company, then the instrument's owner offered it to the travelers, but it seemed none of them could play. As the owner prepared to stow away the lute,

Adrian spoke in quavering tones. "My wife's a modest woman and will not speak up for herself, but despite the arthritis in her joints, she's got a tune or two in her yet."

Startled, Claire could only stare at him.

"Too conspicuous," Graile murmured to her. "Refuse."

"Refusal would also draw attention," Adrian returned as quietly, giving the intelligencer a small, triumphant smile. As the lute was passed to Claire he looked into her eyes. "I have not heard you play."

She was weary and her injured hand already ached from holding the reins. He would not hear her at her best now. But even her best now was a humble thing, and there might not be another time. Claire took the instrument. As she pulled the plectrum from between the strings the tendons of her right hand protested, sending a needle of burning ice up her arm. Hiding the pain from the strangers and Adrian alike, she kept her face resolutely impassive, forcing her right hand to steadily pluck the notes so easily and flowingly fingered by her left. Though Adrian had given the gathering a reason for any stiffness that might mar her music, she was determined not to play badly for him. Still she hesitated, for the galliards and bransles that delighted her best were Court fare. Those she did not dare play.

Then like an echo of sunlight from distant summers she heard in her mind a tune learned long ago from a milkmaid on one of her family's country estates. It was a simple air but sweet, and her fingers remembered it of their own accord, even as hearing it again brought memories of the scent of hay and cattle, a shaft of light through the barn window gilded with dust motes, childish laughter shared over stolen strawberries.

Sharp twinges scraped at her arm, but hearing the forgotten tune well up from the strings, Claire strove to keep music and pain separate, giving herself to one in escape from the other. The trick worked only rarely, but she had schooled herself long and hard at it, and could almost believe this long-forgotten air could cure her hurt. Reaching the end of the refrain, she began again, forcing herself to the embellishment of a counterpoint. The deeper notes sighed beneath the treble like a sadder, more profound knowledge below the sweetness of the tune's ephemeral gaiety. The two voices spoke and replied, repeated and mingled, obeying not her will but some urge of their own. Lifted as if above herself, Claire saw the pleasure in the lamp-lit faces, thoughtfulness in one, a smile hovering on another. Even Graile's face was touched with wistfulness. But Adrian's was turned down, hidden from her.

Perhaps he was disappointed. The many instruments in his London house bespoke a musical ear, and English tunes could seem crude beside the melodious Irish airs. Her playing, too, was not flawless. However fluid the music she heard in her mind, her plectrum hand now lacked the control to reproduce that flow perfectly. But the lacework of sounds she drew from the lute gave her mind wings to fly beyond those thoughts. Both voices, the one like birdsong and the sorrowfully measured one, were her own. She heard them ask and reply to one another, twining together in poignant wisdom, and listened for answers to her doubts, her fears, and her desire, yet she listened in vain.

A shadow lifted on the wall as Adrian looked up. His eyes gleamed from out of their false wrinkles. In the gray beard his sculpted lips were slightly parted. As he met her gaze she saw his own doubts and hopes were also stirred, but stronger still, a raptness beyond those constraints, a pouring out of his soul to hers as if through her music they touched as truly as if they touched hand to hand. He breathed in through his open lips as he had done when he kissed her, as if the beauty of the music were her essence.

As he did, Claire realized the music was indeed her own. Freed of the old tune, it had flowered into a new composition. Her creation. Her joy in it was one with her joy in Adrian. Shaping a pattern she knew she would remember, she let it carry her through a bright rain of notes, then soar upward into skies mapped only by the stars. She gazed into Adrian's eyes as she played. All that her inner voice had to say she offered him, weaving a song of love and hope, the thrumming of the counterpoint like the beating of their two hearts in accord. She saw that he heard, and understood. If he could not bring himself to give in to that harmony, at least she saw how much he desired to surrender.

After the entertainment, Claire was wide awake, filled with excitement at the thought of the music she might compose. Newly attuned to Adrian, she wished fervently that she was alone with him, although Graile seemed oddly mellow after her playing. However, Claire was not ready to be tied to the bed for the evening. Pressing her fingers to her lips, she choked back a burst of laughter. She did not want anger or nervousness to spoil her lingering pleasure. Better to talk for a time. But despite the ease that followed the music, conversation proved difficult. Adrian's past was full of sorrows, and Graile's full of secrets. So many crucial topics seemed forbidden, but she could not bear inanities. Finally she was able to initiate a discussion of the repercussions of the arrest of Mary Queen of Scots, which allowed them to talk of something of substance, as if they were not hemmed by their peculiar circumstances.

They ventured to tell Graile pieces of their own story—cautious, for the intelligencer was mistrustful. Even if Adrian's gift was not engendered by dark sorcery, his mother's madness showed that it could turn dangerous. But Adrian's honesty and clarity spoke well for him. Claire was certain their every word and gesture was measured on some precise scale within Graile's mind, grains of knowledge that weighed the balance of their very lives.

The conversation soon pointed to Edward Quarrell. Taking her chance, Claire asked the intelligencer if Sir Nigel had continued to hunt for the doctor even though he believed Adrian guilty. Graile frowned slightly. After a moment, he said, "I have reason to think Sir Nigel regards the doctor with suspicion. But I was not privy to all the assignments of the intelligencers, any more than they knew of mine."

Obviously, he would say no more about his work, nor should he.

With equal hesitation, Adrian asked, "Sister Mary—did she die as horribly as the others?"

"Yes. She was flayed," Graile answered, not attempting to soften the blow. "Her body was left exposed in an alley near Bedlam."

Adrian turned away, not allowing them to see his face.

Claire's heart twisted for him, but she grasped at a possibility of hope. "When did they find her? Sir Adrian was not even in London this last week."

"They found her body last week, but she'd already been dead a week or more."

Adrian turned to him, frowning. "She was murdered before Penelope?"

"I would judge so."

Rising, Adrian paced the room. "Then it is possible to prove that I did not kill her—to prove it to Rafe and Vivian, at least."

"How can we?" She wanted to leap up and seize him in her eagerness to know.

"You remember the labyrinthine approach to our meeting place?"

"Yes." Claire noted that Adrian kept secrets, too. He did not tell Graile about the Buzzing Hornet.

"Our whereabouts were carefully guarded from the time we escaped Bedlam. Once Viv was pardoned, the location of her hideaway did not matter, but she still protected mine from Edward Quarrell. Night and day, guards were posted, and wrigglers watched the roofs."

"I see!" Claire responded. "The watchers were to keep the hunter out, but they would also know that you never left."

"Yes. And during the day someone looked in on me quite often." Adrian smiled a little. "To check on both my presence and my continued sanity, I suspect. The others were a bit worried, even if Vivian was not."

Graile considered what Adrian had said. "You might somehow have managed to evade them, so it is not enough to convince Sir Nigel. But it is enough to make him reconsider."

"Perhaps enough for Sir James, as well." Her heartbeat quickened. How much easier to hunt for Quarrell if Adrian did not have to hide.

Adrian shook his head. "I don't know. Far easier for James to believe in my guilt than Penelope's collusion with Quarrell."

Claire's anger stirred. "Only because your guilt absolves Sir James of his treachery."

"Yes," Adrian conceded. "That is true. But James loved her. Protecting her memory may be more important to him."

Sir James protects his own illusions, Claire thought. Most would think she had acted far more blindly, but Adrian was innocent. "For the first time, you have solid points to argue in your favor. With this new evidence, perhaps a timely surrender to Sir Nigel would be best."

"You may do better to prove your innocence first," Graile disagreed, surprising Claire.

"I will not surrender—not while I have other options," Adrian stated. "Sir Nigel would imprison me while he investigated. House arrest I could have endured, but I have had enough of locked cells. When I think of them, I think of death."

Graile said nothing, and Claire trusted Adrian's gift enough to shiver with apprehension. "We must find Quarrell," she said simply.

Adrian nodded. "I can hardly do that from the Tower, unless he scaled it to find me."

"If he is even in London," Graile remarked. "If I entertained myself in such a bloody fashion, I would have secured other identities in other cities."

Adrian shook his head. "I believe he will remain until he has completed his revenge."

The next two days went slowly because of rain, but there were no more incidents. They reached the outskirts of London at sundown and chose an inn at the farthest edges of Southwark. After they settled into their room, Graile ordered stewed hare, ale, and fruit tarts. They shared what would be their last meal together in silence, while new rain pattered on the stutters. Claire was caught between eagerness to be free of Graile and concern for Adrian.

When they finished their supper, Adrian asked Graile, "Have you decided what you will tell Sir Nigel?"

"Sir Nigel knows Flaxman was given to drinking and brawling, but presumed I could control him. I will tell him that Flaxman has vanished, and is mostly likely dead in some alley. Since it was also possible he had found you and wanted to claim the reward for himself, I decided to reverse my course. Flaxman could not have been trusted alone with Lady Claire and I felt obliged to search for him."

"That will justify your return," Adrian agreed. "Sir Nigel felt responsible for her welfare."

"Since I cannot reveal your evidence, he may send me hunting for you again," Graile said.

Adrian returned an ironic smile. "He will want to save the Crown and the nobility some trouble and dispatch me rather than bring me back for trial. A corpse will be less of an embarrassment than a living killer."

"The wrong corpse would be a greater embarrassment by far," Claire retorted. "Edward Quarrell will not stop killing."

Adrian nodded to her. "So we must be the ones to stop him."

"There should be no contact between us after we enter London." Graile looked from her to Adrian. "I have returned you safely, so I ask that you fulfill your promise, Lord Roadnight. Now, before I leave."

"Very well," Adrian stood, visibly bracing himself.

"I will stay here while—" Claire began.

"I do not want you here," Graile said flatly.

"We have shared this journey. Surely you do not fear me," Claire argued.

"No." Graile gave a sharp tilt of his head. "Wait outside."

"It would be better if Lady Claire remained," Adrian said, surprising her. She had expected he would have more concern for Graile than himself. Adrian laid his gloved hand on her shoulder and she could feel a slight tremor penetrate through his grip. His fear increased her own. To Graile,

Adrian said, "Some people and the objects they own make an intense impression."

"Like Quarrell," Claire flung at Graile.

"Yes, and like your brother, too," Adrian said gently.

She expelled a pent-up breath, recognizing the complexities that faced Adrian.

To Graile, Adrian said, "I have told you how difficult it can be. I am stronger with Lady Claire beside me."

The words were quiet, but the acknowledgment made Claire's heart bound with joy.

"You did not find it so difficult at Stonehenge," Graile countered.

"Then call it a premonition, if you will," Adrian replied.

At the henge Adrian seemed sustained by some hidden power within the stones. Now he felt safer with her close by. Claire could not be stone, but she would be strong for him. Looking at Graile, she insisted. "I will stay."

"While he holds . . . what I will give him. Then you must leave."

Even the slight hesitation in his voice surprised her. She replied, "Very well. I will stay until Adrian is ready to speak with you."

"You will say nothing of any of this."

"I give you my word. I will say nothing of what I see—unless it means the life of the Queen, or of my family."

For a moment Graile did nothing, reluctance emanating from his stillness. Then he took two small chamois packets from his purse and handed the lighter one to Claire. She opened it and drew forth her dragon brooch. A peace offering? She had not even been sure he would return it, but it mollified her only a little. She took it from him without thanks, for it was hers, and started to put it away.

"Wait," Graile said. He unwrapped the other object and held it out on his palm.

She gasped. It was a brooch identical to the first, a fine golden dragon wrapped round a gleaming dome of amber—save that the amber was a darker shade, blood red.

Adrian sat on the bed, but his face showed no surprise. He must have seen this brooch in his vision at Stonehenge, and so asked Claire to show her own. Curiosity filled her as to their history, and how Graile came to own the twin. Were there more?

Slowly Adrian removed his gloves and laid them aside. He drew a deep breath and released it, then held out his hand. Graile laid the brooch in his palm. A visible shudder racked Adrian's body. Then he went rigid. Only his arm moved, quivering as he raised up his tight-clenched fist as if to strike a blow. He stared, his eyes blank as a blind man's, but Claire knew he was staring inward at the revelations that radiated from the brooch. Time seemed endless, though Adrian held the dragon brooch for barely a minute. Then, moaning, he dropped the jewel and doubled over on the bed. Adrian wrapped up into a ball, his face pale, limbs trembling. A cold rain of sweat drenched his skin. He said something under his breath that Claire could not hear.

"What?" she asked.

"Now you must go outside." Graile's stillness was frightening.

"Not till Adrian is ready." Claire defied him, moving to sit beside Adrian on the bed. He made a sound between a sigh and a moan, pressing closer. When her bare hand touched his cold forehead an aura of darkness descended on her like a pall. Her heart weighed heavy, its cadence slow as a dirge. Sorrow smothered the heat of her anger, but not the warmth of her love. Holding Adrian fast, she made her heart a glowing coal to warm them both.

After a few moments the sense of chill and oppression lightened. Under his breath, Adrian whispered, "Thank you." Then he shifted away from her. She felt bereft when he broke contact. Adrian must have felt the same severance, for he leaned forward with his head in his hands, gathering his energy again. Then he sat up, facing Graile.

"Lady Claire." Graile's voice had softened infinitesimally— still it was a dismissal. Claire reined a sharp surge of anger.

She had given her word. She went outside and waited perhaps ten minutes, questions swarming in her mind. Questions she knew would not be answered. Then the door opened, and Graile stepped out into the hallway.

His face was smooth as glass, yet she would swear he was shattered from within. Devastated. His gaze moved over her, his eyes refusing to truly look at her.

"If we meet again—" he began.

"We have never met," Claire finished.

He frowned, looking slightly puzzled. "I did not thank him."

"I will do it for you," she said, realizing he did not want to go back.

He nodded, and started to walk away.

"Graile," she called quietly.

He turned, waiting, saying nothing.

"Godspeed," Claire said. "May your quest lead you to happiness."

"Happiness," he said. Then his gaze sharpened and he looked at her directly. "Satisfaction, at least."

Then he was gone down the stairs, leaving her alone in the hallway. Quickly, she entered the room and locked the door behind her. She returned to sit beside Adrian on the bed. He wrapped his arms around her and laid his head in her lap. He had come to her, her tired unicorn. A pang of aching tenderness throbbed deep within her. Desire, but desire muffled by exhaustion. They were alone for the first time in days, she realized, embracing in bed. But she would not make the same mistake twice.

And Adrian, she realized, was already asleep.

He did not wake when she stretched them out and pulled the covers over. She slept beside him, hoping her presence would hold the nightmares at bay.

In the morning, they would begin their own quest.

Chapter 16

Another masquerade—and this time Claire was in the midst of the players, sharing both excitement and anxiety. Garbed in sedate blue velvet and brilliant red satin, Rafe and Viv led the way. Claire followed, exquisitely groomed and gowned in borrowed black damask. She looked neither wanton nor victim, but the model of propriety. As they approached the Thorne town house, she gave Adrian a quick smile over her shoulder. He smiled in answer from his place behind their improvised guards, Izzy and a young fellow named Pie. Adrian remained in disguise, gray-haired, wrinkled, and padded to portliness inside Vivian's scarlet livery.

Golden sunshine filtered through clouds thick as clotted cream, filling Claire with hope. So far, the morning had unfolded as smoothly as they could have wished. They quickly made contact with Rafe and Viv, and discovered their friends had reached the same conclusion about the timing surrounding Sister Mary's death. Reassured by that and the message Moll had brought, Rafe had spoken to her parents in hopes of easing if not ending their worry. Claire sent word of her return, but would deal with the havoc she had wrought later. The most important goal was achieved. Adrian had protection again, and allies for his search, and together they had devised this scheme to test his cousin's still unpredictable humor.

"After Sister Mary's body was found, I spoke to Sir James and to Sir Nigel Burne," Rafe said, giving the doorknocker a rap. "Neither was convinced then. Sir Nigel said the testimony of a pack of scruffy pickpockets was worse than none. But I believe Sir James will listen now."

They had an ally within the house as well. Samuel had escaped dismissal and still served as steward to Sir James. Always hoping to prove his master's innocence, he had kept Rafe and Vivian apprised of events at the town house. Many of the servants had deserted after the murder, but Sir James had hardly noticed in his wretchedness. Samuel opened the door to admit them now, all but Pie, who kept watch without. After the rest of their party entered the hall, Samuel went to inform Sir James that Sir Raphael Fletcher had come with important news. Even if Sir James were still angry, he would want to know what that news might be.

But when Sir James appeared, it was obvious that grief had overtopped his rage. He stood at the head of the stairs, hollow-eyed and ill shaven, his clothes stained and disarrayed. "Why are you here?" he asked, his voice slurred with drink. "Have they managed to capture my cousin? Have they found Lady Claire's body?"

"The opposite, Sir James," Rafe answered. "When last we spoke, you told me you would be willing to listen if Lady Claire returned unharmed. Here she is now, before you."

Taking her cue, Claire stepped forward as Rafe and Viv opened the way.

"But you are dead!" James stumbled forward, gripping the banister to keep from falling.

"So I am told," Claire replied. "It has yet to be proved to my satisfaction."

"My cousin kidnapped you—Sir Nigel witnessed it."

James descended halfway down the stairs, staring at her in bewilderment. "Adrian meant to kill you!"

Claire spoke in a calming voice. "Only the first is true, and only in part. I was frightened when Sir Adrian made me get into the boat with him, but he only meant to speak to me away from the others. Once we had crossed the Thames, he offered to let me go."

"Then where have you been?"

She answered with quiet defiance. "I chose to go with Sir Adrian, since it seemed for a time that the whole world had turned against him—"

"But—" James protested.

"My life and my virtue are both intact," Claire cut in. In truth she would rather have sullied her virtue far more. Both Sir James and Rafe looked flustered. A small smile hovered about Vivian's lips, as if she knew Claire's wishes perfectly well. "Sir Adrian tried to dissuade me from leaving with him. But I knew where he intended to go, and threatened to follow alone if he did not take me with him. When we learned of Sister Mary's death, he decided to return, not because it could prove him innocent, but because he owed her a debt of honor."

"Innocent?" Confused, James looked to Rafe. "You said so. I did not believe you."

"Quarrell made a great mistake when he killed Sister Mary," Rafe said. "Now that Lady Claire has returned safely, perhaps you will believe we can account for Sir Adrian's whereabouts."

"I don't know what to say." Stunned, James sank down on the bottom step.

"Mistress Vivian is as dear to me as Lady Penelope was to you," Rafe said. Claire could all but hear him thinking "dearer," but he went on, "Lady Claire is like my own sister. I would never risk their lives for coin, as you accused before. I do not fear for their safety at Sir Adrian's hands—but I do fear Edward Quarrell's revenge."

Claire did not dare glance back at Adrian. She willed

James to listen, to believe. He shook his head, bewildered. "But he seemed deeply concerned with the inmates' welfare."

"For a week after I first encountered him, my throat showed the marks of his concern." Viv gave a snort of derision. "He acted as advisor at my torture."

Sir James stared at Vivian, disbelief slowly giving way to dismay. At last he said, "It is true Master Quarrell has proved himself dishonest."

"He has proved himself a monster." Viv's anger grew visibly.

"We want to find the killer, even as you do," Claire said, moving closer. "Sir Raphael and Mistress Swift have been hunting Master Quarrell for days."

"Is he not at Bedlam?" James asked.

"He disappeared on the morning of Lady Burne's death," Rafe said. "As soon as he discovered Sir Nigel's men were searching for him, he vanished."

"Sir Nigel was searching for him?" James asked, puzzled. "Why did he not tell me?"

"Because of your grief, perhaps, or because he was dubious," Claire answered. "But even though he suspected Sir Adrian, he has continued to hunt for Master Quarrell."

"My cousin has vanished as well!" James cried out suddenly, grief and horror welling over. "How can I know for certain?"

Adrian came forward then, before any promise of his safety was secured. Kneeling beside his cousin, he grasped his shoulders gently. "I am here, James, and I swear on my soul that I did not kill Penelope."

James pulled back, his eyes widening with dread and amazement. But Adrian did not relinquish his grasp. "Look in my eyes, James. I do not wish you harm."

Terrified that James would give the alarm, Claire held her breath, releasing it only as James sagged beneath Adrian's firm grip. For a moment James seemed numbed by shock. Then he shuddered, his face quivering as he would weep. The bulwark of anger sustaining the weight of his grief had crumbled. Then he looked about him and gathered his dignity as best he could.

"I don't know what to believe," James whispered, meeting Adrian's steady gaze. "I wanted you to be guilty, so that I might have revenge for Penelope. Now it seems that all my lies only led to her destruction."

"Let us place punishment where it truly belongs, on Edward Quarrell," Adrian said to him. "He has many lives to account for."

"If he is guilty, he must have fled London by now," James said wearily. The will to fight slipped away with his anger.

"No. He is here. I know it." Adrian looked over to her. A shiver of apprehension crept along her spine.

"He cannot remain hidden forever," Rafe said.

"We will find him, one way or another." Viv began pacing restlessly. "Sir Nigel's men have been hunting, and we have set men searching for him as well."

For Rafe's sake, Vivian had relinquished her crown as Queen of the Clink. Her former captain, Smoke Warren, and his sister, Joan, looked to rise as the new rulers. But Claire knew Rafe would not object if their allegiance were used to good purpose. She exchanged a glance with Adrian, remembering the morning's discussion. Smoke had summoned the other leaders of the underworld, men like Maggot Crutcher and One-Eye Wallace. The doctor's description had been given out, and Smoke impressed on the other lords of rogues just how dangerous the doctor could be. Promises had been made to scour both sides of the Thames.

Just then, Pie slipped through the door. "It's the Queen's rat catcher come calling," he said. "M'lord Burne."

Claire bristled at the insult to Sir Nigel, but this was no time to quibble about it. They had expected to be gone by the time he learned of her visit. Someone must have spotted them en route and rushed to inform him. Izzy quickly beckoned Adrian and Pie down to the end of the hall. At that distance,

Adrian's disguise should be undetectable. The others did not change their tableau, save that Sir James rose to his feet and made an effort to look presentable. Claire wondered if he would hold fast, or crumple under Sir Nigel's scrutiny.

A sharp rap sounded at the door, and Samuel opened it to admit Sir Nigel, with two guards beside him. Bows were exchanged, but there was no mystery who the focus of his attention would be. Claire gathered her composure. Adrian's safety was her greatest concern, but she had not forgotten that nightmare had followed her into Sir Nigel's life. She stepped forward, meeting his searching gaze.

"Lady Claire, I am pleased to see you safe. Pleased and amazed."

"I am deeply grateful for your concern, Sir Nigel, and regret the trouble you have gone to on my account." Her words were formal but sincerely spoken.

"It seemed necessary."

The last time he had seen her, Claire had screamed out to him for help. She did not play lightly in her response. She confessed the truth, even though she would rather have kept it hidden from all save Adrian. "I know my panic increased your anxiety for me, but it was the river I feared . . . because of my accident. I assure you Sir Adrian did not harm me in any way."

"Would that I had known it sooner." It was a rebuke.

"Had there been a way to tell you without endangering Sir Adrian, I would have."

"And where is he now?" Burne asked, an edge to his voice.

Her gaze did not waver. "Until you capture Master Quarrel, he will not come forward."

"He is not here?" Burne glanced toward the end of the hallway.

Claire knew he would recognize Izzy and Pie. Would he suspect that the other man was Adrian? Her heartbeat quickened, though she trusted nothing showed in her expression. She answered with half the truth. "We did not know if Sir James was ready to concede Edward Quarrell's guilt. But he has."

"Have you indeed?" Burne turned to Sir James, eyebrows lifting.

Sir James swallowed heavily, then said, "Yes. Yes, Sir Nigel, they have convinced me. The doctor is the man behind these murders."

Slowly, Burne looked round at them all. "You should know that I myself am more inclined toward Lord Roadnight's innocence. After his disappearance, a window was discovered ajar in my library. It is possible the killer used it to enter the house and kill my wife."

Here Sir Nigel looked down, silent for a moment. Claire ached anew with sympathy. He had suffered greatly at Quarrell's hands.

Sir Nigel faced them again, speaking firmly. "Nonetheless, I cannot revoke the warrant on such flimsies. It would be better if Lord Roadnight came forward. Surrender only works in his favor." He paused significantly, as if waiting for Adrian to reveal himself.

"You forget, Sir Adrian was falsely imprisoned in Bedlam for many months." Claire gave him Adrian's argument. "He will not surrender, and none of us will help you find him."

"But we will help you find the doctor," Rafe moved forward, drawing Burne's attention.

"Anyone with such a blood lust will kill again soon," Viv added.

"So it seems," Sir Nigel said, and then turned back to Claire. "Have you seen your parents yet, Lady Claire?"

His words struck a note of guilt within her. "I have sent word that I am all right, and that I will see them soon."

"Can I escort you home?" Burne asked.

She drew back a step. "Not now, we have plans to make—Rafe and Vivian and I."

"Let me know what they are, insofar as you are able," Burne said, surveying them all. "Let us be allies in this endeavor, and use the men at our command wisely."

"We shall do so," Rafe assured him. "We will meet when there is information to share."

Claire saw Sir Nigel's gaze directed behind her again, with the same peculiar intentness. She feared he would stalk down the hall and confront Adrian.

But all Burne said was, "I will take my leave of you, then."

Claire murmured her farewell along with Rafe and Vivian, sighing her relief when the door closed behind Burne and his guards. Adrian came forward, perplexed. "He was suspicious of me, I am sure of it; but he did not approach to see me clearly."

"I doubt he wanted confrontation with so many of us here," Rafe said.

"He has more men without," Adrian countered. "If he still believed I murdered his wife, he would not have been stopped by so few."

Claire said to him, "Sir Nigel no longer blames you, but he dare not renounce his mission when your innocence has not been proved. He cannot afford to be wrong twice."

"Not in the eyes of his superiors," Rafe agreed.

Viv frowned. "I do not like him, but our efforts should be combined."

Hope surged within Claire. Quarrell would be taken, and Adrian proved guiltless.

"Will you go with your friend, Adrian, or stay here?" James paused, obviously unhappy. "Your welcome is not in question but my own presence is. I should vacate the town house."

"No, James," Adrian spoke quietly to his cousin. "This house is yours to do with as you please. I promised it to you."

"Under duress." Despite the obvious pain of his emotion, James spoke for all of them to witness. "If you still feel bound by your word, I release you from any such promises. The Roadnight barony belongs to you and your heirs. I stole your title, but it was Penelope who I wanted to attain. Instead I've achieved her death, your torment, and my shame."

Adrian reached out to him, but James lifted a hand to forestall him. "Forgive me. I must be alone."

He turned and made his way up the stairs. Even in his distress, it seemed to Claire that James was his own man for the first time. When he turned the corner out of sight, there was an awkward silence. Then Vivian asked Adrian, "Will you stay?"

"Yes, for now. There is something I hope to find."

His mother's bequests, Claire remembered. Morna had asked Adrian if he had seen them. Would they be here? They might have been stolen the night the robber's attacked. James might have thrown them away. She said to Adrian, "I will stay and help you search."

They agreed to meet at the Buzzing Hornet before sunset, then Rafe, Viv, and the others made their farewells. Claire and Adrian were left alone in the hall, with only the faithful steward waiting. He came forward. "If I might have leave to speak, Lord Roadnight?"

"Of course, Samuel. Now and always."

"If you retire upstairs, I will keep the other servants from venturing up there for the time being. Meanwhile, those who are not sympathetic to your plight can be sent to other properties till this disturbing matter has been resolved. I believe I am well acquainted with those who will listen to the new arguments in your favor."

"Thank you, Samuel. I am weary of going about with glue on my face." Adrian ran his gloved fingers along the false wrinkles.

"And I believe you are too young for gray hair, my lord."

"I will go upstairs and wash—I will take the chamber I had as a child," he added the last quickly, obviously not wanting to reenter Penelope's death chamber so soon.

"Yes, my lord."

Adrian glanced at her, and then turned back to the older man. "One other thing, Samuel—do you know where I can find the trunks my father brought back from Ireland?"

"Indeed, my lord, I put them safely away in the attic. I will bring you the key."

Burne rode back toward Whitehall Palace, cursing inwardly. He was certain the third guard was Lord Roadnight.

The disguise was good, but the man was too old to be included in their party when force of arms might be necessary. Burne had been tempted to arrest him on the spot, and to carry through with his original plan to have the wretch die in prison. But now the others had allied with him, more strongly than ever. If Roadnight died under mysterious circumstances, they would all be suspicious—Claire of the death, Rafe and Vivian quite likely of him. And their suspicion could taint Claire. He must not lose her trust.

Burne was pleased to be free of Margaret, but it was the prospect of winning Claire that made the trouble his wife's death caused worthwhile. The havoc surrounding Margaret's demise had delayed the granting of his barony, though yesterday Walsingham had indicated that Sir Nigel would still receive it. He would not be cheated, not of Claire, not of the rewards of his skill. Struggling to control his anger, Burne pieced together his new plans.

If he could capture Quarrell and hold him secretly, Burne could arrange Adrian's death and claim the doctor had murdered him. Then he would rid himself of the deadly doctor and the threat he posed. Burne did not want Quarrell accusing him of murdering his wife. His men were searching every rathole. But if the doctor was never found, or was found by other hunters, how would he dispense with Roadnight? A hunting accident? A fire? Perhaps Burne would arrange something that would eliminate Fletcher and Swift as well. Then Claire would have no friend closer than he.

She had been so valiant in Adrian's defense. Her voice filled with quiet fervor, her hazel eyes glowing with green fire.

Would she ever love him with such fierce, such sweet intensity?

He would not be thwarted. Claire would be his.

The false beard itched. A dozen times in the last few minutes, Quarrell had to restrain himself from scratching at its edges. He peered at Maggot Crutcher's henchmen from behind the dark circles of his glasses and whispered some advice in the fat man's ear. Maggot nodded, his chins wobbling. He would be all jiggly yellow fat when peeled.

Quarrell did not think any of Maggot's men suspected him. They were a stupid lot, on the whole, which was one reason the fat man would never get control of the Clink. Viv had been clever, and Smoke Warren had brains as well. While ruthless with their enemies, they managed to inspire loyalty in the riffraff they commanded. Maggot's men groveled before him and plotted behind his back. Viv had offered a reward juicy enough to tempt any of them, even their leader. For the moment, Maggot was better paid to keep silent and his men would not suspect that he kept a notorious killer so close at hand.

Not that Maggot believed he was a killer. Quarrell had told him in detail about his encounter with Vivian Swift in Bedlam. The details were skewed, of course. He'd made himself naught but an observer to the whims of Viv's old enemy. The man was no longer alive to dispute his version of the affair. Vivian's crueler account Quarrell dismissed as lust for revenge. Instead, he impressed on Maggot that Lord Roadnight was a clever and devious madman.

It was possible that Maggot suspected Quarrell anyway, but did not feel at risk. So far, all Quarrell's victims had been women, and Maggot would care nothing what women Quarrell chose to satisfy himself, or in what fashion he did it. It would not be difficult to find a new victim, even in his current circumstances. No one knew of the existence of Mr. Lamb, or of his house on Hampstead Heath, save for his guard who would do anything if the price were right. If Quarrell took care, he could fulfill his growing need. Yet, despite the increased strain on his temper, he refrained. His rituals of Death provided sustenance for his spirit that he could not long live without, but he did not want to risk being caught for snatching some paltry morsel. To truly sate his craving, only Lord Roadnight would do.

Burne had complicated matters. His intelligencers had been searching for over a week, just as Vivian Swift's men had been, and Quarrell had thought it wise not to be found. But Burne had just quadrupled the reward, which indicated he now believed that Quarrell rather than Lord Roadnight was responsible for the murders. Maggot Crutcher might well be tempted to secure one large lump sum—but not until Vivian and Smoke were dead. And what better ruse than to offer them what they sought—then spring the jaws of the trap once they entered? Maggot would take Smoke and Viv, and Quarrell would claim Adrian. Or so the original plan had been devised. But looking at the pale, greasy hulk beside him, Quarrell grew more dubious of success. What if Maggot fumbled? What if Lord Roadnight did not walk into the trap?

Maggot had kept him apprised of Mistress Vivian's activities and the precious information she shared. And so he knew that Adrian had returned, if not where he was closeted. Vivian had not revealed that to Maggot, not with a price still gleaming golden above Lord Roadnight's head. But Lady Claire was back, and Quarrell guessed Adrian was with her. At the very least, she knew where he was hiding. If he could capture Lady Claire, he would possess the secret of Adrian's sanctuary and the means to lure him from it.

All in all, Quarrell was beginning to prefer this plan to the other. There was more risk achieving it, but less chance of exposure after. And the whole process would be far more entertaining. He needed his entertainments. His breathing quickened and he subdued it. He must show nothing untoward in this company. But if it was to be done, it must be done soon. Smiling, Quarrell rose and excused himself. He had messages to send. People to summon.

After events here were settled to his satisfaction, Quarrell had another identity he could assume, a doctor with property in York. Once Adrian was dead, he supposed he could go there, begin again. But Quarrell found it difficult to envision his life beyond Adrian's death. The pleasure of his early murders seemed pallid compared to the drama of death that had bloomed in such rich crimson hues around Adrian.

Perhaps it was a premonition of sorts, and his life would

come to a close as well. If his days were numbered, Quarrell planned to cause as much suffering as he could. They would all die, everyone who had thwarted him. Through Quarrell's connivance, Maggot would dispense with Viv Swift and her lover. Perhaps a way could be arranged to assassinate Burne as well. Adrian would not have killed Burne's wife, so Quarrell surmised that Burne had mimicked the murders to rid himself of her for some motive of politics or passion. Burne was ruthless enough, even if Quarrell would not have thought him sufficiently imaginative. He bristled at being so used—and determined to arrange a suitable comeuppance.

But all these plans were pretty posies about the grand bloom, small gems to set off the perfect jewel. Once he had summoned Adrian to Claire Darren's rescue, he would destroy her, slowly, slowly, while Adrian watched. And then he would take Adrian himself.

Take him into the dark.

Chapter 17

A lone in the bedroom of his London childhood, Adrian washed the wrinkles from his face, the gray from his hair. The cleansing became a preparatory ritual, discarding the falsehood in which he'd clothed himself for days, readying his mind to search for the truth. When he was done he felt curiously bare, almost empty. Fear hovered like a specter, but for the moment it did not touch him. He treasured this brief respite, knowing it would not last long. He held it at bay as he dressed in fresh clothes that fit, velvet trunkhose and doublet soft linen. He put on his gloves. Samuel had given him the key to the attic, and with it the promise that he would not be interrupted. That they would not be interrupted. . . .

Claire must be with him. After all they had shared these last days, she deserved no less. And he craved her. Craved what might be their last day, their last minutes before parting. The specter moved closer. Adrian shivered as he felt its chill breath on the back of his neck. His elusive calm vanished, and apprehension tightened nerve and sinew. His lungs grew heavy, his breathing shallow. Should he wait? Wait until Quarrell was captured? Claim a few more days, weeks of time with Claire?

But Quarrell might never be taken. And Adrian had said he was through running.

He stood, forcing deep breaths until he could maintain the illusion of courage. Then he picked up a candleholder from beside the bed and opened the door. He did not have to search, for Claire was waiting in the corridor outside his room, ready to demand her place in this journey if he sought to deny her. Despite his apprehension, he smiled a little. "Come, then."

Guided by the flickering candlelight, they climbed the dark stairway to the top of the house and unlocked the door. Inside, a narrow mullioned window sent a shaft of dappled sunlight into the shadows. Ivy leaves brushed against the round panes, their quiet rustling whispering of untold secrets. The dim room was faintly musty, but strangely quiet and peaceful. Samuel ordered a meticulous house, and even the attic floor was swept clean. Adrian had played here as a child. Sometimes being alone had been less painful than loneliness among others.

Adrian saw the chests at once, pushed against the wall on the far side of the room. He put the candle aside and knelt in front of them. Heedless of her black damask skirts, Claire settled on the floor beside him. Love filled him, and gratitude, for her courage and her loyalty. Her very presence gave him hope. Was there a chance he need not renounce her?

But Fear had followed too, descending on him like a frigid ghost. Icy claws raked up and down his spine till he shuddered. His skin wept cold tears of sweat. He might emerge from this attic in control, knowing he was a murderer. Then there would be solitude, penance, and a search for some kind of redemption. Wondering always if insanity would claim him again.

A life without Claire's light, her love, to warm it.

Or the dreadful knowledge of his crime might crack his mind, finally and completely. That was a life too horrible to contemplate. A life from which even knowledge of Claire might vanish. But not the sense of her loss.

His voice low, he said to Claire, "Even if I become violent, I do not think I will turn on you. But protect yourself if I do. Call out for help."

"I am not afraid, except for you, a little." She gave a small nod, urging him to begin.

It was why he was here. Opening the chests one by one, Adrian used his gloved hands to move aside the tapestries and fine linens that lay within. In the bottom of the third was a smaller leather chest. A pang of recognition pierced him like a dagger.

He walked along the Thames past the Tower, the flickering torches in their sconces and occasional light from a lantern guiding his way toward the docks. His father would be waiting on the Kestrel. He was certain—as he was certain his mother was dead.

Adrian shivered again. It had been cold that night, he remembered now.

"What is it?" Claire asked.

"I'd wished for her death," his father said. "For my freedom. My peace."

His mouth felt dry, and he licked his lips. "The night my father returned, I took him to a tavern. He told me my mother had left me a bequest. I ran to the dock, where all the chests were piled, and carried this one back to the tavern."

Adrian lifted out the box and placed it on the floor between them. Carefully, he removed the lid. Inside lay the wooden box with the carved dragon atop. A patch of sunlight gleamed on the dark wood, bringing the coiled dragon to life.

"A maze." Tracing the serpentine spirals with her finger, Claire said, as she had said at Stonehenge, "The dragon is symbol of evil for some, of wisdom for others."

Adrian nodded, staring at the wooden box. As a child, he had traced the fantastical creature just as Claire did now. But he was not a child when last he saw the dragon—

The floor beneath him warped, becoming a table, the scrubbed oak turning dark and wine stained. But the box still sat in its center. The dragon seemed to writhe on its surface. A fragment of light glinted in its eye.

Adrian's breath caught in his throat.

"You remember," Claire murmured. She drew her hand away, yielding the box to him.

"Yes." He reached out toward the box. Even shielded by the glove, his hand hovered over the lid, trembling.

His father watched him, face haggard in the darkened tavern room. The flesh seemed to be sagging off his bones, showing the skull beneath. The patch covered one eye; the other gleamed from the shadowed socket.

Adrian took one deep breath . . . another . . . fighting off dizziness. Whatever walls he had built to protect himself were crumbling. He met Claire's expectant gaze, gentle yet implacable. He must not fail her. If he did not face the past, he would be trapped in this limbo, where he had neither the courage to embrace her or to send her away. Even the worst truth would be freedom. Adrian pulled off the gloves and opened the box.

There was not a great deal inside. He glanced at his father, then picked up the stem of dried flower from the castle hillside. The yellow blossom had crumbled to dust amid the rest. For an instant he could smell its fresh blooming scent, and hear a ripple of his mother's laughter snatched away on the wind. He looked at the other curious treasures. A tiny bird's nest they'd found held a blue feather gleaming with purple iridescence

*and one perfect shell. Gold buttons rolled about, their
complex metalwork in the same knotted mode as the
carving on the box. A small handkerchief was folded to
show the rose his mother had embroidered after the new
bush had bloomed in the garden.*

*Coiled in one corner was a scarlet satin ribbon. He
did not recognize it, but the vivid color gleamed in the
candlelight, drawing his eye. Returning the flower, he
took up the ribbon.*

Adrian lifted out the thin narrow scrap. It seemed to twist
about his fingers like a tiny snake. Like a thin tongue licking
fire. It gleamed scarlet on his fingers, red as flame, red as
blood. Heart's blood.

*Power uncoiled, wrapping around him like a dragon's
tail, pulling him through time, from the attic, to the inn
by the Thames, to the castle in Ireland. The fragile ribbon held a vast skein of emotions twisted together, binding his mother, his father, his infant sister in rage and
terror and grief. Binding Adrian. Their desperate hold
wound tighter and tighter around him. Their pain cut
through him, stripping skin down to nerve and bone,
stripping away his mind.*

*His father's outraged pride choked him, filling belly
and throat like vitriol. He stared down at his infant
daughter, disgusted by her sallow skin and low forehead, by the strange downward drag of her eyes. She
was worse than useless—she was censure, judgment,
and condemnation of all he was. All he should be. Better she die now than dishonor him with her existence.
His father picked up the pillow, his fingers crushing the
satin rosettes and fluttering scarlet ribbons.*

*The babe reached up toward their gleaming bright-
ness and burbled her delight. Innocent bewilderment
transformed to terror as the pillow descended and cov-*

ered her. In the smothering darkness she struggled for breath and found none. Her frantic heart thudded . . . thudded . . . and stilled. She sank down into darkness.

The warmth that glowed in his mother's breast and womb hollowed to cold emptiness as that sweet life was snuffed out. Panicked, she ran to the nursery and saw her husband standing beside the cradle. The babe lay still, her head cradled on the pillow. Scarlet ribbons falling like streams of blood.

"I just found her," he lied. "I thought she was sleeping, but she isn't moving."

Dead. Dead. Dead . . . She stroked the still warm cheek. Touched the single red ribbon caught in the tiny fist. Grief, horror, rage, rushed to fill her aching emptiness—poured out of her. Seizing the ribbon, she turned on her husband, an avenging fury.

"Liar! Murderer!"

She saw that at last he believed in the gift he had so long denied. He had thought he could murder their child and no one would know. She seized the heavy candlestick, flame licking at the tip.

He backed away, out of the nursery, into the hall. She followed, grief twisted with rage. She had loved him, given herself to him, tried to become what he wanted. In return he had destroyed everything! Killed their love. Killed their child!

She lunged forward, stabbing him in a savage blinding thrust. He screamed and clutched his face, blood pouring between his fingers. He staggered back to the edge of the stairs and over. She watched him plummet down, her mind cracking with that ghastly fall. A fall from grace. A falling out of love—the heart plummeting into blackness. Tumbling into hell. He lay still at the bottom of the stairs. With a shrill cry, she ran downstairs, not knowing if she wanted to save her husband or kill him. Despair and fury consumed her.

His father lay still at the bottom of the stairs. Waiting to die. Wanting to die. Hot blood seeped from his eye like bitter tears. Despair and remorse consumed him.

. . . Consumed Adrian.

"Adrian . . ." Claire's voice called to him, soft but fiercely urgent.

He gazed at her, stricken. Her eyes were darkly luminous, full of love and anguish. He pressed his hands to his throbbing temples. The ribbon fell from his shaking fingers, but still images inundated his mind. Ireland and London wavered and rippled like weeds beneath a murky tide. They wrapped around him, pulled him back to the tavern by the Thames.

He confronted his father, filled with his mother's rage.

"Murderer!"

He struck out, a backhanded blow that sent his father reeling against the wall.

His father stared at him, white with panic, then sagged against the wall. "Maeve . . ." He whispered his wife's name, then said, "Do it. Finish what she started."

His father closed his eyes, waiting for the killing blow to fall.

Adrian stood over him, shuddering with fury—

"Adrian," Claire whispered again, drawing him into the present.

His tongue would not form words to answer her. His bones would not support him. Utterly drained, he leaned back against the wall. The terrible brew of memory seethed within him, his own emotions tangled fast in that twisted web, ugly, dark, and ultimately sad. He felt devastated by the death of the innocent sister he had never been allowed to see, scoured by his mother's wrath, and sickened with the endless oppressive weight of his father's guilt and fear. Claire did not offer her touch, only her soothing low voice, and her steadying presence. He wanted to reach out to her, but he did not. Not yet. There was further to go, and he searched for his own strength before seeking the comfort of their bond.

At last, Adrian found his voice and turned to face her. "I remember it all now," he said. "I struck him—one blow it was, but fierce. It is only luck that it did not kill him."

"But you didn't." Claire's response was quiet but vehement.

"No. But for a moment I did not care. For a moment, I wanted him dead. As my mother wanted him dead." He closed his eyes at the memory, turned his head away. He clenched his fists tightly, nails gouging into his flesh. Their tormented emotions were inescapable, knotted into his flesh and mind. Only his understanding was his own.

"But why? Tell me why," Claire cried out to him.

Adrian opened his eyes, unclenched his hands, and faced her. "He killed her baby, my sister, because she was deformed. He took a pillow—" Adrian broke off. Emptiness echoed within him, a smothered wail. He wrapped his arms about himself. "My mother felt her child die at his hands."

"He murdered her child?" Claire's voice choked on a sob. "I would have tried to kill him as well. Perhaps I would have gone mad."

Remnants of his father's torment hung in shreds from his own soul. "My father was ashamed, horrified by the child. He'd defied his family to marry my mother. The babe seemed a judgment against him. He could not endure it. And then could not endure what he'd done."

Claire's face was pale and unforgiving. "You accused him of the child's death?"

"Yes. He only stared—in terror of me," Adrian said. "Until he killed the babe, he had denied my mother's gift, and she, for fear of losing his love and acceptance, had hidden the full extent of it."

"He never loved her for herself, then." Claire's face looked pale as a marble statue of Justice. But the coldness in her gaze melted to warmth when she looked at him.

As you have me, always. Gently, Adrian touched a fold of her skirt, not daring more yet. It rustled in his fingers, a subtle music. He felt nothing but cool silk, still he was comforted. He rested a moment, feeling the firmness of the floor and wall. Dust motes quivered in the shaft of light from the window. Ivy leaves tapped delicately against the windowpanes. Secrets.

"The truth is sadder," Adrian told her, the dull ache of waste and misery permeating to the bone. "My father fell in love with her wildness, her fey spirit. Yet once he captured her heart, he tried to tame it. He did not know how to be free himself, and could not admit how much he needed her just as she was. Instead, she grew ashamed. She tried to dim the very brightness he adored, to hide the gift that frightened him."

"How terrible, to destroy what he loved." Suddenly, her eyes brimmed with tears as sadness welled through her anger. Her lips trembled.

Fighting his own urge to weep, Adrian closed his eyes a moment, overwhelmed by the tragedy that had trapped his parents, a failure of love that doomed them both. Growing up under his father's suspicious gaze, he had shared his mother's growing shame in her gift, her fear of unworthiness. But Claire had found him worthy. Her love had not faltered. She had stood by him, followed after him. Opening his eyes, Adrian met her tender gaze. Her unwavering strength sustained him even without the link of touch. "After she went mad, my father always dreaded to see her power awaken in me. To forestall it, he punished any flicker of her gift in me. And so I hid the gift from him, and from myself."

"Until that night." She drew a breath, gathering her own calm.

"Yes." Slowly, Adrian coiled the ribbon. A tiny red tongue, it had spoken truth. He felt no more from it. He laid it within the box and closed the lid. The dragon still seemed to coil sinuously across its surface, fiercely alive, merciless yet not malevolent—like the quieter, deeper power that rose from the rocks at Stonehenge. His story was not yet done. "I came to myself enough to know that I might kill him. That's when I ran away, out into the alleyways behind the inn, into a dead end. He followed me. I wonder now if he wanted me to kill him. What was left of his spirit died with my mother."

"Such unhappiness," Claire sighed heavily, her pity stronger now than anger.

"He destroyed everything—his child, my mother, himself." Bitterness poured through him, the ache of his own miserable childhood churning with his father's ever suspicious wretchedness.

"He did not destroy you," Claire insisted softly.

"That night . . . I tried to hide in the shadows. I could hear him calling, then his footsteps entered the alley. I was afraid to look at him, afraid I would strike him again. Then he gave a horrible cry. I turned and saw him stagger toward me—blood pouring over his face." Adrian gestured, hand moving over his own face. "But it was not from the wound that I gave him. The robbers attacked—"

"You did not destroy your father, Adrian," Claire repeated. "Those men killed him."

Adrian's voice cracked. "I felt as if I had summoned them somehow—that I could not escape my wish to kill him."

"I understand your guilt," Claire moved closer, speaking with quiet fierceness. "But you did not summon them. They were already waiting for their prey."

Adrian paused for a moment, holding her gaze. The pain of the moment ebbed, and when he spoke again his voice was calmer. "After that there is darkness. I know now they knocked me unconscious and tossed me into the Thames. The water must have revived me, for the next thing I remember is climbing out of the river, stripped of all but my hose and linen. But I did not know who I was."

She nodded, urging him to follow the memory to its end. Sunlight touched the pure oval of her face, limning her perfectly sculpted features with a shimmer of gold, and streaking the fall of her rich chestnut hair. His fingers curled, as if they could feel its rich texture.

He forced himself to go on. "I passed out again. In the morning men woke me with kicks and dragged me to my feet. With every touch, their brutality flooded in. They were angry that I had nothing left to steal, and their anger goaded mine. I lashed out at them like—like the madman I was."

He flinched at the memory, and Claire did as well. "You were wounded," she said. "Wounded in body and soul."

He was not touching her, but it was as if his hand was linked with hers, as if they walked the last steps together. "Guards came to take me to Bedlam—even more vicious than the other men. I tried to find some sense of myself, but their blows shattered through."

"I saw them drag you in." Her voice caught as she spoke of the ugly memory. Then she smiled a little, ironically, as he might. "How strange a meeting."

The journey was complete. Adrian's hands spanned the distance between them, clasping hers. It was like being dipped in purest rainwater, bathed in sunlight. Her love was balm to every sense. "Yours was the first kind voice, the first gentle touch," he whispered. "You were like an angel, commanding yet serene."

"I thought you were the angel, though a very muddy one. Your voice penetrated to the core of me." She pressed one hand to her heart.

"You touched me, brought me back to sanity . . . then darkness swallowed me." He paused as a sudden wave of despondency washed over him. Once he would have retreated, now he kept his hand entwined with Claire's. With her beside him, the shadow passed more swiftly. "My memory suddenly stops for several days. There is only blackness—like being swallowed into the belly of Evil."

"Because Quarrell covered you with his cloak?" she asked.

"His cloak?" Was that the explanation for that terrible plunge into darkness? Not his own madness welling up, but his first contact with Quarrell? Then there was a cause for everything. "The touch of his garment could have wiped all else from my mind."

Another chill swept through him, but he knew it for Claire's fear. Quarrell had obliterated her from his mind. Her hands trembled a little in his, but she said in her calm voice, "Quarrell is the enemy, indeed."

Adrian knew he would only be free when the doctor was captured. In truth, he would only be free when Quarrell was dead. He kept hold of Claire's hands, offering the light of his newly kindled hope. "Because of you, facing Quarrell at last seems possible."

The memories that had first shattered him had been confronted and conquered. He had not killed his father. He understood the terrible forces that broke his mother's mind, and he had reclaimed his own sanity. His gift could be controlled—at least in part.

He could not have done it alone. Claire had been here beside him, her soft voice an anchor no weightier than breath, yet holding him secure in the storm. He would never be complete without her, he knew that now. She was his future. If she was not with him, his heart would remain a locked tower, a cell of loneliness.

Adrian looked around at the old tapestries that had once given warmth to Castle Treise. He laid his ungloved hand on their surface. A vestige of his mother's pleasure in them lingered. Joy wove through the embroidered vines and blossoms that brought the green and gold brightness of spring even into winter. He stroked them slowly, absorbing that faded delight. Perhaps his family curse could truly be a gift. Since childhood, he had run from it, but he no longer wanted to deny it. With its emergence, his fragmented, wandering life had taken on a pattern. If fear and terror were part of its weave, so were hope and friendship and happiness.

So was love.

He clasped her hands in his own and pressed his lips to her

fingers, gazing into her eyes. Like shadowed forest pools, they shimmered with rich bark browns and leafy greens, layers of glorious color—and layers of warm glowing emotion.

"Claire." With the whispered syllable of her name, he pledged himself heart and soul.

And received her soft-voiced murmur in answer. "Adrian."

Chapter 18

It was time. They both knew it without question.

Claire reached up to Adrian, her fingertips stroking the tawny hair back from his face. In the arch of light from the window, the bones showed sharp in his face, and dark circles of strain smudged the hollows beneath his eyes. But the darkness within them had lifted, the irises shone clear as a sunlit stream, alight with motes of green, blue, and amber. Alight with emotion—tenderness, love, and with a deeper yearning. A deeper hunger.

That same hunger hollowed her belly, yet filled her with the ache of longing.

They could go back downstairs, but there they would be one step closer to the demands of reality. Here they were as alone as they had been on the first days of their travel. More so, for then Adrian had stood back from her, guarded and solitary behind his crystalline charm. His own shadow had blocked the light flowing between them. Now that shadow was lifted, that barrier dissolved. She could see, could feel that Adrian was open to her. His defenses were gone, and passion welled to the surface.

The attic was quiet, intimate, a world apart. In silent accord they began to transform it. Adrian unrolled the pallets to cushion the floor beneath the narrow window. Claire spread a rich old tapestry over them, making a bed of tawny arabesques, green twining vines, and yellow trumpet blossoms. Outside the mullioned window, the afternoon sun flickered through the ivy, the dance of light and shadow brocading layers of shimmering leaves across the surface of the fabric. They lay down in their golden bower, the dappled light falling over them like a blessing.

Claire tilted her face up to Adrian's, welcoming his kiss. The world, her own longings, seemed new as Eden. His lips sought hers, his fingertips brushing across her cheeks, her temples, along the arch of her brows. Each touch elicited a tantalizing quiver, strumming soft fire from her fine-tuned nerves, awakening desire within her. His lips were firm, yet warm and pliant as they caressed hers. They kissed softly, delicately at first, sweet notes thrilling with each teasing brush of flesh. Claire could feel her pulse quicken as he stroked the slender column of her throat. Sensitive there, she gave a little shiver, then a sigh that parted her lips. He gave an answering sigh as his mouth covered hers, tasted hers. The moist tip of his tongue brushed along the open seam of her lips, courting her response, delving within when she opened to him. Shy yet eager, her tongue moved to meet his, sensation unfolding with new intensity with the intimate caresses. Warmth filled her, the touch of his lips, his tongue, kindling all her flesh.

Adrian pressed her closer and Claire bent to him like a willow sapling, curving to fit the harder planes of his body. The kiss deepened, tongues gliding and stroking. She drank in the warm, intoxicating taste of him, kissing till giddiness overwhelmed her. Tilting back further, she looked up at him. A soft brimming joy filled her and spilled over into a smile. He answered with a caressing laugh. Her heart bloomed to hear it, the first he had given her. The sound touched her like a melodic caress. His eyes glowed. Like elven jewels they were now, faceted with unearthly iridescent hues, enthralling her with their beauty, their promise of undiscovered rapture. She murmured his name again, the syllables music on her tongue.

Drawing her into his arms, Adrian lifted her effortlessly. She felt as light as windblown thistle in his arms. His strength excited her even as she treasured his gentleness. He carried her to their tapestry bower and laid her on that soft, sun-dappled bed. Wherever skin was exposed to him, he kissed—her face, her ears, her throat. He clasped her hands and raised them, touching his lips to her wrists.

A sweet pang rippled through her. Gently, her hands folded over his, claiming her prize. Pale from their sojourn in their leather shell, still they were more golden than the pale ivory of her own. Taking each one in turn, she caressed his fingers with her own until all his skin tingled as if music played beneath his skin. He caressed her face as she stroked his palm with her lips. Her tongue tip teased the center of his palm, then traced the lines, mind, heart, life, all given to her. She willed her love to permeate him through each pathway to his being. She drew his thumb, each finger, into the lush warmth of her mouth, caressing with the wet silken tenderness of her lips, then sucking with sweet, erotic delectation. Adrian gave a helpless moan, pressing to her. Through her skirts she felt his manhood rise, summoned by her wanton play.

Kneeling back, he untied the ribbons of her sleeves, and drew them off, leaving her arms bare. She tensed when he gazed down the scars twisting along her arm, stark and ugly to her eyes. But Adrian bent to them without hesitation, his lips moving along their length. The softness of his lips, the totality of his acceptance, melted her. His eyes met hers, glowing with love and desire.

When she relaxed, he loosed the bindings of the tight bodice and slid it off, leaving only the gossamer shift of linen and lace beneath. He gazed down at her, his breath catching. Claire could see the dusky rose circles of her aureole visible beneath the transparent fabric. Already her nipples ached for his touch. With his fingertips, he pulled the lacy edge beneath her small, high breasts, framing them. Bending, he kissed each nipple till the peak hardened with a throb of delight. He trapped the nub between teeth and stroking tongue tip, flicking it with wet, tormenting sweet caresses. Bright trills coursed through her with each delicate caress. Her heartbeat quickened, a muffled percussion matching her increasing eagerness. She pressed closer to Adrian, her arms tightening even as her legs liquefied. Arching upward, she moaned to him, the husky sound revealing the deeper resonance of her pleasure.

With a last playful nip, he drew back, murmuring, "I want more of you."

Claire smiled into his eyes, assenting. "All of me."

Grasping one foot, Adrian slid off its slipper, then kissed the arching instep, the dip between the ankles, and licked up the long line of bone leading to the rounded cap of her knee. He planted a kiss there, then slipped off the other shoe and began again, nuzzling and nipping along the slope of her calf. The black damask skirts still draped her thighs, but beneath them he stroked her warm skin. To Claire, her own yielding flesh felt like satin beneath his fingertips. Tentative in her inexperience, yet sweetly shameless, she parted her legs to his persuasive fingertips, gasping as his nails grazed delicately along her inner thighs. Frissons of delight shivered along her spine.

At last, he loosened her skirts and freed her of the black mourning and delicate white linen. She lay beneath the attic window, clad only in the leafy veils of sunlight and shadow, in the soft flush of desire that made her tremble with longing. He kissed her lips again, then followed a slow downward path, evoking a soft gasp with each caress. The ceaseless sigh of the wind seemed hers. The murmuring leaves spoke in her breathless voice. Adrian whispered to her in answer, praising her beauty, coaxing her responses. His hands moved over her, a journey of tantalizing discovery. His tongue traced gleaming outlines on the soft skin of her breasts, the concave curve of her belly, the sculpted rise of her hipbone. His fingertips combed the chestnut hair swirled at the apex of her thighs, then dipped between her tender lips, seeking the liquid fire within. Slowly, he stroked the sleek, wet inner skin, then found the pearl of flesh at the crest. She cried out in amazement as pulsations of fire unfurled from his touch.

He looked up at her, his gaze filled with sweet lust, with wicked delight. His fingers circled there, sending hot spirals spinning through her, out to her fingers and toes, up to her dazzled brain. She gave a small sob as his fingertips slid away from that aching peak, another as he parted the petals of her sex, exposing her to him. Her pulse, her secret heart beat there under his gaze, unbearably intimate.

"A rose," he whispered, "a hot-petaled autumn rose."

She quivered with suspense as he bent and kissed the inside of her knee, then nibbled softly up the tender skin of her inner thigh. The pulsations deepened. She wanted to draw her legs together—to spread them wider still. She trembled with expectance and a delicious trepidation. His warm breath touched her, a sigh against that most sensitive skin. She cried out, amazed, as his tongue flicked over that tight bud of delight. She swooned into darkness as his tongue laved her softly, hot and wet against her secret wetness. Every nerve coiled into a tight, furled core of pleasure, of need. Once again his tongue touched her, precise, devastating. Desire burned bright as a single star glowing in the center of the dark. Again—and the bright star exploded, filling the darkness with a million glittering notes of light, of burning, throbbing pleasure. . . .

Claire lay dazed for a moment, thrumming as the ripples of pleasure slowly dissipated. They did not fade entirely, but left her blood singing softly with delight. She felt luminous, and she saw her glow reflected in Adrian's eyes. They gleamed, alight with triumph and desire. She knew now the sweet goal at the end of the journey. The answer to the unbearable craving was that almost unbearable pleasure, and this utterly exquisite fulfillment.

Claire reached out, tugging at Adrian's doublet with her

stronger hand. He eased back, undoing ties and fastenings, then stripping off both sleeves and the doublet of mossy velvet. She lifted his shirt, her hands exploring the sensitive skin taut over his rib cage. Adrian gasped at the flare of sensation, as if his nerves lay exposed to her touch, and she gloried in the power that lay in her hands. She could feel his flesh vibrating with pleasure as her fingers played through the soft, gilded mat of his chest hair. Her fingers winged out across his chest, fingertips brushing his nipples. They hardened as hers had, smaller but taut and puckered. Her fingernails teased lightly over the tips. He sucked in a breath, tightening his belly muscles. Beneath the rounded knot of his navel, she glimpsed a descending trickle of darker hair.

"I want to see you," she whispered. "To see you as I touch you."

The points of his hose were already undone, easy to peel them off—though she had to lift the cloth free of his eager arousal. He laughed softly, bemused with delight, panting lightly as she stripped them down his long legs and off. She stroked his taut thigh with the stiff fingers of her right hand and gazed at the masculine treasures she had uncovered.

"You are beautiful," she said. He was marvelous, with the strong, lithe grace of a young stag—or a golden unicorn. She had to smile at the myth, for his single upcurving horn of flesh seemed magical, rising from the bronzed hair. The skin flushed dark rose, the branching veins blue beneath. Surely the unicorn's horn was an aphrodisiac. She must taste him, as he had tasted her. He inhaled sharply, a long hiss of excruciating pleasure as her fingers wrapped around the long length of his shaft. She felt his life in her hands, hard yet supple, straining against her caresses. He was like a perfect instrument, satin skin stretching taut over the hard straining thrust of desire. She must play him, as he had played her, with coaxing tongue and sweetly tormenting teeth.

Desire inspired and intoxicated her. Bending down to him, Claire breathed his masculine scent and took her first taste, salty sweet. Her tongue played lightly over the straining length of him, wanting all his skin to know her touch. When she took the hot shaft in her mouth, he made music for her, soft cries and breathless moans. And when she cupped the rounded weight suspended beneath, he gave a deep low moan that echoed down to her core. She moaned in joyful resonance. Whatever music she had lost, she had found what was deepest, truest. He was her song and she his. The first note had sounded with their first touch. The last would die with the last heartbeat.

His response played through her. The pleasure she evoked in him took on new life within her, a rising harmony. Her blood shimmered in her veins, as if she was filled with the same tremulous sunlight that danced through the window. Every atom hummed with music woven from the primal elements. Her earthbound flesh dissolved—in the watery sparkle of sweat, in the air of every sighing breath, and in the melting fire of passion. Deliciously malleable, she flowed with his touch like an endless melody. Adrian eased her back on their golden bed and pressed her thighs apart. She made him welcome there, unresisting as he guided himself to her hidden portal. He paused there to capture her gaze, to be with her in the total intensity of the moment. She could feel the hot press of his erection against her. Her body, her entire being, contracted with need, then expanded with a need that was greater still.

"Now. Come into me now."

Pain shot through her as he broke the last fragile barrier separating them. She cried out. His hands tightened on her. Looking up, she saw her own hurt reflected in his eyes. He held there, barely within her, not moving till the wound of his entry was assuaged by the wonder of his presence. "Yes," she whispered, urging him.

Slowly he pressed forward. She sobbed, first with the hurt, then with a sweeter agony. He stopped, but the promise of pleasure lured her, enthralled her, and she pressed up to him, cleaving the path to her core. Her moan blended with his, pleasure and pain melded, indistinguishable. When he was fully within her, he paused again, waiting for her body to accept him. But the throbbing need of his sex, the aching response of hers created subtle, unbearable friction that demanded they move.

"Adrian," she whispered his name, feeling its music in her breath.

"*Mo cride*," he whispered in answer. "Claire . . . my heart."

He began to thrust, slowly, as if each stroke was too exquisite to bear. It was for her—such piercing sweetness, she cried out with the joy of it. He sheathed himself inside of her, and she clasped him closely, holding him with every part of her. They moved together, the quickening rhythm of desire, of need, pulling them apart only to plunge them closer, deeper. The rising crescendo of pleasure crested to a pinnacle of agonizing sweetness. Absolute joy lifted her for one eternal second. Flesh . . . love . . . music . . . light. No difference.

But she was still flesh, and the ecstasy was too pure, too powerful to contain. The brightness cascaded, flowing through her, decimation and delight. Adrian moaned her name once more, his ecstasy one with hers.

She clung to him as the waves slowly subsided to ripples, and at last even the ripples faded. Yet she sensed an invisible vibration still lingering beyond her human apprehension. Adrian's fingers wove with hers, gently tightened. With him, Claire felt herself part of eternal boundless singing, wedded to love itself. They lay curled in each other's arms, lingering in the hushed wonder of afterglow for long minutes, sharing a precious peace. The fluttering lace of sun and shadow draped them, and they listened to the timbrelle rustling of the leaves.

His eyes drifted shut. He sighed, then murmured something under his breath. She heard. "We'll go to Southwark. . . ."

"Later. Now go to sleep," she said, then smiled when she saw he already was.

But Claire could not sleep for the wonder and the newness and the joy. Watching Adrian, she savored the perfect trust that allowed him to give himself to her quiet vigil. Sated desire had melted care from his face, and sleep smoothed it even more. His lips were parted, his eyelids quivered faintly as he slept. What did he see in his dreams? Nothing fearful, for he sighed with contentment. She caressed his cheek, imparting her love with her touch. Her fingertips followed the angle of his jaw, the column of his throat, and touched the pulse in the hollow beneath. Her hand flowed down his body, feeling again the silky crispness of his chest hair. She traced its faint bronze trail down his torso to where the thatch sprang up darker, wilder. His magic unicorn's horn had become a tender thing, nestled there like a soft bird. She kissed it sweetly, smiling as he murmured her name but did not wake.

Magic, too, were his beautiful hands. Stroking his fingers, long, graceful, and strong, Claire wondered if he would ever go without gloves except in the most intimate situations. Today's revelations had proved his gift was not a curse. Would it in time become a pride, a strength for him to turn to, rather than something to avoid as best he could? How deeply had this day changed him?

Stirred by the wind, the ivy leaves rustled and tapped at the glass, reminding her that all too soon the world would encroach on their serenity. Beyond the haven of their attic bower, danger waited. Claire shuddered, touched by a sudden chill. Once before, Quarrell had taken him from her, body and soul, drowning her memory in his darkness. Claire was loathe to leave here, all the more loathe to risk Adrian now that he was finally hers entirely.

No. Not entirely.

She frowned a little. He had not said the words, but surely he would? Surely he would not have made her his lover if he did not tend to make her his wife? If he feared to have a child with her? Surely, his possession of her had been his gift of himself entire?

But with a lover's sweet greed, she hungered for his pledge.

Another simpler hunger woke in Claire. Breakfast had been a light, nervous meal. As she dressed, she thought what food she would bring up for them to share. White bread and wine. Lush purple grapes. A pomegranate to crack open like a mythic heart, filled with tart-sweet, glistening red seeds. They would each eat twelve, one for each month of the year. So they would live not in winter darkness but in this golden harvest of delight. In their own hearts, at least. She smiled at her own whimsy.

After a brief struggle, Claire managed to fasten the complicated ties of the black damask gown and make herself presentable to the world. She quietly descended the stairs and made her way toward the kitchen to ask for the dishes for their attic picnic. Seeing her in the hallway, Samuel approached. His demeanor was serious as befitted his position, but his eyes showed a smile. He bowed and said, "Lady Claire, a note has arrived from your father. It is on the table in the entry hall."

The world was intruding already, she thought, then felt ashamed. Her father was a most dear part of that world. She had treated both her parents ill, letting them worry so long. She opened and read the message, which asked her to meet him at the tower soon. The missive was brief, curt even, but well it might be after her neglect. Claire read it again, one finger idly tracing the inked *B* with its swooping curves, a mark of Lord Brightsea's eccentric hand.

Trepidation stirred—her parents might have made some drastic pact during her absence. Her father would consider her happiness, but would he judge it the same as she? He would not discount wealth and family connections. Her mother would have been at work upon him. Perhaps the old Earl her mother had chosen would take damaged goods with a lesser dowry. Claire wished she could say that she was betrothed to Adrian, but she could not. She resisted the urge to wake him, and ask him to come with her—to ask for that final commitment to be given before her family, before the world.

Would he still hesitate? Would he insist that Quarrell must be captured first?

Claire frowned. She did not trust her mother not to denounce Adrian and have him arrested. She would insist 'twas all for the best while trying to force her own chosen suitor upon Claire. And even if the cloud over Adrian was lifted, her mother would not choose a man, Baron or Earl, who was half-Irish. Claire shivered. Who knew how long it would be before Quarrell was taken. What if he was never found? Adrian must not be confined in the Tower. Difficult though it was, she would face her parents alone.

"Samuel, I would like to borrow a horse from your stable, and a small escort for protection." She found Samuel's good will toward her so apparent that she did not hesitate to add, "Let Lord Roadnight sleep peacefully for now, but wake him before the sun sets, so that he may reach his rendezvous in Southwark."

"I will attend to it all, my lady," he replied.

"I will leave a note for Lord Roadnight before I go."

Samuel directed her to the library, where she found fresh honed quills, ink, and fine parchment. Claire wrote a tender salutation, followed by a simple message.

My father has written, asking to speak to me. I must needs assure my parents of my well-being, but I promise nothing will prevent me from joining you at the meeting.

She could truthfully tell her father she had given her word to meet her friends to help plan the strategy to trap the murderer. He would be angry, but she doubted he would prevent her from going. Still, after a moment, she added another line.

If I do not appear, you have leave to rescue me.

Claire hesitated. The note seemed silly one moment, fearful the next. And so are you, too, she scolded herself. Nonetheless, she did not tear it up, but powdered the note dry, then folded it and sealed it with a bright red drop of wax.

Chapter 19

Sidesaddle, Claire thought grimly, as one of the burly guards Sir James had provided boosted her onto the mare. She took the reins in her stronger hand and settled her balance. Riding astride had spoiled her. Then she blushed at the thought of mounting so, sore as she was. But sweetly sore. She glanced at the upper windows, wondering when Adrian would wake. She hungered to return to his arms and renew that breathtaking intimacy. Tonight? Tomorrow?

But not now. Now she must explain her impetuous departure to her father. With a nod to her escort, Claire set out along the road toward the tower. The warm sun had been swallowed up. Heavy gray clouds rolled like mammoth bolsters overhead, weighted with rain. As the breeze quickened, the leaves chattered on their branches or skittered wildly about the horses' hooves. Amber, russet, and scarlet, their autumnal hues glowed rich but somber in the muted light. The air seemed to cling to her skin, moist and tingling, foretelling rain. There was a wildness in the air that stirred her blood. In an instant her mind leapt from belated explanations to enticing visions of Adrian. She conjured the supple caress of his lips, the limber play of his tongue against her own, the fiercely tender grip of his hands. A few feet behind her, a horse snorted, reminding her she was in public view. The wanton images made her feel far too naked. Claire forced her mind back to more sober matters.

Remembering how Adrian had made this same journey in the fog and been followed, she took care to check behind her at intervals. But she saw no one, and felt safe enough with two armed men beside her. Reassured, Claire prepared to face her father. She must beg forgiveness for her reckless behavior—and convince him of her need to continue the hunt for Bedlam's master. She must be cautiously honest if—when—her father questioned her about Adrian's intentions. *He is an honorable man. The situation is much complicated by the cloud of suspicion that shadows him.*

He has not asked me to marry him—yet.

Despite her uncertainty, Claire felt a warm anticipation when she turned into the lane of tall, golden-crested chestnuts and approached her father's tower. She and her escort drew to a halt outside the stone wall and dismounted. An unfamiliar but formidable guard in her family livery waited outside the door. Claire was surprised. Her father valued solitude more than safety, and seldom allowed anyone but friends and family into his sanctuary. However, he might well have taken new measures to protect himself after she vanished. Perhaps the guard was only here to protect her. Guilt gnawed at her. She had brought her family pain and scandal. The pain she could heal. The scandal might well continue.

But Adrian's vindication was more important than her reputation.

Knowing she might need her escort to accompany her to the tavern later, Claire asked them to wait, then walked toward the ivy-draped tower. The guard bowed to her stiffly, and then opened the door. "Your father is waiting inside, my lady."

Claire stepped into the shadowed room. She saw her father

bent over an experiment on the central table, his old velvet robe flowing loose down his back, a cap and embroidered coif covering his head. For an instant it was amusingly familiar to see him bent low over his work, too absorbed to turn and greet her. She smiled at the clink of glass as he lifted something.

Then a cold finger traced the length of her spine like a keyboard, raising prickling notes of alarm. She tried to dismiss them, but they accumulated, one after another. She had been gone over a week, presumed dead—worse than dead. Even if her father had believed her safe, how could he be so detached, so oblivious? In this gloom, how could he see what he worked at? Despite the loose flow of the robe, he looked different, broader and heavier.

Instinctively, Claire backed toward the door, grateful for the three guards without.

But if this was not her father, the man at the door was not her father's guard.

Behind her, the door swing shut. Before her, the man straightened and turned, a glass beaker in his hand. Even in the darkened room, she could see now who it was. Quarrell—wearing her father's robe. The prickles of alarm stabbed deeper, icy stilettos that pinioned her where she stood. The doctor smiled, then glanced to the side, to the corner of the room. Her father lay in a heap, blood drenching his face.

Claire cried out, first in horror, then calling loudly for help. Sir James' guards were close, surely they would hear her. As if surprised, Quarrell's henchman opened the door and rushed in—then stepped to one side, his sword drawn.

"It's a trap!" Claire shouted as her guards stormed through after him.

The warning came too late. Quarrell's henchman skewered one guard in the back. The doctor flung the contents of the beaker into the other's face. A splash of reeking corrosive. Screaming, the guard fell to the floor, writhing and clutching his face as the acid sizzled into his flesh. Quarrell's henchman moved forward and finished him off.

Claire bolted for the door, but Quarrell lunged forward, grabbing her damaged arm in a wrenching grip. Pain sliced a path from wrist to elbow. Seeing her reaction, he increased the pressure, twisting across the injured nerves. She gave a cry and sank to her knees, cursing her own weakness as she fought to keep from fainting.

"They are all dead, Lady Claire," Quarrell said. "There is no hope."

She gave a sob of fury and despair, her gaze going to her father lying so still in the corner.

"I wrote and asked him to validate a copy of the Emerald Tablet. What alchemist could resist? He invited me here, greedy as a child for sweets," Quarrell sneered. "All I had to do was copy his note with the smallest changes, and bring you here as well."

Then he gestured to his henchman, who shoved the acid scarred corpse of her guard aside and snatched a rope from the table. Claire fought fiercely as they bound and gagged her. Seizing an opening, she kicked the henchman in the groin. He cuffed her, a dazing blow to the side of the head. Quarrell shoved him against the wall, snarling a warning. Leery, the henchman backed off.

"Hide the horses, then go fetch the wagon," Quarrell ordered and the man left to do his bidding.

Quarrell covered her entirely in her father's cape. The comforting aroma of velvet and vellum, of garden herbs and exotic resins, made her want to weep. She fought back tears, needing her breath, her strength. Waiting, she heard a low, impatient mutter, a strange dull tapping. She pictured the doctor's pale fingers drumming on the table. Then it stopped. Glass crunched as he moved toward her, stood over her. His gaze seemed to sear through the cloak like acid. Involuntarily, she curled smaller beneath. He gave a sibilant laugh, the sound rubbing her raw nerves like sandpaper. Claire bit her lips, fighting her rising fear. A moment later, she heard the clop of a horse, the creak of a wagon. They carried her out the back, and dumped her into a wagon, flinging a wide length of oilcloth to cover her. Claire flinched when Quarrell slid under the tarp beside her.

"In the past I have done my own driving, but now I am more discreet," he whispered, curving against her back and hips with obscene intimacy.

His henchman snapped a whip at the horse and they moved into the road. Quarrell opened the cape but only to hold the blade of a knife to her throat. Every jog and bump left small cuts on her neck. After a few moments, Quarrell eased his body back away from hers a fraction, though the knife stayed close. Such close contact was too human, Claire guessed. Cold metal knives were his desired means of touch. For the moment, she could only be grateful.

Outside, they passed into a more crowded area. Her sense of hearing was acute. Beyond the nasal drag of Quarrell's breathing, the creaking of their own wagon, Claire could hear other horses and wagons. She could hear people moving, talking, and laughing in the ordinary world. So close. If she cried out would they hear her through the gag? She knew Quarrell did not want her to die now. He wanted her to suffer. If she drew attention to them, would he kill her before he attempted to escape?

As if he knew what she was thinking, he pinched off her nostrils. With the cloth stuffed in her mouth, she could not breathe. The bustle of humanity slowly faded into nothingness. The only sound was the mute, desperate sucking of her lungs. Speckles of light, black stars swarmed. Abruptly he released her. Claire lay weak and trembling, inhaling the muffled air greedily. The known, comforting scents of the cape were polluted by Quarrell's evil perfume. He smelled of acid and violets, smoky incense and blood. Her blood, fresh and metallic. Old blood, rotten and corrupt. The wagon rolled on. It began to rain, heavy drops spattering on the oiled cloth covering them. Instead of voices, now she heard the heavy swish of trees in the wind, and caught a faint scent through the cloth. Damp earth and wet green foliage. Life.

Adrian . . .

Claire prayed silently, willing him to hear.

The wagon pulled to a halt. Claire felt the shift in weight as Quarrell's henchman jumped down, and heard a gate open. There was a loud bark without, taken up by more fierce canine voices. Dogs would guard against both escape and rescue. The barking and growling grew wilder as the beasts rushed toward the wagon, then subsided as the guard yelled at them. "They are most vicious," Quarrell spoke with smug assurance. "They can rip a man to pieces."

Could Adrian play Orpheus with his musical voice, the magic of his touch, and tame the savage beasts? She did believe Adrian could find her. Something would show him the way. But would he would find her alive or dead? She did not want to suffer, to die. She did not want Adrian to find her mutilated corpse. She must try to save herself.

Claire recoiled as the gate clapped shut. The guard led the horse forward into a stable of some sort, for the light faded and she could smell a thick aroma of hay and manure. Outside, the dogs snarled. Quarrell flung back the tarp, eased her to the edge of the wagon, and lifted her over. Her feet had fallen asleep and she collapsed into the straw.

Quarrell's smile twisted one side of his face. "I thought you more graceful, Lady Claire."

She fought off tears of humiliation, fury, and fear as she struggled to stand. The doctor leaned down and pulled her to her feet. His renewed closeness unnerved her and she drew back, breath catching in her throat. Quarrell chuckled, then bent and cut the bonds on her ankles. She wished she could kick him, but her feet were numbed from having been tied. A million tiny stings pierced her skin as the circulation returned. Even if she could have disabled Quarrell, there was still the guard, leering. Seeing the direction of her gaze, Quarrell gestured the man out. "Stand watch. I will have a message for you to deliver later."

Quarrell guided her out of the stable, across a covered walkway, and into the house. Claire wondered if the guard knew what his master intended for her. He looked cruel enough to join in rape and murder, but she suspected he thought her kidnapping would bring a rich ransom. No one would trust Quarrell if they knew his lusts. She balked at the doorway, but with her numbed feet, her bound hands, he easily pushed her into the kitchen. The room was empty and chill. No scent of bread or milk or ale made it human and inviting. Again he urged her forward, and she stumbled into a dining room, equally dismal. A faint odor of mold clung to the walls. He steadied her with a hand on her back and she tensed.

"Be at ease, Lady Claire," Quarrell murmured. "You seem skittish—as if a single touch would make you jump out of your skin."

Beneath his hand, her spine branched with ice. She inhaled sharply. Quarrell chuckled, a breathy wheeze. Moving around to face her, he drew a fingernail up one side of her neck, tracing across her jaw, and then descended the other side. The faint pressure scored her skin like the tip of a blunt knife. She glared at him, anger rising over her fear, loathing his depraved cruelty.

Quarrell went on speaking, his voice pouring over her like black oily syrup. "Even though I seldom have visitors, for my own comfort I try to evoke a sense of sumptuous repose. Your family estates must be richer by far, of course, yet these tapestries are fine, don't you think? And my paintings—observe, I am most pleased with this. I bought it abroad."

On the wall hung a still life of perfect flowers, fruit, and vegetables, wrought in minute detail against a black background. A skinned rabbit carcass hung in the center. Claire said nothing in response. It was all a malicious conceit to draw the strings of her fear taut, then pluck them till they snapped.

He edged her forward into the main hallway. She was steadier now on her feet. They no longer felt half-numb. But she kept her pace slow and uncertain.

Pausing by a panel, Quarrell said, "I had this constructed especially. The woodwork is lovely, don't you think? So ornate." He ran his fingers along the top. There was a snick and one long panel sprang open. The ridged and carved edges of the molding had concealed the doorway completely, and the inner side was covered with thick padding. With the candle, he lit the small lantern that hung at one side of the top landing. Light bloomed, casting writhing shadows on the wall. An open staircase led down to a dim cellar. "Although I have taken some care to my comfort above—my true abode lies below. Shall we go down?"

He watched her, measuring her resistance. When she did not move, Quarrell nudged her down onto the steps with a hand on her shoulder. She held back, resisting his push.

"I can carry you, of course, if you prefer."

Fighting nausea at the thought, Claire took one step down, another. Entering the darkness was like descending into a crypt. Quarrell inhaled deeply, savoring the dank, putrescent odor that rose up the steps. "It is such a delight to share this with you, Lady Claire. For I know that you can appreciate it as few others before you could. In the past, I took pleasure in surprising my guests, but this shared anticipation is a new and unforeseen delight." With that, he clicked the door shut behind them.

Unnerved, Claire caught her breath sharply. Behind her, Quarrell gave a rasping laugh. She stared into the dimness below, looking about for any way to flee, but running down ahead would be going deeper into the trap. White cloth shimmered at the periphery of her vision, its pallor evoking a shroud. She could not let herself think on what he would do to her. She must think how to prevent it.

He loves your fear. Pretend it is greater.

How easily pretense could give way to true terror. It clawed at her guts, a panicked thing threatening to break its fragile bonds. She needed her defense of anger, flimsy as it was, against her growing fear, his verbal torments. Yet if she were too defiant, Quarrell would be too wary. She walked ahead of him, feigning unsteadiness. Deliberately, she tripped a step, made a whimpering noise. He gave a small cluck, feigning sympathy.

"Take care not to hurt yourself, Lady Claire," Quarrell murmured, relishing every quiver of emotion she revealed.

The stairs were steep, she thought, too steep for perfect balance. She might easily fall.

And so might he.

She cowered against the wall, half-turning to look back at him. "Don't stop now, Lady Claire," he said, misinterpreting her glance. Quarrell looked down into the shadows below, eager for whatever horrors he had waiting. Let him think on that rather than of her. Let him trust in his balance. Impatient, he prodded her again. She moved down, halted, moved again. Her mind scrambled to make sense of the descent, dredging up childhood scuffles, bits of fencing treatises, Rafe and Gabriel's banter about their tavern brawls.

One more step.

Quarrell murmured a soft-voiced spew of insinuations Claire forced herself to disregard.

She took another step, then paused, sensing the shift of his weight as he followed her descent. Just as his foot was about to land on the next tread, she twisted around and grabbed his wrist. Her hands were bound, the right one weak, but she held fast with the left. Quarrel's foot was in midair, not quite down to the next step, his balance askew. Claire pushed off from the tread, and launched herself down the staircase with all her strength, dragging Quarrel after. He lost his footing and tumbled down. She gripped him as tightly as she could with her good hand.

Pain flared as he rolled atop her, beneath her, atop her again. Claire fought against its blinding flash. Her skirts bunched around her hips, but she was ready for his weight as she hit the floor at the bottom of the stairway. She tucked her knees to her chest, and thrust her left foot up into Quarrel's chest. She let go of his wrist and pushed up and sideways with her legs. Her shove and his own velocity carried him over her. He crashed into the wall at the foot of the stair, and pitched sideways into the room.

Claire scrambled to her feet, gasping for breath. Stunned,

Quarrell tried to stand. He drew up onto his knees, groping at the wall for support. Dashing forward, Claire lifted her skirts and kicked him in the head, once, hard, then leapt back. Quarrel bumped back against the wall, shocked by the force of her kick. He struggled to rise, and sank down, dazed. Claire looked about desperately for something to finish him off. In the gloom, she saw nothing heavy enough for a weapon. Quarrell shook his head to clear his vision. Slowly, ominously, like a bear at a baiting, he began to rise again.

Run . . . run. It's the only chance. She turned and fled up the stairs.

"No," Quarrel bellowed, staggering. "No."

Claire sensed his movement, but put all her focus on attaining the door. No footsteps sounded behind her on the stairs. She reached the top landing. Her heart beat frantically, plucking wild notes of hope and dread as her bound hands fumbled with the latch. It jammed, then opened. *Almost free.* She stepped back to swing open the door. As she reached for the mechanism to open the outer panel, a terrible force closed on her ankle, rooting her where she stood. She tried to pull her foot free, but she could not. Looking back, she saw Quarrel standing on a small table beside the stairs. His hand gripped her ankle like a vise.

"You will not escape me," he hissed at her.

He put his other hand around her ankle, pulling her legs wide and jerking her back off the stairway onto him. They tumbled off the small table and he was on top of her, pinning her to the ground. She fought wildly, jabbing at him with her elbows. She tried to kick him, but now the heavy skirts snared her legs. She dug her nails into one of his hands. Rage and terror knotted in her belly.

He hit her once, savagely, stunning her, then grabbed her arm and dragged her across the room. Pain flashed through her. Lightning strikes whiting out thought. Quarrell laughed. Pulling her to her feet, he slammed her up against the far wall. Here the ghastly smell was thick, the odor of old blood putrid in her nostrils. Dizzy, she struggled futilely as he untied her hands, then lifted them up, locking her into the chains that hung from the ceiling. He jerked the chains and searing pain stabbed along her arm. "Resist me again and I will haul you up into the air."

Afraid of greater pain, Claire stopped moving.

"Better." Quarrell made a show of adjusting the metal cuffs. "Heirloom jewels could not be so beautiful—nor have circled the wrists of so many dead women."

Claire shuddered. How many had been here before her?

A table stood against one wall. Its surface was covered with linen—the flash of whiteness she had glimpsed earlier— and a darker square of fabric lay draped across the center. Quarrell limped over to it. Claire snatched a fragment of satisfaction. At least she had hurt him. The doctor struck a tinderbox, and lit the candles set at either end to reveal blood red satin. He lifted it aside. Light from the candles glittered on the blades of knives, long needles, and the sharp teeth of the saws that he exposed. His fingers glided across them lovingly. At the far end of the table was a carved box. He opened it. Claire could not see inside, but she saw what he took from it—a narrow ribbon of black silk that he laid on the white cloth. He picked up a small knife from the collection. Flame sheared off the blade as Quarrell turned to face her again.

Involuntarily, a gasp escaped her throat. He made a sound too, a hungry catch of breath that echoed and mocked her. With deliberate care, he began slicing away her clothes, until she stood naked in the chains, totally vulnerable. He stepped back, studying her with approval. "An elegant form, delicate yet sensuous. Does our Adrian appreciate it?"

She heard anger seep into his voice. He hated her, she realized, hated her because Adrian loved her. Fear burrowed deeper, into the marrow of her bones. Quarrell smiled with even greater malice. He moved closer, reaching up to loosen her hair and spread it about her shoulders. "Such a lovely color. Where the light shines, it glows like fresh-spilled blood."

The blade of the knife touched her throat. Claire quaked,

almost choking with horror as he slid a caressing touch along her skin. She remembered the white mask of Penelope's face and Lady Margaret's, their white hands and feet, and all the rest stripped to red. But Quarrell's fingers went to the back of her neck, lifting her hair. Carefully, he cut a lock from underneath, close to her nape.

"First I will take this memento, Lady Claire, to commemorate our brief but fascinating acquaintance." Wrapping the lock of hair about his fingers, Quarrell carried it back to the table. He pressed the curl to his lips, and then he arranged it ceremoniously on the table beside the ribbon of black silk. Deliberately, he laid down the knife, and instead picked up a long silver needle. He displayed it with a smile. "This implement was used during the Inquisition to discover witches—or so its vendor told me. Shall we test its veracity? Shall we find some spot on your body immune to pain?"

Claire closed her eyes against his gloating as he approached her, the thin, evil weapon in hand. An instant later, she winced as the needle pricked the inner corner of her eye. "No, no, no," he insisted. "You must watch me. If you don't, I will take up the knife and cut off your eyelids. I had to force Sister Mary just so. Lady Penelope, however, was truly fascinated. She stared all the while."

Gathering her courage, Claire opened her eyes and met his gaze.

"Yes, that is better." His eyes glowed like lamplight through a fog, radiating his obscene delight in power.

All this time, she had not spoken to him. What could be said to such a monster? Nothing would stop him—yet she might perhaps delay him. Delay death, if not pain. But when she opened her lips to speak, he raised his hand, forestalling her. "No. Do not waste words. I want a sweeter singing from you."

The needle glittered as he slid the tip along her cheek. He drew it down her throat and across her breast, caressing her. He brought the sharp metal point to her nipple. "And now, my dear, shall we begin?"

Chapter 20

The bells of St. Saviour's tolled half past four, and still Claire had not come. Once again, Adrian glanced out the window of the Buzzing Hornet. Claire's note, surely meant to tease, troubled him instead.

If I do not appear, you have leave to rescue me. . . .

He hated having her out of his sight. Fear had stalked him since the moment he awoke and found her gone. No doubt she was safe with her family, but he was distressed that she must face them without his formal declaration. Distressed that he had given her his love but not the words themselves. But surely she knew he would deny her no longer?

Fool! He had not meant to fall asleep. Why did she not wake him and have him ride with her? Probably she was protecting him again. Yet he thought her father would believe their new proof. His daughter would not be wedding a murderer.

Adrian savored a brief spark of relief that it was so, then forced his attention back to the meeting. Rafe and Viv, the Warrens, and Izzy Cockayne had gathered to confer with

Maggot Crutcher. Ten minutes ago, Tadpole had announced the crime lord's arrival. Maggot was an enormous bulk, pale as his namesake. His entrance was roundly welcomed when he announced that Quarrell had been spotted leaving a tavern in the Fringes and followed to his hideout—a rented room over a leech's shop. Adrian's excitement was dampened by Claire's absence.

"You say he cut one of the women?" Rafe asked Maggot.

"No—it was only a silly knife fight between barmaids. He left when it started." Maggot pursed his lips. "That's when he got noticed—fleeing trouble most would want to watch."

"A knife fight between women? Yes, that sounds like trouble Quarrell would enjoy," Viv said. "Why would he leave?"

"Perhaps he found it too tempting," Rafe said.

Adrian stood and paced restlessly, fighting his growing alarm.

Maggot heaved himself off the bench he occupied. "We've got Doctor Rat cornered in his hole—and he doesn't know it yet. I thought you'd want to be there to take him, having made such a fuss."

"Of course," Viv answered impatiently.

Maggot puffed his cheeks, his eyes darting to Adrian. "Be quick if you're coming. Rats are fast on their feet. If he scurries out of the trap, don't blame me."

"We're ready now." Viv stepped to the door, Rafe close at her side. The others moved to join them, but Adrian held back.

Rafe looked at him curiously. "I thought you'd want to be part of this capture."

"I did." Adrian shook his head, realizing he could not join them. "Lady Claire promised she would be here. Something is wrong."

"Her mother and father have several hours worth of admonitions to deliver," Rafe said.

Adrian nodded, subduing his anxiety. "That must be it. When you return—"

"When Quarrell is captured we will go speak to them." Rafe grinned. "I will vouch for your character."

"Wait here, then," Viv said to him.

"Take my two guards with you," Adrian told her.

"I will with thanks," she said, "But don't go out without protection."

"Leave them here," Maggot said. "We've men enough."

"Not for catching Rat Quarrell," Viv answered.

"Very well," Maggot grumbled. "Must we wait till he dies of old age?"

In answer, Viv's band pushed him out the door. Adrian locked it behind them, then sat alone in the growing silence. Each second seemed the sharp flick of a scalpel. Just when he could stand it no more, he heard footsteps running up the stairs. *Too heavy for Claire*, Adrian thought, even as he rushed to the door and unlocked it. James burst in. He grabbed Adrian's shoulders, the bare skin of his neck. Panic poured through him. He envisioned a flayed corpse laid out like a bride—Penelope.

Not Claire—

Words poured from James, a jumbled rush. "An attack! At the tower. Claire's father has been found half-dead—and my guards lie slaughtered beside him."

Distress doubled, Adrian's panic rose to swirl with James' anguish. Adrian shook him. "Claire?"

"She is nowhere to be found." James gasped.

"Quarrell has her." Adrian's mind reeled with blood-soaked horrors. Black waves of despair pounded against him, James' and his own. Adrian pulled away, fighting for control.

She's not dead—not yet.

The thought came from nowhere, offering hope. "I must find them."

"Impossible." James seemed to sink deeper into himself, the weight of Penelope's death dragging him down. "There was not a clue to who had been there, or where they had gone."

"I will find one." Adrian's heart pounded. Quarrell would have left some trace behind.

"Don't be a fool. Sir Nigel will be summoned, and Lord

Brightsea's tower filled with his men. He made it clear you were still publicly under suspicion."

"I do not think he truly believes—"

"Adrian, they will say you kidnapped Lady Claire yourself. You will be arrested."

Adrian jerked free of James' grasp and his jumbled emotions. The risk of capture was nothing now, if he could find a clue to point them toward Claire. But would they listen to him? He could not predict his own reactions to touching objects saturated with violence. They might think him mad—or accuse him of witchcraft as Graile had done. Better to stay free and hunt for Quarrell on his own. A sudden dark purpose formed in Adrian's mind, but he saw no way to achieve it on his own. Reluctantly, he turned to James. "We must go to Bedlam."

James drew back, appalled. "If there was some record of his secret refuge there, surely they would have already found it."

"I must look. Will you help me or not?"

"Yes. Yes, I must do something!" James cried suddenly.

"When we reach Bedlam, you will present yourself as a benefactor." Adrian gave his cousin a way to concentrate his mind. "If you appear upset, they will become suspicious."

James nodded. "I will play my role."

They hurried down to the street where James' guard waited with the horses. Adrian sent the man after Rafe and Viv, to tell them the plan. "Even Quarrell cannot be two places at once. Tell Mistress Vivian she may be walking into a trap."

As they mounted, Adrian spotted a shadowy figure flitting behind some of the barrels piled behind the tavern. "Who is there?" he demanded, bracing himself for pursuit.

After a brief pause, a small figure stepped out, sheepishly confessing, "It's me, Lord."

"Tadpole," Adrian called out, cheered despite the grim mood. "You're good luck and we need just that."

"Mistress Viv told me to keep watch over you, m'lord.

Didn't think you'd see me so quick." He looked chagrined.

"A watcher is just what we need. Can you come with us? You can tend our horses—and keep an eye open for trouble."

"I'll get leave to ride old Damson," he said, dashing into the Buzzing Hornet and back out in a flash. Soon he was back, riding atop a dun nag.

Side by side, Adrian and James crossed over London Bridge and rode the crowded thoroughfares toward Bishopsgate, Tadpole following behind them. They spoke very little, but Adrian felt a silent communication growing with his cousin, like a rediscovered possibility, something that might have emerged in their early years had things not bent in other ways.

At one point, Tadpole waved them down a side road. "It's quicker through here, less crowded," he called out and rode on ahead.

James took the opportunity to speak. "How can someone as young as that lad fear so little? How can he need so little to be happy?"

Adrian understood that he was making amends, however obliquely. Perhaps he did not see himself how he was changing. "I do not know, but I hope he can teach me the way of it."

Emerging from the side street, they found themselves close on Bishopsgate. Riding through, they caught sight of the forbidding stone walls of Bedlam. The air reeked from the surrounding sewers. James' face took on a sickly hue, and Adrian supposed he looked little better. Yet the past was not so difficult to face when his future was at stake. And the future had no meaning without Claire.

James averted his gaze from the asylum but forced himself to look at Adrian. "Before this was only a place I wished to escape as quickly as possible. Now I see the prison you had to endure because of me."

"Can you do this?" Adrian asked, gesturing toward the iron gate. He struggled against his own fear and impatience, aware of James' turmoil.

"I must help you, Adrian, as I did not before," James answered him.

When they stopped before the gate, Tadpole was off his horse well before they dismounted, waiting to take the reins and tether the horses. He reached into a pocket and lifted out some bits of metal dangling from a ring—lock picks. He gave them a jangle. "I don't suppose you know how to use these, m'lord?"

"Ah, but I do," Adrian said, managing a smile. "Izzy tutored me while I stayed at the Buzzing Hornet."

"Can't 'ave 'ad no better teacher then, m'lord," Tadpole said with a grin. He handed Adrian the picks.

James halted at the entrance. Adrian nudged him through the gate, and then followed into the courtyard. He startled as the iron clanged shut behind them. His skin seemed to crawl with vermin. Ugly memories deluged him, jeering faces and heavy boots, maggoty food and foul straw. The nightmare insanity of Quarrell's visits. Returning here sickened his soul, but his greatest dread was that he would fail Claire. Adrian tilted his cap low, staying well behind James. But when they entered Bedlam, the keepers saw only Sir James' servant. None would expect to find an escaped madman here.

The new warden hurried forward to greet him. James' responses were blatantly nervous, but the size of his donation to Bedlam provided excellent camouflage. Fawning, the warden instantly acquiesced to his cousin's request for a tour. James waited till they were near the door to Quarrell's office, then ordered Adrian to wait for him in the hall. Adrian took the indicated post as the warden led James up the stairs and out of sight. Heart racketing, Adrian waited until the corridor was empty, then hurried to the door. His gloved hands fumbled with the picks, but the lock was not difficult and the door opened. Fighting his own stifling dread, Adrian entered Quarrell's office and closed the door behind him.

Inside, the sour stench of Bedlam thickened with Quarrell's cloying scent, a sickly perfume of cloves and violets stifling Adrian. The gray shadows quivered, as if malignant spirits watched from the corners, waiting to descend. Quickly, quietly, Adrian began to search through the desk—that too required some lock picking. He did not know what he searched for—some receipt, a note, a bit of jewelry. Anything that might lead him to Claire. If the scraps he found were clues, he could not tell.

Adrian gripped the edge of the desk, praying silently, then slid off his gloves. Even before he touched anything, the skin all over his body prickled. Gritting his teeth, he forced himself to handle object after object. A quill, a paperweight—the simplest things were saturated with vicious lust. Images of brutality and reveling cruelty besieged him, dragging him down into a foul, suffocating quicksand. He inhaled the odors of moldering earth and rusted iron, gangrenous flesh and fresh blood. He thought he would vomit and staggered back, leaning against the door shaking. Clammy sweat covered him like a chill slime. Knowing there was a door out of this room helped only a little. There was no door in his mind. The images were loosed there, crawling through him like obscene worms bloated on death and suffering.

There would be no escape until Claire was rescued from the monster who held her.

On the far side of the desk, there was a chest he had not opened yet. Slowly he moved forward to kneel in front of it. This lock needed a deft plying of the metal keys. Adrian cursed as his fingers trembled, but at last he opened the chest. Inside lay a dark cloak, a starched ruff support, a pair of gray gloves embroidered with silver. He did not want to touch Quarrell's clothes, but he had found nothing yet to further his search for Claire.

Adrian laid his hand on the wired ruff support. Nothing. He did not know if he could endure the cape, and looked instead at the fine leather gloves. His own gloves were treasured protection. Donning Quarrell's would be like reaching into the mouth of a venomous serpent. He started to slide his hand inside. The leather clung and seemed to suck him inward. Then his fingertips brushed something tucked inside.

He snatched back his hand and shook a linen handkerchief onto the cloak. The fabric was too plain and sturdy to be Quarrell's, who would have fine white lawn and lace. It was utterly innocuous—with nothing about it to link it to anyone in particular. Except that beneath Quarrell's omnipresent perfume, Adrian caught the faint aroma of pears. Just such a quiet scent Sister Mary had about her sometimes, bringing a hint of something alive and nourishing into hell. Gently, Adrian closed his fingers around the soft fabric of her handkerchief.

He stifled the cry that threatened to break from his lips, fighting to keep his own awareness as horror engulfed him.

Barking. Barking. Under the dogs' racket, Sister Mary heard Master Quarrell talking to someone, calling orders. "Chain the mastiffs." Long moments, waiting. . . . Please God . . .

Like ravens flapping, the tarpaulin flipped back. Master Quarrell laughed as she cringed back. He grabbed her foot, pulled her toward him. "No witnesses now, good Sister."

I should have spoken out . . . should have told some my fears.

He lifted her from the wagon, set her on her feet. The door was open. Hands tied. Feet free. With a spurt of energy, she broke free and ran into the night. The vicious mastiffs jumped and howled like demons. Escape! Where? The rise of hills . . . everywhere trees . . . the side of a house.

Please . . .

Behind her Quarrell laughed. Footsteps sauntered after her. She dodged to the side, but there was nowhere to run. He grabbed her, spun her round. "You should have given yourself to the dogs, my dear. They would have been quicker. Now I will have to punish you for trying to escape."

Mouth choked by the gag. Mind screaming for help. Screaming as he knocked her down to the ground.

The blow stunned Adrian. Groaning, he fought for control, shaking his head to try and disperse the images, bringing himself back to Bedlam. He stared down at the simple square of fabric. Sister Mary did not have it on her when she died, or he might not have been able to endure the touch of it. She had not known the agony she must soon suffer, but she had seen too much of Quarrell's cruelty to hope for an easy death. Pity welled within him for her terrible end, and gratitude for what she had shown him through her eyes.

"Thank you, Sister Mary," he whispered. "You helped save me once—now I pray you will help save my lady."

Adrian rode pell-mell for the heath, James and Tadpole galloping behind. The roads were muddy from the brief shower and the green fields glistened, strangely luminous under the glowering storm clouds. At last they came to Hampstead, with the wooded swell of the heath rising beyond. Drawing rein, Adrian looked back to see the Thames shining pewter in the distance. The massed clouds broke apart, showing a gruesome sunset of maroon and blood red. He sensed that they were in the right vicinity, but no more than that. There were clusters of houses amid the groves of trees. Would he even recognize Quarrell's hideaway from the brief glimpse in his vision?

The doctor knew his face and James', so Adrian sent Tadpole to ask at whatever hovel or manor they found, if anyone knew of a house where savage mastiffs roamed the yard. At house after house, they met with ignorance. After yet another denial, James said, "The doctor may not be the only one who keeps such dogs."

He shook his head. "I think not so many."

"Why did Master Quarrell tell you about them?"

"He liked to tell me horrors." That was true enough, but Adrian had lied to bring James here, and the lie sat ill. "He whispered many unpleasant things in his visits, James, but he never told me of the dogs."

This cousin frowned. "Then how—"

"I have my mother's gift, James. It woke in me the night my

father gave me her bequests. Too much of her pain, her sorrow, was in them for me to endure. I did go mad that night, and when the thieves attacked me, I forgot who I was for a time."

James swallowed. He looked apprehensive, but he did not withdraw as Adrian had feared. "But your memory came back to you. You asked for your father to come to Bedlam, though he was dead by then. That was when I saw you."

"Yes. It was easy then for Quarrell to make me seem more lunatic than I was. For a time, any strong impression could unbalance me. Perhaps he drugged me to make certain of it."

"And I left you at his mercy," James said.

"I have been afraid of this gift, for at times it is a torment. But my freedom from Bedlam came because of it. My new friends—Lady Claire herself—came to me in its wake." Adrian drew a breath and went on. "I no longer deny it, but use it to the best of my ability. That is how I discovered Quarrell's house and his dogs. They are but images in my mind, yet I am certain I will know them when I see them."

At last, as the sun was sinking, they came upon a lane half-hidden by trees. As soon as Tadpole asked about the dogs, an inhabitant pointed the way to an even more obscure pathway. There was a house there, he said, rented by Master Lamb. Half a mile on, they found it, set back by itself, with four enormous mastiffs chained before the door.

Adrian nodded to wagon tracks marking the narrow path. "Those are recent."

They tethered their horses out of sight in a small grove of trees, but one of the dogs must have caught wind of them, for he began barking ferociously. The others instantly followed suit. A moment later, a guard lumbered from behind the stable, eating an apple. He stood and glared at the dogs, then flung the apple aside and started walking down the drive, his gaze roaming the surrounding trees. Tadpole gestured for them to approach through the trees, then walked brazenly along the road and up toward the gate.

"My master sent me to tell you to keep those dogs quiet,"

he called loudly to the guard, timing his distraction to the progress of Adrian and James. Seeing him, the dogs rushed against the length of their chains, snapping and barking.

"You rump-witted little fool!" the guard yelled furiously. "Nothing will shut their teeth now you've started 'em up again. And why should I care about your bloody master?"

"Oh, but you must," Tadpole insisted, approaching closer. "He'll do something fearsome."

"I hope he breaks a switch on your bum," the guard said.

"He'll come break a staff over your uggsome 'ead, is wot." Tadpole kicked a great scuff of dirt, and the mastiffs' barking took on a manic edge. Tadpole danced gleefully in a circle, checking to see that Adrian and James were in place.

"You puling measle," the guard shouted at Tadpole. "I should loose 'em on you for that. They won't stop for hours." He vacillated between attempting to pummel Tadpole or somehow calm the dogs.

"Spleeny, beetle-eyed, reeling-ripe rat's turd, yerself!" Tadpole exclaimed, displaying Izzy's superior tutelage in his insults. He scooped up a handful of rocks and began pelting both the guard and the dogs. The mastiffs sent up a crazed cacophony, leaping and lunging on their chains. Outraged, the guard charged at Tadpole. The boy gave a whoop and dodged toward the trees. The guard raced after him and right into the force of Adrian's fist as he stepped out from behind his cover.

James sprang out and the two of them tackled the massive guard, who took their blows with angry grunts, and rolled away as best as he could, landing a kick that sent Adrian sprawling. James dove after him, but did not have him quite pinioned before the guard pulled a knife and slashed his arm, splattering him with blood. Adrian leapt to his feet and rushed to seize the guard, wresting the knife from his hand, then twisting it behind his back. Tadpole hurried forward and pulled out a wicked cosh, rapping it across the back of the struggling guard's skull. Once. Twice. Thrice. At last the man groaned and lay still.

James started to rise, then sank back on the ground. Blood soaked his arm. Adrian cut a swatch of the livery and bound it tightly around James' arm. "Can you ride?"

"Yes," James said, "But I must help you." The wound slashed through muscle to the bone. His cousin looked ready to faint.

"No, Tadpole must get your wound tended."

"You should not be alone," James protested.

There was no help for that. Adrian turned to Tadpole. "Guide Sir James back to a safe household in Hampstead, then find a doctor for him."

"Quick as I can, m'lord."

"Once we find help, we will send it in return," James said.

Tadpole fetched the horses while Adrian bound and searched the guard. All the while, the dogs clamored. The man had no key; which was not a surprise, considering what games Quarrell played within. When the boy returned, he and Adrian helped James to mount. "I'll watch out for your cousin, m'lord," Tadpole assured Adrian. "You watch out for those dogs."

"I will."

Trusting Tadpole to find help, Adrian hurried toward the front of the house, stopping short of the mastiffs. He still expected Quarrell to emerge from inside and investigate the raucous howling. But no one came out. With sudden despair, Adrian wondered if Quarrell had some other evil den where he had secreted Claire. Adrian could only find out within. Watching the prowling dogs, he noticed that in their snarling, circling and lunging, the mastiffs could not quite reach each other, no doubt to keep them from tearing each other to pieces. They also were chained such that they could not quite cover all the ground between him and the door. There seemed to be a jagged path through them. Adrian pulled out his snaphance, checked the charge and the powder in the pan, and then started forward between the lunging beasts.

With his first step into their domain, the mastiffs' howling lowered to vicious guttural snarls. They flung themselves at him, tugging at the ends of their chains. Cautiously, he wove a path between the first two dogs. Their teeth snapped within a few inches of him on either side, saliva flying from their jowls. One misstep and their fangs would close, pull him down. He saw the narrow way and stepped through. They snapped at his heels when he passed them and reached the second set of growling beasts.

Then, in the very midst of the raging mastiffs, a curious peace descended. Quarrell was inside. Adrian knew it now. Claire was inside. This test helped him prepare for what lay beyond. He held her image in his mind, like a candle lit against the dark.

Adrian stepped quickly past the inner pair of dogs, to the porch in front of the door. Behind him the mastiffs snarled their threats. He found the door bolted shut. It would not give way to any force or cleverness Adrian could apply. Adrian stepped back closer to the dogs and looked up at a window just above him on the second floor. Quickly, he clambered up a post and managed to pull himself onto the small roof over the porch. He did not hesitate but kicked in the glass and eased through, jumping down into a hallway that framed the stairs.

He listened. All was quiet above, but he could still hear the yammering of the mastiffs. If Quarrell did not come, it was only because he could not hear. The doctor was somewhere where all outside sound was muffled. Somewhere where no screams rose to the surface.

Dim light shone up from the first floor. Adrian checked his weapon again, then descended silently down to the bottom of the stairs. Filled with a sense of abhorrence, he turned into the parlor, walking softly through the chill house. The rooms smelled musty, but there was a perverse sense of life, a dread miasma hovering in the stillness. But this was not Quarrell's realm, only the antechamber. There must be a cellar below, but Adrian had seen no door leading down. He circled back, his eyes searching even as his sense of revulsion increased.

The evil within the house seemed to grow with each step permeating him. He found himself once more in the hallway, and shuddered. He should not have turned aside. Somewhere here was the door into hell. The joinery of the walls and posts of the house were vague in the muted and shadowy lamplight. If there was a latch, there was one way to find it. By feel.

Adrian took off his gloves. It sickened him to touch anything of Quarrell's, but he dreaded the weakness it brought more than the horror. But he must use every sense he possessed to find a way down to Claire. He summoned her face again, recalled the tender, husky timbre of her voice. She was like a glowing light, a mirror bright shield such as Perseus once carried. Only in the brightness of her reflection could he face the monster below, who otherwise would turn him to stone. Stepping silently along the walls, Adrian let the fingers of his left hand glide over the wooden surfaces. With his right hand, he kept a grip on the snaphance. Repulsive images roiled through his mind as he traced the course of the woodwork, but he steeled himself to keep going, letting the darkness roll over him in a loathsome tide.

Then, as his hand passed over a curious small place in the angle of the wall, a deluge of bloody images encompassed him, driving him to his knees. Adrian pulled himself to his feet, fighting the waves of nausea that rose against the carnage and gloating malice. He forced himself to reach up and touch the panel again, searching for the worst place. His fingers found the point of leverage and he swung open the padded panel to expose a landing where a lantern flickered, revealing stairs leading down. Wavering light suggested torches burning out of sight below. Adrian stepped through, and the weighted panel swung shut behind him.

Any surprise he had would now be gone. Quarrell must have heard him. Adrian took three steps down, evil permeating him with every breath. Then Quarrell appeared at the foot of the stairs, his pale face yellow and waxen in the dim light of the lantern.

"Lord Roadnight, this is a pleasure quite beyond the expected," Quarrell mocked him. "How did you defeat both my lovely dogs and my burly guard? I planned to send a message to fetch you, but I was having some difficulty obtaining knowledge of your exact whereabouts."

"Where is Lady Claire?" Adrian demanded. His voice did not betray his sapped strength.

"Waiting below, of course. Won't you come down and join us?" Quarrell peered up the stairs. "It seems you are alone. So it is only the three of us, as I hoped it would be."

Descending slowly, he kept his gun trained on Quarrell as the doctor moved halfway across the room. "Stop there," he ordered, looking desperately around, but Claire was still not in sight. Did he dare kill Quarrell before he found her? Was she buried alive in yet another hidden chamber? Yet something of her presence lightened the swarming darkness of the cellar.

Then Adrian heard a muffled cry.

As he surged forward, he saw Quarrell reach out and snatch something. A gun? Adrian did not fear his own death, only Claire's. The doctor would not kill him now, not when the chance of torture waited. But he might shoot to cripple. Adrian could imagine all too well what would happen, with both of them at the doctor's tender mercy. Then Quarrell wheeled and threw a pitcher across the room. Adrian easily avoided the flying crockery, but it crashed against the wall and splashed a shower of water over him.

"A pitcher of water—not much use against gentlemen and their guns. Unless they find the powder is wet, naturally," Quarrell laughed.

Adrian looked down and saw that Quarrell's ploy had worked. The cock could fall, perfectly abrading the flint against the plate, but no spark could ignite the damp powder in the pan. However, Quarrell stood too far away to be certain of his success. Adrian smiled a little, as he had trained himself to do no matter what he felt.

"A clever attempt, at least," he replied blandly, training the useless pistol on the doctor. Quarrell stopped midmotion, as Adrian stepped off the last stair and moved into the room.

"Come," Quarrell invited. "Admire my fine needlework."

First Adrian saw the table, like some demonic altar draped in white and covered with knives. Another step and he saw Claire, chained naked to the wall and gagged. Scarlet rivulets mazed her pale skin, threads of blood trickling from dozens of tiny wounds. Fighting the surge of terror that threatened to swamp every thought, Adrian's eyes sought hers. There was pain within their depths, but her gaze was alive, intent. He held that visual union for the instant he dared.

"She looks most lovely, don't you think?" Quarrell asked in his most oily, insinuating voice. "The gag is a foul thing, only to prevent her calling out to you—not quite as effective as I hoped. I promise to remove it soon. I want you to hear the sweet screams she will make for me."

Rage almost blinded Adrian. Its hot surge gave him new strength, but he had to fight for control. Quarrell would use any carelessness against him. "I will make you a bargain, Quarrell. I will give you my life for hers."

Claire moaned against the gag, shaking her head in denial.

"Would you do that?" Quarrell inquired.

"In an instant," he replied, briefly meeting Claire's gaze. "If I am assured she is free."

"A pity that would be so difficult to assure," the doctor remarked.

"We can come to terms." Adrian tried to draw out the time. Surely, Tadpole must have reached another house by now. Help would come.

"Can you tell me, my lord, why I should surrender one delight when I can claim two," the doctor murmured, edging slightly closer to the table. "I don't believe your pistol will fire."

"No?" Adrian aimed it at Quarrell's heart. He could see the doctor weighing the risk.

"If you thought it would work, you would have used it by now." Quarrell lunged for the knives.

Adrian pulled the trigger. As he feared, there was only a dry click, no flash, no shot. Gripping the barrel, he flung the gun at Quarrell's hand, knocking away the blade he'd seized. He heard the doctor snarl with outrage. Adrian flung himself across the room, taking hold of Quarrell before he could seize another weapon. Quarrell's hands closed on his arms and they fell grappling to the floor.

Evil enveloped Adrian in a cloak of darkness. He struggled against it, but it covered him, suffocated him, writhing with half-formed unspeakable shapes and hideous desires that insinuated like maggots into his being.

Adrian fled, curling in on himself, trying to hold himself apart from their crawling horror. That was how he had survived in Bedlam—hiding as much of himself as he could beyond Quarrell's reach. It had been victory enough to stay sane, to stay alive. But where could he hide now? Evil spawned around him, within his skin, it invaded his senses, inescapable, unendurable.

Screams echoed and reechoed in the darkness, shrill and wailing, then guttural, thick with blood.
The odor of it drenched the air, suffocating, vile—and intoxicating. Every inhalation filled him with its scent, its taste. Fear resonated around him. Its feverish music sent shivers racing along his nerves, icy hot, fiery cold. It melted him down into a crucible of madness, of terror.

"Look at me." Quarrell's arms gripped him, wrapping round him like thick, squeezing entrails of darkness. Hatred, malice, and lust ate into him, a burning corrosive acid eating away his will, devouring his sanity. The doctor pinioned his head, twisting it back. Adrian stared up into Quarrell's sneering face, into his fog pale eyes. From the center of the gray irises, the pupils expanded into a blackness avid to consume him entirely.

"You're mine," Quarrell exulted. "Mine."

"No," Adrian grated, but the weight of Quarrell's evil crushed his lungs, silencing him. He turned his face away, pressing it to the dirt floor.

Underneath, in the earth, they cried out to him, all Quarrell's dead. Their suffering crushed him, suffocating as earth. Endless pain. He too would suffer, then he would join them. He would be free. Or would he hear them still, sharing their endless agony, eternally crying in the dark?

So many . . . so many had died.

But Claire would live. Claire must live.

"Open your eyes," Quarrell gloated, his triumph all but complete. "Look at me."

Adrian turned his head and opened his eyes. But he looked at Claire. So beautiful. So loyal. So valiant.

"Look at me," Quarrell rasped.

Adrian turned back to him.

Quarrell gave a low, obscene laugh. "You are mine. And she is mine."

"No," Adrian answered softly, implacably. "No."

He belonged to himself. He belonged to Claire. Quarrell would not possess either of them.

Fervent with that resolve, Adrian met Quarrell's gaze, his invading mind.

Deliberately, he opened himself. The mad rage, the darkness, the writhing evil spewed voraciously into him. Endlessly it poured in, filling him, all but annihilating him. But not entirely. Adrian gathered it into the crucible of his own soul, held it there. Captured it. Contained it. Prompted by some unknown wisdom beyond his waking mind, he remembered old tales, the alchemical tapestry in Claire's father's hidden room, his own dreams of the dragons. Adrian smiled as he ignited the crucible of his soul. The elemental fire drew power

*from the wild seas of his mother's Ireland, the rich
earth of his father's England. It drew power from
windswept reaches of the sky, and from the living
breath of Claire's presence. Adrian burned the darkness, melted it in the pure fire of his rage, and the purer
fire of his love. It burned brighter and brighter still, the
black of hatred and scarlet of blood transforming to in-
candescent white. He became a mirror reflecting, mag-
nifying, turning the darkness back on its source. It
collected, gathering and coiling, transforming into a
devouring dragon, a creature of black flame. Starved
and denied any other prey, it gnawed Quarrell's limbs
and soul, incinerating them in an endless burning, blis-
tering conflagration.*

Quarrell screamed, a shriek of incomprehensible terror as
his own darkness burned through his mind. With an eagle's
fierce cry, Adrian twisted, breaking the constricting grip. He
shoved Quarrell away, mind and body thrusting him back
against the wall. Slowly, Quarrell crumpled into a heap on the
floor.

Dazed, Quarrell stared at Adrian as if he'd never seen him
before. With a shudder, he looked away. Slowly he dragged
himself up, staggered a few steps, and then collapsed again.
Wearily, Adrian pushed himself up, starting after him. Something glinted by the doctor's hand. Seeing the knife lying on
the floor, Adrian dove for it. Too late. Snatching it, Quarrell
lurched to his feet and stumbled toward Claire. In a rush of
fear for Claire, Adrian leapt after him, grabbed him and spun
him around. Filled with new fury, he smashed Quarrell's head
against the stone wall and grabbed his knife hand. Quarrell
twisted to plunge the knifepoint into Adrian's chest. Adrian
tightened his grip on the doctor's knife hand and jerked upward, deflecting the thrust. The sharp blade slashed along his
neck, but cut only skin.

Ignoring the slicing pain, Adrian kept hold of Quarrell's
wrist and thrust his arm further up, dragging the doctor far

enough off balance to kick his feet out from under him. As Quarrell crashed backward onto the floor, Adrian let go, lunged for the table, and grabbed a long knife. Behind him, he heard the doctor rise. Adrian whirled into a crouch to fend off his attack.

But Quarrell did not charge him. From his kneeling position, he hurtled toward Claire, slashing at her in mad desperation. She twisted in her chains, barely evading his strike. Adrian leapt on Quarrell, but he struck again, his blade descending for Claire's heart. Adrian flung himself to the side, dragging Quarrell with him, oblivious to the blade now striking at him. Rolling onto the madman, he pinned him to the floor. Quarrell grunted, then screamed, flailing as Adrian's knife rose and descended, stabbing again and again, as long as he felt any movement. Stabbing with the endless force of his hatred.

Claire gave a muffled cry, but Adrian heard her through his rage. He gasped for air, his mind clearing. He looked down. Beneath him, Quarrell lay dead in a wide pool of blood. The pale fog of his eyes clouded with the deeper opaqueness of death. Adrian let the knife fall. He groped for the key in Quarrell's pocket, then struggled to his feet.

Moving to Claire, Adrian untied the gag and unlocked the chains. He gathered her to him gently, kissing her forehead, her tear-stained cheeks. She pressed closer, dismissing her pain. "He was saving the worst for when you arrived."

Adrian kissed her shoulder, and then released her. He went to the table and tore off strips of the white linen cloth, using them first to clean his hands, and then the blood that drizzled from Quarrell's cruel needle piercings. Claire did not make a sound as he ministered to her. That done, he looked for something to cover her. Her clothes lay in tatters, but in a trunk shoved under the stairway they found some of the other victims' clothes. Many of the garments were cut and bloodstained, but she was able to piece together a clean outfit to wear. Gingerly, she began to draw them on.

"He murdered all these women," she said sorrowfully. "He killed my father as well."

"Your father lives, Claire, or was living when we set out."

"Then there is hope." She sagged with relief, but a tired smile curved her lips. "Tonight, I must see him. In the morning we can go to Sir Nigel's and clear your name. I want this truly ended."

"Then we may begin again," he said softly.

"I know it is morbid, yet when I put on these different garments, I feel that I am bearing witness to each of the murdered women," Claire said as she finished dressing. "They did not survive, so now I will speak for them, as best I can. Even as you once spoke for my brother, though I have not your gift of sight to aid me."

"I have only begun to feel it is a gift, not a curse," he said. "What I suffered was worth it, to free you and to bring about his end."

Hesitantly, Claire walked over to the table and opened the box. "Look here, Adrian. He has kept pathetic tokens of the victims."

Moving to stand beside her, Adrian looked and saw the locks of hair, all different colors, and each bound in black ribbon. Two dozen, he thought. "So many dead."

Claire looked up at him, swallowing back her tears. "This hidden chamber, with its chains and gory walls, is proof that Quarrell is the killer. But they must come to see it. The box we can take now, to end all questions."

"Yes. All questions." Looking at the pitiful collection within the box, Adrian knew he must bear witness—not only for Sister Mary, but for all Quarrell's nameless victims. Lock by lock, he would find the identity that Quarrell had stripped away. Some might have no other mourners, but he would try to find their families, their friends or lovers. He would have to judge then if he would tell them what happened. But many would want the release of mourning. He did not doubt it would be painful, but it seemed the surrounding spirits already lay quieter. When that was done, he would bury the box. That would be the true end to the doctor's persecution, and a new beginning for the gift he had always feared to use.

"I will discover their names, Claire," he promised. "Not tonight, or tomorrow, but soon."

He saw the pride in her eyes, and felt it was recompense enough. He felt pride in himself, as well. He had faced his fears, destroyed his devil.

"Let us leave this place of abominations," she said, and together they climbed the stairs.

To their surprise, the gloomy rooms above were lit and others were searching for the hidden chamber. Quarrell's neighbors drew back as they saw Adrian emerge covered in blood, but Tadpole hurried forward. "I've brought 'elp, m'lord, though it looks like you've no need of it."

"Any help is welcome," Adrian said gratefully.

"Your cousin is well looked after, m'lord, down the road. Though you may be wanting a fine doctor to be tending him."

"We can bring him with us," Claire said. "The journey to my home will be shorter, and likely there is a doctor already in attendance for my father."

Adrian nodded his approval.

"We've made the guard shut the dogs up in the kennel," the boy continued. "And the constable's been sent for."

"Good work, Tadpole," Adrian praised.

"Is the villain dead and gone, m'lord?"

"Yes, Tadpole. He is." Slowly, Adrian could feel the weight of that loathsome presence dissipating. "Edward Quarrell lies below," Adrian said to the gathering. "If you dig in that cellar, you will find his previous guests as well."

Thunder rumbled, and Adrian realized the storm had broken. Curtains of rain showed outside the windows. Impulsively, he walked through the door and down the steps, out into the night. Opening his arms wide, he stood in the downpour, letting Quarrell's blood be washed away. Claire came down the steps and into the deluge. She reached out to him, her fingers, her emotions, twining with his own. Liberation overlapped the lingering sorrow, swelling to a joyful peace. Hand in hand, she stood beside him, lifting her face to the falling rain.

Adrian turned to her, free of the curse of fear that had held him in its talons. Cleansed in heart and soul.

Stroking her wet hair back with his hands, he asked, "Will you marry me, Claire?"

"Yes, Adrian, yes," she whispered. "Yes, I will marry you."

Chapter 21

"Sir Adrian, I believe you wish to ask for my daughter's hand in marriage," Lord Brightsea said, propped on pillows amid the rich velvet hangings of his bed. He held that selfsame hand, as he had since Claire had entered his chamber a few moments before, alive and well. He stroked her fingers tenderly.

"My lord, you have become prescient," Adrian murmured.

"Perhaps it is the injury to my head." Lord Brightsea twirled his free hand, mimicking the wrapping of bandages that swathed his head like a turban. His face was bruised, but his eyes gleamed with all their sharp intelligence. "It aches abominably, or I should be more cheerful in my consent."

"May I suggest the first banns be read this Sunday?" Lady Brightsea said from the foot of the bed, a slight frown creasing her brow.

"Indeed, indeed," her husband replied.

Once Lady Brightsea was assured that Claire's injuries were small, both to body and spirit, and the menace removed

once and for all, she had turned her attention to the matter of
her daughter's tarnished reputation. Though he kept Claire
close by him, Lord Brightsea had taken her cue. His approval
granted, Lady Brightsea offered Adrian a tiny smile, to indi-
cate the measure of her favor. With her regal stance and red-
gold coloring, she looked like a miniature of the Queen. Her
face had a delicate beauty, her eyes a hard glitter. She had a
rich but decrepit Earl ready to wed her wayward daughter, and
had been foiled.

Even without Claire's account, Adrian would have marked
Lady Brightsea as a pretty tyrant, well used to bending others
to her will. Adrian found the gloss manners, and even the luxury of opulent furnishings and glowing candlelight, strangely
unreal after Quarrell's dark pit. Yet smiling charm was a familiar mask, one Adrian found easy to don. He was almost
grateful of the distance, even as he longed for Claire's unfeigned sincerity.

"You must gain the Queen's consent first. She may be dis-
pleased," Lady Brightsea said to her husband.

"Her Majesty has been much provoked, 'tis true," Lord
Brightsea replied. "But I believe she will see the wisdom of
the outcome—and cause for rejoicing. Our Claire is returned
safely, and with her comes a noble, wealthy, and handsome
suitor—one to whom she has promised both her hand and her
heart."

The scandal they had caused would soon round to its
proper end. Adrian hoped that Lady Brightsea would see its
wisdom as well. He did not want her as an enemy. Nor she
him, apparently, for her expression and her tone softened
when she said, "Lord Roadnight, my husband and I offer you
our blessings."

"I thank you for them, Lady," he said, his smile easing.

"We should arrange for an audience on the morrow," Lady
Brightsea went on. She viewed her daughter's shabby attire
with distaste. "Claire, you must wear your best black velvet, it
is rich but only enough to show respect."

The lesson of the extravagant gown had made an indelible

impression. Lady Brightsea's concerns seemed utterly superficial after all that had passed, but Adrian had seen her trembling and tearful when Claire at last returned safely. Knowing that Lady Brightsea's brittle façade masked deeper emotions, he did not condemn her, even if he could not warm to her as he did Lord Brightsea.

"Soon, certainly," Claire replied. "But immediately in the morning, we will take our evidence to Sir Nigel, the warrant on Sir Adrian must be rescinded. After that—"

Lady Brightsea appeared quietly horrified. "Perhaps you should do that tonight."

"We have sent word to him already," Claire said to reassure her the Crown's men would not march in and seize her guest.

"We have also dispatched a message to Sir Raphael Fletcher and Mistress Vivian Swift that we are here," Adrian added, forewarning his hostess that the notorious Queen of the Clink might be paying a call.

"Sir Raphael will always be welcome," Lady Brightsea said with a tight smile, "And it will be . . . interesting . . . to meet his betrothed."

"It was most important to make sure you were well, Father," Claire said.

"Well enough, knowing you are safe." Gently he pressed her hand to his cheek. Then he released her and settled back, his weariness showing in a sigh. "Better still after a night's sleep. I suggest you retire as well."

Lady Brightsea turned to Adrian. "You will stay the night, of course. I have ordered a guest room readied for you, close by your cousin."

"I thank you for your kindness," Adrian said, truly grateful that James had been carefully tended. After his wound was stitched and bound, he had fallen into a deep slumber.

"Claire, your maid is ready to attend you in your chamber." Lady Brightsea obviously wished to ensure that the return of the runaways meant the return of protocol and decorum.

A small smile quirked the corners of Claire's lips, but she

curtsied demurely to her mother and father. "I bid you all good night."

The look she flashed Adrian as she left was not in the least demure. The dark fire in her eyes startled and aroused him. Fighting his yearning, he allowed himself to be escorted to his room.

Wind rattled the branches of the tree outside the window, the wet leaves rustling softly against the panes of glass. Adrian pushed aside heavy drapes on the bed, rose, and walked naked to the window. Cool moist air gusted over him as he opened the casement. The rain had ceased, tattered clouds revealed a blue-black sky speckled with stars. A bright gibbous moon seemed tangled in the branches of the tree like a lopsided lantern, its light pouring into the room. Exhausted as Adrian was, he could not sleep. He had conquered his fear, and the sense of cleansing endured. But he was bereft without Claire, as if part of him was missing. How could he have denied her so long? They were one flesh. One soul.

He was not surprised when the door opened quietly and Claire entered. She paused for a moment, a pale, gleaming shadow in her shift of white lawn, her robe of pale satin. Under her gaze, his cool skin tingled with heightened awareness and rising heat. She crossed the room to him, graceful as a swan in the filtered moonlight. Moving into his arms, she laid her cheek against his chest and rubbed softly.

"Your maid is asleep—the ideal chaperone?" he teased, wondering how discreet they need be.

"The ideal conspirator. She is dazzled with admiration for your bravery, and promises to call for me before the household stirs." Claire answered lightly, but she shivered in his arms.

Adrian knew it was not from the cold. "You're afraid."

"Of shadows," she said. "I was fine until I lay in the darkness. The memories are too close."

"I understand," he murmured. "I could not sleep, yearning for you, *mo cride*."

His lips brushed the softness of her hair, freshly washed,

scented with lavender. The sweet, keen fragrance sharpened his senses. He inhaled deeply, wanting to draw her essence into him entire, to feel her within and without. Need encompassed him, wrapping round him as he embraced her. Heat surged through his loins, hardening his sex. Feeling his arousal, she pressed closer, drawing a low moan from his lips.

"Love me, Adrian," she whispered.

He stepped back, gathering control. She looked up at him, her eyes dark with desire. Her satin robe felt cool under his fingers, her flesh warm beneath. He slipped the robe over her shoulders and let it fall. The shift glided after, a lacy froth cascading down onto the shimmering satin. She stood naked amid the fallen garments like a goddess in a moonlit pool. Against the fairness of her skin, her puckered nipples drew his gaze, as did the darker triangle at the juncture of her thighs. The multitude of tiny needle wounds Quarrell had made were all but invisible. But touch would recall pain, and pain terror.

"I want you, Claire," he said softly. "But I would not cause you more hurt."

"The hurt is small enough, knowing what I escaped. It pains me more to sleep alone."

"Sleep is enough," he murmured, nodding toward the bed.

"No," she said, pressing again to his betraying hardness. "Only love is enough."

He did not protest more over what they both desired, but guided her to the bed. Drawing back the blanket, he settled with her on the white expanse of the sheet. The curtains he left open, and the window, giving them the moonlight, the cool, rain-washed air and wind-shaken leaves. He craved the perfume of fresh, living things.

Claire reached up to him, drawing his face, his mouth down to meet hers. Her lips were cool and soft. They parted, her tongue licking warm over his lips, then seeking heat within, exploring. He sucked the supple invader, drinking the taste of her. She joined the intimate play, her tongue thrusting softly against his pull, exploring the depths of his mouth. The touch of her hardened nipples and soft breasts, the curls of her womanhood, sent a lightning flare of desire through him. He tightened his hold, but she flinched when he chanced on some sore place. Easing back, he whispered, "Let me pleasure you."

Taking care, he leaned over Claire, kissing and stroking her tenderly. His lips praised the curve of her brow, her eyelids, her cheek. His loving touches skimmed her flanks, the arched curve of her ribs, the slopes and tips of her breasts. But his gentleness did not soothe her, only made her more frantic. She rolled to him and he heard a faint soft hiss of discomfort, but when he tried to ease away, she only pressed near. She moved restlessly against him, filled with craving that emanated through his own flesh. "More," she whispered. "I need you. I need to be filled so that there is nothing else but you."

It was what he desired too, to press close, to touch every inch of her with every inch of himself, to feel Claire alive against him. But when she flinched again, he could not bear it.

Rolling onto his back, Adrian guided her atop him, her legs aligned to his hips and thighs. Her hair spilled about her, a flood of darkness silver gilt by the moonlight. She gazed down at him. Shadowed by the fall of her hair, her eyes were black pools lit by glittering sparks of desire. Her breasts tilted forward, pointed cups he gathered in his hands, suckling, then nipping the tight-drawn puckered nubs. Soft sobs escaped her with each hungry tug of his lips, his teeth. She opened her legs wider, his hands steadying her hips as she settled over him. Adrian gasped as he felt the first brush of her curling thatch, the touch of tender lips, soft and damp. Claire moaned to him. Her legs parted, wider still. Adrian arched up, as he felt the wet lick of her sex along his, stroking him, coaxing him.

"Yes," she said as he rubbed his straining hardness in that sweet, hot furrow. "Yes."

He sensed her need rising quickly, an almost desperate desire to find escape. She lifted to give him room to reach her. His cock strained up eagerly, swollen with need. The crown kissing her giving portal. Claire gasped at the touch. Adrian cried out as she thrust down onto him, taking him full inside her. Desire enveloped him. He burned in a pool of black fire, lost in the darkness of her need.

The last constraint vanished. The fear, the grief, the anger Adrian had buried so long transformed in a flash to burning joy. A new ferocity filled him, overwhelming in its intensity. Unafraid, he gave way to the tender violence of possession and surrender, claiming and giving. He thrust, each stroke coruscating mind and flesh with blinding light. Beyond pain, Claire matched each quickening stroke, exquisite in her wild abandon. Her cries urged him. His hands clasped her hips, molding to her resilient flesh, every sensation separate yet merging. His hips lifted, lunged up, driving his hardness into the melting heat that clasped and squeezed around him. She plunged down to meet him, the hot wet friction a searing ecstasy. He thrust deeper into her, reaching from deeper within himself, his whole being penetrating, consumed in her embracing core, a furnace to temper the sword of his sex.

This was nature's alchemy, the elixir of life that transformed dross metal to purest gold. He reveled in the elemental power of passion, male seeking female. He marveled in the greater power of love, the singular, utterly transforming wonder of Claire's touch. Desire fused them, their passion a crucible melting them both into one being. Each thrust strove toward a perfect dissolution, a perfect melding. He could not believe the beauty of it, primal and transcendent, filling him with a glory that dazzled sense and spirit, urging him to strive to the ultimate consummation. He plunged into her, again and again, raw energy driving him deeper, burning ever fiercer, ever purer. She met him with a cry of unbearable rapture. Darkness burst into blazing light, bright as a sun at their joining. Mind melted into flesh, then flesh melted into soul. Light and fire radiated, the light growing, expanding, filling every particle of being with obliterating joy. Escaped from hell, they shattered the doors of heaven. . . .

Claire lay over him, her breaths soft sobs of joy. Adrian's hands moved gently over her back, feeling the curve of spine and ribs beneath the wet silk of her skin. His heart still thudded wildly, each beat filling his veins with iridescent light. With each breath the clamor slowed, matching pulse for pulse the echoing rhythm of Claire's heart, till each beat sounded a soothing stroke. They hovered at the glowing pinnacle, then floated back toward mortal earth, drifting softly as two feathers plucked from an angel's wings.

"*Mo cride,*" she murmured the words she had heard from his lips.

"My heart," he whispered. "*Mo cride anim.* . . my soul."

They slept peacefully, wrapped in moonlight and nestled in each other's arms.

At dawn, Mistress Pease scratched lightly at their door. Claire stole noiselessly away, ready to reassume the aspect of propriety. Two hours later, Adrian partook of a decorous breakfast with Claire and her parents. They shared a rich fare of thick beef pottage, white bread with fig and lemon conserves, and brandied peaches. Idly, Adrian imagined drizzling their delicious liquor over Claire and licking her clean, while he listened to the debate on the relative merits of the proposed wedding guests. After the darkness he had passed through, Adrian was pleased to listen to such trivia, and dream on the essential delight of pleasuring his beloved.

As Adrian and Claire made ready to depart for Sir Nigel's, they received a message from Rafe and Viv, with news that all were alive and unharmed. Reassured about their friends' safety, they mounted and set forth to bring the brutal saga of Quarrell's murders to a close.

Chapter 22

Claire was relieved she and Adrian arrived at Sir Nigel's without incident. His steward ushered them into the library, where they found him conferring with Sir Francis Walsingham. The negotiations were not secret, for two guards in Walsingham's livery stood in the corner, and one of Burne's nearby. Sir Nigel and Sir Francis both stood as they were announced. The strain of office and illness had taken their toll on Walsingham, leaving him grim and gaunt, but his dark assessing gaze examined them minutely. Burne looked almost as haggard, but when they entered two patches of color flushed his pale cheeks and his eyes brightened. "Lady Claire, it is good to see you safe. We feared for your life."

His relief for her sake was so evident, she smiled in answer. "Yes, I am alive, thanks to Lord Roadnight. His innocence is proved beyond doubt, and Edward Quarrell has answered for his crimes."

"We are well rid of such vermin." Burne's satisfaction was

so obvious, he might have done the deed himself.

"I regret all that you have suffered, Lord Roadnight." Walsingham bowed slightly to Adrian. "Be assured, the warrant for your arrest has been rescinded."

"I regret that it was not withdrawn earlier," Burne amplified. "Once I discovered the open library window, I knew there was a chance that Edward Quarrell had broken in, just as you said. But I hesitated to act without further proof."

Adrian nodded. "You could not risk being wrong with innocent lives at stake."

"My own anger . . . my grief . . . influenced my judgment." Burne's lips compressed into a thin line.

"The circumstances were extraordinary," Claire said quietly. This time had been appalling for him as well. Yet she could not help thinking how unusual it was of Burne to offer emotion as an excuse.

"I did not ignore your accusation, and the brunt of the search was soon turned toward Quarrell," Burne continued his justification.

Perhaps, Claire thought, Walsingham had been more critical than need be. Sir Nigel could hardly have predicted recent events, yet his mentor would want just such prescience.

"Lord Roadnight, none of our men discovered this madman's alias, Lamb," Walsingham said. "Or his hiding place. How did you find it?"

"When I was his prisoner, Quarrell used to torment me with dark tales. Though my memory of that time was hazy, I finally remembered him whispering about his house on Hampstead Heath, the dogs without, the hidden cellar," Adrian lied smoothly.

"Edward Quarrell confessed all as he prepared to kill me," Claire told them. Adrian moved protectively closer, so she gave him a small, reassuring smile. She was amazed and grateful that so much of the pain and horror of that day had truly been washed away.

Adrian turned back to the others. "Many of Quarrell's victims lie buried in the house on Hampstead Heath. But we have brought other evidence with us."

"Evidence?" Burne asked sharply.

Adrian showed them the wrapped box. "After Master Quarrell was dead, we discovered this proof in his lair."

"Well then, let us see it," Walsingham said, then seemed to realize that such proof might pain Sir Nigel. Claire saw that his lips were indeed pale and tight. Nonetheless, Walsingham would expect him to master his emotions, even as Sir Nigel would demand it of himself.

"They are sad artifacts, but not grisly," she said gently, preparing him. "This box contains hair that Master Quarrell snipped from each victim."

Still, Sir Nigel looked nervous as Adrian placed the box on his desk and opened it to reveal the locks of hair, each subtly different in shade, each tied with a black ribbon. Looking at them in the brighter light of Sir Nigel's study, Claire was suddenly disconcerted. Among the darker shades, there was a token of curling gold, one of silken ash blonde, and one flaxen pale. Burne picked up this last, for the color most resembled Lady Margaret's fine, fair hair. He stared at it, stroking it with his fingers. But Claire saw it did not truly match—it was bleached and coarse. Could grief have so distorted Sir Nigel's memory that he saw what he imagined he must? But when he saw her questioning gaze, he frowned and laid the hair back in the box.

Claire was perplexed. "There is nothing like Lady Margaret's hair here."

"Obviously, Quarrell was interrupted before he could cut it and tie it." Burne shrugged, dismissive.

"No," she insisted. "Before he did anything else, he cut a lock of my hair and laid a black ribbon beside it. It was the first act of his perverse ritual."

"Perhaps he only performed such actions when he was safe in his own cellar," Burne said.

Adrian shook his head. "Penelope's hair is here. I recognize it."

"Then the doctor cut my wife's hair, but lost his prize. He would not have risked capture to retrieve it. There is no other explanation." Burne was too abrupt, too argumentative.

A discord played along Claire's nerves—a strange note that did not fit the pattern. She closed her eyes, forcing herself to picture Lady Margaret as she lay on the bed. She saw her blue-tinged face again, framed by the fair hair on the pillow. "Master Quarrell told me I must look into his eyes as he tortured me. He said he cut Sister Mary's eyelids." Claire touched her own lids, flinching with the memory. "He always forced his victims to watch. . . ."

"But Lady Margaret's eyes were shut," Adrian said, recalling that fearful morning.

"Yes," Claire whispered.

"I closed them," Burne said. Then quickly he added, "When I entered the room, they were open. It was too painful to have her watching me."

Behind him a guard made a hoarse sound, choking the denial that sprang to his lips.

"What is it?" Walsingham whirled on him. Seeing the man hesitate, he said. "I'll have you hanged if you lie."

The guard paled. "The maid went in to Lady Margaret's room first, my lord. She ran out sobbing and begged me to come back with her. It was a horrible sight, but I made myself look. I remember well—I was grateful my lady's eyes were closed."

Silence filled the room. Burne had chosen the wrong lie. Or perhaps, Claire thought, it was the wrong truth. He could not bear to have her dead eyes watching while he completed his crime. "You killed your wife," Claire announced with wretched certainty. She saw the truth of it in his face, as if she had never truly looked at him before. And he stared back at her, betrayal in his eyes. And a terrible pain.

"You did it for Claire," Adrian said, stunned. "You wanted Claire."

Walsingham gestured to his guards, a quiet flick of his hand. Suddenly, Burne grabbed Claire and pulled her against him. She cried out in surprise and from the reawakened pain of Quarrell's shallow but cruel wounds. Burne drew his snaphance and trained it on the others. Lowering his head closer, he hissed, "If you struggle, I will kill Adrian."

Claire stilled instantly, knowing Sir Nigel meant it. His chances of escape were slim, and he would kill whomever he hated most. Quarrell had hated her because of Adrian. Burne hated Adrian because of her. She could not resist—yet.

"There is nowhere far enough for you to go, Sir Nigel," Walsingham warned him.

"You underestimate me." Moving backward, he dragged her out the door, locked it behind them, and pocketed the key. The steward and two guards stood in the hall. They stared at their master emerging with Claire obviously held captive. But they might think her a spy, an enemy who had to be restrained. Burne barked a series of orders, telling one guard to open the front door, the other to watch the library. "Let no one out."

The man knew nothing of what had just transpired in the library, but he knew Sir Francis Walsingham was within, and he moved with obvious reluctance. As Burne ordered the steward to open the front door, thumping began behind them, and Walsingham called out a counterorder to open in the Queen's name. Burne pulled Claire through the door and kicked it shut behind them. A young groom stood tending the visitors' mounts. Burne pointed the snaphance at him, and the boy dropped to the ground.

Seizing her chance, Claire tried to free herself from Burne; but he lifted her and carried her struggling toward the river. The events of the last weeks spun through her mind, weaving the macabre patterns of a nightmare dance. Dark circles whirling, interlocking, converging to this moment—a bizarre reversal of all that had passed.

"This was all for you." Burne's voice was low and furious, as if she failed to appreciate something of great importance. And she had. In a flash she reinterpreted the slightest gestures, the least remarks of his past kindness to her. She should have heeded them more closely.

"All for you," he repeated. His green eyes glittered wildly.

"You cannot escape." Claire was frightened but furious too. He had butchered Lady Margaret, and tried to destroy Adrian because of her.

"Roadnight escaped," Burne reminded her.

What did he think to do with her? He knew she had never loved him. Now he had destroyed every shred of respect and affection that once existed.

"I'm afraid of the river," she cried, as he pulled her toward the dock. In truth, her panic was less than before, but he did not know that. She tried to move him. "Please, I'm frightened."

"You will be safe with me," he said, and Claire could not help laughing wildly. She fought to break free, ignoring the stinging soreness of her wounds. Then Burne gripped her scarred arm, sending a fiercer pain shooting through her. At her cry, he lessened his grasp, but she could see him calculating how the pain could be used to control her. "Do not fight me."

"If you love me, let me go." She faced him with that plea, that challenge.

"No."

At first she had been too shocked by the realization of his guilt to truly assimilate the horror of it. Now in a flash, she loathed his devious cruelty. Loathed him. Killing Lady Margaret seemed an act of madness, yet it had all been calculated toward an end. Sir Nigel had gambled his entire world and lost. He had always been ruthless, now he was menacing. Finally there was little difference between his love and Quarrell's hate.

All for her, he had said. Would he kill her, so no one else could have her?

A boatman in livery waited at the dock, tending two wherries and a barge. He, too, looked startled at his master arriving with a struggling woman. "Cut those two free," Burne ordered, pointing to the barge and the far wherry. When the man hesitated, Burne shouted, "Do as I say!"

"No! Don't!" Claire cried as the man hurried to obey. "He murdered Lady Margaret and is trying to escape."

The boatman stared back and forth between them as if they were both mad. Burne jammed his own gun into his belt, then stepped up to the man, snatched his weapon and pointed it at him. "Cut the lines!" he shouted into his face.

The boatman hurried to slice the ropes. When the other boats began to drift off, Burne motioned him into the wherry with the gun, then dragged Claire in after, forcing her down beside him on the rear seat. The boatman loosed their boat from the pier. "Row!" Burne snapped, and the man leaned into the oars.

Turning back toward the house, Claire saw Adrian running through the garden and down the path to the dock. She started to cry out, but her voice choked as the boat caught the current and surged down the river. Claire felt the pull of the water with a thrill of fear and hunched down, gripping the seat.

Reaching the dock, Adrian tugged off his doublet and boots and dove into the Thames, swimming after their wherry. But the river had them, sweeping them out farther and farther, leaving him behind. Under the threat of Burne's gun, the boatman bent to his work, driving them into the main current and down the river toward the bridge. The soughing wind raised the water. Choppy waves slapped the boat, and Claire's stomach twisted and knotted with each bounce. In the distance, she saw Adrian gain the other wherry and clamber over the rail. Pointing the boat after them, he pulled the oars with powerful, steady strokes. He lost some distance getting out into the current, but once behind them he rowed furiously in their wake, whittling down the gap.

"Faster," Burne commanded his boatman, checking the firing pan of the snaphance.

Glowering clouds hung like a pall overhead. Claire prayed for rain to descend and soak the powder in Sir Nigel's pistol, but no rain came, only a cold wind to raise the waves on the river. Would the flying spray be enough? Panic welled up as the boat dipped and rocked, water sloshing against the side. She could barely breathe against the growing force of her fear.

Behind them, Adrian's lighter wherry moved steadily closer. She watched as he channeled his fierce energy into the rowing, each stroke biting well into the water. Burne's boat had a lead of a hundred feet, but Claire could see it diminishing. He snarled at the boatman to row harder, but Adrian's boat kept gaining stroke by stroke. Burne raised his pistol, sighting on Adrian. Instinctively, Claire surged up, trying to knock the gun out of his hand. He slapped her down into the bottom of the boat.

"Sir, the bridge—I must pull over," the guard warned.

"Keep rowing," Burne snarled.

Claire turned and saw the bridge drawing closer. A chill shuddered through her at the hulking size of it—story upon story of shops, offices, and living spaces stark in the hazy morning light. Below the level of the bridge roadway, she could see the arches where the gray water swirled through, capped with foam. She turned away from the bridge, concentrating on Adrian. He controlled his boat perfectly in the hastening current, drawing ever nearer. If he closed upon them to rescue her, he would come within certain range of Burne's aim. And yet he rowed fervently. She shivered with fear, but it was like a waning fever, a remembrance of nightmare whose power no longer gripped her utterly. Nothing could be worse than facing Quarrell—except losing Adrian. That was a far more compelling fear than the threat of the Thames.

"Hold off," Burne commanded the boatman, who lifted the oars from the water to slow their pace. Adrian had his head down, pulling hard, rowing after them, and the gap narrowed.

Claire rose to her feet as Burne lifted his pistol again. Realizing she would try to disrupt his aim, he twisted her crippled arm cruelly with his other hand. She cried out in agony, sinking to her knees. A shot rang out and the powder flash startled her. Overcoming the dizziness of the pain, she looked back. Adrian had not been hit. He was still rowing on, looking over his shoulder between oar strokes.

Burne relaxed his grip on Claire, but did not let her free as he dropped one gun and drew the next. The boatman resumed rowing to steady their course through ever rougher water roiling toward the narrow gaps of the bridge arches. With terrible swiftness, the bridge loomed high above them. She glimpsed a man standing between two buildings. He pointed down, and another man turned to watch.

"We can still pull to the side, bank at a pillar!" the boatman cried.

"Take us through," Burne commanded. Clearing the bridge was his only hope for a fast escape. With growing panic, Claire saw the boatman hadn't the will to refuse.

Burne trained his second pistol on Adrian. Claire twisted against his grip to look over her shoulder. Burne warned her with another wrench of her injured arm. "Stay back, Adrian!" she cried out against the pain. "He'll shoot you!"

Burne jerked so violently, the shock seared through her entire arm. Claire felt the excruciating flash, but somehow moved outside it, beyond the pain. She knew what she must do.

Adrian had faced his deepest fears, risked life and sanity to rescue her from Quarrell. She had escaped the river once, but perhaps she was meant to die this way. If she could save Adrian in turn, she would sacrifice herself gladly. She could not take her eyes off Burne, who was tracking Adrian with the gun, watching him row directly into the closest range. A strange tranquillity settled over her fear.

Burne checked the hammer of the pistol, then lowered the barrel slightly, aiming straight at Adrian. She crouched to spring, and he twisted her arm again to control her even as he steadied his aim. The pain became a bright burning coldness that brought total clarity.

Now, she thought. *Now!*

Claire leapt to her feet again, crashing into Burne as he fired. He staggered, then almost restored his balance. She grabbed his neck, pushed forward again with her feet and shoved hard. Time slowed, seconds passing in stillness as together they tumbled over the rail of the wherry toward the dark swirling water just as the bridge closed over.

As she went down she heard Burne cry out, "Damn you, Claire."

The river swallowed her, plunging her into the utter blackness. Even with the terrifying shock of the cold water, Claire held her breath. *I'm alive. I'm still alive.* The furious will to survive battled with the mind-destroying fear. But the merciless river pulled her down, soaking her skirts and wrapping her legs in the waterlogged folds. With her good hand she tugged loose the ties and pushed the garment to her hips. The churning water helped for once, yanking the skirts clear of her legs, leaving only the thin shift. The force of the current tumbled her over and over in the water, but she kicked again, trying to follow the flow. Something struck her. Her breath escaped in a bubbling gasp, but Claire fought the instinct to inhale. She levered her arms with a sudden upward surge, driving her legs in another strong kick.

For one instant she broke free to the surface and gasped fresh air into her lungs. Again something slammed into her, knocking out the breath she had just seized. The river threw Burne up before her, his skull caved by some underwater blow, his eyes staring sightlessly. He vanished again in an instant. Liquid claws of water closed about her, dragging her down.

"Claire!" Adrian cried out.

As she went under, she saw him dive. Hope and despair warred as she battled the greedy hold of the river. It wrapped her jealously in its cold black arms, dragging her down, down, deeper than before. *Death's embrace.*

But now in the darkness other arms encircled her and held her close. *Adrian* . . . Claire clung to him, fought off her panic and tried to help, legs scissoring. They moved in rhythm, bursting to the surface. The water foamed around them, but the current carried them forward now, instead of trying to drag them down. As they floated past the rapids, Claire saw the warm sunlight glowing on the bridge behind them, the sky a peaceful blue, tender as a robin's egg. Adrian held her, his warm lips moving over her face, her hair. Tears spilled from her eyes in a joyous, giddy rush, flowing warm over her cold skin.

Burne's boatman oared backward to slow his course down the river. As Adrian and Claire swam to the wherry, he looked carefully around on all sides, but Burne could not be seen anywhere in the water. The wherry moved toward them, and when they reached its side, the boatman held steady as Adrian half-lifted Claire into its safety, then clambered in after.

"It was not my will to take you onto the river, Ma'am," the boatman said in apology.

"I know," Claire absolved him. Her body was a mass of stinging pains and aches. She welcomed every one. She was alive. She was with her love.

Adrian took Claire in his arms again, and she curved herself into the warm circle of his embrace.

"Claire . . . Claire . . ." He murmured her name with his angel's voice, welcoming her not to life hereafter, but to the heaven of life here and now. His lips found hers, and all their joy blossomed into the kiss, filling her heart and soul with glorious delight.

Drenched to the skin, Claire and Adrian returned to the Brightsea town house, where they were told a new coterie was awaiting them upstairs. Viv, Rafe, and their cohorts had arrived during their absence and been escorted to see James. After changing out of their sodden garments, they joined them there. Congratulations greeted their entrance, for James had told the tale of Quarrell's demise. Claire thought Adrian's cousin still looked too pale, but he was nonetheless most pleased with himself and his part in avenging Penelope's murder.

Teeming with energy, Viv began at once to relate the events they'd missed. "The warning you sent arrived in the very nick,

Sir Adrian," she said. "Maggot's supposed sighting of the doctor was naught but a ruse to lure us."

"It was a close thing," Rafe added.

"We were able to reverse the surprise, so Maggot's trap sprang shut on him." Warming to her tale, Viv elaborated on the deadly fight in Southwark, punctuating her account with animated gestures.

"Then, this Maggot is an outlaw?" James asked, trying to stitch it all together with a question.

"Was," Viv corrected. "Now squashed. Utterly squashed," she said, drawling the words with satisfaction. "As from to-day, Smoke Warren rules the Clink, and the Fringes beside."

Claire knew Viv was pleased to leave her old kingdom in good hands, and that Rafe was pleased that it was formally conferred into another's keeping. Now her friends wanted to learn what had transpired at Burne's. She and Adrian told them all that had unfolded.

"Which villain was worse?" Viv queried when he was done.

"Quarrell," Adrian said.

Rafe shook his head. "Burne."

"I should have heeded your warning about Sir Nigel, Rafe," Claire said.

"So you should have," he answered with total satisfaction.

That earned him a blow on the shoulder from Viv.

"I never liked him—nor did you!" Rafe exclaimed.

"But I was not so pompous in my victory!" she scolded.

"Aye, you were, when you bragged of squashing the Maggot," he accused her, aggrieved.

Adrian's gaze sought Claire's, their lips curving in a shared smile.

"All villains are well-crushed," James said, rubbing his bandaged arm. There was satisfaction in his voice, but sadness too.

There was a reflective silence for a moment. To break the somber mood, Claire asked Rafe, "Will you be leaving soon?"

"Yes, today we depart for Kent, to see our new estate," Rafe answered.

"I'm sure it will feel like home," Viv laughed, and Rafe's eyes sparkled at a shared joke.

"We've no patience for the banns to be called, and have obtained a special license for our wedding," he told Adrian and Claire. "You will come share the celebration, won't you?"

"Yes, if you will come to ours," Adrian answered.

Rafe wrapped an arm about Vivian and smiled at them both. "Few bargains are so joyful."

"We will come—if Her Majesty gives us leave," Claire said. For that one last barrier remained to be crossed.

"Lady Claire, you have brought disgrace upon Our honorable service. You've as good as eloped, without the decency to wed!" the Queen thundered, berating Claire for abandoning her duty as she had Adrian for spiriting her off. Elizabeth stalked up and down, a royal blaze of fury in orange brocade and cloth of gold, rubies and diamonds flashing with every movement. On either side, courtiers and ladies-in-waiting quailed before her display of rage. Claire remained kneeling beside Adrian, praying that the true intent of the public scene was to terrorize any other ladies harboring thoughts of a daring elopement. The Queen paused in her tirade, glaring down at Claire. "God's scabbard! I should have you both locked in the Tower for a year!"

Claire cringed at those words, biting her lips to keep from speaking.

"Did you think to escape unscathed?" the Queen demanded. "Well—what have you to say for yourself?"

"I beg Your Majesty, shut me away if you must, but Sir Adrian was falsely imprisoned for so long. Please, do not lock him away."

"Do not bargain with me, chit!" The Queen's eyes narrowed. "And you, Lord Roadnight, how did you dare shame Lady Claire?"

Beside her, Adrian raised his head. His voice was soft, respectful. Its magic flowed, deliciously soothing as warm honey even as he spoke of horrors. "Your majesty, we had witnessed yet another hideous and bloody crime—a crime which was again falsely laid at my feet. My greatest fear was that Edward Quarrell intended to murder Lady Claire as well. When I fled London, I took her with me in hopes it would put her beyond his reach."

Claire said nothing. Adrian had taken a fragment of the situation and presented it as the whole, yet it played well.

"So she escaped death, but not dishonor." The Queen curled her lip.

"I will swear to you on my honor that I returned Lady Claire to London with her person, if not her reputation, intact."

He deserved a buffet for that, Claire thought, though it was the truth as well.

"Is this true?" the Queen demanded of Claire.

"It is, Your Majesty." Slightly sullied, but intact. She hoped the Queen would not probe into what happened once they reached London.

"And you, Sir Adrian, could you think of nothing which would protect her reputation as well as her person?" the Queen asked sarcastically.

"I acted heedlessly in the moment. Now, I ask only to make proper reparation."

"You ask to keep what you have stolen," the Queen accused. Nonetheless, Claire could hear the Queen's anger waning, and with it the enjoyment of her own performance. The other ladies-in-waiting were duly frightened, for the moment at least. Not wanting to dilute her effect, Elizabeth dismissed them and kept Claire and Adrian privately. "Now," she said. "I will have a fuller account from you, Lady Claire, of why you behaved so disgracefully."

Claire told their story simply, keeping silent only on two aspects. She made no mention of Graile. She said nothing of Adrian's gift, substituting the explanations they had devised as events unfolded. If Queen Elizabeth knew of Adrian's powers, she would set her claws into him and never let him free. His life would be a constant confrontation with objects and people Her Majesty wished to test. Claire could not help but feel disloyal, but in this she put Adrian first. If some desperate matter arose in which he could help, he would, but Claire prayed it would not be necessary. And she prayed her omission would not bring her Queen or her country to harm. Though Walsingham must have given his own account, Claire finished with the last frantic boat chase on the Thames, and Sir Nigel's death.

"Seems you must needs embroil yourself in murderous plots, Lady Claire," the Queen grumbled. "One a fortnight."

Scarcely a month earlier, Claire had brought Vivian to the Queen, and helped stave off an assassination. Her part in that affair was small, but not forgotten. Because of it, Claire hoped that the Queen's punishment would be light.

"Even in this debacle, certain circumstances mitigate in your favor. You sought help from the Crown in the person of Sir Nigel Burne, who misused his office." The Queen paused, her eyes narrowed. "I never liked that man. Cold-blooded, venomous reptile."

Claire waited tensely as Queen Elizabeth looked back and forth between them, but it was to Adrian she turned now. "So, Lord Roadnight, you desire to wed the Lady Claire?"

"Both honor and desire compel me, Your Grace," Adrian said quietly.

"Honor requires my consent," the Queen snapped.

Claire's heart faltered. What if the Queen refused? Even if they eloped, she could imprison them as she had threatened, or negate the marriage entirely.

"However . . ." Queen Elizabeth paused, waiting till they were both tense with expectation. "I believe that honor also requires that I give that consent."

After their twin exhalations of relief, before their smiles fully bloomed, the Queen raised her hand. "Nonetheless, Lady Claire, such untoward behavior cannot be tolerated." She paused again—long enough for Claire's heart to quicken to a frantic beat—then announced, "You and Sir Adrian are banished from court for six months."

Claire hoped her lowered head would be taken for dejection, rather than the quick suppression of her full-blown smile. The Queen's decree seemed more reward than punishment. But whichever Her Majesty intended, such banishment opened the way for a most leisurely and sweet honeymoon.

Epilogue

ᕙᕙᕙ

Light was different in Ireland. Color gleamed, more saturated, more vibrant, as if it drank richness from the morning mists, then released its brilliance into the air. Even the clearest, purest air held a soft shimmer, a translucent haze as if the veil to another world could be parted. But could anything more magical lie beyond? Adrian doubted it.

He sat cross-legged near the edge of the cliff, plucking lightly at the lute. Claire curled behind him, her hand slipped under his loosened shirt, her fingers warm against the bare skin of his back. Overhead, a fleet of galleon clouds sailed the vast, luminous blue sea of sky. A tantalizing wind rippled through the long grasses on the cliff top. Spring wildflowers blazed, a million golden candles burning amid the verdant green. White butterflies whirled about their fragrant light, giddy princesses dancing at a ball. The sun sparkled on the ocean beneath the cliff, the waters shifting with variable shades of gray, green, and blue. Waves raced shoreward, tumbling in a creamy froth.

Claire's delight glowed within him, myriad and bright. The joy he'd known here as a child was reborn in her. His own emotions were more poignant, twined threads of love and sorrow. Together they wove their shared love of the land into the strands of a new madrigal. His fingers were more skillful, but without her gift for innovation. Her hands stroked him, and awareness of what she wanted flowed into his fingers. Adrian added a rippling flourish that echoed the soft breath of the wind in a last, lingering sigh. He laid the lute aside and smiled at her. This was their first shared creation.

Soon, he hoped, there would be a child.

Even the hope was a delight.

Their banishment was drawing to an end. If they chose, they could return to court—and return they would. In the Queen's honor, Claire had finished a composition she would play on his Irish harp. Adrian thought its beauty was sure to win total absolution.

Together they had decided to spend a quarter of their time amid the fascinations of London. Claire was close to her father, and Adrian wanted to learn more of the alchemist's lore, perhaps make contact with others who had some unusual gift. Another quarter of their time would be spent tending the Somerset estates he loved. But he was half Irish, and half his time would go to his Irish lands. Memories of the past would always hold a lingering sorrow, but Adrian had reclaimed his love for the land without shame, as he had his love for his mother. As with her, the anguish of Ireland's body and soul hurt his heart. He had so little help for either in their turmoil. But if the Queen could not be convinced to change her policies, Adrian swore that no one who lived on his estates would be the worse for his rule. What help he could give, he would.

A butterfly alighted on his knee. Adrian watched it bathe its fragile wings in the sunlight and smiled. His own fear had been shed like a chrysalis that bound him too tightly. He accepted his gift now. The emanations that reached him were erratic, sometimes intense, sometimes subdued. He no longer tried to deny them when they came, but sought to discover some purpose in them, some good to be wrought. Nothing since had been as terrible as the first encounters of his awakening— the shattering revelations hidden within the dragon box and the cloak of evil embodying Quarrell's power. Learning he had not killed his father freed him to commit his love to Claire. Deeper than that, unacknowledged, lay the anger he had shut away all his life, linked in his mind with madness. To conquer Quarrell, he had needed that untapped reservoir of rage and the strength that came with it. He was stunned to discover the fullness of passion that followed that unleashed energy.

Claire stirred, nuzzling his neck, then nipping softly at his earlobe. He shivered with pleasure as the point of her tongue followed up the rim to the tip. "Faerie Prince," she said. "You've brought me to your magic realm."

Sensing her playful mood, he pointed down to where the sea ponies raced shoreward, tossing their wet white manes and flicking their foaming tails into the air. "When I was a child, I used to swim without a stitch in that cove below."

"Your bare bottom must have been a charming sight then, but it would be even more charming now," Claire said, her lips curling into a provocative smile.

Laughing, he pulled her to her feet. "It was very, very cold," he warned.

"However cold, I believe we have the means to warm ourselves anew."

Adrian led her down the hillside pathway to the sheltered cove, where tawny rocks stretched arms out into the sea. Hidden from the eyes of the world, they stripped and entered the water hand-in-hand, gasping at the chill but delighting in the creamy rush that swirled about them. Claire splashed him, laughing. Adrian caught her and pressed her against him, feeling the thrust of her nipples, puckered tight and hard from the cold water.

He picked her up and carried her back to the beach, setting her on her feet so he could spread his cape as a blanket over the soft sand. She lay down on its surface, reaching up to pull him down to her after. He lay beside her, limbs in a sweet tan-

gle, leaning to meet her eager kiss. Her lips were cool still, but
the hollow of her mouth, the lush stroke of her tongue, were
warm. He pressed her to him, passion heating their sea-cooled
skin.

She was exquisitely slender, supple and lithe in his hands.
He glided his fingers along the curves of hip and flank, skimming upward as softly as butterfly wings. He caressed the
arch of her ribs, like some magical lyre encased beneath warm
skin. Touching her filled his mind and senses with music.
Sweet, sweet, yes—but he loved the wilder rhythms she conjured in his blood.

Claire quivered with breathless sighs, enthralling as a
siren's song. Her wet hair fell like mermaid tresses across his
arm as she lifted her breasts to his lips. He cupped their delicate perfection, the soft mounds crowned with dark rosy nipples drawn to eager peaks. He suckled them, delighting in the
playful nudge of the aroused nubs against his tongue. Claire's
sighs deepened to husky moans. Her eager calling excited him
intensely as her touches sent rippling sweet fire along his
nerves.

Desire animated flesh with a soaring, singing flame. His
heart took flight. His cock reared, fierce as a dragon. It
strained to reach her, to penetrate the pure mystery of her
anew and discover her innermost secrets. Moving atop her, he
entered with swift urgency. She molded to him, arms and legs
wrapping round him in a tight embrace. The sweet wet heat
within her soothed and stoked his own burning need. She
cried out to him as they surged together, a rising paean of
pleasure. The pounding of the waves merged with the wild
rhythm of their hearts, with the beating of the invisible wings
of flame that lifted them up like dragons soaring straight into
the sun.

Adrian sighed with contentment, and Claire's breath
flowed with his own. Her hand reached and clasped his. He fit
his fingers to hers gently, drowsing in blissful aftermath. The
sea sounded, vast power in it depths, nearby soft lappings, a
gentle frothing of bliss.

"*Mo sòlas,*" he murmured. Claire was his pleasure and his solace. His soul. "*Mo anim.*"

She smiled softly. "*Mo cride.*"

Memories of their meeting, of the events and adventures that had led them hither, floated through his mind. In this peace, there was no pain. The terrors were distant, flotsam carried off by the waves. Love liberated and love endured. They had emerged from darkness, cast up from the sea of night onto this sunlit glowing shore, into a heart of light.

Dear Reader,

Warm up with Avon romance! There's something for everyone . . . and I guarantee these books will heat you up on a cold winter's night. And, if you live in a balmier climate, you'll just have to turn up the A.C. . . . So, if you like the Avon romance you've just finished, check out what we have next month.

Let's begin with January's Avon Romantic Treasure, *Too Wicked to Marry* by Susan Sizemore. Lord Martin Kestrel can have any woman he desires . . . but the only woman he'd ever deign to marry is the woman he knows as Abigail Perry. But as a woman in the service of the queen, Abigail has deceived Martin, and when he discovers her ruse she must handle the consequences . . .

Remember that rhyme you said as a kid? "First comes love . . . then comes marriage . . ." Well, sometimes it's the other way around, as we discover in Christie Ridgway's *First Comes Love*, an Avon Contemporary romance. What would *you* do if you found out you were accidentally married? I know, it sounds crazy, but in a romance by Christie anything is deliciously possible!

If you love romances by Lisa Kleypas, you're going to love Kathryn Smith's sensuous and dramatic Avon Romance, *A Seductive Offer*. Lord Braven has saved Rachel Ashton's life once . . . and when she accepts his offer of a marriage in name only, she knows he has actually saved her yet again. But what happens when her passion for him turns to true love?

A bride sale! How can it be? But in *The Bride Sale*, an Avon Romance by Candice Hern, Lord James Harkness stumbles upon this appalling practice, and stuns himself by bidding on a beautiful gentlewoman being auctioned off. James knows he's not fit to be a true husband, but how can he resist her?

I promised these would be hot! I hope you enjoy them,

Lucia Macro

Lucia Macro
Executive Editor